Praise for *Swimming Home*

'This is an excellent book on so many levels, the story is captivating, and the social history of athletic women and how they were viewed at the times was very interesting . . . Highly recommended.'
—*Sydney Morning Herald*

'*Swimming Home* is the beautiful story of two fiercely strong and determined women in their own right . . . Five stars.'
—*Mrs B's Book Reviews*

'MacColl succeeds in bringing all the various places to life, whether it is humid Australia, murky London or exuberant New York. A highly engaging read.'
—*Historical Novel Society*

Praise for *In Falling Snow*

'As Iris recalls her wartime experience, she draws the reader deep into her past, eventually revealing the tragic secret that has shaped the rest of her life . . . an evocative and intriguing tale that encapsulates the horrors of war and the powerful legacy of love.'
—*Australian Bookseller and Publisher*

'At once chilling yet strangely beautiful. The book touches on the contributions made by a group of pioneering women who succeed despite society's bias toward their gender; the strong friendships that develop, particularly between Iris and ambulance driver Violet Heron; Iris' increasing love for medicine and her involvement with a man she meets during the war; the men and boys whose lives are sacrificed for a cause many of them don't identify with or understand; and the far-reaching effects of the war on the generations that follow . . . MacColl's narrative is fortified by impeccable research and her innate ability to create a powerful bond between readers and characters. Well done.'
—*Kirkus Reviews* (starred)

The True Story of Maddie Bright is Mary-Rose MacColl's sixth novel. Her first novel *No Safe Place* was runner-up in the 1995 *Australian*/Vogel's Literary Award. Her first non-fiction book *The Birth Wars* was a finalist in the 2009 Walkley Awards. *Swimming Home*, her recent novel about the first women to swim the English Channel, won the People's Choice Award at the 2016 Queensland Literary Awards. It followed *In Falling Snow* about the hospital established by Scottish women doctors in an old abbey near Paris in World War I. Mary-Rose MacColl's most recent book is *For a Girl,* which tells a story from her own young life. It was shortlisted in the 2017 Queensland Literary awards and the Victorian Premier's Literary awards.

MARY-ROSE MacCOLL

The
True Story *of*
Maddie Bright

ALLEN&UNWIN
SYDNEY·MELBOURNE·AUCKLAND·LONDON

This is a work of fiction. Names, characters, places and incidents are sometimes based on historical events, but are used fictitiously.

First published in 2019

Copyright © Mary-Rose MacColl 2019

All rights reserved. No part of this book may be reproduced or transmitted in any form or by any means, electronic or mechanical, including photocopying, recording or by any information storage and retrieval system, without prior permission in writing from the publisher. The Australian *Copyright Act 1968* (the Act) allows a maximum of one chapter or 10 per cent of this book, whichever is the greater, to be photocopied by any educational institution for its educational purposes provided that the educational institution (or body that administers it) has given a remuneration notice to the Copyright Agency (Australia) under the Act.

Allen & Unwin
83 Alexander Street
Crows Nest NSW 2065
Australia
Phone: (61 2) 8425 0100
Email: info@allenandunwin.com
Web: www.allenandunwin.com

 A catalogue record for this book is available from the National Library of Australia

ISBN 978 1 76029 524 0

Typeset in 13.4/18.6 pt Adobe Garamond Premier Pro by Bookhouse, Sydney
Printed and bound in Australia by Griffin Press

10 9 8 7 6 5 4 3 2 1

 The paper in this book is FSC® certified. FSC® promotes environmentally responsible, socially beneficial and economically viable management of the world's forests.

To Bluey Joshua and Olive Rose

My barn having burned to the ground, I can now see the moon.

Japanese proverb

From *Winter Skies* by M.A. Bright:

London, 1921

There she is on the stone bench that circles the fountain in the centre of the square where she's been sitting since early afternoon, watching and waiting as the church in front of her fades into darkness. The only illumination now is from that lamp on the side of the rectory, right where the nurse at the Sally Ann had told her it would be.

It's April, unseasonably cold; of course it is. The baby in her arms does not stir. Of course he doesn't.

'Fatigue,' the nurse had said. 'You're both suffering from fatigue. Are you getting enough rest?'

She'd almost laughed. Even then, she hadn't slept in—how long was it? She was too hungry to sleep. When had she last eaten? the nurse asked. She didn't know that either.

'I'm worried about the baby,' she said quietly. 'The baby,' she repeated when the nurse appeared not to hear.

'Oh, nowt to worry there,' the nurse said, sniffing dismissively. 'He'll suck the marrow from your bones before he'll go without. Lusty, that one.'

The nurse smiled but her smile was without kindness, as if she'd sucked on the marrow of a lemon and was trying to see the funny side of it. 'You'll perish long before he does, dearie, and keep producing milk until the end.'

That was the funny side of it.

A missing tooth at the lower front might have been the reason the nurse whistled on her esses. It might have been what made the smile look bitter. Perhaps underneath was a soul seeking the light.

'But you can't stay here with a bairn. You must know that, a lass like you.'

A lass like her.

'You'll find it easily enough. They keep the lamp burning all through the night.'

And there it was.

༄

It's one hard thing. That's what the nurse had said, her steely blue eyes. 'It's one hard thing and then it's over.'

She was shivering now. The mist that had gathered around them with the darkness had collected itself into a light rain.

She wrapped her shawl more tightly about the child as she stared at the lamp.

She stood suddenly, awkwardly, as if her mind had made itself up and ordered her body to follow, resistance taking up residence in the large muscles of her legs as she bade them walk.

Above the lighted window was a shallow awning that didn't quite shield them from the rain, and under the awning a window box shaped like a half a wheel. It housed a tiny crib lined with soft straw over which was a blanket. Someone had crocheted a blanket of little squares in different colours backed with thick wool. Someone had cared enough to do that.

She laid him on the straw and put the blanket on top. He didn't cry, even though the rain was still falling and the awning was not keeping them dry.

She bent over to wipe a droplet of water from his cheek with her thumb. He only looked at her, big eyes filled with that light, brightest in babies and the dying, the inner light that ebbs and flows with the passing of years.

Years they would not pass together.

'We don't always know the right thing,' she said, her voice surprisingly true.

The rain was more like sleet now; she mustn't tarry. Quickly, she started turning the handle, her fingers numb with the cold.

The wheel creaked and began to turn inwards. The baby stirred a moment and then settled, eyes closing. As she wound the handle and the crib moved slowly away from her, she felt the rush of cold in her belly, a cold that would never now altogether leave her.

Away from her, towards his life.

He raised a hand, just an involuntary gesture, but she took it as a wave, that little hand, those tiniest of fingernails she already knew so completely.

Her last view was of the shawl, her only shawl, a brilliant blue, disappearing into the church, and a second empty crib that came around from inside to stand ready, a different eiderdown in this one, no crocheted blanket.

Empty.

She walked away and did not look back.

It was a morning, the second day or the third; she couldn't be sure. On the first night, the nurse had welcomed her back at the Sally Ann as if none of it had happened. But time had become solid now, her arms which felt heavy, her breasts which ached or stung and leaked milk when she thought of him, that little hand waving, those light blue eyes.

She must get on. She was dressed and ready to go down to Harley Street, where there was a typing job. She stuffed strips torn from the bottom of her petticoat into her bras, just in case.

She would get the job and go to the church and say she could take him now. Now that she'd slept, eaten, and the madness had left her. Her body knows.

He is hers. She is his.

She will have to hurry because her milk will dry up and she'll not get it back. Once she has the job, she is sure they'll accept her with a child. Of course they will.

She walked into the dining room. The newspaper was on the table. The headline.

ANOTHER BABE PERISHES!

She took in great gulps of the text without breath.

A second baby has died in the 'foundling' wheel at St John of God Church. The church, the only London establishment to have retained such a contraption, is now the subject of an official investigation, Police Sergeant Harold Forth said earlier today.

'Mark my words: there is nothing safe about these so-called foundling wheels,' Sergeant Forth said.

The babe didn't stand a chance, Sergeant Forth said. 'The cold. It was just too cold for a little one.

'He was well cared-for,' the sergeant said. 'He had a blue silk shawl around him, expensive looking, but it wasn't warm enough.'

According to Rector Martin Somerset, the bell installed to warn churchmen of a baby's arrival had failed to ring and the chute through which the baby was placed had failed to close.

'The little tyke just gave up,' Rector Somerset said.

She put the paper back down on the counter, smoothed the creases she'd accidentally made in it.

She couldn't remember what she was doing, why she was standing there at all. The world was moving slowly around her, herself not moving.

One of the other women was behind her. 'Come on, slow coach,' she said. 'Haven't got all day to read.'

She turned. She would remember the woman's face for the rest of her life, cheeks like little cherries, stupid brown eyes like a cow. 'I'm sorry,' she said. And then she fainted.

ONE

Brisbane, 1981

I HEARD A THUMP THAT AT FIRST I TOOK FOR A POSSUM in the ceiling. They remind me of my brothers when we were children in this house, pounding across the wooden floors, screaming at one another over some game or claim. At night I might hear one fall from the jacaranda branches onto the roof—a possum not a brother now—with a thud you'd think would kill any living creature, and yet I know they survive because after the thud there's a pause, and then the scurry of feet. I should do something about them, get the possum man to set traps, but I don't have the heart. I still miss my brothers.

Ed from across the road says they bring fleas. The possums again, not my brothers, who are all dead, boisterous noisy boys, gone too soon. Only me now. Women live longer. It's not necessarily better.

I heard the noise again, louder, and realised it wasn't a possum. It was the front door, someone pounding now on the door with what I took for impatience, which irritated me mightily. My hearing's not as good as it used to be. It can't be Ed, I thought. Too early in the day for Ed, and Ed would never be impatient with me.

Last night's news has altogether discombobulated me. I keep seeing her in my mind's eye, more helpless than the possums in my ceiling, more helpless even than my little boy brothers, in a trap of her own hapless making. After the letter last week, it's almost too much to bear, too many signs all saying the same thing. I am too old for this. I want to die quietly in my sleep. It turns out this is quite a lot to ask of the Lord, who knows every hair on your head and could pluck them all out at once if the mood took him.

Other than Ed, no one knocks on my door but religions and electricals, peddling wares or schemes for redemption, and it's too early for either of them. They don't tend to make such a racket either. I used to like the Pentecostals. Their prayer books have pictures and they don't have a uniform. I joined them the year before last, but I didn't know any of the songs, so I went back to the more ordinary Catholics whose songs have straightforward melodies. Even if you don't know them at the start, you have them figured by the second verse.

I live in a house that attracts a particular kind of religion, one whose followers are nutty for it. Last week, I had the Jehovah's Witnesses and the Latter-Day Saints on the same day, which is a record. Swindle is what religions specialise in, according to Ed. He is cynical. It won't make life any easier, I want to tell him. Whereas believing in a hereafter, where my brothers and I, my parents, and others I've lost will be reunited, might be a comfort when I need one.

'I'm coming!' I called towards the door as gruffly as I could manage. I was in the kitchen at the back of the house, and although I've weaned myself from the walker, I'm still slow, ginger when I'm first on my feet, as if I broke my balance when I broke my dumb leg.

The leg itself has healed entirely, the doctor told me when he sawed the cast off, stressing that word *entirely*, but perhaps next time I might ask the gardener to clear the leaves from the gutters rather than getting up on the roof myself. He was one of those doctors who'd have been pointing a finger at me if all his fingers hadn't been on duty for the sawing. As it was, he was shaking his head, a smug smile stuck to his face like it was a regular visitor. He can't be older than fifty, and he's not my usual doctor, Dr McKellar, who would never be so condescending and would likely encourage me to get up on the roof if that's what I felt like doing, which I did, obviously, or you wouldn't have found me up there and I wouldn't have fallen off. Not only that, the assumption I have a gardener is offensive to me.

I felt like giving him a piece of my mind, the young doctor, but I refrained for the sake of ensuring he finished the job at hand without taking my leg off. It's harder to assert your authority when the object of your irritability has an electrical saw in his hands.

I passed the television in the sitting room. It had turned itself back on—something that should probably worry me—and there again was the picture: a willowy scrap of a girl arm in arm with what I could only describe as a wolf in sheep's clothing. Her suit was the worst of it, a sky blue two sizes too large, as if she'd only bought it that morning for the afternoon's announcement and she had a false impression of her own size in the world. It's more innocent than wedding-white will be, the enormous jewel on her finger shown to the waiting horde like a brand on a heifer. They flashed back then to that other picture, the one that might frighten her, her skirt made see-through in the morning sun, her long legs exposed for all the world to gawk at. Of course it frightened her. That was the point.

'Run!' I shouted at the screen. 'Scream your head off!' But she couldn't hear me and wouldn't know what I was talking about if she could. That was all yet to find her.

Helen. Is that who she reminds me of? Helen, whose adventurousness people mistook for sophistication, or some Machiavellian nature that was not Helen, not in any way. Is this what the world does to women who pretend to be worldly, buy suits two sizes too big? Cut them down to size, shrink them?

I reached the front door just as the pounding resumed. 'Lord save us, I'm coming!' I called out again, exasperated now, for having reached the door, I had to negotiate the locks, three of them, and the chain bolt. Ed says if there were a fire in this house, I would burn before I could get myself out. Minutes, he tells me. These houses burn in minutes. I tell Ed I'd see it as an early but hardly premature cremation. He doesn't find that funny, which I can well understand—he's young yet—but when you get to my age, death looms, an unwelcome guest but a guest all the same, one your very living has invited. Your humour can't help but be gallows. The gallows are what's left.

Forgiveness. I know I will be seeking forgiveness. That's what I like about the Catholics, in addition to songs I know the tunes of. Forgiveness appears to be in plentiful supply. Ed doesn't understand that.

I'm still thinking of Ed and smiling when I open the door and when it's not him, I'm confused momentarily. It's not Ed. It's a tall, strong young man with blue eyes and wavy blond hair parted on the left. Behind him is a perfect sky which frames those eyes. Sky eyes. I look again at his face, trying to work out if I'm supposed to know him.

'Can I help you?' I say, in a way that suggests helping is the last thing on my mind. Big brown boots, I notice, and navy work shorts, the ones with hip pockets, a short-sleeved shirt, a pocket there too, a pen clipped to it, Bic, black, the cap on. Building. He looks like a building. A builder, I mean. He looks like a builder.

'I'm Andrew Shaw,' he says gently. He has a quiet voice you want to hear more of. 'I'm doing the work next door? I'm here to do the inspection. We spoke on the phone.' He's two steps lower, bending his body closer as he looks up at me, nodding.

'Did we now?' The inspection. Trust the inspection to turn up today, after the news.

It was not my idea, as I'd said to Ed when he brought in my bin this week. 'Ed, do you know what they've done?' I said.

Ed had looked towards the house uphill from mine, not unlike my house, with the sign out front we'd read together, which said its purpose was to give notice of a development application, along with the name and address of someone with whom I could lodge objections. Ed was as close to scowling as Ed ever gets. He's a sweet boy, so a scowl is not his first favoured facial expression.

They moved in three months ago, the neighbours, before I broke my leg, and they worried me from the start. He's a solicitor, he made a point of telling me, in a big city law firm. I don't remember the name of the firm just now. She *was* a teacher, she said, as if you can just stop being one, but she was taking time out to raise their children, two noisy beasts, six and eight. I *am* a teacher, I wanted to say, despite not having been in front of a class for over a decade. I retired—it wasn't my idea. I'll always be a teacher.

Based on my early interactions—you would be forgiven for using the word *spoiled* in relation to those children—I decided it would be best to discourage early and with firm resolve. I waited until they were playing in their backyard then went out to my own yard and began howling like a wolf—at least that's what I was trying for—in my singlet and slip. The children looked over, not so much afraid as curious. I redoubled my efforts in an attempt to establish an advantage.

How was I to know their mother was standing on the back porch out of view? She stepped forward and looked at me, smiled and waved weakly.

'A building inspection will be a big headache for you,' Ed had said after he'd read the notice, and Ed should know, because before he was fired for drunkenness he used to work on building sites.

'Can they do that, order your house be inspected?' he asked me then.

'Apparently,' I said, looking at the notice again for some exit strategy the council hadn't thought of.

'I can do the inspection,' Ed said, swaying a little.

'No, you can't,' I said. 'You're not a builder.' And you're drunk most days, I didn't say, because it wouldn't change anything if I did.

'S'pose not,' he said. Ed had been a little drunk that morning, to be honest, and overestimating himself. He'd lost the last job three years before, when someone stole his bag while he was at the pub. Inside was his ticket for the forklift he drove. The next morning, they didn't let him in at the building site. I pretended to believe the story, knowing full well you only had to look at his poor tortured eyes to know he'd been drinking, was always drinking. You wouldn't let him within a mile of a forklift if you had any sense.

Ed had been unemployed ever since he lost that job, sitting on his front steps and drinking. He didn't go out much, only to take his father, another drinker, to medical appointments in a taxi. His mother had already passed.

Ed takes my rubbish bin out every week, brings it in after the rubbish man has been. He's never forgotten, not once in more years than I can recall. That amounts to something in my mind.

'I'm not paying you,' I say to Andrew Shaw now. I notice my arms are folding themselves, a habit I don't much like but don't always have control over.

'I wouldn't think so,' he says. 'Your neighbours are paying.' He's moved up a step now so we are eye to eye, but he's still leaning towards me in the way some young men lean, disarming rather than threatening.

'Why?' I say. 'Are they worried about my safety?'

He smiles and not sheepishly. He has the loveliest smile, white straight teeth and those eyes you want to look at.

My neighbours, who are not kind, have ordered an inspection of my house and sent this boy of a builder.

'You know they've announced their engagement?' I say.

He looks confused then. 'Simon and Alice?' Simon and Alice are the neighbours, Simon the lawyer, Alice the teacher, taking time, she said, while the children were small. 'I think your generation was right,' she said to me. 'My grandmother—' as if I'm old enough to be her grandmother '—raised my father and his brothers. I'm going to be there for Atticus and Scout.' Atticus and Scout! Those are the names of the children, both boys, although Scout was a girl in *To Kill a Mockingbird*. I wondered if I should tell them. I doubt they've read it.

'No!' I say to Andrew Shaw. 'Diana Spencer. This morning. She's going to marry H.R.H. the Prince Charles.'

'Well, I guess you could see that coming,' Andrew Shaw says.

'Indeed,' I say. 'She's nineteen years old. What do you think of that?'

He looks unsure. 'Young?'

'Exactly,' I say. 'Did you see his face?'

'Who?'

'Charles.'

'No?' he says, eyeing me more carefully.

'Good. You seem a nice young man. Don't be like him.'

'Not much chance,' Andrew Shaw says.

'Why?'

'For a start,' he says, 'I'm not a prince.'

'Well, I suppose not, but neither is he,' I say. 'We live in a world where a dog snatches a baby—' I bared my teeth '—in its jaws.'

I can see that smile forming at the edges of his eyes. 'Ayers Rock,' he says, nodding. 'The dingo. I saw it on the news last night, the inquest.' He grins widely. 'And, yes, it was right after the engagement announcement.'

We both turn our heads then, because the fledgling crow that's been making a branch of my front jacaranda its favourite perch has started squawking fit to frighten a cat. 'Don't mind him,' I say to Andrew Shaw, who appears to be looking around for an ambulance. 'He's just a stupid baby crow who wants his mother to feed him. He's been running that routine since the spring. It's high time you grew up!' I yell at the bird.

'Oh,' Andrew Shaw says. 'He *is* just a baby. Down feathers.' He smiles at the bird. I start to think he's always smiling, odd in a builder, odd in anyone really. 'Look at that eye.'

I look at the crow, see what he means; an eye of milky lapis looking not at us but at the future. I'm about to say as much when I realise I can see. Without my glasses, I am seeing. I am seeing Andrew Shaw's smiling face and the crow's milky blue eye. I'm blind as a bat without those glasses. Andrew Shaw has been sent by a goodly spirit, I decide, to help me with what's to happen next, even if what's to happen next is unclear. A beautiful girl like her; she has no idea what happens next either. But I know. Or I know more than she does.

Andrew Shaw is a good omen, a sign from the Lord. I'm fairly sure he's an angel. Or the sun. He has the name of Andrew, the youngest and most favoured apostle. It can't be a coincidence.

'I think we're all right,' he says. 'You see . . .' He looks behind him down my stairs. Two treads have rotted out. When I fell from the roof and onto the steps, the first step gave way. I went over but my leg stayed where it was. It was a bad break, the shinbone exposed, which has turned me vegetarian, the experience of my own meatiness giving me a newfound respect for the meatiness of other creatures.

The worst part with the broken leg was the awful waiting for someone to notice, and it was Ed who noticed, God bless him, not Alice and the children who left in their Volvo, pretending not to hear my cries. Ed called the ambulance and brought me whisky to drink until they arrived. I couldn't abide whisky, I told him, not so early, but would he sit with me? Of course he would, he said, and there we sat, him sipping the whisky. I wish he'd offered sweet tea. But it would never occur to Ed.

Blessed are the poor, Jesus said, and he meant the alcoholics.

'I just need to get my glasses,' I say to Andrew Shaw now.

'You're wearing them,' he says, pointing to the bridge of his own nose.

I put my hand to my face. He's right. Not so spiritual then. He smiles again.

Lovely all the same. An angel, I am almost certain.

TWO

London, 1997

VICTORIA BYRD EMERGED FROM THE TUBE STATION INTO Oxford Street, feeling silly in a mac, the day much brighter than first promised. She'd woken late and a glance at the sky registered the kind of clouds that might give forth, but hadn't.

If we'd been a crow and asked Victoria, as she'd thrust her blonde curls out the kitchen window of her Brockley flat, was there anything unusual about that particular morning, she'd only have said she'd overslept, which was out of character. Also that a crow was asking questions. Perhaps the fight last night was unusual, although perhaps not, and Victoria wouldn't mention it anyway. And there were no photographers down in the street. That was definitely unusual now.

Ben had been celebrating last night. They'd finished the London exterior scenes and that was cause enough. He'd opened a bottle of champagne before dinner, another with dinner, Chinese takeaway because neither of them felt like cooking. Victoria couldn't have drunk more than two glasses, but now she wondered if the edge of a hangover was circling her eyes, flattening the world while simultaneously throwing it off kilter. The world was definitely off kilter this morning. Ben was happy at the start, smiled his beautiful smile, the one that won her over in the first place, that won everyone over. Yet she'd been unaccountably nervous when he'd opened the second bottle.

'It's no big deal, Tori,' he'd said. 'We can live a little.' He was still smiling then.

೬

Victoria had profiled Ben Winter when *Zombie Deader* came out in London last year, his third film as the action hero professor Jack Kessler. Now he'd finished *Zombie Armageddon*, or *Zomb-arm* as he called it in the interview, as if Armageddon were a notion that lent itself to abbreviation. So it's a quadrilogy, he said, a term she could have worked out the meaning of if she didn't know it already, she assured him. *Zomb-arm* was his first film as director, he told her. She already knew that too.

'It's not nothing to save the world, Victoria,' he'd said. He waggled a finger so she'd look up from her notebook. She hadn't known at first if he was joking. She'd thought about that finger waggle at various moments since.

In fact, he'd annoyed Victoria, confidence bordering on brashness, as if he owned the entire world, but she covered her own feelings to draw him out and found something she took for depth of character as the interview went on.

'You seem unimpressed by me,' he said after half an hour, tilting his head in a way she found attractive even as she wanted to dislike him.

'You make zombie films,' she said, surprising herself with her frankness.

'And?'

'They're wonderful films, and my friend's son adores you, but I'm not sure I'm your demographic.'

'Money and power?'

'I imagine you have those.'

'But they don't impress you, Victoria.' He said her name softly. She noted that for the article, his voice somewhat at odds with the almost superhuman nature of the character he played and the initial brashness she'd disliked.

'Why do you want to impress me?' she asked, flirting a little. He was beautiful. The notion he was interested in Victoria's view was terribly flattering, she admitted to her friend Claire afterwards. Claire didn't always like the men Victoria dated, but she'd like Ben Winter, Victoria said. 'I've seen his picture on the side of the bus,' Claire said. 'Quite the yummy.'

'I want to impress everybody,' Quite-the-yummy said, rubbing his thumb along the tops of his fingernails, as if he'd just had a manicure and was admiring the work. He probably had. He probably was. 'Doesn't everybody want to impress everybody?'

And it was this, which she took for self-reflection, that she'd liked.

'No', she said. 'I don't.' She didn't put this exchange in the magazine piece, but when she transcribed the interview, she listened to it three times.

'Does it surprise you that I could believe that?' he said. He had a nice grin that came on suddenly, open-mouthed, one or two crooked teeth. Each time she'd listened, she remembered the grin.

His publicist was giving her the look publicists give to suggest a writer is on thin ice, ice about to give way under the weight of the question. Oh God, he was handsome.

She couldn't imagine his confidence in an English film star, not even back in the days when England had an empire to brag about. She continued to find it annoying, but also now a little thrilling.

He'd phoned that afternoon to ask her to dinner that night, fully expecting she'd have no plans, which she didn't.

Ben had left before dawn. He'd said the night before that they were driving down to Bath to start filming in the ruins. He was wearing dark blue jeans, brown suede boots and a white t-shirt that showed the lean muscle he'd worked on for the role he was playing. His beauty always seemed so effortless. She'd looked at him and thought how lucky she was.

She'd found a croissant from the Brockley baker on the bench in the kitchen just before she'd left the flat. Ben must have asked the driver to take him down there and then brought it back and put it on the little plate for her. Next to the croissant was a single rose, picked from Victoria's garden. Oh, she said, experiencing a feeling that made her heart ache. Oh. It was his way of saying sorry. She peered out the window again. Still no photographers. At least she could go out without being pursued.

She'd noticed the baby crow in the front garden as she walked down the path. She was taking her time, despite being late, luxuriating in how her life used to be when she didn't have to run the gauntlet of photographers in the mornings. And there it was, the baby crow, in the elm that grew into the rock wall, in a low branch, its mother further up in the tree and eyeing Victoria suspiciously. 'Watch out for the cat,' Victoria said as she closed the gate. Not that Martha, Victoria's cat, could catch a bird if her life depended on it.

She'd nibbled the croissant on the way to the train station, throwing most of it in the rubbish. Not the right food at seven am, she decided. Seven thirty, she corrected herself. She would have grabbed a coffee at Brown's but the queue was out the door. If she hadn't been running late, she might have read the paper while she waited. Rushing, she missed the headlines at Waterloo, and the taxi driver—she'd caught a cab at Oxford Street instead of walking—was listening to a cassette tape—Vivaldi's 'Winter'—rather than the radio. When he asked where she was going and she told him Knight News, he'd said, 'Of course. I expect they'll be needing all hands.' She hadn't enquired why; it was clearly something she should already know, and she didn't feel like being informed of the news by a London cabbie. Victoria was supposed to inform the cabbie of the news.

By the time she walked in through the big glass doors of Knight News it had just gone eight. At the desk she flashed her ID and didn't stop to talk to Mac on security as she normally might have. Mac smiled all the same.

'Morning, Miss Byrd,' he said politely. Mac always called her Miss Byrd, no matter how many times she told him it was Victoria, then, after Ben, Tori.

Knight News occupied two seven-storey terraces on Norfolk Square, a glass atrium joining the two buildings across a narrow laneway. There were risk-your-life bridges on level three, where *The Eye* newspaper crossed both buildings, and on level five, where *Vicious*, the monthly magazine Victoria wrote for, did the same. No one except Mac knew that if Victoria had to go from one building to the other, she never used the walk bridge. She took the elevator down to the ground floor and went up in the elevator on the other side of the atrium, passing Mac each time, which was how she'd come to know him so well.

Mac had four kids who'd all studied at the university, he'd told Victoria with considerable pride, showing her a photograph of each of them over several weeks as she walked between elevators. He and his family had come from Nigeria, where the future was much harder, he said.

Here was the face of social change, Victoria would have written, if she'd done a profile on Mac, one reason New Labour was so important, a living example of why Blair's free tertiary education policy—the one Victoria's father had authored—was so necessary. She'd write it without ever seeming patronising. She'd mention her father's name proudly, Michael Byrd, the new prime minister's education adviser and friend.

They put on security a year ago, after the IRA Docklands bombing. Now it was standard for news organisations. A target, that's what the two detectives from Scotland Yard said when they visited afterwards. Media will be a target. Victoria wasn't in the meeting, but Ewan was. Liars, he said later. She worried Ewan might actually side with the IRA, given a choice. You could never tell which way he'd blow on some issues. But ever since Mountbatten in 1979—fishing trip, young children, the bomb directly under an old man's fishing chair—you couldn't side with the IRA publicly. You'd be lynched.

Victoria emerged from the lift on the fifth floor and saw, through the glass doors, more people than she'd ever seen in the magazine bullpen, staring up at the few screens mounted on the walls while talking on phones. Large plate-glass windows flooded the space with London's soft summer light. They'd had an architect in when Harry Knight bought the buildings for his empire, and it showed. The light! The light! Ewan used to say, trying, unsuccessfully, to imitate the architect, who did talk about light more than the average person.

It couldn't be bad news, not today, Victoria thought, the sun having found its way through those awful clouds. But then someone she'd never seen before rushed past her, newspaper galleys in hand. There was never that much hurry for good news, only tragedy. She looked for someone she knew but they were all strangers, other than one or two she thought she recognised from downstairs and a sub from *The Eye*. There were extra phones, she noticed, cords running along the floor.

Victoria hadn't seen this many people in a newsroom since John Lennon's death. She'd been at *The Guardian* in December 1980, just starting out. Everyone was on that story through the night. Journalists were calling friends who lived in New York, family, getting them to go down to the Dakota and call back. It was mad. They held printing then went to print then reprinted.

He was dead. John Lennon was dead.

They'd gone together to an all-night bar near the offices afterwards to numb the emotions that began to wash over them, a deep sadness that felt like a comfortable old cardigan to Victoria. They were all together, senior journalists, subs, cadets. The bar was the kind of place that seemed beyond hope, and with Lennon dead hopelessness might have set in. But someone had a guitar, and they all sang 'Imagine'. Victoria watched the sun come up through the smoky windows. Imagine.

She hadn't turned twenty. Oh God, she was a journalist. She was bringing the news, the truth, to the world. She was at *The Guardian*—the guardian of truth, she believed then. She felt as if her real life had just begun, as if this was what she'd been called to do.

She thought of that night now. It bathed her in a different kind of light.

Victoria looked across to the middle of the space, to the conference room where the morning editorial meeting was already underway. She remembered the taxi driver, 'all hands'. She stopped a copyboy whose face she knew but whose name she'd never learned. 'What's going on?' she said.

'They don't know yet.'

'They don't know what's going on?'

But the young copyboy was gone.

She went to her desk, wound her bag around the chair, hung her mac on the hook on the side of the partition. No Daniella on reception. Victoria looked over towards the conference room again—glass walls, not soundproofed, not vision-proofed, in the middle of the floor. They called it the fishbowl, because you could see the fish. And if you stood close, you could hear everything the fish said to one another. From this distance, Victoria thought, they were not one fish, two fish, or red fish, blue fish. They were more like dumb fish, glum fish.

Victoria grabbed her laptop and a yellow legal pad and pen and walked back across the bullpen. She saw English bobbies on the vision above her head. Somewhere grey, like Liverpool, she thought, from the background, lots of concrete, or maybe Sheffield. IRA? If it was so big the news division downstairs was spilling up here into the magazine floor, it must be IRA. Oh God, she thought. What now?

'Well, here's the lass herself,' Ewan said when she walked in. He was wearing the only tie he owned, tied too tightly then loosened off so you had to wonder why he bothered, with a blue shirt that hadn't been ironed. Black jeans, black gym boots on his feet. Ewan's uniform, if he had one. He was sitting back from the table, legs crossed, a relaxed pose in anyone else but Ewan managed to look tense.

Thin, if not the first word that came to mind, was among the first three you'd use to describe the editor of Britain's most edgy and (on June sales figures) most popular magazine. High-strung would have to be one of the other two, and then maybe intelligent. He smiled at her, but even his smile came out high-strung, full of eyebrow, his dark auburn fringe pushed straight back.

'Nice to see you, Victoria,' he said, with what she took for irritation in his voice. Ewan was one of three people in her life who refused to call her Tori. The others were her father and her best friend Claire who'd always called her Victoria.

Tori Winter, Ben had said on their second date. They were at the rugby final; Victoria had just written a long feature about English captain Will Carling. Tori Winter has a ring, Ben said. They weren't engaged. He hadn't asked her—of course he hadn't; it was their second date—but he gave her his surname. You could go on stage with a name like that, he continued, without missing a beat. He'd called her Tori from then on. She'd liked it so she'd asked everyone else to call her Tori too. Her by-line was still the same though. Tori Byrd was sure to prompt laughs in a way Victoria Byrd wouldn't.

Victoria's colleagues were all there around the table, even some she'd thought were on leave, along with an assistant editor from *The Eye*. There was no story list for October on the whiteboard. There was nothing on the whiteboard. Daniella was sitting at the end of the table next to Ewan. Daniella didn't normally attend the briefing.

'Sorry,' Victoria said. 'What's all this?' She gestured out to the bullpen. She sat down at the nearest corner of the table.

'Got your go-bag?' Ewan was rubbing his cheek, looking at her face.

She dusted her own cheek. It was sore to her touch. 'What?' she said.

'What did you do?' he said, frowning.

'I fell,' she said, remembering she'd caught her heel in the carpet on the stairs and had gone over last night. It was after she'd taken the rubbish out. She didn't get her arm down in time and she'd hit her cheek on the architrave. 'Is it red?' she asked. It gave her a fright to think of it now.

He nodded, still looking at her.

Oh dear. She'd hardly looked in a mirror before she left home. God knew what her hair was like. She felt found out suddenly, as if she'd been doing something wrong. She hadn't been doing anything wrong. She thought of making a joke about sleeping in but decided against it. The mood was anything but jokey today.

'Why do I need a go-bag?' she said, focusing on Ewan. Most senior reporters kept a bag in the office in case they had to travel at short notice. Victoria hadn't used hers since joining the magazine and she'd let it slide. Her specialty nowadays was celebrity interviews; fat-cat journalism, as her father called it, a long privileged way from bringing any kind of truth to the world, although Victoria didn't let herself think about that. She hardly ever faced a tight deadline. She was often at the mercy of her interviewees anyway, especially in the early days. She might have more choice about who she interviewed now, but there were still those whose lives were complicated by fame and success. She was the bottom of the pack as far as they and their publicists were concerned.

Danny Brown, the photographer Victoria might have turned to for advice, was on the other side of the conference room. She'd hoped to sidle over to Danny and find out what was going on before she was put on the spot. She tried to look a question his way, hoping for a hint, but Danny was so stone-faced that he didn't even notice Victoria. Danny took everything in his stride but this morning he looked as if he'd been in a bomb blast. Danny had photographed what to most people would be unthinkably hard even to witness, let alone record. She had no idea what had rattled him, but something had.

'Sorry I'm late,' she said, looking back at Ewan. 'And it sounds like I drew the short straw on something?'

'What?' Ewan said curtly. 'Have you not heard?'

She shook her head.

He sat up and forward, pulling his chair into the table, donned his glasses.

He looked at her, his green eyes framed now by the kind of big dark rims that give a face an odd vulnerability.

'Princess Diana is dead. We're holding the edition.'

THREE

Brisbane, 1981

'YOUR NEIGHBOURS ARE WORRIED YOUR HOUSE IS GOING to fall on theirs.' Andrew Shaw was leaning back now, as if to inspect the house in its entirety right then to form an opinion of its likelihood of toppling, a smile at the corners of his mouth.

'Uphill,' he said, pointing towards the neighbours. 'I just can't see it. Even if it collapses, it's not going to go that way. Anyway, they've asked me to inspect it.'

'I suppose you're going to tell me everything that's wrong with my house.'

'I imagine so,' he said, with a raised eyebrow. 'Can I come in?'

'I'm not sure yet,' I said, seeing Ed barrelling unsteadily across the street. 'I'm all right!' I called out to slow Ed down, my voice failing me a little. 'He's the inspector!'

'Is this your knight in shining armour?' Andrew Shaw asked.

'I sense a mocking tone,' I said sternly. 'His armour may be tarnished, but where were you when I fell off the roof onto those steps?'

'A fair point,' Andrew Shaw said. 'Does he need help getting up them?'

'I think he'll manage, although it depends on how far we are into the day.' I looked across and realised Ed would probably falter. 'Yes, that would be good, thank you,' I said.

Andrew Shaw brought Ed—or Ed brought Andrew, Ed objecting with some energy to being helped—and they followed me inside and along the dark hallway past the boys' room and my parents' room and my room through the lounge room to the little kitchen. Andrew Shaw—call me Andy, he said several times—tested his footing on the veranda floor and again in the kitchen. 'Termites?' he said.

'No,' I said. 'The only pests are the new neighbours and their like.'

He laughed then. 'Well, I'm their builder, so I can't comment on that,' he said.

'You'll need a hand, son,' Ed said, a statement not a question, the room clearly moving for him as he swayed against it.

'I think I'll be right,' Andrew Shaw said, looking at me and then back at Ed. 'Actually, maybe you could hold the torch under the house, if you can get under there.'

'Course I can,' Ed said. It was a job Ed might actually be able to do. Andrew had picked his man and knew his state but treated him kindly.

Poor Ed was thinner every time I saw him. It amazed me that something with so many calories as beer could eat a person's body up the way it did. Wisps of once-red hair were combed back neatly at least; some days even a comb to his hair was beyond him.

Andrew Shaw said he wasn't sure how long it would take, as if I had all the time in the world for him, as if he'd made the appointment for today. And perhaps he had. I told him I'd be on the front veranda and not to bother me unless he absolutely had to.

And then, regretting my inhospitableness, I offered tea. Three sugars, Andrew Shaw said, which I would have guessed, and Ed said I don't mind if I do.

'Did you see the news, Ed?' I asked.

'Yes,' Ed said. 'That's why I came over. Are you all right, Maddie?'

'Of course,' I said, although perhaps I wasn't. I stopped talking then, for tears had started coming out of my eyes.

I see her there, a poor butterfly pinned to a board, a creature even more helpless than those possums in my roof. I watch her sparrow chest rising and falling with each short breath, as if her body is still deciding on flight or fight without her mind having any idea. She gives that lovely smile and talks like she thinks a grown-up should talk, all the while deferring to him with her eyes. Good God! I kept saying to the television, but the television had nothing to say by way of response.

'And after the letter, it's hard to believe it's not a sign.'

I thought I might collapse into Andrew Shaw's arms right then.

'What letter?' Ed asked.

'She wrote to me.'

'Diana Spencer?' Andrew Shaw looked confused. I wondered, was he hard of hearing?

'No,' I said. Had I told Ed about the letter? Perhaps not. 'Nothing,' I said. 'It's nothing.'

But it wasn't nothing. It was everything.

The truth is, Diana Spencer won't have the choice of fight or flight once she knows, her real self in terror. That's the point of pinning them. Run, you say, run as fast as your legs will carry you before he knows you're gone. But she can't hear you, and wouldn't listen if she could.

That's the way of things, isn't it?

Not even knowing from whence the terror is coming. And there it is, sitting next to her on the settee, the chinless cat that got the cream.

It was Mr Waters who said to me that the thing about good people and bad people is that they look exactly the same, and it is true.

Take Ed, nodding at me now. You'd be forgiven for making assumptions. He's a drunk. You'd be forgiven for thinking that's all he is. But the look on his face as he saw my pain was so kindly, I couldn't hold his gaze. I found tears in my eyes again and only shook my head and formed my mouth into as tight a line as I could.

I made the tea, transformative of even the most disturbed mental condition, and I carried the two cups to the dining room and put them on the table. Andy was in the ceiling by then, Ed swaying at the bottom of the ladder under the manhole.

The day was heating up, I could hear the tin roof cracking as it stretched.

'There's possums up there!' I yelled, just as Andy shouted, 'Oh shit, rats!' and came back down the ladder.

'Possums,' I said, 'and that's quite enough foul language. This is not a building site. Here's your tea. I have no cake. And it will be toasted cheese sandwiches for lunch.'

He looked sheepish for a moment. 'Sorry. They gave me a fright. More like rats, I'm afraid,' Andy said, looking at Ed, not me. He took a sip of his tea.

'They're possums,' I said. I wasn't going to listen to nonsense talk. Rats! Didn't he know the difference? Rats thither whereas possums thump. And he claimed to be a builder. For goodness' sake. He wasn't a builder's bootstrap.

'I have a book to finish,' I said, pretending not to notice Ed rolling his eyes at Andrew Shaw. Ed thinks the book will never be finished. But Ed is not a writer, so he would not have any idea what is involved.

And the fact is, she's written to me.

Helen.

She's written to me after all these years.

I don't have long left, Maddie, she writes. *Rupert is gone.*

Mr Waters, I want to say, I'm so sorry I didn't . . . I'm sorry.

I have my desk out here on the enclosed veranda because the middle of the house, the second bedroom where I could keep it, started to feel suffocating, as if I were standing on the shoulders not of giants but of the long dead. Ed helps me to move the desk just inside the door when rain's coming from the north, which is rare. I can drag it in myself, or I could before I broke the leg, but now Ed carries it for me.

Out here, where the front wall is covered entirely with louvre windows, I can feel as if I am part of the air, inconsequential and vital at the same time. My words can flow out of my fingers and onto the page and scatter to the street.

Today, I am looking over chapter one. I need to rethink the beginning.

The woman was still sitting outside the church where she'd been since early afternoon, watching and waiting as day faded from her eyes.

Oh, God! As if day fades from one's eyes.

The woman sat on the bench circling the fountain near the church where she would change history.

Really? Change history?

The woman stood up and felt in her knees she'd been sitting too long.

Perhaps she could spy a rat.

Rats, for goodness' sake.

The little blue envelope is in my top desk drawer, a red-breasted robin in one corner, so like her, that stationery, the loopy M in my name. She was a writer of loopy Ms. You would have guessed that on meeting her.

I know more about rats than most people know about their own faces.

FOUR

London, 1997

'I BEG YOUR PARDON?' VICTORIA SAID.

Princess; he'd said Princess Diana. Ewan never used Diana's title.

'Daniella has your tickets sorted,' Ewan said. 'Flights are full, so it's the tunnel, I'm afraid. I think you're on the eleven thirty. You'll have to get a move on.' He looked at Daniella, who was listening on a call on one of the phones in the conference room, taking notes. She nodded.

'I'm sorry?' Victoria couldn't concentrate on what Ewan was saying. Diana was dead?

'Go!' he said. 'Harry says we're redoing September.' Harry Knight, editor-in-chief of *The Eye* and owner of Knight News.

'Where?' she said.

He shook his head. 'Paris, unless you have a better idea.'

Victoria looked around the room, trying to take it in. All eyes were on her now. 'She's dead?' Diana was thirty-six, Victoria's age. Their birthdays were a month apart.

'And we're covering it?' She looked at Ewan. 'We're pulling September to make Diana the lead?' Ewan despised the monarchy.

'Not the time, Tori,' Meredith said. Meredith was crying. Meredith was from advertising. People from advertising didn't cry.

'How?' Victoria said.

'You really don't know?' Ewan said. 'Car crash. Paris. With Dodi Fayed.' He half choked as he said it. Ewan, her editor, was holding back tears, tears about Diana.

Dodi Fayed was the new boyfriend. Victoria had seen Nathan Ashbury's picture, the one Nathan said *The Sunday Sun* paid him quarter of a million pounds for. THE KISS! He took it after Diana telephoned and told him where she was, or so Nathan told Danny. You could never really trust Nathan, but perhaps it was true. Perhaps Diana had telephoned him and said, 'Hi Nathan, I'm in the Mediterranean on the Harrods yacht. Come photograph me.'

Danny had shot Diana, of course. He was one of the favourites. Sometimes, he said. He'd done that famous picture for *The Sun* in the early days of the royal romance, the one that made her skirt see-through. 'She's one of those women—loves a lens,' he said, which reminded Victoria of something but she couldn't think of what it was. 'Until she's in a bad mood, then she hates it. You can't win with women like that.'

Claire was still working for *The Eye* then. She told Danny he was kidding himself if he thought anyone would like what he and his colleagues did to Diana. Claire was cynical about most things but she'd always been in Diana's camp.

'It's a job, Claire,' Danny had said. 'And I'm fucking good at it.'

Danny did have a kind of mental swagger, it was true. He was a good photographer, but you had to accommodate the swagger if you wanted him to get a shot for you. It was probably the only way you could do his job and not kill yourself. That's what Claire said.

Claire was right about the photographers though. You'd never want anyone doing what they did to you. Victoria was sure about that now.

Diana was dead? The truth kept coming in and out of focus in Victoria's brain, her thoughts as thick and slow as molasses.

She opened her mouth to say something and closed it again.

'Do whatever you need to,' Ewan was saying, 'but get moving. I'll brief you after we finish here.'

'Okay,' Victoria said. She stood to go. 'Hang on. I have a lunch today, the one you organised—Finian Inglis.'

Ewan looked away down to the left and back at Victoria. 'Oh, yes, of course.' He considered it. 'Probably not for us.' He was tapping a pen on the tabletop absentmindedly.

'Why did you set it up then?'

'I don't know, because it might be? Fin Inglis runs Barlow Inglis, the publisher, so he's a somebody. They published

M.A. Bright's *Autumn Leaves*. He says there's a second novel, *Summer Sky* or something.' Ewan rubbed his chin. 'He seems pretty convinced.'

'By M.A. Bright?' Victoria said. 'Well, that would be extraordinary, wouldn't it?'

Ewan was looking out to the bullpen, weighing it up.

'What if it's genuine?' Victoria said.

'I'll eat my hat and yours.' This was Des Pearce, a personal friend of Harry Knight who had a column in *Vicious*. It was hard to say exactly what Des wrote about. What Victoria knew was that he didn't write it very well, and yet month after month he garnered letters, from men mostly, who saw the world the way he did. Right place at the right time was what Ewan said about him. He kept middle-aged men happy, which, apparently, was part of the magazine's job. Dinosaur was what Claire, who now ran her own PR agency, called Des and old men like him who'd been kicking around newspapers when Lord Beaverbrook was a boy beaver, as Claire was fond of saying. 'They just don't know they're extinct.'

Des *was* slightly reptilian in appearance, Victoria thought now as she looked over at him; big eyes, scaly skin, not much hair, a head that sat forward like a lizard, little fingers. Yes, one of those fat lizards on bent legs on that island ... what was it called?

Diana was dead?

More reptile than beaver, for sure. Reptilian. Was beaverian a word?

Des interrupted her train of thought. 'M.A. Bright must be a hundred and fifty if he's a day,' he said. 'It's sure to be a hoax.'

Des knew everything, naturally.

'Oh, put a lid on it, Des,' someone said.

'Ewan?' Victoria said.

Ewan sighed. 'Des is right. M.A. Bright would be old if he served in the First World War. I just had a feeling... Fin wouldn't call for nothing.' He took a breath in, held it momentarily and then sighed. 'Look, do it. If we don't, he might go to someone else and we'd kick ourselves if we let it go. Fin's only contacted me because he and my father were at school together. Go and meet him and see what he says. We'll put you on the first train to Paris after lunch.'

'I can go to Paris,' Des said.

The room went silent. Writers stopped clicking pens, keyboarders stopped tapping keys and all eyes turned to Ewan. The thought of Des Pearce covering the death of Diana didn't bear thinking about.

'No,' Ewan said. 'Victoria, you're going.'

The noise resumed. Ewan looked at Daniella. She was still on the phone, writing something down. She nodded acknowledgement.

'Yes, do the lunch,' Ewan said, looking at Victoria and not Des. 'The dailies will cover the accident scene; we'll be out-of-date by the time we print if we go for that. When you get to Paris you can file a weather piece for Harry for *The Eye* tomorrow. We can work out what we need for the magazine once we know the funeral arrangements. We don't even know yet what the family's doing. This will be tricky for them. I'm sure we'll get something later this morning when the Queen comes down. I'll see what our deadlines look like, how much we can push back.'

They'd locked up on Friday night. It was always a difficult time as Ewan was allergic to closure, a reasonable quality in a writer but a poor one in an editor. Victoria's profile of a young British actress named Kate Winslet was the cover story. Danny had convinced Winslet to have her photograph taken in front of a painted brick wall at Venice Beach in Los Angeles, angels and devils in the background. It was Danny's picture, rather than Victoria's story, that ensured the story was on the cover.

Victoria had the best job in the world, her friends all said, and she made sure she agreed with them. Ben had said last night that she was the same as the photographers who waited outside their flat every morning. Did he say that? She shook her head involuntarily.

'Victoria?' Ewan said.

'Fine,' Victoria said, although she hadn't heard his question.

'Are we really covering this for the magazine?' Des Pearce asked.

Ewan sighed. 'I think we'll have to,' he said. 'She's a major figure.'

'But Diana's so tarnished,' Des said.

'What an awful word to use,' one of the younger journalists said. 'She's just died.'

'Yes,' said Ewan. 'Des, forget it.'

'How long do you want me there?' Victoria asked Ewan.

'Until we know a bit more. I don't even know how they'll . . . bring her home.'

One of the interns burst into tears and excused herself.

As Victoria left the conference room, she heard Ewan instructing Danny to head up to Sandringham, where the family had been on holiday. 'Get the boys. I want the young princes.'

FIVE

Brisbane, 1981

'CAN I USE YOUR TOILET?' ANDREW SHAW WAS STANDING in the doorway to the veranda despite the fact I'd forbidden him and Ed from disturbing me.

'Yes, of course,' I said. 'It's in the bathroom off the kitchen.' I didn't turn around. He could have asked Ed.

'I know that book!' he said, like a child who's seen a sweet.

I did turn around then, with as grumpy a face as I could muster. He was pointing to *Autumn Leaves* on the table.

'My wife read it with her book group before the kids were born. Hers had a different cover. Have you read it?'

'Yes,' I said.

I had always liked the original jacket of *Autumn Leaves*, a daguerreotype of hands not quite joining. You couldn't tell if they were the hands of one person or two. That's what I'd liked.

Mr Barlow had strong views about his jackets, he told me. 'It is, after all, the way we dress a naked book,' he said.

When Mr Barlow smiled, it was a rare gift, as if he were taking you in as his one and only confidante. Perhaps he was like that with all his authors but it made me feel as if I were the only one.

When I think back, he was so very kind to me. There was not even a hint of impropriety when he talked about nakedness and book jackets. It would never have entered his mind to be improper, not in any way.

'She said it was good but I probably wouldn't like it,' Andrew Shaw said now.

'You might,' I said. 'You never know.'

'I don't read much.'

'Well, you may as well not bother living then,' I said. 'Now leave me be. I have work to do.'

'What are you doing?' he asked, ignoring my stern tone, which I didn't dislike as much as I would have preferred.

'I'm writing a letter.'

'Who to?'

'A publisher in London.'

He peered at the typewriter. 'Who's Edward McIntrick?'

'Ed, who's been under the house with you.'

'You're writing a letter for him?'

'Not exactly,' I said. 'More, he's writing a letter for me.' I noticed the *t* in *McIntrick* was more like a plus sign again. The t jams almost every time I strike it now, and it puts me in a mood. Sometimes it strikes below the line and only partially, as now, looking like the plus sign. Sometimes it just doesn't do anything, so there's a space instead of a t. *I will send the manuscrip+, oo, when I hear from you.*

I will have to write without the letter t if it keeps going, and that's going to be a new kind of struggle. For a start, I won't be able to use *struggle*, or *start*.

'Ed doesn't strike me as someone who would write a lot of letters,' Andrew Shaw said.

'Well, you never know people,' I replied.

'Is he a literary agent?' he asked, pointing to the title under Ed's signature line.

'Yes and no,' I said. 'For today's purpose, let's just say he's moonlighting as one.'

'Why?'

'It's easier to be Ed than me. And he wouldn't mind.'

'So he doesn't know?'

'Not precisely. He never has to do anything, just be the name on the letters.'

'That's very strange.'

'Yes, but I did ask you to leave me alone,' I said snippily. Andrew Shaw was very difficult to be snippy with, I was finding.

'There's water under your bathroom floor,' he said, as if I would have any idea what that might mean.

I looked back at the letter I'd typed. I'd told Mr Inglis he could reread the chapter I'd sent to Mr Barlow to get a sense of the style of the new book. Perhaps I shouldn't have said that.

Perhaps that won't even be the first chapter now. Perhaps it won't be the style. I suppose it's the same story, but it's entirely different too.

Until now, you see, I not only didn't have the beginning. I didn't have the ending. Finally, perhaps, I do.

∾

Sydney Central Station was like an ant colony without a queen that morning long ago, or, in this ant colony's case, without a prince. I'd left my aunt Bea's house in Balmain before dawn to catch the ferry, and the sun had risen to reveal a royal day. The prince himself—not Charles, of course, who was yet to be born, but Edward, the Prince of Wales before Charles—wasn't due for another four hours, a policeman told me. It was a Sunday, the twentieth of June, 1920. I already knew the prince was off shooting wild pigs because that had been in the newspaper, along with a dispensation from the Archbishop of Sydney, it being the Sabbath and shooting requiring a gun and some commentator raising the alarm about the possible threat to the royal soul.

There were policemen everywhere around the station, more of them even than newspapermen with their big cyclops cameras, their wide-brimmed hats behind. I had watched those newspapermen enviously for some moments when I'd first arrived, daring to long to be among them, to take up my own notebook and pencil and write what I was seeing. At that moment, they had nothing to do but fiddle with their equipment and bother the constabulary, but soon they would have a prince to write about, a bona fide prince to share with the world. Imagine that!

It was another policeman who read my letter of appointment, delivered the day before to Bea's house by a servant in full livery—livery a term I learned from my mother after the liveried servant left, Bert my brother asking why a servant would wear his liver not his heart on his sleeve, the rest of us erupting into fits followed by a biology lesson from Bea's husband Reg, an architect and apparent polymath.

The second policeman directed me to the platform; Platform H.R.H., as it had been named for the occasion. The royal train was waiting in earnest, porters and guards running about, busy as busy bees. You knew the train because the carriages were painted light blue and ivory rather than the plain brown of the trains we got about in. It was all very grand. The pigeons above us cooed more warmly and fluttered more meaningfully than they might above any other train. The steam and smoke were more like a gentle mist of morning. The smells—coaldust and more universal dust—were more pleasant.

You see, they really should have had me writing about it!

∾

It was Mr Waters who'd interviewed me at Government House two days before, with the governor's housekeeper, a Mrs Danby. Mr Waters was Rupert Waters, the prince's assistant private secretary, he told me; a man of middle height, with uncontrollable sandy hair that he'd made a fair fist of slicking back, and blue-green eyes like those very pure lakes that come from glaciers you see in the pictures. Very true eyes, and a gentle smile, the remnants of childhood freckles still scattered across his nose.

That's who Andrew Shaw reminds me of, I realise: Mr Waters; Mr Waters who, at that time, 1920, seemed old but who, I realise now, was so young, barely twenty-seven. He and Andrew Shaw share soft voices, soft eyes, and perhaps even a belief that the world is overflowing with goodness. That's certainly what Andrew Shaw seems to assume, and it was Mr Waters's best quality, even if it destroyed us all.

Mr Waters is gone now, the letter says. Perhaps he's been reincarnated as Andrew Shaw.

The Buddhists, notable for the fact that they are a religion whose followers don't come knocking at my door, offer a whole different way of seeing, and one I don't much like, frankly. You go to the university and study comparative religion to learn about Buddhism. It is anti-attachment, which to me is entirely counter-existential. Isn't attachment the whole mechanism with which we are anchored to life? Isn't it the same as gravity? I have been unattached for most of my life and, believe me, if it weren't for Ed, I might actually prefer death by now. Why else would I entertain religious nuts?

The housekeeper Mrs Danby was the counterpoint to Mr Waters—so humourless that if you had a humour meter it

The True Story of Maddie Bright

would register in the negative when passed over her. She may well have already learned the skill of unattachment.

There was a seamstress on the tour, Mrs Danby told me when I asked about uniforms—hoping I wouldn't have to pay for my own, as I had no money with which to pay—and the seamstress would fit the *successful* candidate for serving clothes. She stressed that word, *successful*, and then added that it was unlikely, *highly* unlikely, that I'd be needing a uniform because only the successful applicant would need a uniform. She was a person for whom the entire field of italics was invented, the way she stressed certain words. I was in no doubt that she stressed that word *successful* to make it clear that it and me were a long way apart.

She shook her head again in disbelief. 'A pot of tea, you say, on a customer? Well, I never. How does an accident like that happen?' Her face was sour, as if I'd just done it all over again, poured tea, but in her lap rather than the lap of the chap at Christie's Cafe in Brisbane.

'It wasn't an accident,' I said. Why on earth was I telling them this? If I'd wanted the job, as she told me after escorting me from the room, I probably should have rethought that story.

It wasn't me who wanted the job, although I didn't say that to her. It was my mother, who had to find a way to feed the five remaining children in my family as well my father and herself. My mother had brought us on the train from Brisbane to see the prince, but so far all she'd seen was the advertisement at

Government House for serving girls. She'd failed twice to see the royal presence—the day he arrived, with us in tow, and the next day, even after splurging a shilling to stand for ten minutes on a wooden crate. I would warrant she carried some hope that the prince would help us out of our misery just by being. My getting a job serving on his train was the next best thing.

There was no money left since Daddy lost his teaching job, and the only wage now was my brother Bert's and it was not enough. I had a job. I lost it. I had to find another. We were, without putting it too delicately, skint, and it was my responsibility, as the oldest surviving child, to do something.

And now, incredibly, despite my inability to tell a lie, I'd been given a job on the royal train!

∼

Mr Waters had said I was to report to the dining car but I didn't know which car it was. I assumed it would be in the back carriages, close to the prince's private quarters, which I knew to be the last carriage, from the pictures in the newspaper. The train had a little portico on the very back and I'd seen photographs of the prince waving from there as he went from town to town.

Along George Street, I'd noticed, there were still streamers hanging from windows left over from the parade the day before, grubby confetti covering the ground in some places, especially around the bank, where people had mulled in hope of a glimpse of the prince. They'd collected around Government House too,

I saw, perhaps assuming he'd slept there. I didn't know where he'd slept.

I was still standing on the railway platform, wondering what to do next, when a voice behind me said, 'Are you lost?'

SIX

Sydney, 1920

I TURNED AROUND AND SAW A WOMAN, SMARTLY DRESSED in a straight blue skirt and ivory blouse, a blue jacket matching the skirt, pearls, gloves and a hat of navy blue felt. Her shoes were ivory like the blouse. She had soft strawberry blonde curls that surrounded a pixie face. Her skin glowed. I thought she was the most beautiful creature I had ever encountered and, yet, unlike what one might expect, not at all unapproachable. She smiled warmly. I knew immediately we would be friends.

'I'm Helen Burns,' she said, holding out her hand. Her accent was hard to pick. She definitely wasn't English. Her vowels didn't end; they just sort of faded. 'If you've made it this far, I assume you're not a Fenian who might have dastardly intentions.' She was smoking a cigarette, I saw now, as she put it to her lips quite casually there on the platform.

'No, I'm the new maid,' I said. 'What's a Fenian?'

'Irish, from Ireland. They shot his uncle.'

'I beg pardon?'

'Doesn't matter. Are you looking for someone?'

'Mr Waters,' I said. 'He's to meet me in the dining car in fifteen minutes.'

'Rupert!' she exclaimed. 'Oh yes, I know who you are. You're a Bright.'

'I am,' I said. 'And not a Fenian.'

She laughed. 'Your father is the poet, Thomas Bright.'

'He is,' I said, perplexed. 'Thomas Bright, Tom. I'm Maddie Bright. And you're from *Jane Eyre*?'

She looked unsure momentarily then smiled. 'Oh yes, the name. I've never heard that joke before, of course. That's what threw me.'

American, that was her accent, I was sure. She was American. My father had described the way the soldiers spoke and it was just like this, as if they'd made the English language either more or less efficient, depending on the word, stretching out the vowels as a general rule and demoting more than a few of the consonants.

'Well, not in recent times anyway, when I've been in the company of uneducated men. But as it happens, just like Helen Burns, I am an orphan, although fortunately of independent means and inoculated for typhus.' She laughed at her own little joke. It took me a moment more to remember that part of the book; Jane's friend Helen Burns had died of typhus.

'And you're joining us today,' Helen Burns went on. 'Yes, I remember now. Rupert has been called away to some awful business, I should think, given that the prince has been afforded a gun and they sent Ned to supervise. Let's just hope that the prince shot Ned and not the other way around. Black mark for the tour if we kill the prince. Oh my God, I didn't really say that, did I?

'I am the other Helen Burns, the one who is not Jane Eyre's best friend. I am the prince's assistant dealing with the newspapermen, and I am to welcome you.' She bowed her head. 'Welcome to the Royal Tour of His Royal Highness Edward, Prince of Wales, to our dominions, and so on.' She gestured with her cigarette hand. 'You may bow low or curtsy now.' I began to bend at the knees as my mother had taught me. 'Oh, for goodness' sake, I wasn't serious.'

She laughed then, such a whoop of a laugh that others around us turned their heads. Looking serious suddenly, she said, 'Do you take after him?'

'Who?'

'The poet. I mean, you do write?'

'I do,' I said, delighted to have been asked. 'I write stories, and I want to be a journalist.'

'Do you really? How marvellous! Just like moi!' She looked whimsical for a moment. 'Not poetry? What a shame. But I knew you'd write. I told Ned, she's one to grab with both hands. I made Ned tell Rupert.' She looked down at my portmanteau and frowned. 'Is that all you've got?' she said.

My bag held almost everything I owned: a grey skirt, a cotton blouse, smalls and an extra pair of shoes, brown. I wore my only coat, black wool, and my other skirt and blouse, blue. My hair was pulled up into a bun ready for a maid's cap. I wore no hat for I had no hat to wear. I looked nothing like the sophisticated woman before me. All we had in common was curls, and even her curls were better behaved than mine.

'They said uniforms are supplied,' I said.

'How truly magnificent,' she said, 'to be so free. Let's take you on board then. Are your eyes green?'

'Yes,' I said.

'I thought so. Lovely.'

'I'm supposed to meet Mr Waters.'

'You simply mustn't call him that. Both he and I will start looking for his father. He'll want you to call him Rupert.'

I knew this was unlikely.

'At any rate, he's late,' Helen said, looking behind her down the platform. 'I'll show you where he is normally, then we'll go and find him together.' She took a last draw on her cigarette and squashed it into the tile with her shoe to extinguish it. 'All right,' she said. 'So you don't write poetry. I wish you wrote poetry. Couldn't you try, just for me?'

I laughed. 'I don't think it works like that. Are you a poet?'

'Good Lord, no. I am what's called a hack. Anyway, you're young yet. Perhaps the poetry will find you. Your father's work is extraordinary. You've read him, of course.'

'Yes,' I said, 'when he lets me.' I thought of Daddy. Rats. All he wrote about now was rats. You couldn't call it poetry, not even doggerel.

'Does he love that you write?'

'Oh yes,' I said, remembering an earlier time, another life really. 'He used to play this game where we each had to supply the next sentence of a story. Mine were always thoughtful, Daddy said, but my brother Edward was our man of action.'

It was a game we hadn't played since Daddy had come home from France, since Edward hadn't. I had a moment then of wretched despair, the weight of everything, my poor family so brought down in the world, Mummy so desperate to see Prince Edward who would be our king one day, Daddy who'd come home a year ago so changed. And our own Edward, who I couldn't think about without tears, which pricked my eyes now.

I felt dowdy in my skirt and blouse, a cardigan I'd had to darn the night before. I felt sudden terrible shame about who I was.

'I'm not a writer,' I said to Helen Burns to straighten out any misunderstanding. 'I'm a servant.' I said the word *servant* with some energy, not meaning to be disparaging, just meaning to be clear.

'Well, service is honest work,' Helen Burns said, smiling warmly. 'Writing, so often, is not.

'I did not have a father anything like yours, Maddie,' she said earnestly then. 'Mine was a stepfather, about which not enough has been written. It's stepmothers we hate, but stepfathers lurk behind even the best mothers, and their lurking is something we would do well to note.'

She looked at me and grinned suddenly. 'Oh, please don't despair about service, Maddie. For me, it's just lovely to meet someone who's not a sycophant. Fresh. It's fresh. And at least you're small.' She giggled then, more quietly than the previous whoop. She looked younger now, a schoolgirl, as if the sophisticated woman was a mask she donned for the world and those who saw her laugh this way saw the real person. 'I shouldn't really say that, should I? But David's a dear little boy, and he doesn't like big women. You'll be perfect!'

'David?' I said, but she mustn't have heard.

She looked along the platform towards the line of policemen guarding nothing in particular. 'Oh God, it's just so stuffy, the whole thing. I'm sure he'd rather get out on a farm and work than all these stunts they put on for him. I know I would.'

'I went to see him with my mother and brothers,' I said, realising she must be talking about the prince now. 'At the town hall. But he'd already left.'

We had lined up for hours on the holiday for his birthday, hoping to walk past and see him up close.

'Story of his life,' Helen said. 'They have him doing this and that and really it's not in him. He shook over two thousand hands that day. His hand was so bruised they had to fetch the doctor.'

'Goodness,' I said. I looked about nervously. There were people everywhere now and a growing sense of departure seemed to envelop the platform. 'I have to say, it's all come as a surprise,' I said.

'What has?' she said.

'The position. I didn't think I'd be appointed.'

'I dared him.'

'I beg pardon?'

'I dared him to appoint you. I thought it would be fun.'

'The prince?' I said.

'God, no! He doesn't have anything to do with it. Rupert told us your name after the interview. Well, as soon as I heard Bright and Brisbane, I knew you must be related to Thomas Bright the poet.

'I was with *Vanity Fair* at the end of the war, the new American magazine, and we published his poems. Rupert told Ned he couldn't give you the job on account of your being *let go*.' She widened her eyes as if relishing a scandal.

'So I wired your cafe, the one that dismissed you. And then I spoke to the owner on the telephone, Mr Christie. I knew there'd be more to the story. There always is. Ned told Rupert what happened and Rupert thinks you have honour. So do I, for what it's worth.' She smiled.

Just then I saw Mr Waters hurrying along the platform towards us with another man. Mr Waters was unmistakable, even from a distance, those long limbs and that slim frame. He was carrying under his arm a thick wad of papers. His fringe, which he'd kept

The True Story of Maddie Bright

pushing back the day before, was flopping into his eyes. In his mouth was a pencil. When he reached us, he pulled the pencil out and blew his hair up in an attempt to get it out of his eyes. He was wearing long brown pants with deep pockets, a white shirt with the sleeves rolled up and a brown belt and shoes.

'Helen, you found Maddie, thank you,' he said. 'Perhaps you might show her around?' He smiled at us both. 'I'll see you a bit later on, Maddie.'

The other man looked at me. 'You're the tea girl?'

I nodded. I supposed I was.

'Funny story, that.' He smiled. It disappeared quickly.

The other man was the same height as Mr Waters, older by ten or so years, with a moustache that made you think he must have been high up in the army. But he was dressed in a suit with a crisp white shirt and tie, not a uniform.

He turned to Helen. 'We're going over who said what.'

Helen rolled her eyes. 'Well, I didn't say anything. Ned, this is Maddie, and we're not to call her the tea girl. Also, why aren't you shooting pigs? I thought you were shooting pigs.'

'Fine.' He nodded at me. 'Maddie, I'm Colonel Grigg.' He turned back to Helen. 'I sent Dickie to the shoot. I know you didn't say anything, sweetie, but Halsey has wired the King and Dickie says he's upset.'

'The King?'

'The prince.'

Colonel Grigg looked at me briefly again and back at Helen. 'Well, if he wants them to treat him like a prince—' Helen said.

Mr Waters held up his hand, the one that held the pencil, to stop her speaking, and frowned in my direction. 'Very well, Helen. I think that's probably enough.'

'Did you find a correspondence secretary?' Helen asked Mr Waters. 'I can't keep doing it. I'm sure Ned has made that clear.'

She seemed brusque with Mr Waters. I wondered why.

It was Colonel Grigg who replied, 'Well . . .' he said, grimacing, 'perhaps just a couple of days, to help Rupert out. He's in a pickle.'

'So you didn't recruit anyone?' Helen was looking at Mr Waters.

'No,' Mr Waters said, looking down towards the platform as if he'd dropped something. 'I interviewed for the maid job and we got Maddie . . .' He smiled at me then. 'And Maddie, I am very pleased you're here. It's just a bit of a morning, I'm afraid. Anyway, Helen,' he went on, looking at the floor again, 'we've also hired another footman back at the house and a chambermaid. The housekeeper organised those for us.'

Helen said, 'You promised you'd get someone after we left Melbourne.' Mell-born, she pronounced it. 'I already have a job, remember?' She turned to Colonel Grigg. 'And you don't give me any less work. I have two masters, three if you count H.R.H., and I don't like any of them right at this moment.'

'Rupert and I met with four candidates but not one of them is what he needs,' Colonel Grigg said. 'I agree with him about it, although I have no intention of giving you up.'

He smiled. I didn't like his smile. There was something self-satisfied about it.

'Did you forget to mention they have to write like a prince?' Helen said. She was the sophisticated woman of the world again, I noticed, none of the girl now. She'd quite changed with Mr Waters and the colonel; I would have said she'd become hard-hearted, if I'd been pressed to provide a description.

Around the train there was a good deal of anxiousness to leave: porters carrying trunks into the carriages, guards inspecting various aspects of the platform, railway staff polishing shiny brass and cleaning already clean windows, the engines puffing and panting as if taking a few deep breaths before a race. The pigeons were still wheeling above, as if they might have messages for us but couldn't find a place to land. The train itself seemed to be shrugging its shoulders, hunkering down to take its load.

'Of course we mentioned it.' Colonel Grigg looked exasperated. 'But everyone wants the job. So we had the governor's cousin's son, who's just started at the University of Sydney, followed by the police commissioner's nephew, and so on. Lovely lads. Not suitable. There's politics in all this; we have to be careful.'

All the while the colonel and Helen were talking, I noticed Mr Waters was looking at Helen. Those lovely clear eyes. Hope. That was the impression I was forming of him. He was a soul blessed with hope.

'Are you sure not one of them could do it?' Helen asked.

'I can show you what they wrote, if you like,' Colonel Grigg said. '*The prince was right pleased to get your letter and I hope you'll be a good boy in future*—typewritten *suture*, as I recall.'

He waved a hand. 'Poor old Rupert is tearing his hair out. Just look at him.'

Mr Waters didn't say anything. Helen didn't look at him.

'So if you could help, we'd both be much obliged,' the colonel said.

I studied him then, Colonel Grigg. I did not find hope anywhere in his features and perhaps this was why I hadn't warmed to him.

'Well, I'll do what I can today,' Helen was saying to him now.

'Thank you,' he said. 'A thousand times. Come on, Waters—let's face the music, old chap.' And they were off.

'It may appear chaotic,' Helen said as they scuttled away, 'but I can assure you we run a very tight ship here at H.R.H. H.Q. It's just busier than anyone thought possible. In Melbourne—' Mell-born again '—more people came to meet the prince than live in the city. Do you understand what I mean? There were more people on the streets of Melbourne than live in Melbourne. How can that even be? At one stage, he had to be carried out of the crowd by a group of soldiers, in fear for his life.'

I must have looked confused.

'The crush.' She sucked her cheeks in.

I laughed. 'Maybe I should be a Fenian after all.'

'Don't say that,' she said, mock horror on her face. 'It was a Fenian who shot poor Alfred, and he was the Queen's favourite. Victoria's favourite and your people shot him, Maddie. If it hadn't been for his rubber suspenders deflecting the bullet...' She made a cutthroat motion.

The True Story of Maddie Bright

Helen had light blue eyes, and when she widened them as she did now they were awfully big in her small face.

'Alfred who?'

'Prince Alfred. Prince Edward's uncle. Queen Victoria's youngest. You don't know the story?'

I shook my head.

'He was shot when he visited Australia, at a picnic here in Sydney, by an Irishman, a Fenian. It was all they could talk about when Prince Edward was leaving England. Will the colonists shoot another royal?'

'Well, so far, we haven't,' I said. 'That must count in our favour: we haven't shot him.'

'Quite,' she said, regarding me carefully. 'There's more to you, isn't there?'

Helen led me to the second last carriage and I stepped up behind her into what was a beautifully appointed room, so spacious you wouldn't believe it was only the width of a train carriage. The wall panels were white with blue trim, and a rich dark red rug covered the floor. There were two desks with chairs at one end and, at the other, leather-upholstered easy chairs with electrical lights on two small tables that added a homely feel.

'Is this the dining car?' I asked. I wondered where the table was. I could smell tobacco smoke and wood polish.

'Rupert's office,' she replied. She pointed to one of the desks. 'That's him.' She tossed her bag onto the other desk. 'And this is the correspondence secretary. That's the job they keep trying to get me to do.' The second desk was a mess of envelopes and papers in various stages of undress.

She gestured to the door at the rear of the compartment. 'The prince's private dining room and beyond that his chamber, where only Dickie can follow.'

I was still carrying my portmanteau and Helen took it from me and put it down on one of the easy chairs. She pointed to the forward carriages. 'The other staff offices and the newspapermen. Rupert is here because the prince cannot survive without him.'

'And who's Dickie?' I asked.

'The prince's cousin, Louis Mountbatten—eyebrows, perpetually grinning—who's allowed in to see him. So is Admiral Halsey, actually, if the mood takes him. And then there's Godfrey Thomas—*Sir* Godfrey, the principal private secretary, Rupert's boss—and Ned, Colonel Grigg, who you just met, my boss. You'll learn. Rupert is the one who steers the ship, despite its many captains. If Rupert weren't here, they'd never get David to do anything.'

I looked at the blue door that separated the office from the private dining room. I'd be serving the prince his meals for the trip to Canberra, Mr Waters had said, when he telephoned to tell me I'd been successful in my application.

Discretion was the main thing, Mr Waters had said in the interview, although Helen didn't seem at all discreet. 'We're a loyal bunch,' Mr Waters had said earnestly. 'Do you understand what I mean?'

'I think so,' I said.

'Really, Mr Waters,' the housekeeper had said then, 'I don't think this girl meets our requirements. A pot of tea, sir, on a guest.' She had been wanting the interview to come to an end for some time, I surmised, but Mr Waters had kept on with it.

'There might have been mitigating circumstances.' He turned to me, frowning slightly, fiddling with his spectacles on the table then looking up at me without donning them. 'You say it was on purpose?'

I only nodded.

'Did you have a reason?'

'Yes, I did, sir.'

'And are you going to tell us the reason?' Mr Waters asked.

'No, sir.'

'Why not?'

'I don't think it would contribute to your view of me as discreet, sir.'

He'd laughed then, a loud belly laugh that stopped only when he caught sight of the housekeeper, whose visage would wipe rust from steel, as my father might have said.

He'd smiled again as I left. 'Well, Maddie, thank you for coming to see us.' He glanced at the housekeeper. 'I don't think we're in a position to . . . All the best, at any rate.'

'Thank you, sir,' I said.

'When it comes to H.R.H. himself,' Helen Burns said now, taking a seat at Mr Waters's desk and gesturing for me to sit at the other desk. 'Well, the truth is . . . I couldn't say I know how to accurately describe him.'

'I saw his hand,' I said. 'I came in with my family the first day he arrived.'

'Good for you,' Helen said.

'It may have been someone else's hand.'

'Yes,' she said. 'Quite possible. I should say at the outset that I'm not like the rest of them. I'm not born to love him or anything. No King and Country for me. Frankly, I wasn't a fan of the prince. I wasn't in his circle, like Godfrey, or his father's idea, like the admiral, or the P.M.'s voice, like Ned. And I have no stupid loyalty to the throne like Rupert, I can assure you.' She paused, lit another cigarette, taking time to strike the match. She inhaled deeply. 'I'm here because I was summonsed to the palace, as it happens.'

'By the prince?'

'Yes, by the prince. He'd read a piece of mine about the treatment of soldiers after the war, darling. Beastly, it's been in Britain. That's one reason I wasn't a fan. He was part of the empire that did all that. Anyhow, he saw my story, apparently. Frankly, it's hard to believe Mr George is still in office. That's what the prince said to me, a journalist! It amounted to a rift in the separation of powers or something and I could have written it, as we were not officially off the record. Wouldn't it have caused a stink!

'He said that the Prince of Wales couldn't say those things I wrote, and if I worked for him, I couldn't say them either, but we could think them, he said, and we could act on them without saying them. Did I understand his meaning? he asked. He looked at me with those eyes of his that could melt the polar ice cap. I thought I did understand, although he hadn't offered me a job at that stage.

'Actually, he quite impressed me, which I hadn't expected. I have reason to dislike him specifically.' She looked around as if someone might be listening. 'Perhaps he's not terribly bright. Perhaps you just end up on his team out of curiosity and then you come to know him and like him and you forget what you disliked him for. You start to see what others see in him, I suppose. Now I'm even fond of the dear little fellow.

'Anyway, by the time he said he wanted a woman who could handle the newspapermen on future tours of the empire, I was more than willing.'

'So the prince asked you on the tour?' I said. Helen was so very glamorous to my mind, and held such an important role, telling newspapermen what to do! I couldn't imagine it.

'Yes,' she said, as if still surprised, 'and here I am.' She paused then. 'And there,' she said finally, 'when I arrived . . .' she lit up a cigarette, took a deep draw '. . . was Rupert.' She made a little *hmph* noise and smoke came out her nostrils, like a dragon. 'The prince didn't tell me that part, that Rupert was coming on the tour.' Her face hardened. 'Although I suppose I should have known. Anyway, I report to Grigg.

'Truth is,' she went on quickly, a tight smile now, 'H.R.H. is difficult to refuse. Rupert's his favourite whipping boy, as you'll see. He always takes it back, though, because he knows he needs Rupert. I think he knows he has no real compass without Rupert.'

'Compass for what?' I said.

'Living morally for a start.'

'So Mr Waters knows the prince well?'

'He and Rupert are like that.' She crossed her fingers, a bitter smile on her lips. 'They grew up together. Rupert's like the big brother David never had and badly needs. He's the only one of the lot of them who'll take David on when he's in one of his moods.' She looked hard again then, like she'd looked when Mr Waters found us.

'And who's David?' I said, feeling stupid.

'The prince. That's his name, or one of them. It's the one they use at home. We all call him David. He asked us to. He'll do the same with you. He doesn't want to be a royal highness. He's terribly informal. You'll see. He'd prefer none of the pomp. Unfortunately, he was born into the pompiest pomp on earth. As I say, I feel as if I shouldn't like him, but I find that I do.' She gave a little sigh.

'And here: the problem!' she exclaimed suddenly. On the floor beneath both desks there were envelopes, hundreds of them. 'Mail.'

'Mail?' I said. I was finding Helen a little overwhelming to be honest. My mother had said no one would notice me or speak to me. I would be a servant and that meant I was no one. 'Do you understand, Maddie?' she'd asked. 'A servant is no one.' She looked so sad. Yes, I said, I do understand, although in truth I didn't know why it would make Mummy so sad. And now, to have Helen not only speak to me but take me into her confidence so fully was quite unnerving.

'They are delivering it daily from Government House,' she said. 'This is all from Victoria. Sydney is just starting. They write to the prince and tell him their stories.' She sighed again. 'The war,' she said. 'I don't know why they write to him. Perhaps they think it will help. There's so much . . . unhappiness in the world.'

I thought of my father.

'Did you know someone in the war?' I asked.

'Who didn't?' she replied, and laughed lightly. 'But all that is past. Now we are an empire united, happy in our glorious victory.' She didn't look happy. She looked almost teary. I imagined we both did. 'And we have our prince, shining himself upon his dominions.

'Rupert,' she said quietly after another moment, her eyes glistening now. 'I knew Rupert in the war.'

'How?' I asked.

She narrowed her eyes. 'Never mind.'

From *Autumn Leaves* by M.A. Bright:

France, 1918

'You're British?' she asked, lifting the blanket that covered him. He felt the rush of cold air. Any sensation other than pain was welcome. He tried to focus on the cold.

'Last time I looked, yes,' he said, controlling the fear in his voice, which would explode into panic if he didn't keep it in check. He could taste iron in his mouth.

He would keep his voice even. No matter what, he would manage that.

'What I mean is, what are you doing here?' She spoke slowly.

She wasn't British, or she was British with something else. Canadian?

He wanted something rough, not that sweet voice. There was no place for sweetness here.

The True Story of Maddie Bright

He looked up, squinted in the sunlight. He focused on her face, a silhouette at first and then as his own eyes adjusted he saw hers, a pale blue like the sky above her, her pretty face, hair tied back, strands escaping.

'I don't know,' he said. 'I was covered with a French overcoat, I think, and so they mistook me.'

'And now a French blanket,' she said. 'So what's the injury?'

He looked down towards his left arm, thought he might vomit, looked away.

'Don't look then,' she said, patting his right shoulder gently. She pushed his fringe behind his ear. It was such an intimate gesture. He felt her touch warm him. The warmth stayed there. 'You've hit your head too,' she said.

He could have watched her all day, he thought. It was the morphine, or the loss of blood. He must focus.

'I'm the batman to the Prince of Wales,' he said.

'Well, bully for you,' she said. 'I'm the ambulance driver to Royaumont. I think I trump you right now, strictly speaking, as you need a doctor not a prince. And I couldn't care less about batmen, much less about your jolly prince who got us into this mess. But I think we're going to save that arm.' She looked around. 'Close your eyes.'

'Why—'

'I said close them.'

He did as he was told. He heard another voice, male, speaking French. 'Driver, are you clear to go?'

'I'm taking this one as well,' she replied, also in French.

Perhaps she was French. The Canadians were French, weren't they?

'He's English,' the man said. 'He's going to the C.C.S. at Soissons.'

He had been out in the sun for hours, he knew. The longer he was out there, the less likely it was they could save his arm. He knew this too. He had seen the studies, the time between injury and aid being of critical importance. This was why they'd established the C.C.S. system, casualty clearing stations, so that the badly injured could get help. But no help had come so far, he thought bitterly.

'What will happen to him?' she asked.

'We've contacted them. They're coming.'

He heard her voice, annoyed now. 'No,' she said. 'Soissons is cut off again.'

The man didn't reply.

'I know him,' she said. 'He's a family friend. Let me take him to Royaumont.'

'You can't just take every soldier you fancy,' he said, switching to accented English.

'I'm only taking one,' she said. 'I have room.'

'No,' he said. 'We can't make exceptions. He's English. He must go to an English hospital. *We* are funding Royaumont, not the English.'

There was quiet then. He opened one eye. They were alone.

'Don't worry,' she said. 'We're not finished yet, not by a mile. Give me a minute.' She smiled then and she looked so very young. It filled him with hope, which was the most dangerous feeling. He thought he might cry.

He bit his lip hard.

He watched her walk away from him, had the strongest urge to call her back. He was sure he would never see her again. Oh God, how weak he was.

It had been three days since the explosion. His wounds were septic, he suspected. She'd screwed up her nose when she uncovered his arm. He might die, he thought. It might be better than losing his arm, his left. He was left-handed.

Just then two French soldiers appeared, one with a head wound, the other a bandaged leg. They each took one end of the stretcher. She was with them, looking around. 'Are we allowed to do this?' one of them said in French.

'Of course,' she said. 'Quickly now. We must get him to Royaumont. He's a batman.' That smile. In another context, he'd think she was making fun of him. But since she was taking him away from here, she couldn't be unkind if she tried.

∽

The drive was excruciating, long. The track was rutted. Every bump. The morphine had worn off, he could be very sure now, and while he couldn't feel his arm anymore, his right leg, where he'd taken shrapnel, was aching, dully at first and then in full bloom. His head hurt too. He remembered then the unique noise as his eardrum burst, like the sea rushing in. Shocking, unrelenting, its report over and over.

The flash of light at the blast kept coming back in his mind's eye. Was David with him? He couldn't have been. Someone would have told him. David wasn't there, he was almost sure; they'd never have lost him if David had been there.

He heard a church bell in the distance. His life was all about sound now, what he heard, and the sun which shone through the trees and warmed his face. He would die here, in the sun, the distant bells.

By the time the two young orderlies were pulling his stretcher from the ambulance, he was entirely numb again.

Someone was calling out, 'You didn't say which are priority. This one?'

He could see a single pillar of what must have once been a church leaning precariously towards him and, next to it, a vine climbing a high wall.

Had she said Royaumont? Wasn't there an abbey called Royaumont near Paris?

And then her voice in reply. 'Yes, the stretcher is urgent,' she was saying. He heard accents, English, Scottish. Where the hell were they? 'The others are all walking. But get him to X-ray soonest,' she said.

SEVEN

London, 1997

VICTORIA WENT DOWNSTAIRS TO THE READING TABLES to go through the morning editions of *The Eye*. They'd been running them hourly since three am, the page-one headline, and pages two, three, five and six, plus the leader in the latest edition: TRAGEDY FOR THE WORLD.

There were smiling pictures of Diana, Fayed; a badly crumpled car, unrecognisable as a Mercedes; a tunnel entrance. Fayed died at the scene, along with the driver. Diana died in hospital. Too much blood loss, one story said. The impact had torn her pulmonary vein from her heart, Victoria read in another.

The pulmonary vein, that was one that took blood to the heart from the lungs, if Victoria remembered correctly.

She went back upstairs to her desk and dialled her father.

'Byrd,' he said.

'It's me, Daddy.'

'Victoria. I'm just making tea.'

She looked at her watch. 'Yes, I was planning to pop in this morning after the meeting, but I have to go to Paris instead.'

'They've got you on it?'

'Ewan wants to redo the cover so I'm going over to do an hour-by-hour. I've got a lunch first and then I'll have to go home and pack, so I won't make tea this morning.' She normally went over on Sundays.

'Tony's going to make a statement.'

'Someone should. Ewan says the family haven't yet.'

'Apparently.'

'Did he call you?'

'Who?'

'Tony.'

'Alastair. I don't know why really. He said Tony wanted me to come up with something to say. I didn't have anything. There aren't words.' He cleared his throat.

Had he been upset by Diana's death?

Victoria's father was scathing about the monarchy, had written op-ed pieces on the sheer unfairness of a system that saw people born to rule. But Diana; he'd always had a soft spot for Diana. He'd met her once, at a lunch where he'd represented New Labour. She'd sat him at the top table. He didn't know why, but when they spoke she knew about the education policy he'd drafted. 'She talked about being dumb,' he told Victoria later, 'but you would never describe her as dumb. You'd be stupid to make that mistake.'

'Alastair must be over the moon,' Victoria said now. The P.M.'s press secretary had no time for the royal family either.

'It's not like that.'

'No, I suppose not. Even the diehards here are shocked. Except Des Pearce.'

'Are you all right?' he asked. She could picture him sitting in his office chair looking out to the front garden—the garden that had been her mother's.

'Yes, of course. Why wouldn't I be? Anyway, the pulmonary veins,' she said.

'Yes?'

'Are they the ones that take blood back to the heart?'

'Yes. But *The Guardian* already has the line. Diana died of a broken heart.'

He had never liked the fact she'd left *The Guardian* for *The Daily Mail*. She may as well have joined a leper colony. 'Good on them,' she said, wishing now she hadn't asked him. 'Anyway, I must go.'

She told her father she'd pop in when she was home from Paris.

It wasn't until she hung up the phone that she realised. Thirty-six. Diana was thirty-six, the same age as Victoria's mother when she died—the same age as Victoria now.

It was what that psychologist Brad had said. She'd been to see him three months ago, prompted by Claire, who knew of him through a friend. Victoria was stressed and anxious and didn't know why. Brad told her she was suffering from delayed grief, as if he was some sort of detective of the mind and he'd solved her crime. She was thirty-six, and her mother had been thirty-six when she died. Snap! Brad called Victoria a strong woman, she remembered now, said he liked strong women. She'd laughed with Claire about it afterwards. 'I like strong women,' Claire had said, making eyes at Victoria.

But perhaps that had been what had upset her father, Victoria thought. Diana's dying reminded him of that other loss.

She nearly called him back but didn't. What would she say? Her mother was one of the things they didn't talk about.

Victoria went back to her desk and took out a blank notebook, intending to sketch notes for her story for *The Eye*. Reuters were reporting that the bodyguard had lived. He was in hospital, critical. He'd lost his tongue. It wasn't a figure of speech.

Victoria had written one of the first features on the problems in the royal marriage when she was at *The Daily Mail*, in 1987, before anyone was saying anything publicly about Charles and Diana. She'd interviewed five staff at Kensington Palace off the record, and it painted a picture of terrible unhappiness between them. The editor had loved it.

Victoria sighed heavily. What would she write about Diana now? She hardly knew. It was as if bearing witness, the first job of a journalist, reporting what she saw, was now out of reach to her and she didn't know why. She couldn't think, let alone write. Grief, Brad had said, delayed grief. Perhaps he was right.

She recalled a picture she'd seen of Diana taken just a few months ago. She looked like the shell of a person, as if the real Diana had just walked out of her own life. Diana didn't look like someone starting afresh, which was what the stories said after the divorce. She didn't look like someone who was playing the photographers the way Danny described. Alone. She looked terribly alone.

At the time, Victoria had thought of the story she'd written, wondered if in some way she'd contributed to that hunted expression. She'd told herself she was just doing her job. But it had shaken her because she was starting to understand just a little of what it felt like to be pursued.

∾

Ben had said calmly at the start of their relationship, the first morning after they slept together at her flat, that being with him would present a unique opportunity to see what it was like to be on the other side of the notebook and camera. 'Like William Hurt in *The Doctor*,' he said. 'He gets cancer and he picks the surgeon he used to make fun of, the one who speaks respectfully to patients, even when they're asleep on the operating table.'

Victoria said it was a non-story, the newspapers wouldn't be interested in her and Ben, and for the first three months she'd been right. Ben travelled from the US to London to visit Victoria, and she took leave to visit him in New York or Los Angeles. No one knew. But then, one night in early July, they'd been into Central London to see *Batman & Robin*, George Clooney all wrong, Victoria had thought, although Ben said he was perfect. They were dressed casually. Ben wore a baseball cap and an old jacket so he wouldn't be recognised.

They were on the way home. They didn't see the photographer.

The next day, Ben's publicist faxed Victoria the picture from the entertainment pages of the New York *Daily News*, a blurry shot of the two of them walking along the street hand in hand. *Who's the mystery London woman in Ben Winter's life?* You'd never recognise Victoria in the shot.

She didn't mind all that much. In fact, it was a little bit exciting to be the subject of speculation like that. It was funny. They both laughed about it.

The next week, Ben had gone back to Los Angeles for the premiere of *Zombie Armageddon*. He'd wanted Victoria to go with him but she had to work, she'd told him. He'd been annoyed about it.

On the Monday after he left, Victoria was heading out to ride her bike to work. She opened the door and suddenly she was blinded. She could hear the flashes firing.

Her response was to step back. As a journalist, she knew perfectly well what it was, but still, her mind had trouble taking it in. She stumbled and had trouble wrangling the bike inside. She was slow to get the door closed.

She stood there, inside, behind the closed door. Someone was calling her name from the other side of the door, her front bike wheel on an angle to fit in the small vestibule. Her heart was pounding, she realised.

She didn't know any of them from work, not the voices anyway. She couldn't see their faces because of the flashes.

The True Story of Maddie Bright

There might have been three. There might have been ten. She didn't know.

They wouldn't come onto the property, she knew, because that would be illegal.

Once she calmed herself, she figured out they were wanting to photograph Ben. She was wearing a bike suit. Her hair was tucked up under her helmet. You might be forgiven for making the error. They'd have no interest in her. She wrote about people like Ben, but her own life was of no interest to anyone. When the photographers realised their mistake, they wouldn't do anything with any shots they'd taken.

But, no, they knew her name. It wasn't Ben they were after. It was Victoria. How did they know her name? Why were they photographing her?

She was about to open the door and ask them when she realised if she did, they'd photograph her again. Victoria carried her bike back up the stairs, took off her helmet and gloves, and went inside. She peeped out her window and saw a van and two men—standing on the other side of the road now—smoking cigarettes and talking. They made a ruckus for two, Victoria thought. Then she saw another two, further up the street.

She decided to wait them out. She emailed Ewan. *I'm going to work from home this morning*, she wrote. She didn't tell him about the photographers.

She made herself a cup of tea and toast and started work. They couldn't use the photographs they had so far. She wouldn't even be recognisably human in her bike gear, surely.

By lunchtime, when she came out again, they'd gone. A win, she'd thought. She felt silly then. She could have just asked them what they were doing. They had spooked her.

The next day, she checked for photographers outside the flat before going down the stairs and then felt even sillier because no one was there. She'd had a telephone call with Ben and she hadn't mentioned it to him. Now, she was glad she hadn't.

When she arrived at work, *The Daily Mail* was on her desk, open at page seven. There was a picture, captioned: *The Spiderwoman who's moved in with Zombie Man.*

She looked around the office, wondering who had put the paper on her desk. Heads were all down.

It was Victoria the photographers wanted after all, she thought, almost dispassionately, as she looked at the picture. Ben had said this would happen, but Victoria hadn't believed him. He'd said they would find out about her, and they had. Not only that, they were wrong; she hadn't moved in with Zombie Man, Zombie Man had moved in with her.

Her father saw the picture. He called her later that day. He read all the papers in case Blair phoned, she knew. 'And so it starts, Victoria', he said. 'Tony says you should get yourself a good lawyer.'

She had taken Ben over to meet her father for tea on the Sunday after they got engaged. Ben had made a joke about not knowing if he should have asked her father's permission before proposing. It fell flat. Her father warmed to him, though, just as

Victoria had. Ben was his charming best, and her father sparred with him about something—Victoria couldn't remember now what it was.

Still, the meeting had left Victoria strangely uneasy. They hadn't been over there together again. Her father didn't mention Ben when she visited. She couldn't understand why not.

In the photograph, you could see her bike pants legs and skin-tight bike shirt, her helmet and plastic goggles. They included her name. They called her *Ben Winter's secret London flame, Victoria Byrd, more a spider than a byrd*. More a stick insect, she thought, which would have been funnier. They didn't mention that she was a journalist, a journalist who'd once written for *The Daily Mail*, the newspaper that was now invading her privacy to fill a page. She was just the spider woman, the byrd.

She'd done this to people, hadn't she? Or something like it. She'd told photographers what kind of shot she wanted. In close to show intimacy, close in a different way to show guilt. More room to create doubt, chin up, chin down, from above, from below. They knew exactly how to photograph a person to create an effect. In a second picture, she was falling back through the door and it looked as if she were trying to hide something. There was a picture of Ben, from their files, his teeth at attention in a perfect smile, an open-necked shirt, a man in control of his destiny.

There was no story, just the two pictures, the caption and a single para.

Is this the new woman in Ben Winter's life? What Tuesday Mail wants to know is when she'll start spitting webs from her wrists.

She looked around the office again. Shame, that's what she felt. She felt shame.

Ewan saw her later in the day. 'It's what we do,' was all he said.

'How did they find me?' she asked when Ben arrived on the Friday.

'I think one of the photographers followed me from the airport last time,' he said casually. Ben had a car and a driver pick him up.

'Why can't you just get a taxi like normal people?'

'I'm not normal people,' he said.

'Well, I wish you were.'

'Let's not go there,' he said. 'It's a job. It's a fun job. I like it. Parts of it are stupid. Parts of every job are stupid.'

'Daddy says I should get a lawyer.'

'He doesn't know shit. You have a free press, remember? You're even part of the free press. So's he, in a way.'

That was how Ben saw it. 'It would be easier if you'd let my guys look after you,' he said. His bodyguards. His publicity team. That's what he meant. She couldn't imagine anything worse. She wanted freedom, she told him.

'It is freedom,' he said. 'We can do whatever we want. Go anywhere, do anything.'

'Except out my front door,' she said.

The True Story of Maddie Bright

'Yes, except that,' he said. 'This is the wrong kind of place, Tori, wrong kind of door.'

He said she shouldn't have a front door that opened to the street. She shouldn't catch the train. She shouldn't get coffee at Brown's.

When she put her foot down and said no, he told her to wait a while and see what happened. It might blow over, he said. But what happened was that it got worse. If you didn't give them a story, they made one up. He'd been right about that too.

To people like Ben, the photographers who took those pictures of her were like Victoria; they were involved in the same kind of work. But what they wrote about her and Ben was nothing like what she wrote about people, she tried to tell him, even doing profiles. What they did was to fabricate a story, without even a grain of truth at its core. They would take a picture and invent a story to go with it and make up sources to fill the story. Fiction, pure fiction. She wouldn't do that. None of the journalists she worked with would do that. It really was different, although when she tried to talk to him about the differences, her arguments all went to water.

Victoria's phone rang at her desk, bringing her back to the present with a start. 'Hey, babe, me.' Ben. 'Just thought I'd call and check you're okay.'

'Yes,' she said. 'Fine. You?' She was still thinking about the photographers.

'Did you get my little present?'

'I did,' Victoria said, realising she should have said something. The fight last night, the croissant by way of apology. 'That was lovely. Sorry. I'm just . . . the news.'

'Yeah, I heard. Diana.' He breathed out heavily. 'I'm on a break,' he said. 'Clouds, so we're waiting.'

'How is it?'

'Oh, you know—meaningful.'

The Resurrect, the film Ben had come to London to star in, was a different role for him, more nuanced than the *Zombie World* films that had made him famous. 'Why me?' he'd asked his agent, Anna, when she'd forwarded the script for *The Resurrect*. 'This guy's their Coppola.' Ben had agreed to read the script because it meant he could stay in London with Victoria—they'd only slept together once and it made Victoria dizzy that he would make plans around her.

'Everyone wants you,' Anna had said. He'd put her on speaker so Victoria could hear the call. It was the kind of thing Anna said. Everyone wanted him. If you were an actor you were nothing but an ego wandering around in a pair of Levi's, or so people thought. 'But there's more than ego in these Levi's, honey,' Ben said to Victoria after he got off the phone.

And he laughed. That was the thing that redeemed him. It always did. He could laugh at himself, laugh at all he'd become.

That was true, wasn't it? It had been totally true, Victoria was sure.

'I'm sorry about last night,' she said on the phone now.

'Yeah,' he said. 'Me too. So sorry, babe. I'm just so mad about it. It's not fair on you. We gotta fix it. I guess I tried to tell you they'd find us so I was stupidly frustrated. I get so mad at them. That's who I'm really mad at. I shouldn't take it out on you. It must be awful when you're not used to it.'

'I just didn't think we rated as news,' she said. 'Shows what I know. Daddy thinks—'

'Yeah, anyway, leave it with me. I'm going to fix it. Gotta go. I love you.'

'You too.'

'See you tonight.'

He was gone.

She hadn't told him she was going to Paris. She could ring back, she thought. But she wouldn't. She knew she wouldn't.

She looked up to see Ewan on the other side of the partition, looking at her.

She jumped.

'Sorry,' he said. 'I didn't mean to scare you, and I didn't mean to be short with you before. It's just you're never late. I think I was in shock. Are you okay?'

'I'm the one who should apologise,' she said quickly. 'I slept in, and I hadn't seen the news. You were right to be annoyed.' She wiped her eyes. 'I was just on the phone to my father.'

'Is he over the moon?'

'No, he's not.' She wondered whether to mention her mother but decided against it. 'He never liked the horrible stories about Diana. When did you come in?'

'I got a call about two from Harry. A photographer called him, he said. He had a pic of the wreck to sell. He didn't know much, only that there'd been a crash. They were operating, we heard next, at around three, I think. It was supposed to be minor. That's what the P.M.'s office was saying. And then Alastair Campbell phoned Harry to say she died.'

'I noticed they made the second edition,' Victoria said.

He grimaced. 'There was a picture.'

'A picture?'

'Her,' he said softly.

'After?'

He nodded slightly. 'In the car. The agency pulled it before Harry saw it.'

'Thank God. He'd have run it.'

'Yes, he would have.' He smiled. 'And you slept in?'

'First time ever. I think I must have drunk too much.'

'Looks sore.' He tapped his own cheek. 'You sure you're all right?'

She nodded. 'I know I've been off my game, Ewan, and I'm really sorry.'

He'd dumped a story she'd written from August, about teaching adults to swim. She hadn't found the heart of the piece, she knew, and when he tried to restructure it, it just fell apart.

'Oh God, it's not that,' he said. 'Everything all right otherwise?' He looked at her carefully.

'Oh yes,' she said. 'Ben's back here now, filming, so it's much better.'

'Good then,' he said, nodding. 'Are you still getting pestered by the lads?' He meant the photographers.

'Not this morning,' she said.

'I bet. They're all on flights to Paris, although God knows what they'll take pictures of.' He reached out as if to pat her head, pulled his hand back and turned and left her to it.

He was halfway back to his office when he stopped and turned. '*Winter Skies*,' he said. 'That's why I came over.'

'Huh?' Victoria said.

'That's the name of the new book from M.A. Bright. It's supposed to be a sequel to *Autumn Leaves*. Just check it out.'

'I think you called it something else before.'

'I did, but it's *Winter Skies*. I checked. Anyway, glad you're all right.'

She sat there for a moment after Ewan was gone. There was something on the edge of her consciousness. She rubbed her eyes. Nothing.

EIGHT

Sydney, 1920

HELEN POINTED TO THE PILE OF LETTERS ON MR WATERS'S desk. 'Oh God, there's all this as well. I think that's only today and yesterday. He hasn't even put it on the correspondence desk. I have a speech to finish by this afternoon and there's some government chap wanting a photograph approved. I don't have time.'

'Are you American?' I said. I'd thought that was her accent before but now I was less certain. She might be English after all.

'Yes,' she said. 'Good guess! My mother anyway. She remarried when I was ten and we moved to England, so hardly anyone picks the accent. It's all over the place. Since coming on the tour, I've become British, or Welsh—Prince, Wales—but at home in New York I become quite the American.

'Actually, when the prince asked me to do this, I was on my way back to New York.' She picked up an envelope absently, took the letter out.

'I'm not sure what I'm supposed to do with you now,' she said then. 'There's a chief steward somewhere but I don't think he's back on the train yet. He went to Government House to chastise the cooks over something I don't care about. There are two other girls and Fanny, whose place you've taken. Well, enough said.'

Perhaps she had poured tea on someone, I thought.

'Is Mr Waters nice?' I said. I had liked him very much. I hoped he wasn't one of those sorts of fellows.

'Rupert,' she said softly. 'Rupert is all about loyalty.'

She started to read the letter she had removed from the envelope. 'This one. Poor fellow was denied access to the speech the prince gave at the university in Melbourne. He's a graduate and they couldn't manage to get him an invitation. I mean, really. He served with the Fusiliers. What should the prince say? I think he takes every war injury personally. It absolutely exhausts him.'

'He should treat the fellow to a train ticket to the next speech he gives.'

'Yes, that's rather good. Excellent, in fact. Of course that's what he should do. Aren't you the clever one? He's a prince. He can do anything. The minions are part of the do-minions, of course. Can you draft the letter and we can tell someone to arrange it?'

'All right, I will.'

'And then, while we're waiting for the steward, why not just go through and see if you can sort them into some sort of order? I've really got to draft his speech for tomorrow. Our prince must deliver some remarks that the colony will think appropriate.'

He could start by not calling us the colony, I didn't say.

Helen sat me at the desk to start reading the pile of letters. We talked through two or three and agreed what I'd do and then she left me there to go to her own office to start work on the prince's speech. She told me to come and find her if I had any questions.

I quickly lost interest in the world around me—what would happen, when I'd get my uniform, where the kitchen was, why the steward hadn't come for me—because the letters received by the prince were so engaging. I entered the worlds of these people who had written to someone who might care. Their families were not unlike mine. They wanted to tell their stories to the prince who had touched their hearts. Perhaps that was why my mother had insisted we come down here. Perhaps she wanted some acknowledgement of what our father had lost, what we'd all lost.

There were so many people harmed. That was the thing that struck me powerfully, skimming the letters. You would never have known it that first day of the prince's visit, looking out at the sea of people in Sydney who were captured by the great joy of the visit. But there were letters from mothers, from fathers, from brothers and sisters of those who'd fallen; loss the experience they had in common.

From what Helen had said, the prince would want to help them if he could. I wanted to help them too, and that first poor fellow, the one who'd missed the talk, gave me an idea. We could lend a hand where possible, and acknowledge what people had written where there was nothing to be done.

By the time Mr Waters came back from his meeting, I had the pile divided into three, starting with letters that could be sent a form reply based on one I'd seen on a file on his desk—although it was terribly formal, and from what Helen said the prince was not one for formality, so I rewrote it to some or other variant of:

> *Thank you for writing to me. It means so much to His Majesty the King and all his family to know that we share so much in common with our friends in Australia. In our hour of need, none was braver than the Australian 'digger' who volunteered to fight side by side with his British comrades, because of our long historical bond of friendship. Of all the titles I have been awarded, none surpasses 'digger prince'. I know our peoples across the great Commonwealth have suffered, and I feel their suffering.*
>
> *I wish you every happiness in the years to come and may God bless you, Edward.*

'What's this, Maddie?' Mr Waters asked.

'That's a draft reply, sir,' I said. I was proud of what I'd achieved in a short period of time.

'But what are you doing in here?'

'Helen asked me . . .' I hesitated.

'Asked you what?' he said.

Just then, Helen herself came through from the next carriage. 'Oh, Rupert, you're back. Look at Maddie Marvel here.' Helen had come in during the morning and I'd shown her what I was doing.

'I'm sorry,' he said to Helen. 'I don't understand. I thought *you* were going to help me with the letters today. I came in and here's Maddie at the desk.'

He looked slightly irritated.

'Yes, and she has made tidy your terrible mess, Rupert. She has taken all the letters we've received, the ones sitting in nooks and crannies on your desk, the secretary's desk, the floor. She has expeditiously opened them and read them and now she is setting about replying to them.' Helen smiled brightly. 'Maddie is doing this because she is clever enough to do it, which is what Ned told you, I believe.'

'But, Helen, she's a servant. We hired her to serve in the dining room.'

'Rupert, did Ned not tell you this morning that the girl you'd put on serving dinner is a Bright?'

'Yes,' he said, 'but I'm not sure what that has to do with anything.'

'Her father is Thomas Bright, the poet. You really don't need to know any more.'

He looked incredulous. 'So you're saying that Maddie, who I interviewed as a maid, is to be my correspondence secretary?'

'Yes,' Helen said.

'Because her father is a poet?'

Helen nodded. 'I know his work, and the literary editor of *Vanity Fair* counts him among the greats.'

'But I thought you could do it, Helen. Grigg has promised he'll do more of the speeches, and you're so very good at the letters. We might work together on them.' Mr Waters looked at her, his eyebrows raised, a weak smile.

'I don't want to,' she said coldly. 'And you know I don't.'

'I see,' he said. 'Well, I just thought it was something you might . . .' He trailed off, took a breath in and held it for a moment, then breathed out. 'Well, that's that then.'

He'd picked up one of the letters I'd drafted a reply to, from a mother who'd lost a son, and he still had it in his hand. He read in silence now, narrowing his eyes. After he'd finished reading, he looked at Helen, and then at me. 'All right, Maddie?' he said.

I nodded.

'Good then. Keep going. We are getting dozens every day and H.R.H. is determined that each should receive a personal reply. Do you type?'

I nodded. 'My father taught me, sir.'

'Excellent.' He turned to Helen. 'Then I will ask Mrs Danby to send one of the girls from the house with us on the train and Maddie can help out with the correspondence. When we get back to Sydney, I'll find a proper correspondence secretary to join us for the rest of the tour. Is that what you'd prefer?'

'Yes,' said Helen.

He looked again at the draft in his hand. 'This,' he said, tapping the piece of paper in his hand, 'this is him.'

Helen just rolled her eyes.

∽

It was late afternoon by the time the train pulled out of the station. A few minutes before, I thought I'd glimpsed the prince, walking hurriedly past the window with a taller willowy young man at his side. There was a frisson around them, a silent, excited moment as they passed, the crowd of railway staff quietening and moving aside.

I didn't poke my head out the window to see where they went, although I wanted to. I could hardly believe I was here, on the train the Prince of Wales was taking to our new national capital, now in charge of writing letters in his name. (In truth, I wasn't in charge, Mr Waters was, but I felt as if it was all up to me now.)

The prince must have entrained in one of the forward carriages. Mr Waters soon flashed by, on his way to join the prince, I assumed. Not long after this, the train rolled out of the station, quickly picking up speed, the whistle blowing its farewell to the city of Sydney.

∽

We were passing through the outer settlements of the city—people waving us by with flags in every village—when Mr Waters came back to the office. He put some papers down on his desk.

'I managed to get us a maid on loan from the governor,' he said. 'This is Ruby Rivers.'

She came in behind Mr Waters, all breast, hip and bright red lips. She wore jewellery on her wrist and neck.

We said our hellos, and Ruby stood waiting for Mr Waters. 'So, Maddie, you've changed jobs and we'll have to talk about your recompense,' he said.

'I don't mind,' I said. I was loving what I was doing and didn't want to stop. I knew the work of a maid would be harder. 'Is it a lot less?' I thought of my mother and how much she needed these two days' wages.

He laughed. 'This pays more,' he said. 'We'll—'

The door to the carriage in front of us opened then and there was a hush that preceded the beautiful young man who stepped into the light. He commanded every speck of attention in the room. He was smaller than Mr Waters, not much taller than Helen or me, and it contributed to an impression of boyishness you noticed and then forgot, because you then remembered him as tall until you saw him again.

Dressed in a dark tweed coat and slacks, with brown brogues, he smiled at Mr Waters and then his gaze fell on me. 'I'm David,' he said. 'Rupert tells me you're going to get us out of a fix with all these letters we've been receiving. I'm so very happy.' I might have melted into a puddle on the floor, but he extended his hand for me to take and I managed to make mine do what it needed to. I couldn't speak. I took his hand, so soft and warm, mine all calloused and cold, I was sure.

I thought then, I will cherish this moment as long as I live, the light coming through the window to our left, late afternoon, the look on his face, the soft chug of the train. My mother would have fallen into a dead faint, I was sure.

Up close and in real life, he was even more beautiful than his pictures, especially when he smiled, as now. It was a smile that lit up a room. I had no knowledge of the world in which to place this new experience. He looked just like an angel, I thought, with his rosy cheeks, eyes of a blue I'd never seen before and I've never seen since, a cherub mouth and that blond hair.

'I believe your father served,' Prince Edward said then. 'God bless him, Maddie. And your brother made the ultimate sacrifice. I'm so very sorry.'

He knew my name. He knew my father had been in the war, my brother. I thought I might cry.

'Sir,' I said, my voice high and reedy.

He smiled again, smaller this time, and then turned from me and it was as if the light had been sucked out of the room. I could see only black. I heard his voice again. 'And who's this now, Rupert?' My vision righted directly and I saw his gaze had fallen on Ruby, the serving girl Mr Waters had found at Government House, who was grinning like a lunatic.

Mr Waters was about to introduce them when Ruby herself curtsied perfectly and said, 'I'm Ruby Rivers, sir.'

'Your initials are R.R.,' he said. 'If I pick Richard as my regal name, I will be R.R. too.' He laughed. 'And how old are you, Ruby Rex?'

'I'm nineteen, sir,' she said. 'But it's Rivers.'

'Well,' he said, looking at Mr Waters.

Helen had come in behind the prince.

'Rupert, tell Helen that we can't deliver that speech,' the prince said.

'I'm sorry, sir, but it's what we discussed last night,' Helen said. 'Colonel Grigg is convinced you need to speak on the issues again.' She looked to Mr Waters, who was studying the floor. When Helen was around, I'd noticed, the floor often needed Mr Waters's total attention. 'The Bolshies are everywhere is what he said.'

The prince laughed. 'I bet he did. Well, I won't do it. It's boring. Let's find something else to say. See what we said in Ottawa—that went down a treat. Grigg wants to whip them with the empire at every turn. People are in terrible pain, in case he hasn't noticed.' He looked over at Mr Waters, and his mouth moved as if to smile but it was more of a twitch, a grimace almost.

'Of course,' Helen said. 'So what do *you* want, sir?'

He smiled properly then, that lovely boy's smile, and his eyes moved to Helen. 'There are so many different wants on this train I find it best not to want anything.'

He left us there, Mr Waters looking concerned, Helen totally deflated, and Ruby Rivers with a grin as big as the train itself.

NINE

Brisbane, 1981

THE LETTER IS IN THE TOP DRAWER OF MY DESK WHERE I am sitting to write. It radiates enough light that I don't need the lamp on.

I have often said to people that I am not a person who carries regrets. The word *regret* becomes *egret* without the *r* and an egret is a bird nothing like a crow. It has a *t*. It is an odd word. It sounds sad. It sounds like you lost everything. I am not a person who carries regrets. Perhaps they carry me.

I am not an egret.

I let my memories settle as sludge at the bottom of the pond of my mind, so that only every now and then are they stirred up by what happens in the world.

Dare I revise them?

It has been my whole life since I first met them. My whole life.

There are things we might wish to discuss. That's what she said. *There are things we might wish to discuss.* There is nothing I would wish to discuss with her. She says she would love to hear from me. *Please*, she says at the end. *Please write. I don't have much time left.*

What on earth would I say after all this time, Helen? What would I say to you? I had thought you were my friend.

∼

'If this were the three bears story, I'd be the porridge that's just right,' Helen said to me the first day we met.

'Am I too hot or too cold?' I said.

'I don't know yet.' She turned her head to one side to regard me, a gesture I would come to know then imitate.

Sometimes, in the autumn, I have the strangest feeling of yearning. It wells up from the depths of me, or perhaps from outside, from the earth's turning, the sun on its journey away from us, the sea already cold. It's as if I knew, as if I've always known in some small part of myself, some small place where I kept my disbelief, where I kept my hope, that the letter was coming.

I look at the drawer, a plain brass handle. I might take the letter out again one day soon. I am not a person who has egrets.

∼

Andrew Shaw came in to say he'd finished for the day. It wasn't quite three pm. I was back in the past, but no longer the painful past. I had placed my thoughts elsewhere. Sometimes you can do this. I learned it in one of the books from the Pentecostals with the picture of Jesus, his glowing heart exposed in his chest. Heartburn, I would never say aloud to them.

Now I was recalling, of all things, having a bath in the kitchen sink, the same kitchen sink I had washed the teacups in an hour ago. Mummy would bathe us, one after the other, me then Edward then Bert, John. By the time the twins arrived, I took over bathing the little ones. I could make lighter work of it than Mummy, who'd bathed enough children for a lifetime, she often said. She wasn't built for bathing children, I'd have said. She didn't have the mindset you need, which has something to do with not minding water all over a floor.

Sometimes now I climb up on the bench and into the sink to write. All that fits are my two feet, but it makes me feel like a child again, before anything happened to grow me up. I'm not sure it helps the writing but my feet feel delicious.

It was early for Andrew Shaw to finish, I didn't say. How he expected to make money without doing much actual work escaped me, but I didn't say anything about that either. What business was it of mine how he spent his day? I wasn't paying him.

'There's a bit of work needs doing,' he said.

'And I suppose you're the one to do it?' I said.

'Not necessarily, but some of it . . . I made a list.' He gave me a sheet of paper torn from a spiral notebook. The first item was steps. He was frowning fairly convincingly. 'I'll do up a proper report and drop it off.'

'Well, the steps are perfectly serviceable,' I said.

'In terms of treads, you mean,' he said.

I nodded.

'Yes, except for the two eaten out by rot, they're all right, but I think they're going to fall down unless you rebuild them.'

'Do you now?'

'I do, and your knight in shining armour agrees with me.'

Ed, who should have sobered a little during the morning, was behind him. He stepped into view. 'He's right, Maddie. There's things need to be done here.' I don't know why he was still swaying. He couldn't have taken a drink in these four or five hours unless he sneaked home or brought a flask, and yet he swayed like the newly drunk. Perhaps drink never really leaves you once you reach a certain stage of pickling.

'Well, I don't have time to think about all this right now.'

'No, I just wanted . . .' Andrew Shaw paused. 'Let me do you a quote, at least, on the bare minimum.'

'Am I going to be forced by the neighbours?'

'No,' he said. 'Of course not. Your house is no risk to theirs. And their plans are nothing to concern yourself with. It's . . .' He looked at Ed. I felt ganged up on. 'Like, look at the second one. Termites. We have to get rid of your termites.'

'For the neighbours,' I said.

'No, for you,' he said, seeming a little exasperated. 'Just because you've got termites doesn't mean you'll give them to your neighbours. Termites are everywhere.' He looked around. 'And they've plenty to be getting on with here without having to move in next door.

'Good news is, they probably won't touch your foundations. Termites like an easy life and you've got a hardwood frame. It's the cladding under the aluminium we should be worried about. Pine. Some of it's gone out back there where the walls connect to the earth. It's easy for them to get up. Really we ought to dig it out and cap it.'

'It's your conflict of interest that concerns me,' I said—cleverly, I thought. 'Not your ideas.'

'When I say falling down,' Andrew Shaw was saying. 'I mean it in the literal sense rather than some metaphorical falling-down.'

I liked that he said metaphorical. 'I see,' I said. 'How old are you?'

'I'm twenty-six,' he said, looking bewildered.

'Well, I'm seventy-eight,' I said, 'so I know things.'

'Of course,' he said. 'I might call in later in the week and see where you are.'

I didn't like him pushing me. 'No,' I said. 'I will call you if and when I want your help. Now leave me be.'

'Best go then,' Ed said, nudging Andrew Shaw in the back.

'I'll just get the ladder,' Andrew said. 'Thanks for your time.'

I wouldn't say he looked hurt, just resigned. I suppose times must be tough for builders. But he's not my problem, I thought. The last thing I needed was another person sucking my savings from me. When you get to my age, you don't know how long your money has to last you.

After he went out to pick up his ladder, I looked at Ed. 'I would have expected a bit more support from you,' I said.

The True Story of Maddie Bright

'But, Maddie, he's right. You have to get a bit done or the house is going to come down around you.'

'Well, I can think of worse outcomes than that, Edward.'

He hates when I call him Edward.

'Maddie, there might be possums up in your ceiling but there are rats too. He's right about that. And you can't ignore termites. And there's a leak in the bathroom floor, and a—'

'Stop, Ed,' I said. 'I have the list. I'll look at it. But right now, I want to be left on my own to write.' It upset me to hear talk of my house as old and decrepit, for the house was exactly my age.

'All right, love. I'll pop back later in the evening.'

Ed would be drunk later in the evening and forget, but I didn't mind.

Andrew Shaw came through then and said goodbye. 'I'll drop back when I get a chance,' he said. 'It doesn't have to be me who does the work. I'm not trying to railroad you here. But you should think about getting it done.'

'I will,' I said. 'And tell those people next door to mind their own business.'

I didn't want to be so difficult. Andrew Shaw seemed a lovely young man, but I know the world.

❧

After they left, I went into the lounge and turned on the television. I put in the videotape I recorded last night and began to watch.

She was as beautiful as she would ever be, her arm tucked under her prince's arm, her eyes so hopeful, looking up towards him constantly to see if she'd been a good girl. A child. She looked more child than adult. She looked as if she had won a prize.

Little did she know there would be no prize for her, not now, not ever, only heartbreak and loss. I could see it as plainly as that. Who was it said, If only youth knew, if only age could? I didn't know when I was her age either. Now I did know and couldn't act to save her.

It was the prince I wanted to look at when I played the tape a third time. You might mistake him for a coyote or a wolf, but you might equally see him as a rabbit caught in headlights.

Perhaps he had no idea either. But he should have. He was thirty-two years old. He should have known better.

TEN

London, 1997

VICTORIA WALKED INTO THE JARDINE CLUB DINING ROOM behind a waiter who'd met her at the door and told her Mr Inglis had already arrived, as if she were late and he, the waiter, took it personally. He was young, with a pretentiousness that might grow old with him and become far less endearing.

Victoria had heard of the Jardine, of course. Women were allowed as guests on certain days, she understood. Her father had lunched here—many politicians on both sides were members. 'The real problem with those clubs is the food,' he said once. 'They don't seem to have changed the menu since the thirties.'

'Not the sexism?' Victoria had said.

'That too, I suppose,' he said. 'But I could put up with the sexism if the food were better.' At least he smiled as he said it.

Victoria surveyed the room. 'More dinosaurs per square yard than Jurassic Park,' Claire had said when Victoria mentioned she was lunching here.

She was trying to work out which of the old men looking up at her was Finian Inglis when a tall slim fellow stood, a serviette drifting from his lap. He bent down to pick it up before the hovering waiter could, smiling affably as he stood again.

He had a fresh pinkish face surrounded by wisps of snowy white hair, as if he'd patted himself with baby powder that morning. Pink was a good descriptor for him more generally, Victoria thought; its softness, perhaps. He wore a tailored black suit over a crisp white shirt with cufflinks and a colourful tie, and yet managed not to look smart. There was no swishing dinosaur tail as far as Victoria could see. More absent-minded professor than apex predator, more avuncular than prehistoric, and not quite at home here in a men's club with its port and cigars, she was relieved to learn.

When Finian Inglis had suggested the Jardine for their meeting, Victoria pictured the sort of man Claire described, the kind for whom the seventies had never happened, for whom *Nine to Five* was a zany comedy rather than a rallying cry: Des Pearce from the magazine—or Harry Knight himself, come to think of it. Every woman knew at least one or two of them, the kind who wouldn't think twice about whether they should stretch their hand around your waist in a group photograph and find some breast and dig in. Not charming in any way. Did they think women liked this? Did they care?

Finian Inglis didn't look like that sort at all. His publishing house, Barlow Inglis, had a reputation for quality. They'd picked winners in the past, punching well above their weight, although Victoria seemed to recall they were faltering financially nowadays.

Of course, none of their big-name authors was bigger than M.A. Bright, whose novel *Autumn Leaves*, a poignant love story set against the horror of World War I, was likely penned by one of the war poets writing under a pseudonym, Victoria had read in a two-pound novel guide last night. When it was first published in 1922, there was enormous speculation as to the identity of the injured captain and his ambulance driver lover. They were unnamed—Victoria's Cambridge boyfriend had done a PhD on why, but she couldn't remember the conclusion.

'Finian, please,' Finian Inglis said when Victoria called him Mr Inglis. 'I'm so glad you could make today. May I call you Victoria?'

'Of course,' she said, charmed. No one else asked. 'Tori.'

Finian Inglis spoke like her school English teachers, stressing every consonant, clipping every vowel to its minimum length. He went to shake her hand, forgetting he was still holding the serviette, and then had to swap it to his other hand before they shook. 'Actually, I thought you might cancel,' he said. 'After last night.'

'Yes, I'm going to Paris this afternoon,' she said.

'Awful,' he said. 'Imagine those boys waking up this morning. The younger one's twelve. A terrible age to lose your mother.'

She nodded. 'Yes, terrible.' Was there a good age? she wondered. Victoria had been almost twelve. She hardly thought of her mother now, she would say if anyone asked. Not that they asked very often. Her grandmother had done everything a mother might and more, she always said, smiling broadly. People rarely understood what it was like.

It was like being a bird growing up without wings.

'I just mean,' he went on, as if she'd spoken her thoughts aloud, 'in that family, she'd have been the only bright spot, don't you agree? She had a bit of spark. Imagine it. *You'll be all right. Granny and Granddad are here.* Good God!' He shook his head.

'I suppose so,' Victoria said, although that hadn't been her experience. Her grandparents had filled the gap marvellously. They'd been to everything at school when her father wasn't available and often when he was, driving for hours just to see her play in an ensemble or act as a tree in a pantomime. She'd spent most holidays with them up in Craster when her father was working. They'd been grandparents and parents both. Who could know that the Queen and Prince Philip wouldn't be the same?

Victoria surveyed the dining room. Not another diner under seventy, most well beyond that.

'It's like trying to stop an historical film that just keeps running, I'm afraid, closing places like this,' Finian said, noticing her gaze and gesturing around the room. 'I often feel we're already an exhibit.' He laughed quietly.

'Yes, that's a good way of putting it,' she said.

They both ordered fish and drank water from a crystal pitcher on the table.

The waiter hovered. Victoria wondered if waiters at clubs were tipped. She didn't want to ask.

Finian Inglis chatted amiably, in no hurry to get to the point of their meeting. The fish came, overcooked, in a buttery sauce with green beans whose day was long gone. Finian didn't comment but didn't eat with relish either. Victoria felt queasy, having missed breakfast and now looking at the glistening sagging blob of white on the plate. She pushed it from one side to the other, took small bites, hoping to cover it with the serviette when the time was right.

'So Ewan told me you wanted to discuss M.A. Bright?' Victoria said.

'Tell me about you first,' he said. He knew she'd written for *The Guardian*, he said. She explained she'd gone from there to *The Daily Mail* and then to Knight News.

'Quite a trajectory,' he said.

'That's what my father says,' she replied. 'Although downwards after *The Guardian* to his mind, so perhaps a reverse trajectory. I think he had visions of me as an investigative reporter, Woodward and Bernstein for the eighties.'

He laughed. 'Fathers and daughters.' He added quickly, 'I have daughters,' as if it to qualify himself. 'And I knew Michael at Cambridge, of course. What a mind.'

'Yes,' she said. 'But if you're wondering, I think I take after my mother, not my father.'

'She was the microbiologist?'

'Yes, she was,' Victoria said, wondering how he would know that. 'They met at Cambridge.'

'So the way I see it, no slouch in the brain department on either side.' He smiled.

She felt she was being assessed for something but didn't know what.

'I also knew your grandfather,' he said then. 'Michael's father. Not well, but he nearly did a book for us, thirty years ago maybe? One of Sir Antony's.'

'A book? What about?' Victoria said.

'I don't know. An explorer? Antarctica? Does that ring a bell?'

She shook her head. Victoria's grandfather had been a history teacher and he did love the explorers. 'I didn't know that.' She wiped her lips with her serviette and then covered her plate with it. 'He used to take me fishing when I was little but I wasn't any good. I felt too sorry for the fish so we had to throw them back. He said they didn't feel any pain with the hook. I think he was lying.'

Finian laughed. 'We all lie,' he said.

'Anyway, *The Guardian* was Daddy's version of a newspaper, as you can well imagine,' Victoria said. 'It would have been my grandfather's too, I think. I never knew he wrote.'

'And at Cambridge, you started in Classics?' Finian said.

'Yes,' she replied, wondering how he'd know that too. 'I switched to journalism at the London.'

'So now you're everywhere.' He smiled.

Had he seen the pictures of her? She felt mortified.

'I'm sorry,' he said immediately, seeing her reaction. 'I just mean, we all read you at Bingles.'

'Oh, that's nice to know,' she said, relieved he didn't mean the photographs. 'Bingles?'

'Our nickname,' he said fondly. 'Barlow Inglis, Bingles.'

She seemed to recall doing a profile on one of their writers, the Icelandic poet Mik Snikliw. That must be how he knew her name.

'I've been very lucky,' she said. 'I wrote a profile of Blair when he took over the Labour Party—before he was Blair, in some ways. That was syndicated, which got me quite a bit of notice, actually.'

Finian Inglis was nodding. He'd read it, he said.

'I mean, I didn't create Blair or anything, which is what people said afterwards. I just gave him more of a heart than he'd had previously, or showed the heart he already had. *Finding a soft spot in hard Labour* was the headline. After it ran I moved from *The Eye* to *Vicious*.'

'And *Vicious* was not quite *The Guardian* in Michael's mind?'

'No, but not as bad as *The Eye*. Daddy knows Ewan, who was features editor of *The Eye* when I started, but the rest of the paper he always said he didn't bother with. He liked *Vicious* at first. We caught a wave, women wanting something more in their reading—and, actually, we have a fair swag of male readers, according to Ewan.'

'Yes, it's good Ewan is still with Knight,' Finian said. 'Keeps him honest.'

'You know Harry Knight?'

'We were on a panel together last year, the future of publishing. There's one every five minutes at the moment.'

'Ah,' she said. 'Yes, he and Harry have pretty different politics, but Ewan has such a sensibility. He predicts the zeitgeist.'

Victoria still felt like she was being assessed, as if this were a job interview, but she didn't know what the job was.

'Anyway,' she continued, 'when Harry started *Vicious*, Ewan went up as editor and asked me if I'd come.'

'And now they pay you so much it's impossible to think of leaving?'

'Something like that,' Victoria said. 'I wish!'

'Well, there's not a lot of money anywhere in publishing anymore,' Finian said.

Barlow Inglis had survived against the odds, he said. 'We're a teeny fish in a smaller and smaller pond. We get by.'

The Barlow, Sir Antony Barlow, had been the publishing muscle in the house, Finian explained. 'He discovered M.A. Bright, after all. When he retired, my father did well to reinvent us as an academic publisher. Since Father died a decade ago, I've managed to keep us afloat,' he said. He took a sip of his water, savouring it like wine, as if he'd forgotten it wasn't. 'So far.' He smiled weakly, his forehead more of a frown.

'So what did you predict for the future on your panel with Harry?' she said.

'I don't think I even hazarded a guess,' he said. 'We're a cottage industry now. We'll adapt or die. But change is coming.

I just don't know what it looks like yet. Harry was more upbeat, of course. But he would be. He runs his own show, and he's got family money to do it with.'

Victoria thought this unfair. Harry Knight was rich but he also knew how to sell newspapers.

Finian put his glass down, as if he'd made up his mind about something. 'So, *Autumn Leaves*?' He looked nervous, Victoria thought, as if unsure where this might take them.

'Yes.' Victoria had read *Autumn Leaves* at school. Everyone had. It brought the realities of the Great War home to generations who'd never experienced war. It was at once personal and universal, as Victoria's form five essay had attested, she told him. The protagonists were lovers of their time, but also timeless. 'Although, come to think of it, I can't remember much of the actual book at all.'

He laughed. 'Did you know it's one of the bestselling books this century?'

'No, I didn't,' Victoria said.

'That's worldwide, yes. My father was terribly proud. Other publishers—I could name them if I were indiscreet—said Sir Antony should have rejected *Autumn Leaves* on ethical grounds.'

Victoria looked at him quizzically.

'In those days, no one was writing anything that brought the royal family into disrepute, even by association. Some publishers saw it as too sensationalist. Even some of the reviews said it was a book that shouldn't have been published. There were libraries that banned it.'

'Goodness,' Victoria said. 'I bet they all ate their words.'

Finian laughed. 'Probably not. Self-righteousness rarely results in self reflection, I've noticed.'

'True, but it's still selling.'

'Oh my, yes. More than ever. This year is seventy-five years since the original publication, and although it's a way off, I suspect World War I will only get more popular as we move towards the centenary, so it will be out there again, I should think.

'It was Sir Antony who kept it in circulation and then, after he died, my father. It did reasonably well in the thirties but disappeared after the second war. And then it was on school lists from the sixties, so it sort of took on a life of its own.'

Victoria sneaked a look at her watch.

'And you have things to be getting on with today, of course. I'm so sorry. You must be wondering why we're here.'

She was but didn't want to be rude.

'I won't keep you. To be honest, I've been spending this hour working up my courage. I wanted to get to know you a little because I have a problem I need your help with.'

Victoria nodded.

'It has to do with M.A. Bright, as I said on the telephone to Ewan. M.A. Bright, by the way, is Madeleine Bright, who now lives in Australia.' He paused. 'I'd always assumed she was English for some reason.'

'I'd assumed she was a he!' Victoria said. 'Madeleine?'

'Yes, Madeleine. I knew that much, that Bright was a woman, because my father always referred to her as Miss Bright. But

I assumed English. Anyway, Madeleine Bright may be English, or she may have always lived in Australia. I really don't know. I've never met her and no one in the house has ever met her, but it seems there's another book finally, and she wants you to interview her.' He exhaled.

'Another *Autumn Leaves*?' Victoria asked.

'A sequel, I think,' he said. 'The first edition of *Autumn Leaves* previewed a sequel, and Sir Antony always hoped. But it never materialised beyond a prefatory chapter. Novelists can be like that. They shouldn't make promises.'

He looked at his hand on the table and then at Victoria again. 'There's a lost baby.'

'A lost baby?'

'Yes, you know, as a plot device.' He frowned. He looked at his hand again, as if it might run off if he didn't keep an eye on it. 'Although this one dies, so perhaps not quite an effective plot device.'

'Really? A lost baby is a plot device?'

'Oh, yes. Think of it.'

She couldn't think of one example, she realised, but didn't say so.

'So, why us?' Victoria said, intrigued.

'Ah, well, yes, this is what I mean about fame. That's why I asked all those intrusive questions. M.A. Bright knows you,' he said. 'Or knows your writing.'

'How?' Victoria asked. She wasn't published in Australia, as far as she knew.

'Apparently, you wrote a feature in an Australian women's magazine she read.'

'I don't think so,' Victoria said.

'It was something about Diana, actually. Does that ring a bell?'

Of course it did. The story Victoria had done on Charles and Diana ran in Australia first. It was a women's magazine. Victoria couldn't remember the name now. Then they ran it back in Britain. That way, if they were sued, they could claim they were quoting an existing publication.

But that was ten years ago. She hadn't done anything in Australia since. *Vicious* might have an audience there by now. Perhaps people read her in the magazine. And she'd done other stories on the Waleses. For a time, she'd been seen as a royal expert. Oh God, she thought now. The things we do.

Finian Inglis went on. 'As far as I know, the new book—*Winter Skies* is the working title—has a link to the royals; not Diana and Charles, earlier, Edward VIII, the one who abdicated, set when he was Prince of Wales. As I say, a sequel to *Autumn Leaves*, with some new characters. Do you remember the main character in *Autumn Leaves* was the batman to the Prince of Wales?'

She didn't.

'It doesn't matter. Bright very much liked what you wrote about Diana, apparently.' He paused. 'I'll be honest. I assumed she was dead. Her royalties go to a bank account set up by my father here in London at the beginning. I don't know if anyone draws on that account.

'Sir Antony, who knew the author personally, was silent on the subject of Bright, and my father was reluctant to talk too. Or perhaps he was ignorant. I don't think Father ever met her in person.

'Anyway, I thought M.A. Bright had died. I expected we'd hear from an estate. We'd done everything as we should, paying the money when it was due. I want to assure you on that score. It's still a selling novel for the house.

'We heard nothing—' he leaned in to speak more quietly '—until about fifteen years ago, when we got a letter from an agent in Australia, an Edward McIntrick.' He said the name softly. 'And this McIntrick said Madeleine Bright was his client and she was finishing the second novel.

'McIntrick didn't mention the royalties for *Autumn Leaves*, which was odd. You'd think that's the first thing an agent would do. But he just said there was a second novel she wanted us to look at, the long-awaited *Winter Skies*.

'I was thrilled but wary. Was it real? What was the novel about? How could we be sure? All of that. We talked, my senior editor and I, and agreed we would proceed with caution and anticipation in equal measure. The letters came soon after my own father's passing, and Bright was in her late seventies then, so I was cautious on a number of counts. On the other hand, M.A. Bright might have a new novel! Worth a risk, I'd say.' He grinned.

'McIntrick and I corresponded over several months. We were preparing to meet the author herself—I planned a trip to

Australia—and then the correspondence stopped. I was finalising dates for my visit and I got no reply. I sent further letters to the post office box but, again, no reply. To be honest, I assumed M.A. Bright really had died and I was sure we'd soon hear from the estate.

'There wasn't much more to be done other than start some sort of intrusive search, which was never an option. My father had asked me to respect M.A. Bright's privacy ahead of everything else. That was the last conversation I had with him about her. It was paramount in relation to M.A. Bright, he said.

'At any rate, it was not the way of Barlow Inglis to chase her, no matter how good the new book would be for us.'

He sat back, sighed. 'I heard nothing, and so there it lay. Every few years, we've followed up with a letter. No reply.

'Until three months ago. We received a letter, not from Bright's agent but from a fellow named Shaw, Andrew Shaw, who claims he's a friend of Madeleine Bright. He used the same post office box address that the agent used fifteen years ago.

'This Shaw fellow says M.A. Bright has had the second novel for some years and now wants it published. I wrote and asked politely about the delay and he wrote that she'd been tweaking it. That's the word he used. Tweaking. Fifteen years of tweaking.

'Shaw isn't an agent, he says. He knows nothing about books, but he knows M.A. Bright well, he claims. There's no email, no phone number, just the post office box again. But it's the same one. I'm more wary than thrilled this time, but a new novel from M.A. Bright after all these years would save Barlow Inglis in the current climate. The long-touted sequel to *Autumn Leaves*? I'm willing to take that risk. You bet I am. Especially with a lost baby.' He sipped his water as if it was whisky this time, to give himself the courage he needed.

Victoria looked at him. Was he serious about the lost baby?

'M.A. Bright wants you to interview her, the letter says.' He smiled. 'You know she's never been interviewed? Not once. And she picked you.'

'Really? What about when *Autumn Leaves* came out?' Victoria asked, ignoring the flattery. 'The publicity.'

'In the twenties and thirties, we didn't care so much about who wrote a book. All press requests came to Bingles and Sir Antony did the interviews. You'd never get away with that now. Talk about a cult of the author.'

Victoria sat back. 'So, have you read the new novel?' she asked.

'I don't have it yet, just the first chapter on file which McIntrick had enclosed with his letter.' He leaned down to a red leather briefcase on the floor, flicked it open and took out a yellowed envelope.

He handed it to Victoria. She took out a sheaf of unbound paper, a yellowing letter on the front. It smelled not musty but sweet, like honey. 'What's wrong with the t?' she said.

'I don't know.' He sighed. 'To be honest, this is all a little beyond me. My degree is in art history. I called Ewan when they mentioned your name.'

Thanks, Ewan, Victoria wanted to say. It sounded so preposterous. Ewan surely wasn't taking it seriously.

Victoria picked up her glass, put it back down, skimmed the letter quickly. *My client ... another manuscript ... chapter earlier forwarded ... world rights.* She had a picture of Ewan's face in her mind, a study in mockery. It was probably a hoax, or some wannabe author taking advantage of Finian's good nature. Why didn't Ewan just say that instead of sending Victoria along today, especially given she had to get to Paris?

On the other hand, what if it were real, M.A. Bright producing a new book decades after *Autumn Leaves*? What a scoop!

'But how will you test its authenticity?' Victoria asked. 'The book, I mean. How will you know Bright wrote it and not this Shaw fellow?' Victoria didn't know where you'd start. 'And what's been going on for the last fifteen years?'

'If it's not genuine, it's an awfully sophisticated ruse. In the first letters, the ones from the agent, there were details about the publication of *Autumn Leaves* that only Bright would have known. But you're absolutely right. We can't be sure. I think meeting her will help. She has that voice in *Autumn Leaves*. That would have to be reflected in the author herself, I think.

'As I say, initially it was an agent who wrote to me. Ed McIntrick struck me as a pretty tough cookie. I don't think he'd be easily fooled. He doesn't seem to be in the picture now though. At the time, when we went searching for his agency, we couldn't find him, not through other publishers or through the local society of authors. If he was Bright's agent, she was his only client, I suspect.'

'And you don't know Bright personally,' Victoria said. 'She must be in her nineties by now.'

He scratched behind his ear and frowned. 'I know. It's all a bit far-fetched. I've made it clear to Shaw that if we are to publish, it cannot be on condition of anonymity. I can't make it work, not these days. I have to meet M.A. Bright. And she has to stand up as the author. In the end, that may prove too difficult.

'The newspapers leave her alone now because *Autumn Leaves* is old. Even if they knew how to find her, they're not motivated. But if there were another book, I think they would go looking and they would find her. Your folk, I mean. She has to be robust enough in mind and body to withstand that, I should think. I won't do this if she's lost her marbles, say, and this Shaw fellow is just taking advantage of her. I don't want to be accused of anything here. Barlow Inglis couldn't survive one of those literary hoaxes. I won't be tricked. Bright must agree to be revealed as part of all this. We must be convinced.'

'That's fair.' Victoria sat back in her chair. 'So, you're going over?'

'Yes. I had hoped I would precede you. But I have commitments here—actually, my son is singing in the opera in Vienna,' he said proudly, 'so I'd suggest I follow on from you if the story appears to have veracity. Ewan has agreed that Knight will fund an airfare now, and we'll fund one later, nearer publication. This one's a fishing trip, for both of us. But Ewan wanted you involved now because he thought there would be a process story about the new book and you'd need to be in on it from the start.'

'Really?' Victoria said. Ewan must have some inkling the story could be real to fork out for an airfare. Strangely, Victoria had a feeling that there was truth in this somewhere too. While she was still sceptical, it was too weird to be entirely false. It had to have something to do with the real author. And even if there was no book, it would be a great feature for *Vicious*: *In search of M.A. Bright*.

'Well,' Victoria said.

'Well, indeed,' Finian said.

'At least it's a consistently awful title. *Autumn Leaves* followed by *Winter Skies*,' Victoria said.

'Quite,' Finian said. 'Probably no need to say all this must remain between us. You can speak to Ewan, of course, but no one else.'

'Of course,' Victoria said.

He breathed out. 'I was relieved Bright said she wanted you.' Victoria looked quizzically at him. 'You're Michael Byrd's daughter. Some of your colleagues, I wouldn't trust.'

Victoria didn't respond. Some of my colleagues, she thought, *I* wouldn't trust. She looked at him. And if I were you, I wouldn't trust me either.

ELEVEN

Brisbane, 1981

I AM THINKING OF CONVERTING TO THE LATTER-DAY Saints. They came today—I thought it was Andrew Shaw when I heard the knock—and one of them had the loveliest smile. It is possible I called him Andrew, because whatever I called him surprised him.

It is now a full month since Andrew Shaw came to the house. He said he would be back but he hasn't been back. Perhaps he's decided to do as I asked and leave me alone. I've seen his truck parked outside the neighbours' house. I find myself hoping he might visit without knowing why as I also know I will be difficult to get along with if he does.

I saw him get out of the truck last week, early in the morning, and I nearly called out but stopped myself.

The other Latter-Day Saint reminded me of my brother Edward. He could be funny, our Edward; he had such a good way with accents. He used to lean in close and train one eye on me and tell me people were threatened by his intellect. 'I am very intelligent,' he would say. For some reason, it never failed to make me laugh. I often wondered, did he make his jokes over there in France? Did the other boys value him the way we, his family, did? Was someone with him at the end? It's the kind of thing you wonder about.

I'm sure he'd have made me laugh about those poor lost boys from the Latter-Day Saints.

I had seen the preview for the news earlier in the day, or at least the tail end of the preview. The writing has been going more slowly than I'd hoped. The television is surely the invention of the devil, who hates books.

On the news preview, she was on the screen again, up close and broken down in tears. It's a wonder the camera didn't bump her, although perhaps they had a special lens. Perhaps the photographer was some distance away. She looked forlorn, just like a startled deer, even before she cried, her beige hair and jumper against a rainy English day. I didn't have the sound on so I wasn't sure what had happened. But, frankly, it's no surprise to me. She's lost weight too, I've noticed when I've seen pictures of her up at the newsagent. She's on all the magazine covers looking like she needs to eat.

They finished the preview with a picture I've seen before, many times, the first picture I saw of her after the newspapers got wind of her relationship with the prince. She was at work at the child-care centre, wearing a skirt she never bought to be see-through, a skirt you'd never pick as see-through, with one child on her hip, another holding her hand, a young photographer named Danny Brown having his fun by photographing her with the sun behind her so you see her legs straight through the skirt.

We might put a picture of you in the paper in your underpants, Danny Brown, with danny brown stains on them, I said to the screen when the picture came up. I had made a note of his name the first time I saw the picture, in case I might have need. If I met him at the library, for instance, I could whack him with my bag. Who takes a picture of a young girl like that? Is this the world now?

Nineteen. She's nineteen years old.

When I said to Ed earlier today that she was going to be on the news tonight and she'd lost weight, he said it was the wedding, planning for the wedding in July, just three months off. I said she was in a leg trap. Ed didn't disagree. He's gone home now. He's not well, he said, and I noticed he has a cough on his chest. I didn't say he ought to give up the cigarettes. He probably knows that, and if life teaches you anything it's that the last thing people need is unsolicited advice about how they might live it. In my experience, even when people ask for advice, advice is not what they want. They want someone to say they're all right.

I've had no reply to my letter to Mr Barlow. Perhaps, like Mr Waters, he's no longer with us. I imagine he might not be. He'd be well into his nineties now. Perhaps the new owner doesn't want a second book. I should send a new first chapter, and I would if I'd actually written a new first chapter. It's the right place to start, I think, and I also think I know where to finish, but the middle is a problem, and also the television, which keeps calling me.

In the evening, I turned the television back on so I could watch the news itself. I was getting my glasses from the study when I heard a knock on the door. Another religion! I thought. I had started to wonder if, knowing about the broken leg, or knowing about the letter, some whisper from God above, they were circling like happy reapers, competing for my soul. It can't be too much longer, they might say to one another.

Not now, I muttered. I want to watch the news.

I left the television on and went out to answer the door. My leg no longer bothers me too much. I am faster every day, and when I opened the door to Andrew Shaw I must have been grinning like a duck with pride at how quickly I'd managed the journey. Andrew Shaw grinned back, although he can't have known why I was grinning. He's that sort of person, the sort who grins for no earthly reason, just to return someone else's grin. We all know those people. They are an insult to grumpiness.

I tried to whip the grin from my face quick smart and did my best to look stern. Because he was employed by the neighbours

I dislike so much, and because he was employed specifically to make judgements about the reliability of my house, I very much wanted to dislike Andrew Shaw. But he makes that task difficult. He is like the sun, making everything around him more bright, including my worst moods, which seem to flow out to him and pass away. This was the source of my conflicted feelings for him. I wanted to dislike him only a little bit more than I wanted to like him.

Confronted with his lovely smile, my most worked-up stares of anger turn to the kind of idiotic grin I couldn't get off my face now. It's something to do with a silent energy our bodies must emit, and his positive energy is stronger than my negative. That's what I said to Frank at the post office after Andrew Shaw's first visit, although Frank looked at me oddly, as if I'd suggested he and I get married.

'I've just dropped a written report next door,' Andrew Shaw said, 'and I promised I'd drop off a copy of what I found in relation to your place.' He handed me a substantial document, twenty pages at least. 'I'm sorry I didn't get it done until now. I've had a few dramas.'

He'd already told the neighbours that my house was not a threat to theirs, he said, but he wanted to make sure I was aware of what was needed in terms of work. 'Just to do the right thing here,' he said. He nodded, looked concerned.

Oh no, I thought then. He was after a chance. I had allowed myself to hope he was a good man, but he was just the same as the rest of them. Well, I wouldn't be so easily fooled, I thought.

There was a summary page; no costings, of course. That would come later, I was sure.

I glanced at the summary. 'It looks to me like so much work is needed I may as well bulldoze the house,' I said, more worried about the seven o'clock news than the house, to be honest. When you don't see the beginning, you never know what's come before, and I didn't want to miss her.

'Not at all,' he said. 'It's an old house in need of maintenance. That's all.'

'The back wall eaten out by termites? That's maintenance?'

'Not the frame,' he said. 'As I said last time, I don't think there's structural in that.'

'But it needs to be replaced?' I said. Back walls wouldn't come cheaply, I didn't imagine. I turned my head, trying to hear whether the music had started for the news.

'Well, treated first,' he said, 'and then, yes, there's work there. But it's not all bad, Miss Bright. Can I call you Maddie?' He was standing one step down from me, just like the first time we met, which I liked. We were at the same level.

'No,' I said. 'The news is on. Do you want to come in? She's lost.'

'Diana,' he said.

'Yes.' I found myself pleased he remembered.

'Look, you don't have to get me to do this work,' he said, without coming in or acknowledging the news. I noticed his hair was longer and more unruly, and he looked tired. 'It's not that. But you should get it done. Is money the problem?'

Here we go, I thought. He'll have a friend who can
me the money. I know about these types. I was about to start saying as much when I noticed his truck parked down on the street was moving from side to side. Not very much, and at first I thought I must be imagining it, but it kept going, which made me think I couldn't be imagining it.

'How is it that your truck rocks like that?' I asked, pointing.

He looked at the car. 'I've got my kids in the back,' he said, 'and they want to get home.'

'I should think so,' I said. 'How old are they?'

'Two and four. The dog's with them.'

'And you locked them in the car? With a dog? Have you not seen what happened at Ayers Rock?'

He sighed. 'To be fair, I wasn't planning to be long and, yes, I need to get them home for tea. How about I call you in the next few days and see how you're travelling with this?'

'I don't think so,' I said, feeling quite stressed about the news and also pressured by Andrew Shaw.

My brain had been right, despite what my stupid body did by way of response to him. He was just a crook like the rest of them. And his crookedness was about money, the most disgusting crookedness there is, the way of greed, that basest human instinct.

'Where's their mother then?' I said, looking down to see a dear little face at the window under the streetlamp. I couldn't help but smile as a tiny hand came up to wave. I waved back.

'She died,' Andrew Shaw said then, and his own face, not unlike the little face in the car window, looked as if it might crumple into tears.

I knew then that he would become a part of my life. Of course he would. Who needs money when children are without their mother? And who needs the news when someone has shared their truth with you?

TWELVE

Royal Train to Canberra, 1920

I STAYED UP LATE DRAFTING REPLIES, FEELING A JOY I doubt I could convey here without exclamation marks, which my father would have been shocked to see me use. He was against semicolons too, and colons, come to think of it. He felt commas and full stops were the punctuation of pause needed in order to provide clarity and conciseness. I had inherited his hatred for those other less-used marks, which Mr Waters found enormously amusing.

'What's wrong with the poor old semicolon?' he said, as he inserted one to replace a full stop of mine. I had to confess that I adopted without much reflection my father's view that writers who used semicolons were indecisive and those who used colons were show-offs.

'I've never thought of it that way,' Mr Waters said. 'I've always been a fan of the semicolon. Does it make me indecisive?'

'I'm sure it doesn't, sir,' I said. 'My father has many quirks.'

Mr Waters smiled. 'The semicolon,' he mused, shaking his head softly.

Mr Waters was a different kind of writer from my father, I was already learning. If Daddy's verses approached meaning from an angle, providing plenty of points where a reader might create their own from his words, Mr Waters liked as little ambiguity as possible. He was different too from Helen, who, I was to learn, wanted always to create a ruckus of interest with her words. It was the nature of their tasks, I suppose, but Mr Waters, who simplified everything I ever wrote for him, was also a kind of poet. It wasn't that my father had been a writer of the overwriting tendency—far from it—but Mr Waters brought such simplicity to my writing. It was thrilling in its way. 'The prince likes to be direct,' he said that first night. 'You'll be perfect. You have no noise of your own style getting in the way.'

Mr Waters had asked the stewards to remove the upholstered chairs and bring in a card table which I could use to sort the mail into piles. He set up the typewriter, which had been on one side of his desk, for me to start typing the replies. I sat by the long window, although it was pitch-black by six pm, and went to work drafting.

Mr Waters was at his desk, writing notes in pencil on the side of a typescript while the train continued west. His job was harder than mine with the moving train. 'The schedule for Tasmania,' he said when he spied me looking over—I had tried to look away and pretend that I wasn't snooping but he only smiled. Everything interested me. I was madly trying to keep a note of whatever I could, thinking I would write it all down in my notebook as soon as I had a chance.

'We have to cut the number of functions in half,' he said, 'and so I am the bringer of bad news to one half of Tasmania, which is now two islands: one that sees H.R.H. and one that doesn't. They don't realise that the prince is one young man not twenty. They have him meeting people from dawn until dusk, official balls every night. We specified hours, numbers, everything, but they have misread by a factor of ten what we meant.' He sighed. 'This has happened everywhere. It's such pressure on one person, even a prince. The admiral is doing his best, but he doesn't seem to be able to control them, and Grigg couldn't care less really.' He said this to himself more than to me. I just nodded.

He sat back in his chair, looked over at the door to the prince's private study. 'Let's hope he likes the speech. We're running out of time to rewrite it.'

'Helen said you've known the prince for a long time,' I said.

'My father is his father's equerry. The prince and his brother, Prince Albert, and I all did our lessons together, and then we all went to school together until they left for the navy.'

'Helen says you're the only one Prince Edward listens to.'

Mr Waters smiled. 'People say things like that but they don't understand. He's born to be king, Maddie. Imagine that load on a person.'

Just then the door at the other end of our carriage opened. It was Colonel Grigg, the man I'd seen with Mr Waters in the morning. He was dressed in his military uniform now, khaki, the leather of his shoes and Sam Browne belt gleaming. 'Rupert,' he said, doffing an imaginary cap. He wore a pistol on his side. A pistol!

'Ned,' Mr Waters said, his expression hard to read.

Colonel Grigg had to approve all the public speeches and the official meetings, Helen had told me. He was in charge of public functions and liaised with the P.M.'s office back in London on all aspects of the tour.

The colonel didn't acknowledge me as he walked through to the door of the prince's study. 'Are we close?' he asked Mr Waters, smiling.

'I think so,' Mr Waters said. 'I hope so.' He looked at his watch.

'It's not me, Waters. It's your lad and bloody Helen. They want poetry. Silk purse, I say.'

'Well, he likes what he likes, Ned,' Mr Waters said. He glanced over to me. 'He likes what Maddie and I write. And we ought to be thankful for that, don't you think?'

I beamed with pride that he included me with him as a writer, although I knew the prince was unlikely to have seen anything I'd written yet.

The colonel had been standing at the door, looking back at Mr Waters. 'I suppose, but getting him to like what we write isn't the job, is it, man?'

'It is for me,' Mr Waters said, and turned back to the papers on his desk.

The colonel rolled his eyes, looking over at me. I had no idea what he meant to convey, but I averted my gaze and went back to my letter-writing. Already I knew where my loyalty lay.

The colonel knocked on the door gently now. I heard a voice within call, 'Come!' He went in.

Just after seven, Helen came out of the study. Mr Waters looked up.

'Ned's going over it with him,' Helen said. 'I have exhausted my considerable store of metaphors, I'm afraid.'

'Never,' Mr Waters said. He smiled up at her and there was such tenderness in his eyes. In a very short time, I had become fond of Mr Waters. He seemed to care so much about what he did, a lot like my father had been before the war.

'A city on a lake,' Helen said, looking at me. 'Isn't that a line from somewhere? Anyway, we're debating whether to say lake or body of water. I mean, really. I suppose "lake" might raise the prospect of Arthur and Excalibur, and Ned might see a downside for the empire in that. But the prince is not a man for colour when it comes to language. Call a spade a spade, he says.'

Mr Waters laughed. 'Hear, hear! I'm not a man for colour when it comes to language either. Maddie's father doesn't like semicolons.'

Helen looked at him.

'Maybe it's too many cooks,' he said. 'Maybe you should help Maddie and me with the letters and leave the speechwriting to Ned. He loves all that intrigue.'

She looked over to me. 'Dinner?'

Mr Waters started to answer and then saw that Helen was addressing me and nodded instead.

Helen took me to the dining carriage through the other staff offices. They were richly appointed: dark wood panelling, leather upholstery, heavy velvet drapes, much more ornate than Mr Waters's office. I said as much.

'Yes,' Helen said. 'Rupert does what David does, and David likes simplicity. This is all terribly fussy, don't you think? I'd say the admiral and Ned probably did their own decor.' She laughed.

In the dining room, which was in the middle carriage, we were served pea soup with bread and sweet, lukewarm tea. I realised I'd hardly eaten any breakfast and no lunch and so the food was sustaining. There was fresh bread and a slab of butter each.

'How are you enjoying the H.R.H. circus?' Helen asked.

'It's all so extraordinary,' I said. 'I didn't want to say in front of Mr Waters, but I've never done anything before. I was at school, then at Christie's, and now . . .'

'Oh, that's dear,' Helen said. 'Truth is, it's we who are fortunate to have you, Maddie Bright.'

I'm sure I beamed.

We were about to leave to go back to work when a tall slim naval officer in whites strode through the carriage from the front.

'Dickie!' said Helen, stopping him in his tracks just after he'd passed us by. He whipped his head around. He had a happy face, eyes that looked at a person directly. 'I thought we'd conspired to leave you in Sydney,' Helen said.

He walked back to us. 'Sadly, no,' he said. 'Although the Old Salt may have tried.'

'Halsey?' Helen said.

'Yes, Halsey. He and Grigg are now officially convinced I am a bad influence on H.R.H. It's my great achievement to be the cause of something they actually agree on.'

He leaned down and spoke more quietly so that only Helen and I would hear. 'As if David needs any influencing at all to be bad.' He laughed at his joke. 'But unfortunately for me, Halsey has written to the King that I am the problem, and Grigg has done the same with the P.M. It was my poor mother who told me. Me, sweet boy that I am. Let's face it. If we were to talk honestly, I think you and I know what's what.' He flashed a Cheshire cat grin.

He noticed me then. 'And who's this?' he said, to Helen not me.

'I'm Maddie,' I said, 'sir.'

'You don't have to sir Dickie,' Helen said. 'Maddie, this is Louis Mountbatten, Prince Edward's cousin. Dickie, Maddie Bright is the daughter of the poet Thomas Bright. Will you sit with us?'

'And I know Thomas Bright?' He sat down beside Helen, who shimmied over to the window to make room for him.

He smelled fresh, like Sunlight soap.

'You should,' Helen said. 'If you read poetry you would. Maddie's taken on the role of correspondence secretary for a few days until we catch up.'

'Well, good for you,' he said, smiling at me. 'I was brought on the tour to write those letters, according to Grigg yesterday. At least, *he* thinks I was.' He laughed then. In fact, I realised a slight smile hadn't really left his face since he'd come into the carriage. 'I'm more the black sheep of the family sort.'

'That's the royal family,' Helen said, 'where the sheep are generally pretty white.'

'Just so. Anyway, I am on my way somewhere, but you two have made me forget where.'

'To remove the admiral's head on behalf of us all?'

'Never,' Dickie said. 'He's on our side.'

'Your side,' Helen said. 'I wish I knew how to get on with him. He treats me like I'm stupid.'

'I think it's Ned, not you,' Dickie said. 'Ned's always trying to make hay out of everything. Tomorrow's speech, a case in point. The admiral and I say we should talk about a new nation, a new capital, one of our friends—like in Ottawa—and that's it, or don't talk at all. Poor David's had enough of all the nonsense. But with Grigg, it's whether the communists are in control or the Fenians or the other Bolshies. Are there any other Bolshies?'

Helen laughed. 'Ah, so it's you and the admiral getting in David's ear. I wondered. Well, Ned has to think of the political ramifications, and I'd just like a bit of poetry.'

Dickie laughed. 'The secret with the admiral is to act as if you're interested. It sort of soothes him, I think.'

'Is that what you do?'

'I'm his best student, he told Mama. Seriously. He's like all of us. He just wants to feel he matters.' Dickie took out a cigarette and offered one to me, which I declined, and Helen, which she accepted. 'He was Fourth Sea Lord and commanded a fleet in the war. Now he's a babysitter. Who'd want to play that particular role on this particular tour?'

He leaned in to light Helen's cigarette and then lit his own.

'He does seem to like you, Dickie. I'll concede that.'

'Grigg doesn't.'

'No. He thinks you're stirring the pot. And you are! Do you know what he told me the other night?'

'No, do tell.' He looked at me as he spoke. 'Maddie and I love gossip, don't we?'

I nodded and giggled. It was as if he'd read my mind.

'David wrote to his mother that he had to give you a dressing-down after one of the balls in Melbourne. He told Ned he'd done that. Something about you and the drink being too well acquainted. Anyway, Ned told me the only reason David likes you on the tour is that there's someone who behaves worse than him.'

Dickie laughed, throwing his head back. 'Ah well, David knows what's really happening, and so does the admiral. And Waters has always been decent to me. I'm not worried. I can afford to have an enemy in Ned.'

He stood then. 'Maddie, it is such a relief to know someone is writing those letters. I was terrified they were leaving it in the hope I'd become suddenly inspired. Ships. I like ships. I'm so glad you're here.' Leaving his cigarette between his lips, he reached out a hand. I shook it.

He took the cigarette from his lips and blew smoke up to the ceiling of the car.

'Helen, I'll see you tonight, I hope.'

He left us.

'Dickie is so dashing,' I said.

'He's just a sweet boy, really,' she said. 'This is all a bit beyond him. Let's face it, it's beyond me, and I *know* how the world works. Dickie's nineteen, just a baby.'

I didn't remind Helen I was even younger, seventeen.

∽

It was late that night before Helen finished working with the prince on his remarks for the next day. She came out of his private study and into our office.

'Finally, we get a speech he's happy with,' Helen said to me. 'And then, five minutes ago, he said he really doesn't need to speak at all tomorrow. Has the admiral been in to see him?'

I didn't know.

Mr Waters, who'd been working at the desk beside me, looked up but didn't say anything.

'I'm serious. We're back to, "I don't want to do this." I don't think the week off helped at all,' Helen said, looking at Mr Waters now. 'I think he's worse.'

'He'll be fine after a good night's sleep,' Mr Waters said. 'What's he doing now?'

'James is in there.' James was the prince's valet. I'd met him during the afternoon when he came in looking for the prince. 'I think he's planning to go to bed. But I am serious. The admiral and Dickie have been bothering him about what to say.'

'Good then,' Mr Waters said.

'No, not good then. There are too many whispers in his ears. It's my job and Ned's job, not theirs. Or yours.'

Mr Waters didn't reply.

'You're still up,' Helen said to me. I didn't like to say I didn't know where I was sleeping and hadn't wanted to ask Mr Waters. I didn't even know where the servants' compartment was. I was happy to keep working, but I was getting tired. My little bag was still beside the desk. I hadn't stopped except for the quick dinner break.

I'd started typing once Mr Waters had read the first twenty draft replies and pronounced himself happy with them. He made changes along the way and it helped me learn. He said we'd give typed versions to the prince, 'in the hope he doesn't change them'. He smiled as he said it. 'But, Maddie, he probably will. He's quite particular about some things, and no one can quite work out what they'll be on any given day. I did show him the standard letter and he was awfully happy, so bravo.'

I didn't care if he rewrote them from scratch. Having a chance to write something he would read was enough for someone who, until a week ago, had one experience of work: having been fired from Christie's cafe for bathing a customer in his tea.

'Come on,' Helen said now. 'You need your sleep.' She looked at Mr Waters. 'No one likes a sycophant, do they, Rupert?' Her voice took on an edge.

'Certainly not,' he said, either failing to notice the edge or choosing not to. 'Off you go, Maddie. To bed.'

I picked up my bag and followed Helen down the corridor past the other offices, the government carriage and the dining carriage and kitchen.

Helen was the only woman on staff and she had a large compartment at one end of a carriage with its own bathroom. The train had been fitted out for the prince's tour and they'd specified the need for female staff accommodation, she said.

'I got the steward to make up the second bunk. I hope you'll be comfortable.'

I knew that Helen would have had the whole compartment to herself if it hadn't been for me. 'It's very kind of you,' I said. 'Are you sure?'

'It's like school. We can be just like school chums.'

'Really, I'd be more than happy to sleep with the servants.'

'It wouldn't be right,' Helen said. 'You're one of the prince's personal staff now. You bunk with the staff. Anyway, I'm glad for the company.'

We changed into our nightdresses—mine poorly mended, Helen's a lovely apricot silk with a matching long gown she draped neatly on the hook behind the door—and crawled into our bunks.

Helen hung her head over the edge of her bunk. Her blonde curls fell around her face. 'See? Like boarding school.'

'I never went to boarding school,' I said.

'My parents sent me,' she said. 'I think Mummy wanted me out of the house after she remarried. God, I hated it, but home was worse by then—a horror, actually.' She looked terribly sad, and I wasn't sure what to say. 'I just wanted to go back to America. I hated England. I hated it.'

'Didn't you say you were an orphan, like the other Helen Burns?' I said.

'I did,' she said, 'but only for the sake of a good story.'

I laughed. 'You can't just make your life up.'

'Why not?'

'I loved school,' I said, thinking suddenly about Daddy, who'd taught us English. I sighed.

'Did you tell me you knew Mr Waters before?' I said then, wanting to change the subject. I had spoken to Mr Waters during the evening while Helen worked with the prince on his speech. I had noticed him watching the door to the prince's study.

'Yes, in the war,' Helen said. 'Rupert was wounded in France. I was working at a hospital.'

'That sounds like a plot for a romance,' I said.

'Not really, no,' she said. 'I . . . It doesn't matter.'

'Yes, it does,' I said. 'We're writers! So is he Rochester to your Jane, or Heathcliff to your Cathy?'

'Rupert? Heathcliff?' she said, as if I'd suggested he was a peacock. 'No, no, no. He's Edgar. No, not Edgar. St John. He's St John not Rochester. Can't bend.' She sighed. 'Do you really want to know?'

She looked upset.

'Yes,' I said. 'He seems so kind, and so sad.'

'He is kind,' she said. 'Rupert is kind to a fault. And he *is* sad.'

She sighed heavily, looked away from me, out into the black night. 'Rupert and I fell in love,' she said, looking back at me. 'But it wasn't enough.'

'What do you mean? Enough for what?'

'It wasn't enough to cleanse me.'

From *Autumn Leaves* by M.A. Bright:

France, 1918

'Will you walk with me?' he said.

'You're not supposed to be over here. This is the drivers' quarters. Some of the women don't like your type.'

'What's my type?'

'Male.'

'I see. There's not much I can do about that.'

'You can leave,' she said, but she was smiling. There was a tooth, on the left, a little crooked.

'I knew you'd look fetching in that coat up close.'

It was early Sunday morning. She was wearing her goatskin. Miss Ivens had ordered them for the drivers in the second winter. She didn't care what it looked like. On those frigid nights, it was a relief to be warm.

'From a distance, I took you for a bear, a Russian one,' he said.

'I'm not sure I like that,' she said. 'And I don't know why it has to be Russian.'

'Standing on its back legs. Or perhaps a centaur rather than a bear.'

'Is that supposed to make me feel better?'

'No.' He smiled shyly. 'Please, will you walk with me?'

The look on his face. There was something uncomplicated about him, something altogether good, she thought.

She could tell him about complication; complication that would knit his brow more or less permanently. But instead she smiled and said, 'Yes, let's walk.'

She wanted uncomplicated, she thought to herself. But it wouldn't be fair on him. He was a gentleman. She knew that much. She was never going to be with a gentleman. She'd been spoiled for that. It was the perfect word, spoiled. It was what happened to rotten fruit.

∽

He had survived. Against all odds, he had survived, and he had her to thank for it.

'You're very quiet,' she said.

'I need time to muster up my courage,' he said.

'Is the muster worth waiting for?'

He nodded. 'Oh yes. It's the quiet ones who have wisdom.'

'That makes no sense,' she said.

They walked across the abbey grounds in silence, towards the village. There was a mist low on the ground, although the sun would soon burn it off and already the chill was lifting.

They came to the edge of the forest. 'How do you think the trees work out where they should stop?' he asked.

'What do you mean?'

'How come the forest is always this big?' He gestured with his arm, the one that wasn't injured. 'And we are in the forest or out of the forest. There's no partly forested.'

'I suppose it's soil that changes,' she said.

'I never thought of that. I thought it was an intelligence that only trees have. They know how to live in a community.'

She laughed. 'I think I prefer your version.'

She picked up a twig. 'Last year, there was a craze among the French soldiers to make bracelets out of pine needles. They wove them together and gave them to the nurses and drivers. They'd sing songs to us. It was rather sweet. Perhaps the trees here do know how to live in community. You may be right,' she said.

She looked across at him. 'Have you rounded up your courage?'

'I have,' he said, turning to face her. He tilted his head, shaking it lightly. He held up his left hand, the injured one. She wanted to tell him to be careful. He smiled. 'You saved my life. I don't know how to repay you.'

He was stuttering. He wanted to punch himself.

She didn't seem to notice. 'I drove you here,' she said. 'Miss Ivens saved your life, or Henry. I think Dr Henry did your surgery. I didn't even know how ill you were until we got here.'

'Still, you were supposed to leave me there.'

'I was,' she said.

'Why didn't you?'

'I'm not very good at doing as I'm told. That's the first thing.' She had a flash of memory then, her stepfather the last time, the time she screamed as soon as he came into the room.

She still doesn't know where that scream came from, how she managed it.

Her mother was at the door then. 'What's wrong?'

'A nightmare,' she told her mother while looking at her stepfather. 'I had a nightmare. I don't want those nightmares anymore.'

Her mother looked at her stepfather, said nothing. Nothing.

'And if I'm perfectly honest, I liked you,' she said to him now, putting thoughts of the past away.

'So if you hadn't liked me, you'd have left me there?'

'Quite possibly,' she said.

'I like you too,' he said.

'But that's because I saved your life. You are beholden to me.'

'No,' he said, serious now. 'I want to tell you this. Since we met, there hasn't been anything else on my mind but you.' He flexed his jaw. He must get these words out.

'No,' she said, putting a finger to his lips. 'We mustn't talk like this. We mustn't.' She could smell the soap on his skin. 'There is nothing there.'

'In you?' he said, incredulous. 'You feel nothing for me?'

'No,' she said. 'Yes. Nothing like that. I feel you were a soldier who was wounded and I drove you to the hospital, which is my job. Your feelings are perfectly understandable but they're really nothing to do with me. You are grateful. Be grateful to Miss Ivens. She established Royaumont. Be grateful to Dr Henry. She saved your arm.' She swallowed hard. 'But now, you must talk about other things.' Her voice was strained; she could hear it.

Other things? He had thought of nothing else but her, the way her hair fell forward onto her face when she bent down to him, the way she spoke, the sweet smell of her breath.

He'd found out what he could from the nurses. Most of them wouldn't talk to him, but there was one who'd been her friend. She's the life of the party, the nurse said. Always up for a good time. You'll have trouble with that one, mark my words.

'All right,' he said. 'I'll stop the talk, if you tell me about yourself.'

'Nothing to tell,' she said. 'Nothing you'd want to hear about anyway.'

THIRTEEN

London, 1997

AFTER THE LUNCH WITH FINIAN INGLIS, VICTORIA TOOK a cab back to her flat and threw some clothes into an overnight bag. There were still no photographers outside, she was relieved to see.

Victoria had no blouses ironed and Martha was sleeping on her favourite jacket in the bathroom. Victoria had meant to take it to the cleaners. Now cat hair was added to a red wine stain. Maybe cat urine as well, she thought when she picked up the jacket.

Victoria couldn't chastise Martha, a rescue cat with difficulties the Royal Society vet said were probably caused by early traumatic experiences. They were the reason she played at three in the morning on the bed, toileted just about anywhere but in the litter, and slept on Victoria's favourite clothes during the day if Victoria left them on the floor.

They'd been together for three years now and Martha was improving, Victoria told herself. At any rate, she was family so that was that.

Victoria took the waiting cab to Claire's flat in Peckham on the way to Waterloo.

'Flying visit,' she said when Claire answered the door, knowing a flying visit to Claire was almost impossible. Her friend was wearing track pants—the kind, if they'd ever seen an actual track, had long since retired—and a fuchsia t-shirt. She had baby Max in her arms.

Claire's husband, Tony, who was finishing his PhD in politics and caring for the kids while Claire established her PR business, was nowhere to be seen. This was not unusual, Victoria knew.

Claire put Max on a mat on the floor while Victoria made tea.

'Fuck,' Claire said when she came back in. 'Jordan's sandwich.' She opened the toaster and took out something black. 'Baked beans and cheese with pineapple, his favourite. Do you think it's salvageable?'

Victoria shook her head. She wasn't sure if Claire was serious. You wouldn't feed what was on the spatula to a dog.

'You're right. Jordan, honey!' she yelled. 'I'll do your sandwich a bit later. That's the end of the pineapple anyway so it will be something else.'

'I'm going to Paris,' Victoria said. 'Can I borrow your black jacket?'

'Sure,' Claire said. 'Oh, hang on, mine's got vomit on it.'

'Damn,' Victoria said. 'Mine's covered in Martha hair. I'll just have to be colour-blind and wear my brown.'

Claire sat down. 'It's unbelievable, isn't it? I've been crying all morning on and off. It's just thrown me completely. I told Tony to go to uni. I couldn't face work today. Poor you.'

'Why?' Victoria said.

'What do you write? Everything just confirms the view that we did this.'

'I suppose,' Victoria said. 'Did we?'

After the *Panorama* interview the year before, Claire had said she thought they'd cornered Diana, that the family were threatening to take the children from her and she didn't know what else to do. While most of Victoria's colleagues decided that interview was the end for Diana, Claire said it was desperate. She said the royal family were like the mafia, only worse. 'It's all about how things look, not how they are.'

'What did you do?' Claire said then. At first Victoria thought she was talking about Diana, how she had contributed to Diana's death, and she was about to mention the story she'd written all those years ago, when Claire leaned across and touched Victoria's cheek.

'Oh, that. I fell last night. I tried some cover stick. Didn't work, obviously.'

'No,' Claire said. 'I'm really sorry I haven't called lately.' She waved a hand at the kitchen, which was still a mess from dinner the night before, overlaid with breakfast. 'It's the bolognese years.'

Victoria looked over at her friend, bit her lip. 'I . . .' She had the strongest urge to cry. She held it back.

Claire sat down. 'What is it, Victoria?'

'We're engaged.'

'Engaged! Oh, wow, that was fast. Ben?'

Victoria laughed. 'Yes. I don't have a list.'

'No, it's just sudden.'

'I was planning on telling you. I just . . .'

Victoria did start crying then, one of those messy noisy sobs that comes out whether you like it or not.

'What's the matter, love?' Claire leaned over and took her hand. 'Are you thinking you don't want—'

Just then Jordan came in from the lounge and asked for his sandwich. Victoria managed to compose herself. 'Hey, Jordy.'

'Hi, Victoria,' the little boy said. 'I'm hungry.'

'In a minute, sweetie,' Claire said. 'Go put the telly on, will you? I think it's *The Flintstones*.' She looked at her friend. 'Desperate times!'

Jordan toddled off.

'What is it, Victoria?' Claire asked.

'I don't even know. I'm just upset and anxious and, until today, it's been every day outside the flat.'

'What has?'

'It's Ben. The papers. They all want pictures of him, and me. They chased me down the street on my way to work one morning last week. I felt like a criminal. I didn't even look to see if they ran the pic. I suppose they won't bother now, with Diana filling pages, but that will pass and they'll be back, won't they?'

'Yes, you could probably see it coming,' Claire said. 'I saw a shot of the two of you somewhere. You looked great, if that helps.' She smiled weakly.

'Ben says we have to get out in front, tell them we're engaged, control the story.' She sniffed.

Claire thought about this. 'He's probably not wrong about that in one way. It doesn't look like you'll have the option of privacy.'

'Why not?' Victoria said.

'He's a big deal,' Claire said. 'Who knows why?' She paused. 'But you're engaged, and happy about that?'

Victoria didn't respond.

'What is it?'

'Nothing.' She wiped her eyes, made herself smile. 'Nothing. Just stress.'

'You know, you don't have to get married,' Claire said. 'You know that, right?'

She nodded, smiled tightly. 'The thing is, we're everywhere together,' Victoria said. 'It's six months. I'm now Ben Winter's girlfriend.'

'So? Do you think it would help if you went back and saw the psychologist?'

'I like strong women,' Victoria said.

Claire laughed.

Just then the baby cried and Claire said, 'Give me a minute. Sorry.'

When she came back, the baby on her breast, Jordan asking for his sandwich again, Victoria apologised for barging in. 'It was really just the jacket. Ignore all the other stuff. I have to go or I'll miss my train. Love you.'

'I'll call you tonight,' Claire said as she was leaving, still looking concerned.

Victoria knew Claire probably wouldn't call; she had too much on her plate as it was. Victoria shouldn't be burdening her further. 'I'm fine,' she said. 'Paris!' She did her best to smile, and left.

~

Victoria checked in with Ewan before she boarded the train at Waterloo. People were gathering at the palaces, he said, leaving flowers. Ewan didn't make a wisecrack as he normally might have. 'The city's really quiet,' he said. 'It's almost like a great darkness is coming down on the world, like evil has been done. You don't think the family . . .'

'No,' she said. 'They're the royal family. You're starting to sound like Claire.'

'They'd have means,' he said. 'It's what Danny reckons. He reckons they bumped her off. And they had cause. She was so much trouble for them.'

'Ewan, I need you to be normal,' Victoria said. 'Meredith can cry and Claire can tell me they're the mafia. But I need you to stay Ewan, the Scottish republican bastard I know and love. I'm about to go under the channel.'

He laughed. 'The tunnel,' he said in a ghostly voice.

'Stop,' she said. 'Look, I really don't know what I'll write. I'll call from Paris. But I don't feel I'm the person for this.'

'You're perfect for this,' he said.

'No one could do it justice,' she said.

'No one else,' he said. 'When you're on, Victoria, there's no one better.'

She sighed. 'Thank you for saying that but I'm not on much lately.'

He ignored what she'd said. 'Harry wants you to go to the hospital when you get there,' he said. 'I'll get the name. It's where ... the body. Mark will pick you up. He's already sent some shots back but there's nothing for the magazine that I can see. I want something that won't date. I think the hospital might work, depending what you write.'

'Will you look at whatever I do tonight before you give it to Harry?'

'Of course,' he said. 'But where's your brash confidence, Victoria? You usually eat stories like this.'

'I don't know. I think this one's different.'

'I suppose. Anyway, we'll get through. Oh, Ben called.'

'Yes?'

'No, nothing. He just didn't know you were in Paris. I might have mucked things up.'

'That's okay. I haven't had time to call him.'

Ewan didn't say anything.

'Hey, before you go?' she said.

'Yes?'

'The lunch with Finian Inglis,' she said. 'You think it might be real?'

'What do you think?'

'Well, that's the thing. It's almost too odd to be made up.'

'I thought that too. Fin's a good guy. Maybe not savvy, like I am, but a good guy.'

'You're not savvy.'

'No. It was probably a figure of speech.'

'He wants me to go to Australia.'

'Yes.'

'And he says you're paying the airfare.'

'Yes.'

'Why?'

'Great story, if it's true. Imagine the shots of this fossil who wrote *Autumn Leaves*. And is it autobiographical? Did he have an affair in World War I? If so, who was the woman? Is she alive? What's the new book like? Is it as good, or better? There are so many angles.'

'It's not a he. M.A. Bright is a woman.'

'Really? I'd have sworn he was a he.'

'That's what Finian said anyway. Ewan, wouldn't you normally go yourself to check this out?'

'Maybe. But Bright didn't ask for me. She asked for you.'

As the train began to move, Victoria stared straight ahead, repeating a mantra in her head: I am not afraid of the tunnel. I am not afraid of the tunnel. Fear rose up and swallowed her mantra whole. Breathe, she told herself. Just breathe.

Ewan had said Mark Staple would be there to meet her. He was a good photographer, but what would he shoot in Paris? Victoria wondered. The site of the crash? Maybe that was what people would want. It was five years since Victoria had worked on a straight news story and what constituted news had changed so much. News is whatever readers say it is, Harry Knight had said when they'd debated whether to run the tapes of the telephone call between Prince Charles and Camilla Parker Bowles. 'And you can't tell me you weren't curious to know what they said to one another in private. It's fucking news.'

Harry had a point. If people didn't want to know, they wouldn't buy the paper and the editors would lose their jobs. It was their job to sell papers because increased circulation led to increased advertising which made their money. Simple as that.

But led by Knight, led by Victoria herself, when she thought about it, they'd taken the gloves off in terms of the royal family. Some time between when Diana married Charles and now, what they reported about the royals changed. There was no longer any such thing as going too far. The public interest had always had a dark side, but now newspapers fed it. Perhaps it *was* news, but sometimes what they reported was without even the most basic respect for human dignity.

Where would it end? her father asked. Where does the public interest become uninteresting, or worse?

It ended in a Paris underpass, Victoria thought bitterly now.

It had bothered Victoria when Ben said that she was no different from those photographers who waited outside the flat. She knew he was wrong, but she also knew he was right.

She hadn't called him before she left London. She knew she should have. He'd be annoyed that Ewan had been the one to tell him she'd gone. He wouldn't like it, she knew, and that was the reason she didn't call. She didn't want to have to explain herself.

'You know, I only took this role because you told me too, Tori,' he'd said at some stage last night, and it had irked her, not least because she hadn't told him to take the role. If she were honest, she'd been relieved to be back in her flat without Ben after she'd left him in New York the last time. She felt less anxious on her own, she realised. Then she felt guilty for thinking this way. He was her fiancé. She should want to be with him, shouldn't she?

She did want to be with him.

Didn't she?

They would be married in two months. The invitations would go out next week. New York, at Victoria's insistence; the middle point between Los Angeles and London, and everyone could have a holiday at the end. He'd wanted a gala at his ranch in Wyoming, but she said they'd honeymoon at the ranch, just the two of them.

Ben wanted Victoria to quit her job once they were married. He'd said it before and last night he'd become angry about it. He didn't like Claire either. That was what he'd said last week. Victoria wanted Claire as her matron of honour. They'd been friends since Victoria started at *The Daily Mail*. Ben said Claire was a smart mouth. That was after the second time he met her—dinner at Claire's place, Jordan banging on saucepans, Max wailing in Tony's arms, Tony watching Ben with a mixture of adulation (the Zombie movies) and suspicion (Tony had adopted an overtly fraternal role in Victoria's life after he married Claire, not altogether unwelcome but not much help with Ben). It was true Claire was a smart mouth, but she was only a smart mouth because she was so smart. When Victoria said this to Ben, he said, Whatever. I don't like smart mouths.

The conductor was standing in front of her, Victoria saw, wanting to see her ticket. 'Sorry,' she said. She found her ticket and he checked it and kept going.

It was Victoria's job that was the main problem now as far as Ben was concerned. The photographers had found them, as he had said they would. If she'd listened to him at the start, none of this would have happened, he'd said last night. That was his logic.

She'd told Ben she didn't sign up for this. It was a threat, wasn't it? She didn't mean it to be a threat, but of course it was a threat. I didn't sign up for this so now I can opt out. That's what would come next, wasn't it? Was that what she was thinking?

After the first picture ran of Victoria in her bike gear, Ben came back from Los Angeles and the photographers came back with him. The day he landed, they were in front of Victoria's flat in the morning. She took the fire escape stairs at the back of the flat and went out into the garden. She climbed over the fence into the yard behind, taking treats for the dog. She walked down the side of the house to the street and from there to the station. Ha! she thought. She'd fooled them.

And then, she and Ben were going for a run early on the Saturday of that week. Victoria came out the front door first. 'Hey,' she'd said, blinded momentarily by the flash. When her vision cleared, she saw Nathan Ashbury.

'What are you doing here?' she asked.

'Come on, give us a smile, Victoria,' Nathan said. 'You look great.' He was taking shots the whole time, talking to her in a way she'd heard him talk to people who didn't want their photograph taken, coaxing.

Victoria was wearing track pants and one of Ben's sweatshirts, no make-up. She hadn't even combed her hair. It was somehow worse that he was someone she knew.

'I'm sorry, Nathan, but this is private property,' she said.

'I'm not on your property,' he replied. 'Ben!' he called out.

Victoria turned and saw Ben waving and smiling.

'Hello there,' Ben said. 'How about a quick picture and you leave us alone to run?'

'Great,' Nathan said. 'Thanks, man.'

The shot they used, page five, wasn't the smiling picture Victoria found herself acquiescing to. It was one of the first ones. BEN WINTER'S TRYST was the headline, Ben handsome, his beard one of those fetching shadows over his cheeks and chin, Victoria in front of him like a rabbit caught in headlights. Ben couldn't see how unreasonable it was.

Fear. She felt a moment of fear then. She looked through the train window to the blackness. It passed quickly. The photographers frightened her. She knew them, or knew what they did. But when their lenses were trained on her, it was entirely different.

Was that it?

'It will only be like this until we take over the story,' she remembered Ben saying last night, his eyes tired in the dim light. That was his solution, to take over the story. He thought he could manage everything. He thought his money could manage everything. And perhaps he was right. What would Victoria know?

Ben operated in a world where beauty, or some hard-to-define quality that was related to beauty, was what made the difference between success and failure. 'Harrison Ford,' he'd said to her. 'Harrison Ford was a carpenter. He's everyman. A lot of guys look like Harrison. Brown hair, eyes a colour you can't remember later, bit angry round the mouth. But not one in a million can close their mouth and raise an eyebrow and look so afraid and so competent all at once. That's the guy. He's just the guy.

'You have no flaws,' Ben said the first night they slept together.

'That's a good thing, right?' she said, wondering where he was going.

'Yes and no. Think of the most beautiful woman in the world to you.'

'Kate Winslet, this month.'

'See, she has flaws.'

'I suppose so.'

'Her cheekbones are not what you want with those lips. It combines as the gift.'

'The gift.'

'Our looks are a gift, just like anything else.'

'Well, if it's a choice, I'd rather brains than looks,' she said, narrowing her eyes at him. Was he stupid? she was thinking. Talk about gifts. God, he was gorgeous. Black hair going silver at the sides—it wasn't dyed, and she'd liked that. Big dark eyes that looked straight at her. He had a tan, but a lazy one, as if he never really had to work at it. It just happened in between takes.

What was he doing with a woman like her? she wondered.

She'd met many people like Ben before as part of the job: presidents, film actors, musicians. Someone else was always managing the environment for them, picking up the tab, keeping fans at bay, telling them names and reasons for meetings. Researching their interview, she read that Ben had two personal assistants with him at all times while he worked. They did shifts, a team of six young people he'd selected, four of them African American. 'I get bright kids and give them a chance in the industry. I have a pretty high turnover, but the few who stick it out a year generally get something out of it.' It had been written up in the liberal press as a form of slavery, the rich white guy employing poor black guys to carry his bags. 'I don't care,' he said. 'They don't just carry my bags. My contract with them stipulates that they have to attend acting school, and I pay for that. One of them is about to open on Broadway. Another is doing set design at NYU. It's not an empty gesture, and it's certainly not slavery.'

He wasn't stupid, she decided . . . and yet those films. 'You don't like superheroes?' he asked when she made a joke early in their relationship.

'I've never given them much thought,' she said.

'Fair point. What do you give thought to?'

She found herself uncomfortable, accustomed to being the one asking the questions. 'I don't know. Books.'

'You say that in a way,' he said, smiling.

'What way?'

'Suggesting films are somehow less.'

'I love the cinema.'

'Just not the cinema I love.'

'Perhaps,' she said. 'What's the point of superheroes?'

'It's the only thing,' he said. 'Good can triumph over evil. Is there anything else that matters in this world? The only stories that matter are the ones that dabble in that.'

He had a way of reducing arguments and she'd liked that at first. It seemed dependable.

Ben had grown up in a trailer park outside Sebastopol in California, he told her on their first date. His father had left his mother when he was four and his mother decided she wouldn't work full-time and leave him without a parent to care for him. So they lived in a trailer, surviving on what work she could do while he was at school.

He never wanted for anything, he said. 'Mom was everything. She's an amazing woman.'

'Why didn't you tell me all this for the story?' Victoria asked.

'Because it's not the story,' he said.

'But it's so great. You came from nothing. It's the American dream.'

'Okay, for a start, I didn't come from nothing.'

'I'm so sorry,' she said, realising how insensitive she'd been.

Ben told Victoria that if his teachers were ever mean to him, his mother would go to see them and explain what they needed to do differently. If they didn't, she kept him home and then shifted school. He changed schools four times because teachers weren't doing him any good.

'And then I bombed out of school pretty badly,' he said. 'I felt terrible. I knew what Mom had given up for me. She didn't have much of a life and here I was, blowing mine.'

And then at an acting school she'd paid for, he'd been picked for a part and then another and another until he won the *Zombie World* role.

The photographers hadn't really left them alone since Ben had been back. If Victoria accompanied him to a function, which she started doing at his insistence now that she'd been named in the press, they were photographed. Victoria didn't feel comfortable playing the role, but it wasn't these planned situations that frightened her; it was the unplanned ones. They ran a picture of the two of them in jeans and t-shirts one weekend and called them grungy zombies—Victoria hadn't even seen the photographer. They took another picture of her leaving the flat for work—again, she didn't see the photographer—and questioned whether she was putting on weight. The picture was cropped to emphasise her belly.

It was unsustainable. She knew it was unsustainable. 'I think if we led from the front foot, released a few pictures of us together, announced the engagement, it would be easier,' Ben had said. 'Otherwise, we'll have to tell them afterwards that we got married and it looks like we have something to hide.'

'Why do we have to tell them?'

'They're outside the door because they think it's a story, you and me. If we tell them the story, we control it.'

He sounded like his publicist, like any number of publicists Victoria had listened to. 'That's PR speak,' she said.

'It's also true,' he said. 'If you would just let me look after you like I said, this wouldn't have happened.'

He meant quit her job and move to a secure house. That's what looking after her would mean. A secure house in London, a secure house in New York, a secure house in Los Angeles. That's all he talked about now. She wouldn't work anymore. He'd gone from 'you need bodyguards' to 'you need to stop working and stay home'. But Victoria didn't want that. She didn't want to live in a secure house. She wanted to keep working at the magazine and not have her picture in the paper. She wanted, badly wanted, her independence.

'That's not an option,' Ben said calmly. Had he told her to shut her mouth? She had a memory of this but surely not. It was all hazy.

She wanted to go back to how things were before the photographers found them. Maybe she even wanted to go back to a time before she met Ben. She couldn't believe she was thinking this way. But it was different, she thought. She found herself afraid, inexplicably afraid because she was a journalist and should know better than to fear them.

Those photographers who wondered if Victoria was putting on weight? They were wrong. She wasn't putting on weight. She was pregnant, eleven weeks. She'd done three home pregnancy tests, three different brands, in the last week, and each time she sat on the toilet in the white bathroom at home and stared at two pink lines like train tracks to a new future. She hadn't told Claire. She hadn't told Ben. She could barely tell herself.

New York three months ago. She'd been careless. He'd said it doesn't matter. We're getting married anyway. She'd been swept along.

A child, like Jordan, Max; a child that would grow inside her, that would fuse her and Ben together forever.

She should have telephoned him. She knew she should have. But she hadn't.

Victoria looked out the window to the farms giving way to the outer settlements of Paris, green spaces punctuated by giant houses in clumps, the middle-class spread, the remaining trees green against a pale sky. She hadn't even noticed the tunnel.

FOURTEEN

Canberra, 1920

WE HAD STOPPED OVERNIGHT NEAR THE TOWN OF Bungendore and I slept soundly until I heard a kookaburra just before dawn. When the train started to move forward, I wiped icy mist from the window and looked out as we chugged up next to a red-brick building festooned with blue and white streamers.

The first kookaburra was joined by a chorus, laughing at the world for a few moments, stopping abruptly when a band of sulphur-crested cockatoos wheeled by above the station, their own wails more like an alarm than a laugh.

There were no houses I could see, and so much bush surrounding the station building that even though it was dressed up, it felt lonely. The grass was yellow now in winter and the scraggly gums a silver-grey green, with just the occasional boulder or dark shrub to break up the monotony. It was a sad landscape, I thought.

I rose and saw that Helen was already up, her bed made. I dressed quickly, made my own bunk and went to the office.

Helen soon came in from the prince's quarters. 'Halsey's in with him,' she whispered. 'There's trouble. Maybe you should go and find Rup—'

I was about to ask what she meant when she put a finger to her lips to shush me. She was looking beyond me. I turned around and there was one of the newspapermen Helen had pointed out the day before, Mr Murdoch from the *Times*. She didn't introduce me but she did say he was her favourite among the pressmen. 'At least he has a brain,' she said. 'The others are so easily fooled. If I'd known it was this easy, I'd have become a turncoat years ago.'

'Morning, Keith,' Helen said now, walking towards Mr Murdoch, a bright smile on her face. 'Are you coming out for breakfast?'

'I-i-i-s he c-c-coming out, m-m-more to the p-p-p-point?' Mr Murdoch said. 'Th-th-there's no one in your office.' Helen had mentioned his stutter, and said that in print, he was razor sharp. He refused to toe the line like the other newspapermen. Helen admired him, I could tell.

'Of course he is,' Helen said. 'You'll be happy, Keith: there's bacon from the pigs he shot yesterday.'

Keith Murdoch smiled. He was tall and imposing. The day before, he'd had his hat pulled low over his face, but I saw now his eyes were dark and perceptive. He looked from Helen to me.

'This is Maddie,' Helen told him. 'She's our new correspondence secretary. And a very good one, too. Her father is Thomas Bright.'

'The poet?' He spent considerable time on the *p*.

'Yes, the poet himself. And Maddie has decided to give up her own writing to help us. You might think of such service one day, Keith.'

'Not on your life,' he said, smiling again.

Suddenly, I heard a raised voice from within the prince's private chamber. Mr Murdoch heard it too, looked inquisitive. I didn't know whose voice it was, but it was not Mr Waters or the prince, I was fairly sure. 'He's not in there,' Helen said loudly to cover. 'He's up the front with the admiral. Let's go and see who else is up.'

She walked forward, forcing Keith Murdoch back through the train. She turned to me as she left. 'Just stay there in case you're needed to jolly him along,' she said.

I nodded, although I didn't even know who she meant me to jolly—hopefully not the prince, because all I could imagine was falling through the floor with embarrassment about how stupid I'd been the day before when I met him.

Ten minutes passed uneventfully and so I went back to work on the letters and soon dropped into the world of the people who looked to their prince for help. I kept hearing voices through the door to the prince's chamber, low and soothing, a little more excited, occasional outbursts. I couldn't make out words.

I noticed people had begun to arrive at the station and the scene became brighter because of them. Music started, quietly at first, growing louder as more band members arrived. By the time the sun was high in the sky, there was an enormous buzz outside the train. I'd been on my own in the office for an hour, every now and then hearing raised voices in the chamber beyond. No one emerged.

I heard the band play 'God Bless the Prince of Wales' and so I assumed the prince had gone out the back of the carriage and down to join the party.

Helen came back and told me to come down to breakfast. She looked towards the closed door of the prince's quarters and frowned.

'Where is he?' one of the newspapermen asked when we came out.

'Sleeping,' Helen said. 'He was up so late reading your stories that he's having to catch up on his sleep. Come, let's have breakfast.'

We had eggs on fried bread at tables set up in the station building.

'Are they all here to see him?' I asked Helen. There must have been two hundred people around the station now. I had no idea where they'd come from. But not one of them had seen the prince. I thought of my poor mother, how terribly disappointed she'd been.

'Yes, of course,' Helen said, a smile at the corners of her lips. She turned to Mr Waters, who had come over to our table.

'Maddie does have a point, Rupert. It's happening again. You told Ned once we'd had a week off—'

'It's hard to understand the pressure on him,' Mr Waters said.

'But all these people have come to see him, and he's not here. They couldn't care a fig for the Australian government. They want their prince!'

'Helen,' Mr Waters said. 'Please.' The look on his face was pained, as if he himself wondered how he'd got here.

The prince did not emerge at Bungendore and we finished what had become a subdued breakfast and entrained to make the short journey to the railhead nearest the capital site.

After we stopped again, Helen came through from the front carriages, looked to the closed door and said quietly, 'Ned talked to the admiral. David kicked up a stink about what to wear.'

'What to wear?'

'He wouldn't put on his uniform.'

I didn't say anything.

'Apparently, the admiral was insisting the prince put on his dress uniform and he refused. The King hates it when the prince doesn't dress properly, and the prince hates dressing properly. The poor old admiral is in the middle. So there you have it. Rupert can normally soothe him, but he was somewhere else, and I had to deal with Mr Murdoch. The admiral of the fleet was trying to dress the group captain and it was a total disaster.'

The admiral's must have been the other voice I could hear in the prince's quarters that morning.

'After the Bahamas,' Helen said, 'we had a wire from the King, marked urgent, that came in a diplomatic pouch, about the creases in their trousers, the prince and Dickie. They'd had sharp creases fore and aft when we went ashore, which I assume is front and back. The King said it was raffish. I'm not joking.'

'Where were the creases supposed to be?'

'On the sides? How would I know?'

∽

At Queanbeyan, the closest town to the capital site, we stopped again and the prince emerged from the train to attend an official reception with the councillors of the shire. He was wearing a suit of dark brown and a hat, the same brown shoes I'd seen the day before. I couldn't make out whether there were fore and aft creases in his trousers or not, but he'd had his way on the uniform.

Admiral Halsey was with him, and Mr Waters and the colonel. I hadn't been introduced to the admiral, but he was easily recognisable in his formal naval uniform, dress sword and cocked hat. He was probably only a little taller than the prince, although the hat gave him an advantage today.

Colonel Grigg was on the other side of the admiral. His face wore a bit of a smirk, I realised now, or perhaps a slightly bemused look, one eyebrow higher than the other, a small smile.

'It's a symbol, sir,' I heard the admiral say.

The prince looked at him coldly. 'You think I don't know that, Admiral? It's the fucking symbol I can't abide, man.'

'Yes, sir,' the admiral said. 'I think the doctor said to use the left hand again today. Give the right a bit more rest.'

Again, it looked as if an entire town had turned out to see the prince, along with the mayor and officials. His staff kept trying to get him to move to greet the officials, but I noticed the prince spent most of his time talking with the returned soldiers who had started in a loose parade outside the station. He bestowed the warmest of smiles on them, tilting his head to listen to their stories.

One poor chap made me think of my father. He didn't look like Daddy, who was taller and more solid of build, but there was something in his manner that was the same. His hands were at his sides and held slightly out from his body, not in fists but not relaxed either. He was wearing the Australian hat, turned up on one side, medals pinned to his chest. He was very thin and about the prince's height or a few inches taller. They leaned in to one another, as if they were in a private conversation and the crowds around them didn't exist. I watched the man for a long moment after the prince shook his hand and moved on. The prince had brought comfort in some way. The man's shoulders were more relaxed, his breathing more easy. The image stayed with me.

'What a shoddy bunch,' I heard Dickie say as they walked away from the men finally.

'You'd be shoddy too if you'd seen what they have,' hissed the prince, clearly annoyed at his younger cousin.

'I'm sorry, David. I was just trying to lighten the load.'

'Well, don't,' he said curtly.

༄

Following the reception, the prince returned to the train, emerging not long after in uniform, khaki breeches, long leather boots to the knees and a coat with an officer's hat, his chest lined with medals. Although the uniform fitted him very well, he looked more like a boy in his father's clothes than an officer. It reminded me of the pictures in the newspaper of the day he'd arrived at Farm Cove, when he'd worn the big hat like the admiral's and the dress sword of a naval officer. Unless you knew it was a uniform, you'd have said he was a child playing dress-ups.

Helen had lent me an outfit for the official function and I'd changed before leaving the train too. It was terribly kind of her to realise I'd have nothing to wear and not make a fuss. She probably knew I didn't have the money for fine clothes, but all she said was, 'You'll have been expecting to wear a uniform like poor David so you won't have brought anything fine.' It was a navy skirt and jacket and a cream silk blouse, and she said it suited my dark hair better than her blonde.

At the top of the hill, the prince was to deliver remarks to the government of Australia and people on behalf of his father the King. It was the speech that had caused all the trouble the day before, Helen explained. The admiral had told the prince that all he had to do was to lay a foundation stone, that there was no need for a speech if he didn't want to speak, but Helen had prepared remarks and the colonel had rewritten them and then the prince and Helen had rewritten them again and then the prince had decided he wouldn't speak, as the admiral had suggested.

'Who knows what will happen?' Helen said. 'Sure to be splendid, if only in the newspapers tomorrow.' She smiled and winked at me.

The prince soon arrived and emerged from the car. Again, he largely ignored the official party—government ministers for the new national government, and the New South Wales premier—and went instead to the small group of women all in black who'd come out to see him.

'H.R.H. always stops for them and offers his family's condolences,' Mr Waters said to me. 'It's the part Colonel Grigg doesn't really understand.'

Although the prince hadn't noticed me since introducing himself the day before, I felt I was now a member of the team of people who supported him, with Mr Waters and Helen including me in everything. I'd read so many of the letters to the prince and I saw now what those letter writers saw, hope after so many hopeless years in which everyone experienced loss. Now I'd seen for myself how decent he was towards those he met, especially the ex-servicemen and families.

I thought of my father. Daddy would be so proud of me now, writing as a prince and attending an important speech.

I reminded myself to note it all in my book. If you're going to be a writer, you write down everything, Daddy had drilled into me from an early age. I was already behind on the events of the day before. I didn't want to miss anything.

Running over an hour late now, the prince joined the official party on the top of the hill, where a tent had been set up for lunch. They'd constructed a wooden stand and the foundation stone was an enormous thing, held in place by chains the prince would release.

Several ministers of the federal government spoke about the remarkable progress that had been made in constructing the new capital. I had seen the cartoons in the newspaper about the capital site, for a first foundation stone was laid in 1913, but seven years had passed and nothing more had happened. The ministers spoke at length. The prince looked bored.

Finally, it was the prince's turn to speak. He stood at the dais and it somehow grew him. He took a good long moment to look around him, as if conjuring the capital in his own mind. He'd visited Canada the year before, he said, where Ottawa was already built. 'Canberra is to be built as a capital from the very first, and offers a splendid opportunity to Australian architects. I hope they will be proud of what they do here.'

'It's always like this,' Helen said to me. 'He knows he has to do a speech but he doesn't want to, then he's forced to make it up on the spot. You never know what will come out.' She was smiling. 'That's what Ned hates. He wants a seamless empire, and he's got never-know-what-will-happen-next David. I'm just glad I got something ready now because today, for once, he's following my script!'

The prince was standing in front of the gathered dignitaries, wearing that smile once again, full of youthful joy but tinged with sadness. Perhaps it was the weight of the responsibility on him, the throne that sat immutable as his destiny, but it was the sadness under the smile that made him beautiful.

People had moved to the surrounding hillside to get a view. There were hundreds now, a sea of hats and coats, to listen to the prince.

'I consider,' he said, 'that it is a very great privilege to be asked to lay the foundation stone.'

'Uh-oh,' Helen said. 'We're veering off-script again.'

He paused for a long moment. 'In fact, I understand that, at the present moment, Canberra consists chiefly of foundation stones.'

He paused, the crowd laughing and applauding.

The prince nodded and waved.

Just then, Colonel Grigg walked up behind us. 'Was that yours?' I heard him say to Helen.

'Nope,' she said. 'That's him, Ned, all him. So if you have a problem, I suggest you take it up with your future king.'

Colonel Grigg snorted. 'All him? All Halsey, more like.'

'Halsey doesn't do humour,' Helen said. 'He does what he's told.'

'By David?'

She shook her head. 'Anyway, I suspect Halsey thinks this is all nonsense. He'd prefer we sail around Australia with our guns and not actually stop anywhere.'

'The admiral is from a world that's gone,' the colonel said. 'The reality is, this country is at risk.'

Helen turned to regard him. 'From those koalas?'

'Yes,' Grigg said. 'Koalas and the Bolshies. We're here to fix it.'

Helen laughed. 'Then God help the empire,' she said. 'If it's you doing the fixing, I mean.'

'Do you know, if you didn't write so brilliantly, I wouldn't put up with you?' Colonel Grigg said.

'If you didn't put up with me, I'd be reporting directly to David, my dear,' Helen said.

'Is that right?'

'It most certainly is,' Helen said. 'And we'd probably all be just a little happier.'

Colonel Grigg smiled widely, but he looked just like a big circus bear trying to smile and it was anything but friendly.

The prince was finished now. The crowd roared approval. He took them all away, including the newspapermen, and no one but Colonel Grigg seemed to mind his little impromptu joke about foundation stones.

'That was fair enough,' Helen said. 'This is the *seventh* one that's been laid. Anyway,' she added, 'they love him.'

'Yes, but at home, they won't love this. They won't love this in any way,' Colonel Grigg said. 'I wish I could just make him do the right thing.'

'Maybe a puppet would help,' Helen said.

He laughed. 'That, my dear girl, is an excellent suggestion.'

After the ceremony was completed, they showed the prince the sites for various buildings, the parliament, the war memorial. I didn't accompany them. I excused myself to Mr Waters and returned to the train to keep drafting the replies to the letters. Helen told me later it was all just bushland so it was hard to get a sense of how the place might look. But the crowd seemed to have swelled during the day so that, when they were leaving, in every direction there were just hats like mushrooms that grew from the ground wherever the prince had walked.

Helen and I ate dinner together in the staff dining car—roast beef with mash and peas—and then the train left to return to Sydney. I didn't see the prince again. I don't know where we pulled up for the night. I worked my way through over two hundred letters, and I could probably still tell you exactly what I did with each one, by subject if not by name.

Helen told me we could do whatever we wanted, within reason, and so I made a note, clipped to each draft reply, for that first boy to receive a train ticket to see the speech, another family to have a set of commemorative cups (for they'd missed out), still others to have a personalised letter about their personal experience of loss. I suppose, looking back, each time I helped one of these families broken by the war, I helped my own family broken by the war, or thought I did.

I hardly noticed the return journey on the train. According to Helen, we made a stop at Bungendore so that the prince could meet the people he'd missed in the morning. We then stopped at two other small towns where people had driven for miles to catch sight of him. He spent more time in these places than he had at the capital site.

'Did you not notice the fires?' Helen asked when she came in with tea. In many places along the route there were enormous bonfires lit in his honour.

'I've been trying to get these finished,' I said. I was feeling the weight of responsibility, for I only had a few hours left. If I could at least catch up, they might be able to manage from here.

I drafted replies and suggested action on all the most difficult letters. Most of the remaining ones really only needed some variation of the agreed form letter. I also had a list of instructions for the staff at Government House; this one to be refunded a train fare to Sydney because he'd come to see the prince but the visit was cancelled when the schedule changed, that one to be included in the meeting with charities organised for later in the week in Sydney as they'd missed out on shaking the prince's hand when he visited Jervis Bay and they had run a canteen during the fighting in France.

Mr Waters could assign a typist at Government House to the form letters and focus on making sure that the things the prince had said would happen actually transpired. I hadn't finished the job, I knew, but I would leave them in much better shape than where they started.

The next morning I ate a quick breakfast in the staff dining car—porridge with brown sugar and cream—and returned to my desk to keep going with the letters. I'd noticed Ruby Rivers going back and forth from the prince's private dining room with trays. I was glad I was doing this other job; a more important job, I knew.

Helen came in from her office. 'Did you sleep well?' she asked.

'Like a log,' I said. 'The rocking.' We'd gone to bed while the train was still moving. It didn't stop until the prince was ready to retire.

'Yes, it works for people our size.'

Without waiting for my response, she said, 'There's something I really should have mentioned yesterday, and it's rather delicate. Actually, it woke me in the middle of the night with terror and I nearly woke you then.'

She had a letter in her hand that she'd taken from the pile. 'You see these letters with the spider seal?'

I nodded. I'd noticed the seal the day before but hadn't got to the letter yet. She handed it to me.

'Thank God,' she said. 'We don't open those. He opens them himself. I shouldn't have left that one there.'

'Who are they from?' I said, looking at the pretty handwriting.

She put a finger to her lips, widened her eyes, plucked the letter from my hands.

Then she said, 'H.R.H. writes back and uses the same seal. He and his . . . friend each have one. We post them and receive them. We don't even record them. They don't exist.' She smiled.

'And his letters go back with the diplomatic pouch. That's the one that goes straight to London, using every ship and train at His Majesty's disposal to be quick about it.'

I looked at the back of the envelope. 'They must be very important,' I said. 'So, can you tell me who F.D.W. is?' These were the initials on the back, with an address in London.

She put her finger to her lips again. 'Sometimes there are a lot of letters,' she said. 'But if there are none, make yourself scarce.' She grinned.

I sniffed the envelope. It was perfumed.

'Exactly,' Helen said. 'I didn't say mistress.'

Just then the prince came in from his private study. 'Here are the busy bees,' he said. 'What are you girls doing?' He was wearing a cream cardigan over a light blue shirt and the brown slacks today, with slippers on his feet.

'We're just talking about the mail, sir,' Helen said, taking the envelope with the spider seal from me and tucking it under the rest so he wouldn't see it. 'We can't believe the number of letters. You have quite a following, Maddie tells me.'

'Is that right?' he said to me. 'Fools. They have no idea who they're writing to.' He made a noise, not quite a laugh.

I blushed, found myself tongue-tied once more. I longed for Helen's confidence.

'Well?' he said, still looking at me. 'You think they know their prince?' He looked more calm this morning, I thought. Helen had said the night before that the stunts stressed him and then he had to take a few days to get ready for the next one. But the trouble was there were no gaps in the schedule in which he might actually do that.

'I do,' I managed to say. He had such beauty, those light blue eyes, that blond hair and a glow to his skin as if he were lit from within, the sadness of that countenance at rest.

Mr Waters came in behind him then and rescued me. 'It's Maddie who writes all the replies, so she should know, sir.'

'How very splendid,' he said. 'You know, I noticed last night that the letters were more modern than they used to be. Rupert is such a stick-in-the-mud when it comes to how things are done. I like very much that we are friendly as far as possible. Is that you?'

I nodded, still dumb.

Helen laughed. 'Her father is the poet,' she said. 'Thomas Bright. I know his work. It's uplifting in a time of sorrow, although you might not know she's related to him to talk to her in person right now.' She elbowed me subtly. 'Maddie seems to have lost contact with her normally vivacious self.'

'Well, it's wonderful to have the daughter of the poet among us,' the prince said. He smiled so warmly I felt the honour of it. I felt he must be used to people being tongue-tied in the royal presence and he was making it as easy as he could for me.

'Sir, thank you,' I said. 'I am so pleased to serve.'

'So am I,' he said. 'So am I.'

He stood very erect, I noticed, and his hands kept going to the front of his trousers as if to smooth the creases, or perhaps correct them to keep his father happy.

His gaze remained on me, his expression turning quizzical. 'I'm sorry to be staring, but do I know you?' he asked.

'I don't think so, no, sir,' I said. 'I came to see you with my family when you arrived, but I doubt you saw me as we were several miles away. I may have spotted your hand waving from a carriage.'

He laughed then. 'I knew I knew you. You were one of the twenty thousand. I have a memory for faces.'

I must have looked shocked.

'A little joke,' he said, grinning now. He regarded me a moment longer and then turned behind him to Mr Waters.

'Have you seen the telegram? It seems I was right about His Majesty on this occasion.' I could hear from his voice that he was not smiling now. 'He's got Bertie going to see my friends, man. I assume it wasn't your doing?'

'Of course not, sir,' Rupert said quietly. 'On the other hand, he agreed we might postpone India, and that's been positive.' Mr Waters attempted a smile but it quickly faded.

'Quite,' the prince said, nodding tightly. 'I understand Mr George is still pushing. Perhaps you might speak with Ned.' He turned back to me. 'Maddie, isn't it?'

I nodded again.

'Well, Maddie, it's wonderful to know I have such a talented correspondent with me. It will come to me, how I know you. I'm sure it will.

'And now, Helen, perhaps you and I could take some time to work on my remarks for tomorrow.'

'Certainly,' she said.

He opened the door to his study and she walked through. He followed and closed the door behind them.

I looked at Mr Waters, his eyes fixed on the closed door. He looked back at me. 'Nothing,' he said, although I hadn't asked a question.

From *Autumn Leaves* by M.A. Bright:

France, 1918

It was a pantomime. She had played an angel, a crow that turns into an angel, from black to white, from a long yellow beak to long golden hair.

The pantomime was a comedy but that part made him sad, as if she were better as a crow. He didn't know why.

It had snowed earlier in the day, and his mind would not rest, not even in the time he spent looking out the window at the large flakes which fell softly.

He had come to one of those moments in which your life is arrested suddenly, stopped on what had always appeared to be its straight and true road. You might reflect, or not. You might find yourself wanting. You might glimpse another road, a road you might have taken, might still take.

You might act.

It was a month since he'd arrived here. The surgeons were saying he needed a further month, perhaps two, to recuperate. He was glad of it.

But now the prince had found him. It had taken a few weeks but he'd had a wire that morning, reminding him he'd have to go back to all that, the life he'd been chosen for.

He was getting stronger every day.

It wasn't fear he felt. It was resignation. The life he'd been chosen for.

୬

From the wings, she watched him watching the pantomime. He'd said three times now that he wanted to marry her. She could no longer tell herself he was deluded. He loved her truly, it seemed, and she found herself loving him back.

୬

'I think I will have to go away,' he said.

'Batman?'

'Yes.'

'What does Miss Ivens say?'

'She says my arm is slow to heal.'

'Can you feel your fingers?'

He shook his head.

'Then I'd suggest you listen to Miss Ivens.'

She leaned in and kissed him then. Her body flushed with desire and, with it, a terrible sadness.

She withdrew from the kiss. 'I could tell you things,' she said. She thought she might cry.

'I could tell you things,' he said.

'Not like mine.'

'Maybe not,' he said. 'But I'm weaker than you.'

'I don't think so.'

'I wouldn't have saved your arm.'

'Well, luckily, it wasn't my arm that needed saving.'

'What needs saving?'

She didn't answer, put a hand to her heart.

'You're strong,' he said. 'And I can help with anything else. I don't care about anything else.'

'You might,' she said.

'But I don't.' He looked at her.

'Is truth better or a dream?' she said.

'Truth,' he said.

'There's no one in my room,' she said. 'Quickly.'

A dream. A dream is always better.

FIFTEEN

Sydney, 1920

THE TRAIN ARRIVED BACK AT CENTRAL STATION AT teatime. It seemed like an age since I'd seen my family, and yet it had been no time at all.

Helen had let me keep the skirt and jacket I'd borrowed. 'Truly, I have two of each,' she'd said the evening before, after the official function was over. I was wearing them again today, with my own blouse. 'And you just look a picture, Maddie, a proper correspondence secretary,' she said when she gave them to me.

I hadn't managed to clear the backlog of letters altogether, but I knew it would be easier for Mr Waters to do now that a system was in place. He would need a typist, I'd told him when he came into the office during the morning. He didn't seem terribly interested. There had been more stops on the way back to Sydney than on the way to Canberra and he had been kept busy with those.

No one had come back to the office to say goodbye and I wasn't quite sure what I was supposed to do. Not that I expected a farewell, but I'd have liked to see Mr Waters and Helen. I didn't know how I was to be paid either. I didn't want to ask but I would have to. We needed the money. And I didn't know if I was supposed to turn up the next day to serve at Government House while the prince was staying there. I didn't much fancy the idea of Mrs Danby as my supervisor.

I waited fifteen minutes more and then left a note on the desk for Mr Waters. I assumed they'd forgotten about me so I collected my little bag and went down to the platform. I decided I would catch the ferry at Circular Quay and go back to Bea's. I would come back to Government House tomorrow to see about wages.

I was trying to work out which direction I should go when I heard a voice behind me. 'Maddie!' I looked out and saw my brother Bert. Behind him and beyond a makeshift barrier were the other boys, John and the twins, George and Henry. Every time I saw them all together like this, I felt the stab of who was missing: our brother Edward.

Mummy was there, and Daddy too, I saw, with the younger boys. Bert had jumped the barrier to come to me. He hugged me tightly, although I'd only been away for two nights.

'Daddy arrived this morning,' Bert said. 'We saw the prince was coming back, so I said we should wait for you.' He was grinning, and his narrow face, a carbon copy of his father's, reminded me of Daddy in better days.

Bert was sixteen, a year younger than me, but a head-and-a-half taller now, and I'd swear he'd added an inch in those two days. We'd grown up in each other's pockets, Edward those couple of years older. Bert left school when I did and got a delivery job with the iceworks at Ithaca. It was heavy work, lugging blocks of ice wrapped in canvas into people's back kitchen iceboxes. Nicer in summer was all he said about it.

I felt a stab of something then: fellow feeling—these were my kin—shot through with something else, embarrassment, which took a moment to register. I was embarrassed. I looked past Bert to the rest, huddled in their odd little group. I felt as if I'd grown up and away from them in these two days, and here they were, mixing in with my new life. How quickly we change our allegiance! It was me on the official side of the barrier. They were on the other. In truth, I wanted to be in neither place right then, but if I'd had to choose, I'd have stayed on the train side with the prince.

I gave a little wave and smiled and went over to where they stood. I hugged Daddy across the barrier that had been set up to stop gawkers from coming onto the platform. When one of the policemen started making his way towards us, Bert jumped back over to their side.

'You made it,' I said to Daddy.

He'd told us before we left Brisbane for Sydney that he probably wouldn't come. He said he was finishing a poem. I don't know if Mummy believed him. I knew better, having been into his study.

'Your mother might have wired me you'd been kidnapped by the monarch,' he said. 'I gleaned what I could from Bert here and thought I'd better see the situation for myself.'

He was trying hard for his old humour. It was awful when he was like this, as we saw a glimpse of the father we'd once had, the wicked grin, the sparkle in his eyes, but we knew now he could not stay.

'Something like that,' I said. 'The heir.'

'It's possible that's worse,' he said, looking at me carefully, as if I might be a spy now. 'It's all so grand,' he said. 'And you pretty grand yourself.'

Helen's skirt, I assumed, made me more grand, or perhaps because I'd been among such important people I'd become a little important too.

I hugged each of the boys, Bert for the second time. I felt better then; they were my family and I loved them. I felt more normal again, ready to go home with them.

'Oh, how wonderful this all is,' Mummy said. 'The prince himself!' She smiled and I saw how proud she was. 'But where's your uniform? What are you wearing that skirt for?'

Before I could answer, I noticed Mummy was looking behind me, smiling still. I turned around and there was Helen.

I felt the embarrassment again now, more acutely. I turned back to my mother, whose dress, brought across from England in 1900, had originally been ankle-length. She'd hemmed it mid-calf but the skirt flared too much for that. It was overmodest and unsuited to both the climate and the current fashion, as I now knew. Her little boots were all wrong too. They were well cared for but old.

My mother was standing there, looking at us expectantly, Daddy next to her dressed in his old tweed coat, a gift from a family at the school and not quite long enough in the arms, his corduroy pants from St Vincent's, also not quite long enough, his worried expression, narrow face so vulnerable. They looked like a travelling theatre troupe rather than a modern family.

Daddy looked afraid, I realised then. His arm was shaking too, I noticed, never a good sign.

Helen looked at me.

'I'm so sorry. Helen Burns,' I said finally, 'this is my family.'

'I'm Emily,' my mother said in her best English, almost a different accent from the one she'd acquired from living so long in Australia. 'My husband, Thomas. So very pleased to make your acquaintance.' My mother's manners, like her clothes, were from another time. She hadn't needed them for twenty years. We were never in this kind of company, only the parents of the children at the school, who were all struggling to make a life in a new country, like we were.

Helen pulled the barrier away immediately, waving Mummy and the rest to come on to the platform, nodding at the police officer to let him know they were with her.

'Mrs Bright,' Helen said, 'the pleasure is all mine. Maddie here has been invaluable to us on the visit.'

Mummy turned to me.

'And I didn't pour tea on him once,' I said.

Helen laughed. 'Well, that's not quite true, is it, Maddie?'

Mummy looked horrified for a moment.

'We're just joking,' I said to my mother. 'I'm actually doing a different job.'

Helen turned to Daddy who had remained where he was. 'Mr Bright—may I call you Thomas?' She didn't wait for his answer. Perhaps she could see he wouldn't answer. 'I am Helen Burns. You wrote for *Vanity Fair*, where I was on the staff. If I may be bold, your poetry changed lives. You showed me what writing can do. We were all in awe of you, even the senior editors.' Helen grinned like a girl, like she had the first time I'd met her. She looked so much younger and less sophisticated.

I saw just how much she admired my father. But Daddy seemed hardly to register her presence. 'Well, good, then,' he said gruffly. 'Maddie, time to go home. Bea's waiting.'

I'm sure Daddy didn't mean to be rude. I could see he was becoming agitated. More people had come onto the platform now that the train had arrived. The barriers were not holding anyone back.

Daddy looked around nervously. I saw Mummy grab his hand and hold it tightly. 'Of course it is,' Mummy said, looking at Helen and smiling. 'Bert and John, take your father outside, would you? We'll meet you on the corner where we waited this morning. All right, love?' she said to Daddy.

'I want to see inside the train,' John said.

Helen smiled at him. 'I bet you're John,' she said. I couldn't believe she'd be able to tell the boys apart from the little I'd told her, although I had said John was the scallywag and he did look the part, his shirt untucked, a determined grin on his face, grease under his fingernails. On the other hand, all four boys met any reasonable definition of scallywag. 'I think we'll be able to get you on the train once H.R.H. is off.'

Mr Waters came up to us then, and so getting Daddy outside was going to be impossible for a little while longer. Mummy looked worried and this worried me. She knew best what Daddy could manage.

Around us porters were unloading the train. There wasn't as much of a crowd as the day we'd left because, Helen had told me, they hadn't announced the prince's return in the newspaper, but there were enough people to worry Daddy. Crowds bothered him now, and noise, and the station was filled with both.

I noticed his hand, the one Mummy wasn't holding, had started to open and close into a fist slowly.

Mr Waters nodded at me and then looked at Daddy. 'You must be Maddie's father. I'm Rupert Waters, H.R.H.'s man. Mr Bright, I know you served, and Prince Edward would have liked to be here to thank you in person. I know he would have. I also want to tell you that your daughter has been of great service . . .' He trailed off, looking at Daddy more carefully.

Daddy, for his part, had started jiggling his leg now in a way he had. I knew he wouldn't last much longer. Soon, he would begin to sweat, despite the winter day. And then he might begin to make noises, moan or cry out, and we would have to do something.

He took the hand Mr Waters offered. I knew his own would be clammy. Mr Waters noticed, God bless him. He looked at me and back at Daddy and nodded.

He didn't even acknowledge Mummy or the boys. He smiled warmly, his eyes still on Daddy. 'Mr Bright, can I suggest we step into the private lounge which is just to our right? Very quiet in there. Pop under the ropes. That's right. You too, Mrs Bright, children. I think you'll find it will suit us better.' He looked at Daddy again, narrowing his eyes. 'Actually, Helen, perhaps you could follow with Mrs Bright and the family in a few minutes. I'm just going to take Mr Bright inside for a moment.'

He took Daddy's arm and all but lifted him off the ground, as if he knew what state my father was in.

'So, John?' Helen said after they'd gone. 'I do think you need to meet the train driver.'

She looked over at the policeman in charge. He nodded. The prince had already been taken off the train, it seemed. Helen had said they sometimes took him on the track side in order to avoid the crowds.

'Yes, I do,' John said to Helen.

Mummy turned to Helen to say something, and then I heard her sharp intake of breath, for there was Prince Edward himself in front of her, with his cousin Dickie behind him.

'Helen,' he called softly, so as not to arouse interest. 'I seem to have found my way back to the train. They brought steps onto the other side and I was supposed to sneak off.' He giggled. 'We got lost. Guilty as charged, but you can be sure I'll blame the flag lieutenant if the admiral gets wind of it.'

He pulled a face then, his mouth downwards, his eyes wide, like a clown.

Dickie laughed. 'I am always to blame, David. Always.'

'Your Royal Highness,' I heard my mother say in a shaky voice. Even the boys were standing up straight, staring. The twins were smaller than him, but Bert was taller and John was the same height as him. They were all in awe now, seeing Mummy begin to curtsy.

He shook his head. 'Please don't,' he said. Mummy obeyed him and stood back up awkwardly.

He looked around the platform and pushed his hat down over his eyes, pulled up his coat collar. 'Just a boy.' He grinned, then looked at Mummy more intently. 'But I know you, don't I?' he said.

'Yes, sir,' she said. 'You came to Fox Hall with Bertie. Prince Albert, I mean. I can't believe you remember.'

'Of course I do. You had the mean horse.'

'Yes,' she said. It was extraordinary to see the transformation. She was a lady again, on her father's estate. I felt pride and a stab of deep sadness. I saw something of the girl she'd been before she came to Australia, something of what she'd lost.

'Spirited was how I thought of him,' she said. 'Bertie fell but you told me not to worry at all because, even though he was a small boy, he was made entirely of rubber.' She smiled and it was as if she were a different person.

'I remember,' he said, holding out a hand to take hers. 'Emily is your name.' He watched her as he kissed her hand. 'Bertie and I both had a little crush on you. Now, tell me what on earth you are doing here.'

'Maddie here, my daughter, has been in service on your train,' she said with considerable pride.

'The writer?' he said, looking at me and back at Mummy. I was chuffed he'd remembered but Mummy just looked bewildered.

'Of course she is,' he said. 'I knew her face, Emily. I did. When I first met her, I said to Rupert, I know that face. Your Maddie, according to my man, has single-handedly transformed our life these last two days.' My mother looked even more confused, clearly wondering how a serving girl might transform anything. 'So you are here in Australia, Emily.'

'Yes, sir,' she said. 'We came here before our own Edward was born.'

'And your husband is the poet?'

'Yes,' she said.

'And all these lads?'

She nodded. 'Yes.' She looked more ashamed than proud, smoothed her skirt with her hands, as if she might hide one or two of them under there given a chance.

'And which one is named for me?' he said cheerily.

'He's gone, sir,' she said. 'Missing, presumed dead since 1918.'

'Oh,' the prince said. 'How thoughtless of me. I knew that. Of course I did.' He looked pained. 'Emily, I am so sorry.

On behalf of my father, I am sorry, and I am personally sorry.' He looked suddenly as if he might cry.

'Thank you, sir,' Mummy said, and I saw there were tears in her eyes too. She always said 'missing, presumed dead' when she mentioned Edward, and I wondered now if she still held out some hope, which could only be a vain hope by 1920, but who would blame her?

The prince looked away then along the platform, where people were starting to notice the group of us. 'Well, I must away to Government House,' he said, 'or you'll soon be in much worse shape, Emily. They will mob us. They always do. It is delightful to see you again, Mrs . . .'

'I'm still Emily, sir.'

He nodded. 'Then I'm surely still David.' He took her hand and kissed it again lightly. 'Emily. Helen, make sure Emily and Mr . . . Emily . . . are on the list for the dancing tonight.'

'I think, sir, the plan is there won't be dancing after tonight's dinner,' Helen said.

He smiled. 'Of course there will.' He leaned in further, bringing both my mother and Helen into a huddle with him. They stood cheek to cheek. 'Dickie, here, is a magician. He has managed to convince the admiral to allow the ship's band to come to shore again, so it's going to be quite the party.' His eyes were bright. Dickie was behind him, terribly proud to have made his cousin so happy. 'Rupert couldn't manage it, too afraid of Grigg and the Bolshie unions, but the admiral said, "Why not!"

'Maddie must come too, Dickie, don't you think?' He grinned, his eyes on his young cousin. 'Make sure you do,' he said, smiling at me.

I think I blushed.

'Emily,' he said. 'So lovely to see you again after all these years.' He pointed to his chest and gave her a final look of sadness.

'Sir.' She started to curtsy.

He shook his head and put up a hand. 'I'm just that scallywag boy with the terrified brother.' He took her hand again, shook it this time, and gave her one more long look before he went off with his cousin.

'Well, I never expected this,' Mummy said when he was gone, wiping her eyes now.

Nor did I, I wanted to say. But I was worried about Daddy now. Mr Waters had gone off with him and I hoped he was all right.

∾

I found them in the private lounge which was set up for the prince's visit. They were drinking from crystal glasses we had on the train that Ruby told me had come with the prince all the way from England.

Some of the colour had returned to Daddy's face. 'Ah, Maddie,' Mr Waters said. 'We've had a good chat.'

'About the war?' I knew Daddy didn't like to talk about anything to do with his time in France.

'Goodness, no,' Mr Waters said. 'About you, as a matter of fact. I've promised your father we'll look after you.'

'You have already, Mr Waters, and it's been a grand—'

'It really has,' Mr Waters said, cutting me off.

Daddy hadn't spoken. He was looking at Mr Waters almost pleadingly.

'Tom,' Mr Waters said as he stood and put down his glass, his drink unfinished. 'I will say again, it has been a great honour to meet you. Our Helen says your poetry is remarkable, and I know from experience your daughter has been a great help to us. And now I know you myself.' He smiled and picked up his hat and coat from the chair. 'It gets easier with time, man,' he said softly.

They shook hands, Daddy nodding acknowledgement.

After Mr Waters left I asked Daddy, 'Are you all right?'

'I think so,' he said. 'The whisky came in handy. He's a decent fellow.'

'Yes, he is,' I said. 'He loves semicolons.'

'Ha! If only I'd known that. There's always something wrong with the King's men. I hear you're writing for them now though.' He smiled weakly. 'Imagine your mother!'

'Yes,' I said. 'She saw the actual prince outside and nearly fainted.'

'Did she now?' he said. 'That will have made her happy.' He looked awfully sad then.

'It did.' I nearly mentioned my brother Edward but held my tongue. 'Writing for the prince was enormously fun, Daddy. I did everything you taught me.'

'I didn't have to teach you anything, Maddie.' He was so proud of me. 'It was all already there.'

Mummy and the boys soon came to join us, and Helen asked if I could come back to Government House for the afternoon to make sure all the instructions we'd given in relation to correspondence would be carried out by the governor's men.

I told her I didn't feel I had the authority to instruct the governor's staff. She said anyone who could pour tea with the accuracy I did ought to be able to instruct anybody to do anything.

'Just come and see me if you have a problem,' she said. 'But I'm fairly confident they'll be fawning all over you.'

I told Mummy I'd meet them back at Bea's and explain all. I noticed Daddy had already withdrawn again, his poor frightened eyes staring into the middle distance.

SIXTEEN

I WALKED UP THE HILL FROM THE STATION TO GOVERNMENT House. I saw Mrs Danby at the kitchen window, scrubbing something in the sink with vigour. I waved and smiled but a response was beyond her.

I went in through the same door I'd come through for my interview just a few days before. I stopped a moment now. Who would think that I, Maddie Bright, would find myself writing letters for a prince? I would have been amazed to serve in the dining room as planned, let alone act as his written voice. And my letters were now on their way to the prince's men in Australia to be acted on—actions I, for the most part, had suggested.

The footman who'd shown me where to go for the interview was in the hall. 'Mr Waters is looking for you, miss,' he said. 'I'll take you.'

He led me to the door of the room where I'd been interviewed. It had been set up as the staff office for the duration of the prince's Australian visit.

I thought of the interview, Mrs Danby and her stony face, Mr Waters and his stifled laughter. Wasn't I lucky it had been him? Someone else might not have taken the chance.

'Come,' I heard Mr Waters call from within when the footman knocked. He opened the door for me.

I went in and there was the prince sitting back in a chair with his feet on a desk, his boots over the papers. Mr Waters was standing at the French windows with his hands in his trouser pockets. He looked handsome in the winter light through the window.

The prince's private secretary, Sir Godfrey Thomas, was sitting on the other side of the desk. Helen had pointed him out to me at the national capital site. He turned to look at me but didn't stand up.

'I'm sorry, sir,' I said to the prince. 'I didn't realise you were here.'

'No, no, come in, Maddie,' Mr Waters said, gesturing with his hand. 'We need to . . .' He looked at the prince and then out the window.

On the desk was the day's mail, another thick wad of letters. They were still coming from Victoria, and now the letters from New South Wales had joined them. Poor Mr Waters, I thought.

'We want you to stay,' the prince said. 'And your mummy is my old friend! I can't tell you how pleased I am, Maddie. You are the image of her as a girl. I was just a little boy, and she was so very beautiful. I thought she would be the best big sister for a little prince.'

'Stay, sir?' I was still on his first sentence.

'Rupert here needs you but he doesn't quite know how to tell you. He thinks you might have other plans and he's not sure your old dad will want to spare you. But I think your mother will be pleased. She was very kind to me.

'So I'm telling you. I'm your prince. You must listen to me. The empire needs you, Maddie Bright! Doesn't it, Godfrey? Ned agrees with me, by the way.'

'Well, yes, sir, he does,' Sir Godfrey said. 'But Ned agrees with anything that might advantage his cause, and I think Rupert and I could hazard a guess as to why he agrees on this particular matter.' He had a slight smile as he said it. It might have been mean.

'Why?' Mr Waters asked. He had turned to look at Sir Godfrey.

'I think the colonel wants Helen to himself, doesn't he? He doesn't want her working with us, Rupert.' He smiled again and there was no meanness in it.

'Doesn't he?' Mr Waters said.

Sir Godfrey just looked at him and shrugged. 'I notice things. I'm sure you do too.'

'Really?' the prince said. 'Ned? Well, I never. Isn't he a bit—' He didn't finish the question.

Sir Godfrey looked across at me. 'Actually, Maddie, we were just discussing the idea of you continuing with us, and it certainly has merit.' He glanced over at Prince Edward. 'Do come in. Sit down.' Sir Godfrey stood and indicated for me to sit in the chair he'd vacated. I remained standing.

I had not officially met Sir Godfrey, just seen him in the distance. Up close, his face was sweeter, I thought, with big dark eyes and an aquiline nose balanced by a generous mouth. He was the same age as Mr Waters or a few years older, I decided. We hadn't been introduced and now I imagined we were to assume we knew one another.

'For God's sake, Godfrey,' the prince said. 'Rupert's say-so is my say-so.'

Sir Godfrey was Mr Waters's boss, so I didn't really understand what the prince might mean, and Mr Waters hadn't said anything since Helen was mentioned. He was looking back out to the garden.

'Maddie.' Sir Godfrey smiled. 'I understand you have been a great help to Rupert here, and to H.R.H.'

'A great help,' the prince echoed.

Mr Waters remained silent.

'And we value your help,' Sir Godfrey said. 'But I also know you came to us in odd circumstances.'

'Sir?' I said.

'You were let go from your last position.'

'Yes, sir, I was.'

'There was tea.'

'Yes, sir.'

'On a customer.'

'Yes, sir.' I looked at him. 'But it wasn't hot, sir.'

The prince burst out laughing then. 'Hear that, Godfrey? It wasn't hot. Enough said.'

'If you don't mind, sir, I would just like to clarify what happened,' Sir Godfrey said. 'Do you understand, Maddie?'

'After all,' the prince added, before I could respond, 'we can't have the heir to the throne at risk of being tea-ed.' He got up suddenly and went over to stand with Mr Waters. 'Oh, look,' he said, 'there's Helen. That's what you've been doing, Waters, ogling the staff. You can't have her. She's Ned's, apparently. Come on. You'll get Maddie. We just have to convince Godfrey.'

I had not replied to Sir Godfrey. I had stood there, mute, while he watched me. Only Mr Waters seemed uninterested in my response. He continued to look out towards the garden.

It was the prince who spoke, finally. He was still standing next to Mr Waters by the window. The light was on both their faces. 'Forget it, Godfrey. We don't need to hear the story. Maddie, the empire is calling. What do you say?'

I was confused. 'I still don't understand,' I said. 'Why does the empire need me?'

'I'm joking, Maddie,' he said. 'The empire doesn't need you. Rupert does. I'm sorry. My joke appears to have fallen flat twice, Rupert.'

The prince looked at me again. 'Rupert is going batty with all this mail. So we'd like you to stay on for the rest of the tour. We've had a marvellous few days, largely because Rupert has been able to focus on his job instead of these jolly letters. He's kept the admiral happy. Godfrey here is my friend again. Even Grigg is leaving me be, and we look like being able to run our own affairs.'

He stood and smiled. 'That's good then.' He turned to Mr Waters. 'See? It wasn't that difficult.'

'Very well,' Sir Godfrey said. 'There is one more thing, sir, while we have Rupert with us . . .'

The prince was walking towards the door. He looked back, inquisitive.

'We . . . Rupert and I . . . I'm just having trouble remembering the name, Rupert.'

'You mean Ruby?' Mr Waters said.

'Yes, just so. Sir, Ruby has had to leave us here in Sydney. She won't be serving in the dining suite for the remainder of our visit. We'll be getting someone else from Admiralty House, I believe.'

'Ruby Rex?' the prince said. 'Oh, she was good fun. She could dance, Godfrey. Rupert, do you agree with this?'

'Godfrey said she resigned,' Mr Waters said. 'I thought she was happy, David, but apparently not.'

'I did have a word with her, as a matter of fact,' Sir Godfrey said. 'Mrs Danby has promised we'll have someone who's more suitable for the role.'

'Ruby left me without saying goodbye?' the prince said. 'Hmph.'

The prince walked past me towards the door. He smelled fresh and new, like summer-cut grass. 'Although I am the Prince of Wales, Maddie, at times my aides think I am not competent to make decisions. But you are one decision I feel entirely certain about. And Rupert is with me.'

He and Sir Godfrey left then, and Mr Waters and I were alone. He sighed, then walked over to his desk and sat down. He gestured for me to take the chair on the other side, which I did.

'We leave at the end of this week for the west of Australia, and I want you to come with us and take over as H.R.H.'s official correspondence secretary. Your recompense will befit the position; it's a senior role. Which reminds me, I must go to the clerk before you leave and see you're paid for the days you've already worked.'

I was shocked and thrilled at once. I had been happy to help out Mr Waters and Helen as well as those who wrote to the prince. And the pay would be such a help to Mummy.

'Do you not want to?' he said.

'Of course I want to!' I almost shouted. 'It's just a surprise,' I added more softly.

He was smiling at me now. 'I didn't want to say anything until we were back here,' he said. 'I took the opportunity to speak with your father. You're so young, Maddie, and I knew he'd want to be sure that we'd look after you. I assured him we would, of course. I know your father has already made many sacrifices, and I didn't want to add to his burden.'

'Mr Waters, my father's not himself at the moment.'

'I assumed so,' he said. 'What happened to the men over there, Maddie... It was pretty rugged. We—the prince, actually—took every opportunity to visit the front.'

'Is that where you were wounded?'

'Yes,' he said. 'How did you know that?'

'Helen mentioned it.'

'Did she? Yes, awfully bad luck. A shell blast. I was waiting for H.R.H.' He rubbed his arm gently. 'I think they hoped he was in the car but they got me instead. I thought Helen might have forgotten.'

'No,' I said, looking back at him. 'No, she hasn't, Mr Waters. She hasn't at all.'

Helen was sometimes hardhearted towards Mr Waters, and I didn't know why, but she'd said they'd fallen in love, and I believed she might love him still. I had also seen the way he watched her whenever she was in the room, the way his eyes sometimes couldn't meet hers.

His expression cleared then. 'Bit of a target, the Royal Standard. An obvious mistake on our part. We took to getting around in ordinary cars from then on.'

'Mr Waters, did... did something happen between you and Helen in France?'

'I beg pardon,' he said, looking irritated with me. 'Why would you ask that? What did she say?'

'Nothing. It's just... you are both so aware of one another.'

'I'm sure I have no idea what you're talking about, Maddie. Helen is here on the tour to help with the newspapermen, and she is on the staff of Colonel Grigg. There is inevitable friction between the prince's political role and his own feelings; between, I suppose, his public and private selves. Sir Godfrey and I work for the private prince, Colonel Grigg and Helen for the public prince.'

'Of course. I'm sorry. It's just that Helen talks about you a lot. And you notice Helen whenever she's around you.'

'Really?' he said. 'I'm not sure I notice Helen at all. I have too much to do to think about anyone in particular. And I'm quite sure she doesn't spend any time thinking about me.'

'Oh, no, Mr Waters. She does. I can tell. I have a finely tuned sense of these things. I'm going to be a writer.'

He smiled across at me. 'No, Maddie. You *are* a writer.'

I felt a flush of pride. 'Thank you, Mr Waters. You know, if you did have feelings for Helen, I am very confident those feelings are returned.' I was sure I was right about this, with all the worldliness of a seventeen-year-old whose knowledge of love was gleaned entirely from romance novels.

'Maddie, if I did have feelings, I can tell you for absolute certain that they are not returned. And that is all we'll say on the matter.'

'Yes, sir.'

Oh, I thought then. Could it be that Mr Waters is sure Helen doesn't love him, and Helen is sure Mr Waters doesn't love her, and they love each other? Oh, my goodness. It really was a plot for a romance, but in real life!

'Mr Waters, are there other men like Daddy?' I said then, wanting more than anything to interrogate him further but knowing he had forbidden discussion. For now, I thought.

He nodded. 'Many others.'

'So if I do this, when will I be home?'

I'm sure he knew what I was thinking, that I didn't want to leave Daddy for too long.

He nodded. 'Of course. You need to plan. We go from here to Western Australia by ship, and then we come back across the continent by train to Adelaide. From there, we meet the *Renown* to go to Tasmania, and then Sydney and from there by train to Brisbane. Brisbane's where you're from, is it not? We could leave you there and go on because after Brisbane, we'll return to Sydney and then we sail for home. It's only a month. It would be an enormous help. So, what do you say?'

'I say yes, Mr Waters.'

He smiled with his whole face. 'I'm pleased, Maddie. The rest of the week we'll spend here at the house working while the prince finishes the Sydney engagements, and then we sail. There are spare staff rooms here where you can stay. And before I forget, I'll go to the clerk now to fix you up for these two days you've already spent with us.'

'Thank you, Mr Waters,' I said. 'You've been so kind.' I stood to leave.

'No, Maddie. You've been so clever. That's what's happened here. You have saved me, and His Royal Highness. Oh, and Maddie?'

'Yes, sir?'

'Not a word about that other business, all right?'

I knew exactly what he was talking about. 'Of course, sir,' I replied.

Hah! After he excused me, I ran outside to find Helen in the garden out the back of Government House, intending to tell her everything Mr Waters had said. Not a word about that other business? Not on your life! I thought.

First I told Helen that I would be staying for the remainder of the tour, and she squealed with delight.

We sat together on a swing in the garden that looked as if it had never been used.

'Helen, you have to tell me now what happened between you and Mr Waters in France,' I said, using my legs to push us off. It was a beautiful day, and the gardens were full of birds.

'Why?' she said.

'Every time I mention your name, he goes all sad-eyed. I've just been in the office and he spent half the time staring out the window at you. What happened?'

'The prince happened,' she said.

From *Autumn Leaves* by M.A. Bright:

France, 1918

She was with Miss Ivens in the office when an orderly appeared at the door.

'The prince is in the foyer,' the orderly said to Miss Ivens.

'Which prince?' Miss Ivens said, looking annoyed.

'Wales.'

'Edward?'

'Yes.'

'Well, what the devil is he doing here?' Miss Ivens demanded.

The orderly shrugged but didn't answer.

'The arm, Frances—the British captain,' she said.

'What?' Miss Ivens looked at her.

'Remember? The British captain, left arm, looked like we'd lose it. Last month, when we had the quiet spell. I brought him from Criel. You got into trouble afterwards.'

'Yes, yes, I had to go and explain, as I recall. That was you? The thing is, they have no idea what this is like. Henry did the surgery, didn't she? What of it?'

'He's batman to the Prince of Wales.'

'Oh,' Miss Ivens said. 'How do you know that?'

'He told me,' she said.

'Well, I should change into my dress uniform. Who can we send to stall him?'

'Iris?'

'Good, yes, send Iris. And Dr Henry, since she did the surgery. She's in X-ray, so she should be presentable enough, and she can talk about the arm. I'll be down as quick as I can. Another thing?'

She turned.

'Don't you go. He has a reputation.'

'Sorry?'

'He likes pretty girls.'

'Who?'

'The prince. Who else?'

'Iris is pretty.'

'Yes, that's a good point. Find someone older—old older, not young older. Perhaps Berry. She'll be a foil for poor Henry. She can give him a lecture on public health in Wales. Get her to go as well.'

'All right.'

'I'll see you directly.'

David had come himself instead of sending a man. 'I heard you were skiving off at some old abbey. I didn't know it was full of girls!'

The prince was uncharacteristically coy, scuffing his boot on the gravel as he spoke. 'Fact is, we need you back in London, old friend. My father assures me he can get you home safely and then you can convalesce as long as you need. He says I might still be a target when you're with me, but it's worse when you're not. And I miss you.'

He didn't reply.

'Besides, we can't leave you with all these girls forever!'

'But, sir, if I stay here—'

'I won't hear another word. We'll take you home and get you well.' The prince smiled. There would be no discussion.

There was no time to find her to say goodbye either. He quickly scrawled a note, folded it and gave it to one of the girls while David was thanking the doctors.

'The Prince of Wales,' Iris Crane was saying. 'Oh, goodness. I nearly fainted. He is so handsome. He talked to me. He actually spoke to me personally, asked my name, where I was from. He has beautiful eyes. Hah! Violet is furious I met him and she didn't!

'He said it wouldn't do to leave his dear friend among the French, no matter how good the lady doctors were,' Iris said, adding, 'Miss Ivens was fairly ropable. I don't know if it was that the prince was ordering him moved or that he called her a lady doctor.

"'I'm sorry, sir," Miss Ivens told him, "but I don't think it's advisable to move the patient."' Iris was giggling at Miss Ivens's speaking so to the prince. 'But he—the patient, that is—stood and told them he was well enough to leave.'

That's what Iris told her now.

'Oh, I nearly forgot,' Iris said. 'He gave me a note for you. The batman, I mean, not the prince. I didn't even know you knew him.'

She had watched him from the top-floor windows as he and the prince walked together along the drive. He looked behind him once and then smiled across at his prince. She watched him go.

She took the note and put it into her pocket.

It was late that night before she had time alone to read. Three lines.

Dearest,
Please understand I must go now, but I will be back just as soon as time permits. I love you. I love you so much. I am yours. We are promised.

SEVENTEEN

Sydney, 1920

I LEFT GOVERNMENT HOUSE FOR THE DAY AND TOOK THE ferry to Balmain. On the harbour on my own in the Sydney winter sunshine, I felt like a bird that had just taken its first flight. Until a week ago I had been unable to keep a serving job, and now I was writing letters for the Prince of Wales. I had a sense of destiny, or what I thought was destiny. This was what I'd been born to do, I told myself. And now I had been invited to join the rest of the tour, entirely on my merits. They knew me, knew my writing, and they had singled me out. The prince had singled me out. I could have sung to the ferry crowd.

Before leaving, I had tied the remaining letters that needed replies into three bundles—those for a standard reply, those that needed thought, those for which action was required. I took the action pile and sat down with the clerk and steward to give them the prince's instructions. The clerk was an employee of the governor, a middle-aged man with a grey beard and glasses, and the steward, a government appointee lent to the prince for the duration of the tour, was not far behind in age and seniority.

It was amazing to me that these men would do as I asked. This fellow is to get a refund on his train ticket (went to see the prince but the prince wasn't there). This one is to be sent the official cup and saucer (lost a grandson in the fighting) plus a personal reply, and this one—I paused, for it was the one that had touched me the most deeply—is a little boy whose father has come home terribly unwell. He is coming to Brisbane with his mother to meet the prince in person, I said.

'Yes, miss,' was as much as either of them said in reply.

I couldn't wait to get back to my aunt Bea's house in Balmain. While I had seen Daddy earlier in the day, I very much wanted to tell Bea what I'd been doing as part of the prince's personal staff. She would be so proud of me, I knew, even prouder than Daddy.

I had been relieved two weeks before when Mummy said Bea had sent money for tickets to Sydney for us all. I thought if anyone could help with Daddy it would be Bea. She was his older sister and she'd all but raised him. Bea had always been in our lives.

On the second morning after we arrived in Sydney, Mummy had gone in early to see the prince again and Bea said I could come into the library with her on the train—she had planned I would work there with her once I completed my matriculation. She hoped that, like her, I would study at the university.

Bea had been thrilled when I'd won a scholarship to the state high school. She said it was a new era for women after the war and I would be able to do whatever I wanted. I hadn't told her I'd left school, that I'd never complete my matriculation now as I must work, that university was a dream.

That day we went together into the library, Bea already knew something was wrong with Daddy. I tried to tell her what was happening at home.

'Is this after Edward?' she said, not understanding.

'It's everything,' I said, shaking my head. I was nearly in tears. 'Daddy has these nightmares, and he becomes afraid, or sometimes angry. Sometimes they happen in the day. He doesn't know who we are. It's like he's not there. Ask Mummy.'

'Your mother would never tell me anything about it. She's too proud. Is he writing?' Bea asked.

I shook my head. 'Rats,' I said. 'He writes about rats.'

'Poetry about rats?'

'More like essays. He describes the different sub-species in detail, noting characteristics, habits. He draws them, writes about them. Please don't tell Mummy. She doesn't know.'

'Has he talked to you about it?'

'No, I go into his study. Mummy thinks he's working on a collection.'

'That's what she told me—that he quit teaching to write.'

'He was sacked,' I said. I was crying now, my eyes filling with tears, my voice unsteady. 'He tweaked this boy's ear very hard. Daddy never did anything like that before.'

Bea looked out the window of the train. 'Poor Tommy,' she said.

∽

I walked up to Bea's house from the ferry just as night was falling. While Mummy was full of excitement about my working for the Prince of Wales, while the boys were just happy to have their big sister back among them to help, Daddy was lost to us again. I found him out on the veranda, sitting on his own on the porch swing, back and forth, back and forth.

'You should still be at school, Maddie,' he said, his jaw set tight. 'I don't know how I've let this happen.' He looked so very upset. 'You're clever, and you're going to write. I had more schooling than you have, and I had no parents to provide. I've let you down.'

'I don't mind working, Daddy. I really don't. The tour might be fun. And I'll be home in a month.'

Daddy's hands were shaking. I took them in mine. 'I think it won't always feel like this,' I said. I could see the sweat beading on his forehead. 'I think it will feel better one day. You'll come back to us.'

He smiled bitterly. 'I don't want you to go, Maddie. I don't feel right about it. Not after everything.'

If I'd thought it would have helped Daddy, I would have said no to Mr Waters in a minute, or at least I hope I would have. But I knew in my heart that we were in no position financially for me to refuse this job even if I'd wanted to. When my mother ran off from her parents' estate with my father, Edward already forming in her womb, her family cut her off altogether. We had nothing, and no one to fall back on but Bea, who for all her kindness could not support five hungry children and who, I realised that night, was at a loss about how to reach her poor brother now.

Early the next morning, I rose before the sun and washed and dressed in my only good dress, a pale grey linen, and my sturdy black boots. I went into the room where the three youngest boys slept peacefully. I gave them each a shield of kisses on their brow and told them in a whisper I'd be home before they knew it. Only John stirred. He mumbled something and smiled in his sleep, such a beautiful boy. The twins smelled of Bovril.

I crept out of their room and went into the room Bert slept in, our uncle Reg's office. Bert was already awake. 'So you're going?' he said.

I nodded and smiled.

'You're a good sister, Maddie.'

'And you're a good brother.'

We hugged and I had a lump in my throat, as if I would never see Bert again.

I went down the stairs and out the front door.

Oh, stop! you want to say to your young self. Just stop a minute and think! Do not do not do not walk into danger's arms. But she can't hear me and wouldn't listen if she could.

EIGHTEEN

Brisbane, 1981

IT HAD BEEN A MONTH SINCE SALLY AND FRANK HAD started coming to my house each day. I found they could spend hours happily playing out in the garden with the chickens, which was where I was with them now.

Sally is the younger one, two and three quarters, as Frank is fond of telling me. He's much older, he says, at four and an eighth. I wondered how a four-year-old understood fractions, but I suppose he didn't. I suppose he mimicked his father.

To lose your mother so young. 'I was older than you by more than twenty years and that was hard enough,' I've said to Sally, although she doesn't know what I mean. I suppose I shouldn't say things like that to a two-year-old, even given the three-quarters. I seem to be losing my ability to censor myself.

The True Story of Maddie Bright

I don't mind the children being here. In truth, although I tell them to rest while I work, I like the noise in the house. It brings back memories of the little boys when I was young. It's the constant noise of children, busy with the living of life right now. I miss my brothers. I miss them still, maybe more with the passing of time, not less.

Making children rest is impossible. Perhaps I never tried with my brothers, but Andrew told me the children should rest in the middle of the day. Frank made a jungle vine of the venetian cord yesterday, swinging back and forth over his little sister while she emitted shrieks of terrified laughter, until I gave up and let them out of the prison I'd made for them in the spare bedroom.

I've seen it all before, I could tell them, every possible thing a child could come up with, although we didn't have venetian blind cords when the twins were four and an eighth.

While the children have played here, Andy has replaced the front stairs, put a beam under the house for some reason I didn't understand, even after he'd explained it, and had the termite man in to kill the remaining termites. The rats in the ceiling were quickly exterminated by poison thrown up there. He assured me the possums would not eat rat poison. 'But we should get them out too,' he said. 'I have a trap at home.' He scratched his head, looking up towards the manhole.

'Possums have to live somewhere,' I said.

'Fair enough,' he said. He sighed. He is getting used to sighing in relation to me.

He is shy about sending me a bill, so I have told him I am a millionaire.

He doesn't believe me.

'I worked as a teacher for forty years,' I said, 'and I have no dependents and own this house. I can afford to pay you.'

Andy came out to the garden where the children were playing now. Frank, who'd been trying to climb the pine tree, ran to his father and hugged him around the legs. 'Can we do building?'

Andy smiled. 'When we get home.' He laughed and pretended to fall over from the tackle. 'Maddie, I reckon I'm done,' he said as he got up.

'But you'll be back tomorrow?' I said, a little too eagerly.

'No, I mean, I've finished all the things we agreed I'd do.' He was looking at me with that smile of his.

I had loved having him and the children each day. I'd hardly noticed what building work Andy had done. For all I knew, he could have stayed under the house running a saw and drill into nothing to give the semblance of building. It wouldn't have bothered me really.

'What will the children do tomorrow?' I asked.

'How do you mean?'

'While you're at work. What will they do?'

'Go back to child care,' he said, as if that was obvious.

'Sally doesn't like it, and Frank doesn't like it much either.' While this was true, it wasn't the only reason I said it.

He looked uncomfortable. 'Well, I—'

'Why can't they come here?'

'I'm finished here, Maddie. It's been lovely and all, but I have to get back on the next-door job. The plans have been approved.'

'So why can't Frank and Sally come here while you're next door?'

'I couldn't ask you to do that. It's not fair. And you have your book.'

'Well, yes, that's true, but a book takes time. Anyway, it's not for you to say what's fair.' I hesitated then, because I wasn't sure I could trust my voice. 'It's for me.' I set my mouth tight to let him know I meant it.

He nodded. 'I see.'

Just then Sally came up behind me and grabbed me around the legs. 'I love you, Maddie,' she said.

And so it was settled.

I became the children's carer during the day while Andrew was at work. He paid me what he paid the child-care centre and later, when his business picked up, he paid me more. It was enough, with my pension, so that I didn't have to dip into my savings, which made me feel independent.

At some stage, he told me there had been a lie.

'My wife,' he said. 'I wasn't completely honest with you.'

'In what way?'

'She didn't die. Well, not in the way I said.'

'I see. She left you?'

He nodded.

'And the children.'

'Yes.'

'Well, okay,' I said.

'She was killed in a car accident six months after she left,' he said. 'Her family blames me. I thought you might like me less if you knew.'

'You were wrong about that,' I said.

'Before she died, people used to say she was a terrible mother to leave the children.'

'People don't know shit,' I said.

We sat there together in silence for a while until I said, 'I think we both need tea.'

NINETEEN

Sydney, 1920

THE DAY I LEFT MY AUNT BEA'S AND MOVED INTO Government House to join the royal tour, Helen and I went into the city to purchase new clothes—for me, principally, although Helen acted as if it were a shopping trip for both of us. All the prince's staff had a uniform allowance, Helen said, and when she joined the tour, they extended the allowance to frocks and suits 'suitable for a royal tour'. I didn't know if this were true, or if they'd made special arrangements for me, but I was in no position to be proud.

We went to David Jones on George Street, and Helen helped me pick out two readymade dresses, silk stockings, and one pair of low heels which would do for day and evening wear. Helen said I could borrow some of her shoes if needs be. She also talked me into a linen skirt and two blouses for day events.

Helen wanted a jacket to go with the skirt but I said I could get by with my cardigan. She paid for everything from the tour account, insisting that this was part of the job.

After we finished shopping, we went to the tea rooms further along George Street which a footman from Government House had suggested to Helen.

We had scones and jam and cream with our tea. The only time I'd ever had anything so special was when I'd come to stay with Bea on my own and she'd taken me to the tea rooms near the library.

'You and Mr Waters have been so very kind,' I said.

'Yes, kindness is Rupert's middle name,' she said.

'You're not going to tell me about what happened, are you?'

She sighed. 'I already told you, Rupert and I were in love,' she said.

'Were?' I said.

She nodded sadly. 'It all feels like an age ago, darling. I really don't want to talk about it. It's the dreadful past I never ever think on.'

I sighed. 'Tell me about the hospital then, the one where you worked.'

'Royaumont?' she said. She struck a match and lit up a cigarette, pushing her plate to one side and dragging an ashtray over. She was the only woman smoking in public, I knew, but she didn't seem to care.

'Oh, it was a marvellous place. I went over at the start of 1915, just after they opened. I had a car, you see, that my stepfather had bought for me. I think he only bought it to get rid of me, frankly, but that's another story.

'Anyway, they gave me a job as an ambulance driver. At first the *Croix Rouge* said women couldn't drive in a war zone but they soon got used to us. Eventually we bought proper ambulances but, at the start, you had to bring your own.'

She took a long draw on her cigarette and blew the smoke above us. 'Did I tell you already that I ran the little school for a time?' she said.

'No,' I said. 'I thought it was a hospital.'

'Yes. But Miss Ivens—she was our chief—was very keen that we do whatever we could to help the villages around the hospital. The school master from Asnières was off fighting and there was no one in the village who felt able to continue a school. I have a degree in the arts, and my French is rather good, so Miss Ivens said *I* could teach the children. I'd never been near a child my whole life except to make funny faces at them so they'd giggle.

'But dear Miss Ivens knew more than she let on, I think. She was always one for finding things you could do and getting you doing them.' She sighed. 'It was marvellous fun. I didn't know what they were supposed to be learning so we just made it up.

'I remember one little girl in particular, a dear thing, six years old, her father off fighting, half scared to death the first few days. But she turned out to be very smart.

'Children are the true gift,' she said then, looking sad again. 'That's certain.'

'You clearly haven't spent enough time with my younger brothers,' I said. 'They would change your mind quick smart.'

'No, they wouldn't,' Helen said. 'They wouldn't. I loved them all.'

∽

I had been working for more than an hour in the office at Government House later that afternoon when I heard someone walk quickly into the room behind me without knocking. I turned around and there was Prince Edward.

He was dressed in the long shorts he wore for running, and long white socks, with a button-down shirt and a cardigan. He looked like any young fellow you might meet, perhaps less stylish, closer in age to my brother Bert, sixteen, than his own age of twenty-six.

'Maddie!' he said. 'What a treat.'

'Yes, sir?'

'Just hello,' he said.

'I am skiving off today,' he said, 'and the admiral is fit to fry a cat about it.'

I had stood up when he came in and he gestured for me to sit back down, which I did. He took a seat himself in the easy chair on the other side of the room, looking out to the garden.

'My father has written to me,' he said. 'And it's made me glum. But seeing you has quite cheered me up.'

'Glum, sir?'

'I am to buck up.' He sighed. 'And my friends; my father doesn't like some of my friends. He didn't want me to appoint Godfrey, who he thinks is too young, and he only tolerates Rupert because Rupert's father is his equerry and so he can't possibly reject him. And now he's angry with me for not wearing my uniform to a parade in Melbourne. He saw a picture in the newspaper and said I had brought shame to him and the family.'

'Oh no, sir,' I said. 'I think our parents always wish we were better than we are in some way. And if you're the Prince of Wales, I imagine that's multiplied a thousandfold. But do you mind me asking why you don't like wearing your uniform? It looks very well on you.'

'No one's ever asked me that,' he said, looking stern.

'I'm sorry,' I said, realising I'd overstepped a boundary. 'Sir.'

He smiled then and his whole face was illuminated. 'Oh, don't be silly,' he said. 'It's a very good question and speaks of an enquiring mind which I find I rather like. That must be why you write such fine letters for me, eh?'

He sighed again. 'I think it might be that the uniform separates me too much from normal people. My father would see this very differently, mind. He is a king. He understands he was born to be a king. Perhaps I don't share his confidence about all that, or his confidence in the people's confidence about us. It's not as if we've earned it, not in any way. And you only have to look across Europe, every one of my cousins is either exiled or dead.'

'I didn't even fight,' he said then. 'I wasn't allowed to. They sent me to the command centre in Paris.

'The last thing the men who did fight need is a royal family expecting adulation. If they need a royal family at all, it's one that can understand their plight. I can best do that by being among them. My father . . . he puts a great store in doing things properly.

'Do you know the peculiar thing?' he said suddenly. 'I feel terribly comfortable talking to you. Do you suppose it's because you've been me?'

'I beg pardon, sir?'

'You write as me. You are me in those letters. Perhaps it makes it very easy to talk with you.'

I nodded. 'Yes, sir, I do understand. I feel I know you because I write as you.' I smiled at him. He really was very sweet.

'Helen writes my speeches, and she strikes me the same way. With you, I feel it more so, because your letters are a better version of me than I am. And yet I don't feel you ever look down on me—on me as myself, I mean.

'Actually, Helen rarely makes me better than I am. I'm funnier than she is at any rate.' He laughed, as if he'd made an enormous joke. 'She is a dear one, though. She looks after me very well.'

He drew on his cigarette and blew out, and then ground the butt into the clean ashtray on the side table.

'But uniforms are a particular problem with me. Perhaps they rankle because I'm not really a soldier, and therefore not really a prince.'

'You're more a prince of the people than your father,' I said. 'I think even my father would agree with that.'

'I doubt it. I'd pick him for a republican. The entire New South Wales government are Bolshie, according to Grigg. And Queensland, where you're from, is supposed to be even worse.' He smiled. 'I might be a bit of a Bolshie myself, come to think of it. I do feel for the men.'

He went on, 'Rupert liked your father though, very much, and Rupert is a good judge of character.'

'Yes,' I said. 'He was different before the war. I hope that with time . . .'

'Yes,' he said. 'I hope so too, Maddie.' He looked pained then, as if he took personal responsibility for my father's plight. I admired him greatly at that moment.

∾

The next morning, I was in the offices starting work on the pile of letters that had been waiting in Sydney when Colonel Grigg came in. Without addressing me, he asked Mr Waters if I might accompany the prince with them on the appointments for the day; if I had more experience of official functions it might help in drafting replies that took account of the political situation. Mr Waters rolled his eyes towards me, but to Colonel Grigg he said yes, of course. We had time for me to do that now that I'd joined the team for the duration, he said to me. I may as well go.

I was thrilled to have been asked. On the way down the steps, I told Helen she must tell me what I needed to do. I knew we were to attend a display by schoolchildren at the Sydney Cricket Ground—not so long ago I might have been a participant in such a display—and I wanted to do the right thing as a representative of the Crown.

'Oh, we do nothing, darling. Not one thing but keep H.R.H. a happy chappie. I'm just so glad you're coming,' she said. 'I'd be bored otherwise. Ned is terribly serious about all this, and David likes a laugh. He'd much rather Dickie was with us, but we can still have some fun.'

The prince himself had been the one who'd suggested to Colonel Grigg that I be asked, she said. 'He likes your spunky nature, I think.'

There had been a run of fine days for the prince's visit and again today there was not a cloud in the sky. As we approached the waiting motor, Helen stopped me, put her hand on my arm and said quietly, 'Can you be a true darling and sit next to me? I don't want to sit next to Ned.'

'Is Ned the one who we need to be on tea alert for?' I said.

'No, nothing like that. He's . . . I think he might think he and I . . . It doesn't matter. He's just a tricky trick, all right?'

I nodded.

Colonel Grigg was in his late thirties, I'd have said. I knew from Helen that he was unmarried and I had wondered about his feelings for her on the Canberra trip. He admired her writing, I knew, but perhaps it was more than that. Sir Godfrey had intimated as much the day we'd arrived back from Canberra.

The True Story of Maddie Bright

In the car, I sat facing the colonel, with the prince beside him. Helen, beside me, faced the prince. On the way through the city, crowds lined both sides of George Street and there were people leaning out the windows of all the buildings. I had never seen so many people, all looking at our car.

The prince waved to them as we drove by. 'What on earth are they here for?' he said. 'This isn't even a parade day.'

'They read the newspaper and guess your route, I suppose, sir,' Colonel Grigg said.

The prince shook his head but kept smiling. 'Fools, the lot of them.'

∾

At the cricket ground, the prince was taken by car to the official welcome area. Helen and I remained in the stand with the newspapermen. There were perhaps a dozen photographers behind us, and down in front, half-a-dozen journalists with notebooks and pencils. The air was full of excitement.

To our left was the bandstand. The children stood in the centre of the ground. From where we were, you could see them milling around like ants and then, suddenly, as the band struck up, they very quickly formed into the Australian flag. It was a tremendous demonstration, as if every single child were connected to a machine that moved them to the right place. Soon the flag dissolved into a mess of colour and regrouped into the three feathers surrounded by the colonies. At the bottom was written, in children, *Many Happy Returns*.

Songs were sung: 'God Bless the Prince of Wales', 'God Save the King' and then 'Happy Birthday', which the children fairly roared out.

The prince came over to where we were while the display was reorganising back to the flag. I was about to wish him a happy birthday—I had thought his birthday was the week before; there had been a holiday to celebrate it—when he said to Helen, 'I want to meet the children, but that idiot Davidson is telling me there's no provision to go among them. Can you fix it?'

Sir Walter Davidson was the New South Wales governor and the prince found him pompous, Helen had told me. Mr Waters had had to intervene more than once to avoid a situation.

Helen looked at Colonel Grigg. The colonel just shrugged.

She scanned the field. 'The band, sir! Why don't we go over there to the band and you can climb up to the conductor's stand so the children can all see you? You won't be going among them but at least they'll all get to see you properly. They'll love it!'

'Perfect,' the prince said. 'You are my champion, Helen.'

And that was what he did.

He stood there waving and smiling for at least ten minutes. The children waved back and cheered wildly. It was a delightful scene and the newspaper photographers snapped picture after picture.

After the display was finished, we quickly returned to the car, which waited on the ground.

When we were away, Helen said the *Many Happy Returns* was odd. 'Perhaps it was originally scheduled for last week,' she said.

'It's because it's my birthday today,' the prince said.

'Oh, I didn't know that,' Helen said.

'No, neither did I,' the prince said, smiling sadly.

'Why did we celebrate your birthday last week?' she asked.

'Because it's what we did,' he said.

'Happy birthday, then, dear David,' Helen said warmly, and leaned over and kissed his cheek. She held his hand in both of her own for a moment and I saw there were tears in her eyes.

Colonel Grigg leaned forward then. 'Steady on,' he said to Helen.

Helen just kept smiling, a tear rolling down her cheek.

'Thank you, Helen,' the prince said. 'You're the only one who treats me like a person, not a relic.' There were tears in his eyes too, I saw now.

'I'll kiss you too, if it will help,' Colonel Grigg said.

It wasn't funny, what the colonel said, especially after Helen's tenderness.

∽

Next, we were taken to the University of Sydney, where the prince was to receive an honorary doctorate. I knew that for the prince and Colonel Grigg and Helen these places were ordinary, but for me the Great Hall was a wonder, those large stained-glass windows, the enormous space filled with members of the colleges in their colours.

In the robing room where Helen and I would wait, the prince was dressed by a valet in a gown of red and purple and gold. It was quite a complicated affair. I heard him ask the chancellor if the gown had been made specially for the occasion, as he couldn't imagine anyone wearing it willingly. The chancellor said it wasn't. Then the prince made a joke about how many honorary doctorates he'd been given.

'It's like when I served in France,' he said. 'I was never allowed to truly serve, and now I am honoured with a degree I haven't truly earned.'

An uncomfortable silence fell, as if the dignitaries didn't know how to respond.

The prince himself redeemed the moment then by going on to speak about the small good even the most humble person could do for his fellows. 'Yesterday, I met a young soldier who had lost his two brothers in the fighting. I was able to thank him on behalf of His Majesty and, while it could never ease his burden, never, I hope it made some small difference. We can all do this,' he added. 'All of us. We must. Because it's what we can do.'

It was such a heartfelt thing to say, I thought. Even the crusty old chancellor was moved.

Helen and I waited at the back of the hall with the newspapermen while Colonel Grigg and the prince went to meet the returned soldiers who were graduates. One of the press men asked Helen about the evening before. 'I hear he danced with Mollee Little all night, and Lady Margaret is none too pleased.'

'Well, that's just the silliest thing I ever heard,' Helen said. 'There was no dancing at all. The prince had the bank dinner.'

To me she said, 'He had the night wrong. It was two nights before that David acquainted himself with Miss Little. They didn't dance though. Rupert wouldn't let them.'

This must have been the dance the prince had invited my mother to. Mr Waters had stopped them going ahead.

'Who's Miss Little?' I asked.

'Oh, I'll tell you later.'

We were soon back in the car—not before the prince shook the hands of many in the crowd—to return to Government House.

Even more people lined the route along George Street now. The prince, glad that the 'stunts', as he called them, were over until the evening, waved out the window at people with his left hand, nursing his right on his lap. You could see the bruises livid on the top of his hand.

'We'll get some ice back at the house,' the colonel said.

Helen was telling a story about the children who'd wandered away from the display at the cricket ground and had to be herded back, and the prince was laughing. I noticed Colonel Grigg watching her as she spoke and I thought she was right: he had feelings for her.

∽

We were about halfway along George Street when I noticed that the police on either side of the road had thinned out in numbers and the crowd had spilled out onto the roadway in front of us.

The prince kept a smile on his face and waved as Colonel Grigg turned to the driver, who was slowing. 'We mustn't stop. You know that, don't you?'

'I'm sorry, sir,' the driver, a young officer, said. 'But there's nothing I can do. The police aren't keeping them back. I can't run them over.'

'I don't see why not,' the prince said.

I must have looked as horrified as I felt, for the prince then said, 'Just a little joke to lighten the mood, Maddie.'

Helen had laughed. She didn't seem worried about the crowds, but I was feeling apprehensive. There were people everywhere and they were closing in on us now. Some were running next to the car and in front, forcing the driver to slow.

Suddenly, a young man jumped onto the running board of the car. 'Your Majesty, give us a handshake, would you?' he shouted.

The prince smiled before Colonel Grigg half stood and leaned out the window and shoved the fellow off.

We had slowed to a crawl now. They were everywhere, banging on the roof of the car and the doors. Colonel Grigg had turned the keys to lock the doors and pulled up the windows, but I worried the banging would soon smash them.

The prince looked over at me. 'Oh, Maddie, the look on your face, you dear little thing. Please don't worry. The police will catch up eventually.' He seemed terribly cool about it. 'Won't they, Grigg?'

'I'm sure they will, sir.' But the colonel was looking over his shoulder to see what Helen and I could see, the mob behind us moving quickly now to overtake the car. 'Oh dear,' he said. 'The fellow I pushed off the running board is coming back with a few friends. We might have to defend the women, sir.'

'I'm your man,' the prince said. 'It would have to be better than standing on that dais shaking bally hands again.' He shook his right hand and I noticed the palm was bruised too.

Just then, we heard whistles, and police on horseback trotted up to flank the car, and they were soon joined by others on foot. They cleared a path, using their batons liberally, and we sped up again and left the melee behind us.

I was relieved and so was everyone else in the car, I was sure. But judging by the responses of Helen and the prince, it wasn't the first time this had happened.

By the time we arrived back at the house we were laughing about the predicament we'd found ourselves in.

'When I try to brief the Home Office on what this is like, they simply don't understand,' Colonel Grigg said to Helen, and to the prince: 'It's like you're a god, sir.'

'Well, if they really knew me, they'd know differently, eh Ned?'

We were still laughing as we all climbed out of the car.

'Maddie looked as if she thought they were going to crush us,' the prince said.

'Well, we shot your uncle, so anything's possible,' I said.

Colonel Grigg looked shocked by what I'd said and so did Helen but the prince laughed loudly. 'And, Grigg, you were no help, pushing that fellow off. What if he'd caught up?'

'I was ready for him,' Colonel Grigg said, taking a boxer's stance, his fists up, moving from foot to foot.

Mr Waters was standing at the top of the steps watching us, I saw now.

'Oh look, it's old stuffed shirt himself,' Colonel Grigg said.

Helen laughed loudly, that hard laugh of hers I didn't believe was truly her. But even the prince giggled. Mr Waters looked down and while he didn't hear what was said, I was sure he knew they were laughing about him.

I couldn't join them. Mr Waters looked so sad I couldn't make fun of him. And I couldn't understand how Helen could. She saw my reaction, stopped laughing, shrugged a little. I saw pain there in her features then, and it occurred to me that I didn't actually understand anything at all about what had happened to Helen and Mr Waters.

TWENTY

Paris, 1997

MARK STAPLE WAS WAITING AT GARE DU NORD. HE'D taken the first flight that morning, he said. 'Been up since four.' He'd been sending images back all day. He smiled wearily.

Victoria had always liked Mark. His wife Kerry called their four young children their 'tribe'. I better get this tribe out of here. Come on, tribe. We'll have the tribe with us. Is it okay if I bring the tribe? Whenever they arrived at staff parties, chaos ensued.

Mark had been to the accident site, he said. 'Not much to see but I got a couple of shots. I'll have to go back and get them again at night, I think. It really is just an underpass. Do you want to come with me after the hospital?'

'Of course,' Victoria said. 'What's happening at the hospital?'

'Charles. He's come over to collect her body, with the sisters.'

'Oh God,' Victoria said. 'It makes it so real.'

'It sure does.'

As Mark drove through the Paris streets, he told Victoria what he knew so far. 'Word is, the driver was drunk. That's what the bellhop at the Ritz said.'

'*The Guardian*'s blaming you,' Victoria said, 'or maybe me. Tabloids. They're blaming tabloids. They're blaming anyone who's not *The Guardian*.'

'Nathan got spat on today. He was shooting the flowers around the palace and someone spat on him.'

'Gee,' Victoria said. She might not mind Nathan getting spat on, she decided. 'Well, maybe we *are* to blame.'

'I'm not the guys in that tunnel last night,' Mark said, anger in his voice.

'No,' she said. 'You're not. Of course you're not. Maybe I meant I am.'

'Danny Brown told me that Nathan earned two million pounds last year,' Mark said. 'Two million.'

'Really?' Victoria said.

He didn't respond straightaway.

'I saw her on the street a few years ago,' he said then.

'Diana?'

He nodded. 'I've been thinking about it all morning. Shot of my career.'

'Where?'

'Charing Cross Road. Can't even remember why I was there, but I had a camera so I must have been on a job. She came out of St Martin-in-the-Fields. She was on her own, no security that I could see, no friends, no one. She must have been at a concert. It was around the time Charles did the Jonathan Dimbleby interview and everyone wanted to know her reaction. Do you remember?'

Victoria did.

'The morning after the interview, we ran that picture, the short black dress, as if she didn't care about anything. One of Danny's. It bumped Charles into oblivion, really, and everyone said that's what she'd wanted it to do. But in the week that followed, everyone was mad for pictures of her. What did she really think? They all wanted to know.'

He took a breath in and held it a moment, then exhaled. 'She had tears in her eyes, so it was perfect. She looked . . . She looked beautiful, Victoria. I was quite overcome for a moment.'

'You didn't get the shot?'

'No.' He smiled sadly. 'I know. I should have. I'd been retrenched from *The Sun* after the takeover. I was freelancing for a bit. Prices for pictures of her weren't what they are now, but still.

'I watched her and I'm thinking about the shot, the light, and then she saw me and, I don't know if she recognised me or saw the camera, but her eyes just pleaded. She shook her head no, a little shake. I just stopped and held the camera there against my chest and nodded.

'No,' he repeated. 'I didn't take the shot.'

'Did you regret it?'

'Huh?' He looked at her as if he'd been somewhere else momentarily. 'You kidding? Of course I did. Kerry said she'd have killed me if I'd done it. Then she said she should kill me for not doing it.' He sighed. 'Life would be a lot easier for us now. I wouldn't be getting up early for Harry Knight for a start. And the boys would be in a better school.

'She just smiled at me. Through her tears she smiled at me.' He shook his head slowly. 'Choices you make, eh?'

'Yes,' Victoria said. 'Although it's our job, Mark. It's what we do.'

'Maybe. Have you ever looked back at the video footage when they got engaged?'

'No,' Victoria said. 'But I remember seeing it at the time and thinking how lucky she was. I think every girl my age thought the same. They looked so happy.'

'I pulled out some old tapes while I was waiting for the car at home this morning. Have a look before you write anything. Make sure you do. It really hit me how young she was. Frankly, she looked not much older than my eldest, and he's an idiot.'

'I think she loved him,' Victoria said, 'or maybe loved the idea of him. I think she thought he'd make everything better.'

'Yes, she probably did,' Mark said. 'That's the way it usually goes. Didn't you do a big story about them, back in the day?'

Victoria sighed, feeling a heaviness in her chest. 'Yes, I did,' she said.

Mark looked at her. 'The paramedics couldn't get to her for a bit. There was a doctor, a passer-by. He had to fight his way through. The guys were still taking shots.'

~

They arrived at the Pitié-Salpêtrière hospital, which was where Diana had been taken after the accident. Mark parked in a side street. He left Victoria at the gate. He was going to make his way up to a small rise to the left to get a shot of the arrival of Prince Charles. Someone had phoned him in the car. They had ten minutes, he said.

Victoria joined the throng of journalists kept back by a line of police. She could see the steps leading up into the hospital. Other people were gathering in the nearby street behind makeshift barriers. The scene was sombre, the weather doing its best to match, dark clouds forming above.

This was where her body lay now, Victoria thought, looking up at the building, trying to get a sense of Diana alone here in a strange place. How had her story changed so quickly, this girl raised to organise country fundraisers and shooting parties, who was now all alone in a hospital bed far, far from her home? How had she drifted so far from who she was supposed to be?

In the middle of the fifth floor Victoria saw a window with a dark covering. That might be the room, Victoria thought. She looked back over at the hill where Mark stood. It was just a sea of lenses on a makeshift scaffold, photographers and their gear everywhere, ladders, boxes, camera bags. Victoria watched for a long moment as they trained their lenses towards the hospital. This had been Diana's entire life, Victoria thought. Her most common social interaction was with a camera lens.

A black four-wheel drive pulled up and then another. Prince Charles emerged from the first car and Diana's two sisters from the second. They were like gazelles, one tall and willowy, the other smaller, and they were like Diana too, both of them. Charles stopped to greet the official party waiting at the top of the steps, the French president and his wife, a colonel from the French military, a priest. The two sisters walked past without stopping and went inside.

There was a to-do about something outside the hospital. The president and the military fellow had turned to deal with it, leaving Charles on his own. Rain had started to fall softly. Charles didn't notice, not even as umbrellas went up around him. He was looking out at the rain, his eyes unfocused. Did he know the world was watching? Did he not care? He was so small, she thought, there in the rain.

And then the moment was over. An aide was by his side, an arm slipped under the prince's elbow. They walked together up the steps, followed by the president and his wife.

⁂

It was only another twenty or so minutes before the party emerged, the prince first and, just behind him, Diana's sisters, one of them crying, the other staring into space. Charles was more composed now, although Victoria could still see the lost part of him, shoulders sloped, suit baggy, as if any minute the mask might drop again.

French guards formed a line down the path. Despite their neat uniforms, their gold-and-black caps and white gloves, it looked as if they'd only recently got out of bed. The crowd in the street was growing. Victoria had no idea how they knew where Diana had been taken or that she was now departing.

Soon the priest was there—the hospital chaplain, Victoria assumed, Catholic—followed by four undertakers in suits and peaked caps. On their shoulders they carried the coffin, but it was all a bit shambolic. Even the group of undertakers looked stitched together hurriedly, their sad faces in the soft light. People were sobbing loudly. Someone screamed. It was unreal, as if Diana's body emanated something of the woman herself, her essence, going from the world.

The coffin was draped in the Royal Standard, Victoria realised suddenly. Someone had thought to bring the Royal Standard. Diana was going to be taken back into the bosom of the royal family, the family that had left her on her own for the years of her marriage and beyond, the family that, according to Claire, wanted to take her children away from her. Now, in death, they would claim her as their own.

Charles stood with the president and his wife. He was swaying slightly, looked as if he might be sick. There was nothing of the confident young man who'd married Diana about him now.

He avoided Diana's two sisters, or they avoided him.

The undertakers loaded the coffin into the hearse, a minivan with large windows.

They were away quickly, Charles in a car behind, the Spencer sisters with him.

As the hearse passed, several people cried out or moaned loudly. Victoria wondered if people would line the route all the way to the aerodrome.

After the cars were out of sight, Mark found Victoria and said they should go. He wiped his eyes and then his nose with a handkerchief. 'We'll get some shots at the aerodrome. It's outside Paris. I can get there before them.'

At the aerodrome, Mark parked away from the terminal itself. They managed to sneak through an unguarded gate to the edge of the tarmac, hidden by a hangar. They could see the Queen's Flight and the English guard standing at attention waiting, their white belts and dress uniforms perfect. There was no haphazardness here, no put-together-at-the-last-minuteness. It was British to the core, as if Princess Diana's death had been planned for years.

They'd been the ones to bring the Royal Standard, Victoria realised. She watched their commanding officer, his face unmoving. He was the one keeping the young soldiers at attention, his sword drawn.

Soon the hearse arrived. There was another quickly pulled together French guard, berets and machine guns, lining the route to the rear of the plane.

And then the British soldiers moved forward two by two in perfect formation and each took a handle of the coffin, still draped in the Royal Standard. They hoisted it onto their shoulders, linking arms underneath, and began that slow march that would take Diana home.

Those poor young soldiers took the weight of her, Victoria saw, England's most loved and hated princess.

It all happened quickly from there. The prince boarded, the two sisters. The plane rose into the air, a perfect sunlit afternoon now, as if the clouds divided in her wake.

The hearse would be driven in from Heathrow and there, as in Paris, the route would be lined with hundreds of silent mourners, drivers stopping their cars to get out and bow their heads for Diana, coming home for the last time.

TWENTY-ONE

Brisbane, 1981

BEFORE HE DIED, MY FATHER HELPED BUILD THE WAR memorial on Cooks Hill at Ithaca. We didn't have money to contribute but he helped clear the land to make way for the cenotaph and plaque. It's the only World War I monument that has a clock, and you can understand why there aren't others. The dead don't need to know the time. I don't know why the town of Ithaca thought they might.

I go to the service on Anzac Day morning every year and I notice the clock, which generally keeps good time. I don't go for Edward, and I don't go for my father, and certainly not to be thankful for anyone's sacrifice, which they wouldn't have made willingly. When the speakers talk about sacrifice, I close my ears. No, I go to mark death, to mark loss as the experience I've known most in my life.

The True Story of Maddie Bright

It's in late April, the service, and the sun is starting its slow journey away from us and towards the northern hemisphere. Ed used to come with me, but today I couldn't rouse him from his stupor so I came on my own. My leg is healed altogether and I walked up from home without even thinking, just a twinge when I stopped and started again.

I used to stand at the back during the service so I could weep unnoticed. Now I go to the front and watch the young soldiers who make up the catafalque party. They're the ones to watch. You see yourself in them. You see your brothers. You'd see your children if you had children, I imagine. Their uniforms change, their guns, but their fresh faces are as fresh as they were in the all the wars we've sent fresh faces to fight.

Today, the students from Bardon State School came along to sing a version of the poem 'In Flanders Fields'. The larks, still bravely singing. The crows, who mark death for all of us, still sadly rarking this morning.

I stare at his name, engraved in the stone, *E.T. Bright*, my brother Edward, whom I once thought I could not possibly do without, and yet I did, and below the line, on the new plaque they pasted there after a new war was over, the twins *G.M. Bright* and *H.L. Bright*, killed in training when a bus went off a cliff in Victoria, before they'd even been to war.

I always think those two boys, the twins, killed so senselessly, would never have thought to go to war if not for Edward going, and Edward wouldn't have gone but for Daddy. And perhaps Daddy, who had no fealty to the Crown himself, would never have gone to war except for Mummy, whose life was not the life she'd been born to because of him. War became part of our family by accident and then destroyed us altogether. They may as well put T.G. Bright up there with Edward, for the war, the empire, the prince and his family, surely killed my father too.

People would often say to me when I was teaching that I seemed to have a special understanding of children. Some would venture to say it was rare in someone who didn't themselves have children. When you're a teacher, people feel they can comment on your personal life in any way they want, particularly if you are teaching their child. It's like being a member of the family they don't necessarily understand or approve of but have to accommodate.

I tell them I had four younger brothers I helped raise, so there wasn't much I hadn't dealt with.

I retired from Ithaca school in 1970. I was past the retirement age but, still, I wouldn't have retired if they hadn't made me. There was a new principal who had an approach I couldn't abide. He cloaked it in educational reform but it was plain cruelty and anyone with a heart knew it.

He took my class one day when I was sick and when I returned it was a little girl of five who told me he had made Jack Stanley stand in the corner while he lectured the rest of a class on the kind of person Jack was—a liar, he said. He had then left Jack there for an hour while Jack cried silently, the girl said.

She offered to give me an explanation of the boy's lie but I told her I didn't need it.

Jack was from the kind of poverty that meant helping children learn not to lie was low on priorities. Not starving was about all his poor mother could focus on.

I told Jack I was sorry for what had happened and I'd do my best to ensure it didn't happen again.

I went to the new principal and said if he ever did that again I would find a way to hurt him and I would use shame as my tool like he did. I would find something to shame him with.

The end of that year came and he moved me out. Of course he did. I have never been a good strategist, for what use was I to Jack then?

I should have shot the new principal instead.

When I was teaching, I liked the little ones like Jack Stanley best. They are so unformed and yet so much their own little selves becoming. How could you make them ashamed for being those selves? It eludes me still.

❦

It was after I returned from the Anzac Day service that I knew what to do about the letter. It came to me and it was entirely the right thing to do, even if it wasn't yet the truth for me. It would become true. I would make it so, for it described the feelings of the person I wanted to be and, by writing them, I would go some way to becoming that person.

Dear Helen,

You were kind to reach out to me after all these years. I can't imagine how difficult it must have been to write the letter you did.

I was sorry to hear Mr Waters has passed. He was a great teacher and a good man, I still believe, in spite of everything.

I am glad Autumn Leaves *found its most important reader. While my way of understanding the world has been to write about it, I am no longer that seventeen-year-old girl on the train. I am older and I believe wiser.*

I know I should thank you for what you did, but I can't quite bring myself to that point. Perhaps I could say we are both old now, and I for one would let bygones be bygones. I've been to the Anzac service this morning. My brother Edward's name is there. His father's should be too. There are two other brothers on the lower part of the cenotaph. They died in the next war.

I lost everyone, Helen, including you, but I'm old and the fact is I'm afraid of what might happen if I know any more of the truth.

I'm sure you of all people would understand.

Your letter has spurred me on to revise the sequel to Autumn Leaves *I started many years ago. I've called it* Winter Skies. *You are not the main character although you are one of the most interesting, which won't come as a surprise to anyone except perhaps yourself. I am hoping if I can write down the events as I recall them, they will have less power to do harm, especially to others.*

The thing is, it's such a sad story I don't quite know if I can tell it. But I thought that about Autumn Leaves, *and if I were to rewrite it now, I'd give it a happy ending.*

In writing this letter, Helen, I am releasing whatever debt you feel you owe me.
With love and friendship,
Maddie Bright

When I told Frank at the post office the next day I needed to post a letter to England he said, 'Is it that novel of yours again?'

'No,' I said. 'This one's a true story.'

TWENTY-TWO

Sydney, 1920

THE NEXT MORNING, HELEN AND I WALKED FROM Government House to the barge that would take us to *H.M.S Renown*. Our bags and the boxes from the office in Sydney had been taken on by staff.

I had read in the paper that morning that there had been five thousand people lining the street the day before, completely unexpectedly. There was no mention of the car stopping, and yet I knew we had been moments from real danger. It wasn't a joyful crowd, despite what the newspaper report said. It was a mob, and while they adored him, they might just as easily have torn him limb from limb.

Even if you were bitter and upset after the war, even if, like Daddy, you didn't care for the monarchy, I feel certain you would still be taken in by the spectacle of the two gunships, *H.M.S.*

Renown and H.M.S. *Repulse*, at the ready. On the *Renown*, the sailors were lined up in their shiny black shoes and white caps, all perfectly turned out and standing at attention. Behind the men, standing next to a large ship gun, were the officers in their suits and hats, also standing to attention. On the *Repulse*, the scene was similar.

'I'm guessing that, given all this fuss, H.R.H. is on his way to ship,' Helen said. 'We better make ourselves scarce or we'll get caught in the pomp and be unable to escape.'

Helen had said earlier that there was a to-do about the prince's spider letters. 'I heard the tail end of something Rupert was saying to Ned. I don't know quite what's happened, but we'll just lie low and hope for the best.'

We went down to the staff offices on the lower deck. Helen told me that Mr Waters and I were in one office, and we went there first. It was spacious and simply furnished, desks along one wall and along the opposite wall a bench seat with cushions in blue. On the floor was a woven mat and a low table. At the far end of the room were two armchairs, leather, with a blue throw rug over the back of one of them.

'That's you,' Helen said, pointing to the desk at one end. I had my own desk, and it was already set up with a typewriter, inkwell and paper. I felt a swell of pride.

Helen and Colonel Grigg were closer here on the ship than they'd been on the train, in an adjoining office, I soon learned. I was glad Helen would be nearby.

We could hear the band playing above us so we knew the prince had boarded. Soon I felt the ship's engines beneath us.

'That was fast!' Helen said. 'I imagine he's in a mood.' We rushed up onto the main deck and saw crowds up the hill and around the point, waving, throwing streamers.

We left Sydney and it was grand to be on the harbour and watch the boats that came out to see the prince away. There were two navy ships to escort us through the heads, as well as private boats from which people cheered and blew their horns. The sky was cloudless once again. I made a mental note of everything to include in my notebook that night.

I was surprised the farewell hadn't lasted longer. 'He just wants to be away,' Mr Waters said when I found him on the main deck. 'Someone's brought the mail from the house, Maddie,' he added. 'More letters.' He was shaking his head. 'And I need to get you to draft some other things for me today, if possible.'

'That's fine, Mr Waters,' I said. 'I'm ready.' I smiled my most confident smile.

'Also, I need to talk to you about something.' He held his finger up in the air as if weighing up what to say, but he said nothing.

'Rupert,' Helen said then, 'Mr Murdoch telephoned me at the house this morning. I can't find Ned and there's a story about the dancing last night, a different story from the other one, and it would be lovely for David to speak to Mr Murdoch, I think. I can ask Godfrey if you want.'

I had spent the night before at Balmain with my family. Daddy was resigned to my going now, and Bea thought it was a brilliant opportunity. Mummy was over the moon. It was only the little boys who cried and said they'd miss me. I assured them I'd be back before they knew it.

'Miss Little again?' Mr Waters said.

Helen nodded.

'No,' Mr Waters said. 'Godfrey already said no. The story isn't a nice one, in case you haven't heard it. He and the admiral are of the view it's better to let Mr Murdoch be Mr Murdoch and give him no access.'

'Can I talk to him then?' Helen said.

'Not today, Helen. There's more from the palace regards F.D.W., and it's going to cause a ruckus.'

On the prince's instruction, we docked at Jervis Bay to wait for the day's mail. Our escort left us there. Helen said we needed to hope for a spider seal and there were three. Relief! she said. 'I'm sure these will make H.R.H. very, very happy. Hopefully, we'll have an uneventful trip.'

I'd never been on a ship before and, while I found it all very exciting, I knew I must focus on my job and do the very best I could. I began to work my way through the new letters that had arrived, as well as finish off the ones I hadn't got done in Sydney over the preceding days. For the prince, six days at sea would mean a break from official functions and meeting people but, for the staff, it was a time to catch up on the work that underpinned the tour. I already knew from Mr Waters that the prince himself read every single letter we wrote for him, and changed them too. There were times he told Mr Waters to send a cheque to this person or that, to make sure this one got a handwritten letter which he penned himself. It meant I often had to retype the letters I'd already written. I couldn't have been more happy that he took so much interest in what we did.

Mr Waters came down after lunch on the first day. He put his briefcase on his own desk before coming over to me. 'All right, Maddie. The time has come to explain one or two things.' He had an envelope in his hand. 'H.R.H. has a special friend back in England.'

'The spider letters.'

'Ah, so you know.'

'I know the spider letters must go straight to the prince and I am not to open them or say anything about them to anyone.'

'Quite,' he said.

'Helen said they're from the prince's mistress.'

'Helen should hold her tongue. The prince has a dear friend, Mrs Freda Dudley Ward, who is married with two children, so she's hardly likely to be a mistress to anyone. It's that kind of talk that makes my blood boil. I will speak to Helen.'

'She didn't actually say that,' I said. 'She hinted. I don't want to get Helen into trouble, Mr Waters. But the prince writes a lot of letters to F.D.W. I'm very glad he's not . . . doing the wrong thing.'

'Yes, he does write a lot of letters,' Mr Waters said. 'She is a dear friend, as I've said. But now the Queen has written to H.R.H. and suggested that his friendship with Mrs Dudley Ward is . . . that as people are talking—people like Miss Burns, who should know better—they should perhaps not be friends anymore.'

'And that's made the prince unhappy?'

'Yes, along with other things. The King is very keen for H.R.H. to travel to India soon after he arrives home and some of us, certainly Sir Godfrey and I, think it's premature, that H.R.H. needs some time off between this tour and another. But it gets complicated because now, I believe, Mrs Dudley Ward has written and she has taken the Queen's view too in respect of her friendship with Prince Edward. She's more or less cut him off as far as I can glean.

'H.R.H. is already under enormous pressure, as you are well aware.' Mr Waters looked as if his head were being squeezed gently in a vice that was getting tighter by the minute. 'I think Mrs Dudley Ward has been encouraged to agree with the Queen on this issue, that Prince Edward's brother Prince Albert has been involved in some way I don't yet understand, and now Mrs Dudley Ward wants to end her friendship with Prince Edward.

'Prince Albert also had a friend, an Australian as it happens, Sheila Chisholm, who is a friend of Mollee Little, the Sydney girl that the prince has been so pleased to see. Prince Albert ended that friendship and has been made Duke of York for doing so.'

'They made him Duke of York for ending a friendship?'

Mr Waters shrugged. 'They are not free to live their lives as ordinary folk are.

'And now the prince, Prince Edward, is worried about all the correspondence back to England in relation to the tour,' he went on. 'Admiral Halsey has written to the King, and Colonel Grigg has written to the Prime Minister. So poor H.R.H. has all of England worried about him. And he feels, I think . . .'

'Ganged up on?' I suggested.

'Just so, and we all need to be aware of that and do what we can to help.'

'I will write the best letters yet, Mr Waters.'

'Oh, Maddie, that's exactly the kind of care I am talking about. I will let H.R.H. know. I am sure it will come as comfort to him.'

'Mr Waters, can I ask you a personal question?'

'I don't know. I don't much like your personal questions.' He was still smiling though. 'What would the question be?'

'Helen. You seem to like Helen very much, and she seems to like you, and I don't understand why you don't just . . .'

'Don't just . . . ?'

'Tell each other!'

He looked at me. 'That is not just a personal question. It's highly personal.' He was blushing, I realised. 'But it has a very simple answer. Because you are wrong, as I've explained before. All right?'

'I'm absolutely not, Mr Waters. I've seen Helen's face when you are stern with her. I told you I have a finely tuned sense for these things.'

He gave me a look.

'Just listen to me!' I implored. 'Helen loves you, Mr Waters, I'm sure she does. You couldn't be as nice a person as Helen is, and yet as mean to someone as she is to you, if you didn't love them.'

He looked hopelessly confused then.

'It's in all the novels,' I explained, uselessly, as his confusion only increased. 'I can guarantee it . . . I'm fairly certain she loves you.'

He looked more upset than confused then, and I wished I hadn't said anything.

'No, Maddie, she does not love me,' he said, 'unless she tells you more about her feelings for me than she tells me, and that is unlikely. I am not without a sense of these things either.'

'But how can you be sure?' I asked.

He sighed heavily. 'Because when Helen started on the tour, I asked her to marry me and she refused, so on this occasion your finely tuned sense of these things has failed you.'

He looked as if saying those words had shocked even him.

'Oh, Mr Waters, I'm sorry. I didn't mean to pry. I don't know why it is that she would refuse you, and I know it's none of my business, but it seems to me that she thinks you don't care for her, not the other way around.'

He smiled sadly. 'Well, she has refused me four times now, and I have accepted the umpire's decision, so to speak. I thought if she came on the tour, I might . . . Anyway.' He looked up towards the window. 'You can lead a horse to water . . .'

'Yes, sir, you can,' I said. 'And, mostly, it will drink.'

'No more personal questions, Maddie.' He was looking annoyed now.

'Of course not, Mr Waters.'

I felt terrible, vowed never to bother him about the matter again and also to stop meddling in other people's affairs. I would focus on the job at hand, to write the very best letters for Mr Waters and the prince.

An hour later, Mr Waters came back to the office and asked could he trouble me for some assistance.

'Of course.'

He looked around, closed the door between our office and the press office. 'I've been thinking about our discussion earlier.'

'Yes, sir?' I said when he paused.

'I wondered if you could tell me what it is that makes you think Helen might have feelings for me. I'm sure you're wrong, of course, but what is it exactly that you know?'

'Well, sir, she gets quiet whenever I ask about you, and looks sad, and when I asked she told me about meeting you in France, and said something happened, but I don't know what it was. She did say you were in love with one another.'

'I see,' he said. 'She told you this?'

'Yes, she did,' I said. 'She did, Mr Waters.'

He nodded and I saw a flicker of hope in his eyes. 'I'd prefer if you didn't tell her I was asking, Maddie,' he said then. 'It's quite a delicate matter, as it happens.'

'Mr Waters, mum is the word.'

What on earth had happened in France? I wondered again.

'Mr Waters, if there's anything else . . .'

'No, that's more than enough, Maddie. That will be all, truly.'

༄

I hadn't seen the prince during that first day, although Helen said he'd been running on the main deck and playing badminton with Dickie and seemed quite happy. After dinner, he sent Dickie to call us to the lounge on the main deck for games. When Helen arrived and saw Mr Waters, I noticed the change in her, that hard heart she always turned towards him. You fool, I wanted to say! He loves you and you love him!

The prince picked Mr Waters, Helen and me for his team. He was in good spirits and I wondered if in private he was upset or if the letters he'd received from F.D.W. contained good news rather than bad.

We started with a game where you name an animal and the other team has to think of an animal's name that starts with the last letter: zebra, antelope, eagle, egret, tiger and so on.

'They give me animals, you know,' the prince said to me.

'Who gives you animals, sir?' I said.

'The Australians. Your countrymen. I had a bear but I gave it back because it belonged to a little girl and she was devastated when she had to give it up. I have a kangaroo called Digger somewhere on board. I also have a tortoise in a tank below.'

'What do you mean?'

'I have them all somewhere on the ship. There are two lizards as well. Rupert suggested we wait until we sail out of the harbour and throw them over. I don't think I could do that.'

'You mustn't,' I said. 'It would be cruel to the animals.'

He laughed. 'And there you have the difference between us,' he said. 'Isn't that right, Waters?'

'Sir?' Mr Waters said.

'I am kind to helpless creatures, and you are not.'

'Exactly so,' Mr Waters said. He was smiling.

'What sort of bear was it?' I said.

'A koala,' the prince said.

We played charades then. Mr Waters surprised me for he was immensely funny. He acted out *War and Peace*. His long slim frame was made for movement, I saw. It wasn't something you'd pick about him straightaway. He did war marching like a soldier, rhymes with saw, the sawing motion, and then peace as piece of a pie. It was quite clever. Even Helen was smiling at him.

I noticed when he finished that he looked over at her sheepishly. What's more, she didn't stop smiling! I held my breath!

Perhaps they would overcome whatever it was that kept them from their true feelings.

The prince and I had the next one, and it was *Jane Eyre* of all things.

I hoped Helen would guess if I mimicked typhus, pretending at a sore throat and fever, but it was harder than I imagined. The prince and his cousin were in fits of laughter watching me gag and wander about the stage, looking like Quasimodo more than someone afflicted. I barked like a dog as well and that just made them laugh more.

The prince himself soon came up and told me he might try something new. He did air for Eyre, blowing out and gesturing, which Mr Waters got straightaway and then his first word, sounds like pain, and Helen got to Jane.

'Have you read *Jane Eyre*, sir?' she asked him.

'Of course I haven't. Who has time for books?'

'I do,' I said, quite forgetting that I was a servant and he was the Prince of Wales.

Mr Waters looked a little taken aback but the prince just laughed. 'Well, I should hope so,' he said, 'given that you're supposed to be a prince when you write.'

I smiled. 'I'm sorry, sir. I just forgot myself.'

'No,' Helen said. 'Don't be sorry. He should be sorry for not reading! If you read more, perhaps you could write your letters yourself.' She looked at him, her eyes hard.

I knew Helen had gone too far; I knew before I saw on the prince's face that she had gone too far. There was a hint of mockery in her tone and he picked it up immediately. His face darkened.

Oh, why did she turn this hard heart of hers to the world when what was needed was softness? I didn't know.

Mr Waters said, 'You can't be expected to do all H.R.H. does and write silly letters to all those folk who want him to write to them.'

The prince looked ready to say something, but Mr Waters kept going. 'What we need to focus on is the tour and what it's about, and H.R.H. is the only one of us who's doing that properly.'

'Well said,' Dickie chimed in. 'Come on, David, let's get ourselves something to drink.'

The look on the prince's face was hard to read now. He didn't look angry, as I would have expected. If anything, he looked sad. Dickie stood and they walked off together. If I hadn't known he was the prince, I'd have said he was about to cry.

'I'm so sorry,' Helen said to Mr Waters after the prince and his cousin had gone. 'I just didn't think.'

'Well, you need to start thinking,' Mr Waters said, getting up to follow the prince and his cousin. 'Because I have enough on my plate without you upsetting him like that. You know what's happened with Freda.' He walked away.

༄

I found Helen on the main deck in one of the chairs, her legs curled up beneath her, looking at the moon reflected on the sea.

She had been crying, I was sure.

'I don't think Mr Waters meant to be harsh,' I said.

'Of course he didn't,' she said. 'It wouldn't even enter his head that it would bother me. But we can't possibly hurt David's feelings because that would be the end of the world.'

'The prince did look upset at what you said.'

'Yes, he did.' She sighed.

'And maybe it was a bit mean,' I said.

'He's a prince who doesn't read books. I don't think it's necessarily poor form to point that out.'

'He did seem more upset than it warranted. You only really told him he should read and, let's face it, he probably should if he's going to be King.'

She smiled weakly. 'Exactly. I think he thinks I find him inferior, and perhaps I do. He knows he's not Rupert. He's not Rupert's bootstrap. That's what really rankles him probably.'

'But he's so marvellous with the soldiers, with everyone.'

'Yes, but it's only half of the sky that is the Prince of Wales,' Helen said.

She sobbed then and it was such a heartfelt sob.

'Maddie, it's no use.'

'What's no use?'

'Rupert and me. It's too hard for us.'

'But he loves you, Helen. I know he does, and you love him.'

'Well, maybe he does, and maybe I do, but it won't be enough.'

'Because of the prince?'

'Yes, that, and what happened.'

'What did happen? He says he asked you to marry him and you refused.'

'He told you that?'

I nodded.

She sighed heavily. 'Could we just sit here together and watch the night?'

I nodded again, not daring to break her reverie, caring deeply for my friend and also hoping she might tell me more.

If I'd wanted to help Mr Waters and Helen, I'd have done well to study *Wuthering Heights* or *Jane Eyre* a bit more thoroughly, for love is never so simple as it is in penny romances.

Helen didn't tell me the truth that night. She didn't tell me until much later, and by then it was too late to help them, too late to help any of us.

TWENTY-THREE

Brisbane, 1981

I HADN'T SEEN ED IN NEARLY A WEEK, AND AFTER ANDREW left with the children I thought I should go and check on him. His father was away for a few days, and it wasn't like Ed not to visit me every day.

My leg had started aching again when the weather began to cool down for the autumn, and it twinged on the way down the stairs. I decided to first walk up to the top of Paddington to the post office to get some blood flowing.

When I got there I found a letter in the box from Mr Inglis, which was a matter for great excitement and so I forgot all about Ed.

Mr Inglis is the son of the Mr Inglis I met when Mr Barlow offered to publish *Autumn Leaves*. They are both gone now, Mr Barlow and old Mr Inglis, but young Mr Inglis, who seems very like his father, is now running the publishing house, he said. That's how many years I've been on the planet. The executives have changed generations.

I did meet old Mr Inglis once, although he wasn't old then. He was a tall slim fellow with a good head for figures, that last being something Mr Barlow told me about him when he met me to tell me they would publish the book. I haven't met the younger Mr Inglis. His letter is very polite. I don't know if he inherited his father's head for figures but he said something about royalty payments and a bank account. I hadn't realised that *Autumn Leaves* was still earning money for anyone.

I had told Mr Barlow everything, and he told me he would take my secret to his grave. I wouldn't have to talk to anyone about *Autumn Leaves*, he said. He would do that for me. He would look after everything. He was very kind.

The only thing Mr Barlow asked of me was that I write the next book, the book I told him I might write—the sequel, as he called it.

As far as I know, Mr Barlow kept his promise as he is now in his grave and there has been no scandal. Sometimes, in some small part of myself, I wish he had blabbed, or someone had. I wish there had been a scandal, especially now. It would make my writing task easier. Perhaps it would ease Helen's burden too.

The letter says young Mr Inglis is keen to see the manuscript and to meet me in person. He looks forward to publishing the 'long-awaited sequel' to *Autumn Leaves*. He's read the chapter I sent and he's very excited to see what became of that 'poor mother of the lost baby'.

I suppose my life has been a sequel of sorts.

Action–reaction: the first rule of physics.

Action–reaction: the first rule of life.

∽

The next morning, I telephoned Ed's house and no one answered, which was not unusual. But, by afternoon, I still hadn't heard from him or seen him and it was late and it's bin day tomorrow and he always takes my bin out the night before. I managed the bin myself, not wanting to bother Andrew Shaw when he rushed in to pick up the children, although it nearly carried me off down the driveway in its wake, heading for the car belonging to my terrible uphill neighbours, a Volvo they park all over the street and not in their own driveway, something about not wanting to run over the children. If they didn't want to run over the children, then they should look where they were going rather than park all over the street.

Proud I'd stopped the bin in its tracks, I walked across the road to Ed's house.

I knocked on the door. I noticed the front veranda was swept, work boots neatly under the eaves as if he was about to go to work at any given moment, which I knew was impossible.

No one answered the door after a few minutes and I could hear no voices within.

I called out.

No answer.

I went around the back and found the door open.

Inside, the little kitchen looked as if no one had ever used it. The cups and saucers were in a display cabinet above the bench. They were lined with dust but not as much dust as I might have expected. Someone had used them, or taken them down and dusted them.

Light came in through a curtain on the right. It was worn thin but looked clean.

I called Ed's name again and I thought I heard a noise like a throat clearing.

I walked down the hallway. I didn't even know which room was Ed's. The first door on the left was closed. I listened but heard nothing. I knocked on the next door. I heard the noise again, like someone trying to talk underwater, so I opened the door.

Ed was not in the bed. He was on the floor, with sheets wrapped around his legs and torso. He was wearing striped pyjamas and I could see his ankles, blue, and his manly hair through the open fly of the trousers. His face was a terrible colour, blue-grey, more grey than blue, and his eyes were glassy. I could smell the metallic smell of sickness in the room.

'Maddie,' he said, although he didn't quite get the word out.

I sat down on the floor beside him, felt his forehead which was hot. 'Don't talk,' I said. 'You're sick. I'm going to telephone the doctor and get you some water to clear your throat.'

Having gone to Ed without thinking, I hoped my leg would not fail me now as I attempted to get up from the floor.

He only nodded and closed his eyes.

Then I saw, shoved under the bed, the handkerchiefs, half-a-dozen of them, covered in blood.

I advised my legs to stand me up quick smart and run me to the telephone to call for the ambulance. They did not let me down.

TWENTY-FOUR

H.M.S. Renown, **Southern Ocean, 1920**

I WAS ON MY OWN IN THE OFFICE ON THE MAIN DECK ON our first full day at sea. Helen and the trip photographer were taking pictures of the admiral and officers for the official record. Dickie was with them as he was keeping the unofficial trip diary for the prince.

I had seen Helen briefly that morning and she seemed a little brighter. Hope, she said to me. 'Perhaps I still have a glimmer of stupid hope. Perhaps Rupert and I can overcome.'

She looked as if she might cry.

'You're right,' she said, although I hadn't spoken. 'There's no hope.'

'No,' I said. 'I'm sure Mr Waters will be different today. He's under enormous pressure with the tour. It's not you. I'm sure it's not.'

She made herself smile. 'Ned said to me this morning that he thinks I am the loveliest woman he's ever known.'

'Perhaps I should I tell Mr Waters,' I said. 'It might wake him up.' I tried a smile.

'No,' Helen said, tears threatening again. 'That's not what this is about, Maddie. And poor old Ned is not my type, I'm afraid. He doesn't . . . believe.'

I thought I knew what Helen meant. To me, Mr Waters was twice the man Colonel Grigg was. Mr Waters was loyal. His sense of duty was written into his bones. Colonel Grigg's loyalty was much harder to discern. Perhaps he reduced everything to its political meaning and manipulated it for political gain. Perhaps even Helen, if it came to it.

*

I was working away at the letters Mr Waters had asked me to draft—for his signature rather than the prince's—when the prince himself came in. He was smiling, his blond hair combed back, wearing gaiters over his pants and sporting shoes, as if he'd just been for a run around the deck.

'Mr Waters is with the admiral, sir,' I said.

'I know. I just left them after they took my picture. They're all being terribly sweet with me today. It's you I wanted to see.'

'Me, sir?'

'Maddie, I'm terribly sorry about last night, deserting the team and all. We were doing so well.'

'You were doing well, sir,' I said, deciding to ignore his apology, since I had no idea how to respond to it. 'Your Pain Air got *Jane Eyre* across better than my typhoid.'

'Is that what you were doing? I thought you were choking to death. I didn't know the book, as we later discovered.'

'Well, yes, but it really only affects a minor character and I will know next time that acting out typhus is not a recommended option for charades. You were the quicker thinker.'

'Was I?' He looked as if he meant the question.

'Yes, sir,' I said. 'You played the better game by far.'

'Well, thank you, you're very kind. Too kind, as it happens. But that's not why I came down. I apologise. I am doing my very best to behave as befits my office, but sometimes I hit a snag. I have a dear friend, Mrs Dudley Ward, whom you may have heard about.'

I didn't say anything.

'And my father is doing his best to stop our friendship out of some archaic view of propriety. As if I would ever act any way but honourably.' He looked angry.

'I don't believe you would, sir,' I said. I nearly added that Mr Waters had explained the nature of the prince's relationship with Mrs Dudley Ward, but I wasn't sure whether it was said in confidence so held my tongue.

'Well, I shouldn't have left last night without excusing myself, no matter what the circumstances. I am, after all, the Prince of Wales. I just . . . Sometimes it all gets too much. Do you know what I mean?'

'I'm afraid I don't, sir, although I imagine it would be very hard to have so many people wanting things from you.'

'Exactly,' he said. 'It is exactly that, and one needs to be more like one's father to really do well.'

'I don't know, sir. I think anyone as kind as you were towards those soldiers in Canberra and the ones in Sydney couldn't help but feel sad sometimes. It would have to affect you.'

'You think that? You really do?'

'Yes, sir, I do. And I don't know your father the King, sir, and I know it's very bad to say anything against him and I wouldn't do that, but I can't imagine he would ever be as kind as you were with those soldiers. I can't imagine anyone could do that as well as you do, sir.' I had tears in my eyes as I spoke, and I'm sure he noticed.

'Is that right?' he said, smiling tenderly.

'It is, sir, and—'

Just then Helen came in.

'Your Royal Highness,' she said. 'I am so—'

'Stop,' he said, smiling. 'Please. I am the one who's sorry, Helen. You are terribly good to me and put up with an awful lot. Don't think I don't know what you gave up to serve me. And yet I find myself unable to laugh at a joke that really was rather funny. I am sorry, Helen, and I will be a better little prince from here. And I may even learn to be book-read.'

Helen's face softened. 'No, sir. I was entirely in the wrong.'

'Well, perhaps you were,' he said, 'and if I were my father the King I might have your head chopped off. But as I am not,

I want to apologise for going off in the middle of a game I am sure Maddie and I were winning for our team.'

Helen smiled. 'Yes, you were,' she said. 'Typhus?' She looked at me and laughed.

'Well,' the prince said, 'I must get on to my laps for the day. Goody good.' And he was gone.

Later in the day, the weather calm, Mr Waters and I were working through the correspondence I'd drafted replies for and a few letters I was unsure about. There was a very difficult letter among them from a boy whose father had died in France and his mother had died since the war. The boy was twelve and the oldest. He had written and said the children were to be split up now and put in homes. He wanted them to stay together and wondered could the prince help. Mr Waters wasn't sure how we should respond to him either.

Mr Waters hadn't mentioned Helen again and I hadn't broached the subject with him, fearing the worst, that Helen was right and he really was angry with her. I felt he might be as Helen believed, inflexible, and once you'd done your dash with him, your dash might stay done, like Mummy's father who had cut off his own daughter.

'What to do?' Mr Waters said to me in relation to the letter. He sighed. 'It's clearly very difficult for this poor lad. Let's talk to H.R.H.'

The prince came down to the office mid-afternoon and Mr Waters told him about the boy's letter. 'Oh, that's terrible, Waters. Will we have the opportunity to meet him?'

'I don't think so, sir. He's from Melbourne. He brought his brother and sister in to see you when you arrived.'

'I want to find out how I can make a donation to their estate.'

'Yes, sir—though I'm not sure that there is an estate.'

'Well, find out what to do. I'm sure there's a way we can set up a trust that ensures they have food and lodgings until this boy reaches his majority. From my personal funds, mind, not the government's, or Grigg will tie it in knots and the boy will never see a penny.'

I was stunned by his generosity.

'Yes, sir,' Mr Waters said. 'The thing is, the boy is twelve. His majority is a decade away, sir.'

'Of course it is,' the prince said then. 'You're right. What are they to do? We can't let three children starve to death because of my family's war. We will not.'

After he left, Mr Waters looked at me, beaming with pride.

That same afternoon Dickie came down to ask Helen and me if we would care for a game of volleyball. 'It's officers against the prince's men,' Dickie said. 'Or me against David. Anyway, it would be awfully grand if the teams included girls.' He grinned. 'By order of H.R.H., I'm afraid.'

When we got up to the main deck, I saw they had rigged the net to run from the lifeboats to the main guns and drawn a court in chalk.

The prince smiled. 'I'll be Maddie's partner. Helen, you can have Dickie, which is a big advantage given his sporting prowess.'

'Ha!' Dickie said. 'Come on, Helen. Let's make short work of these two and then we can have a drink.'

Dickie served the ball to me, figuring I was the team's weakness, I'm sure. It was a long way back from the net and I had to turn and run but I knew I was closer than the prince. Still, I saw he looked as if he might try to return instead of me.

I yelled, 'Mine!' as I would with any other player, forgetting for a moment who he was. I hit the ball with my upturned wrists. I was still facing backwards and so didn't know if I'd got it over the net.

The first I knew of it the prince was clapping as his cousin had missed the return. 'Well landed, Maddie,' he said. He turned to me then and smiled. 'You are quite the extraordinary young woman, in more ways than one.'

'Sir,' Helen said then.

'Yes?'

'Are we playing volleyball?'

'Possibly,' he said, still looking at me.

And then we all stopped because the little wallaby Digger appeared at the top of the ladder to the lower decks and then hopped all the way across our court. I didn't know how he knew not to jump into the ocean.

The prince laughed. We all joined him.

The sun was low in the sky and the sea was burnished bronze and moving softly beneath us. I thought I would never be in a more beautiful place in life. The prince's face, ruddy with the sun, broke into that smile when he saw Digger. It lit up the entire world as far as I was concerned. I smiled back, so proud of myself right then.

He was still smiling as he served the ball. Before he moved to the other side of the court, he said quietly, so only I would hear, 'I want you on my team, Maddie, always.'

That smile of his, that boy's smile, would melt the hardest heart and my heart was anything but hard.

My heart was as soft as the down feathers on the crow outside my window, as soft as the eyes of Digger the Wallaby.

We are all doomed, probably.

∾

That night in bed, I wrote to Daddy.

> *Firstly, Prince Edward is nothing like you thought he might be. He is not a dandy or a flibbertigibbet. Mummy may actually be right about him. He is enormously kind to those who have little. Wherever we go, he makes a beeline for the injured soldiers and the grieving families, and he just listens to them. He seems to understand people's suffering and I think he takes it all onto his shoulders. I would say he feels terrible about the war and the suffering.*
>
> *The big news from me is that I have an idea for a story. Helen, who you met in Sydney (she was the one who worked for* Vanity Fair *and knows your poetry) knew Mr Waters during the war when he was injured in France and she was an ambulance driver in a hospital. They are like the heroes from*

a novel. He is like Mr Rochester, although she isn't as loyal as Jane Eyre for some reason, so might prove difficult to figure out. But she is heroic. I'm sure she is. I just need to get to the heart of the story to be sure.

I haven't started writing yet, and it may not go anywhere but I find myself liking Mr Waters and Helen immensely.

Anyway, I'm not sure I'll ever write it but it strikes me as a story people might actually want to read!

I hope you are feeling well, Daddy, and the boys are looking after you in my absence.
With all my love,
Maddie

The weather turned bad the next day and everyone was sick except Dickie and me who were more fish than human, as Dickie said. We had rough seas from around ten in the morning and we shut up the offices and spent our hours in the main deck lounge watching a fierce battle the ship fought to overcome the sea. The prince remained in his state room and then moved to Dickie's room because the motion bothered him less there, Dickie said.

In the night, I woke to hear a mighty groan of metal and then what sounded like a loud slap. I thought the ship had cracked in two. I rose from my bunk, put on a gown and left my cabin and went to the bridge. It was a difficult journey owing to the motion of the ship. I looked at the deck and saw no one was out there now. The ship was not in two pieces at least.

'What are you doing here, miss?' the first officer said to me when I came up the stairs to the bridge.

The admiral turned to me. 'Get her below, Ensign.' He looked angry.

'I thought we'd stopped,' I said.

'Green water on the deck, sir,' I heard one of the sailors say, his voice nervously loud.

The ensign took my arm to escort me from the bridge. 'The admiral ordered the engines cut,' he said quietly. Even the young ensign looked afraid. 'It's the only way we'll get through. But I'm sure we'll be all right now that he's on deck, miss.' He smiled weakly. 'Neptune wouldn't dare sink us while the admiral's awake and staring him down.' His eyes widened. 'Though even the admiral's not seen seas this big, he says.'

I told the ensign I could find my own way back down to the sleeping cabins.

The prince himself was coming up the stairs to the main deck as I was going down. He must have been woken by the noise too. 'Well, here's the weather,' he said, looking quite relaxed, if pale. He'd been sick all day, Dickie had told me. 'Don't worry, Maddie. The old salt won't let me drown. My father would bring up his body from the depths just so he could cut off his head.'

He kissed me on the cheek and smiled.

'Sir,' I said.

By the next morning, the sea was so calm you wouldn't believe the night before had happened. In the far distance, I could see the cliffs of the coast. I hadn't slept again until the weather settled at around four, and then I'd woken with the sun and found Mr Waters already at work in our office—Helen was there too with Colonel Grigg as water had got in and ruined the press office overnight.

Colonel Grigg looked up cheerily enough to greet me. 'Maddie, dear girl,' he said. It was the first time he'd addressed me since we'd set out.

Mr Waters and Helen had their heads down. They were like blocks of ice that would break if they came together. There seemed little hope they would ever resolve their differences. I still didn't even understand what the differences were.

Colonel Grigg stood suddenly. 'Helen, darling, we're supposed to be up on the bridge to help him with the weekly address,' he said. 'Quick.'

They left. Helen hadn't said a word.

'Are you quite all right, Mr Waters?' I asked after they were gone.

'Of course, Maddie,' he said. He looked anything but all right, his face grave.

'You don't look yourself, sir,' I said, genuinely concerned. 'I know it's none of my business but, Mr Waters, Helen didn't mean to hurt the prince's feelings.'

He looked confused for a moment, and then said, 'Oh, the other night. Of course she didn't. That's of no consequence.'

I nodded.

'The fact is, we can probably all celebrate.'

'Sir?'

'Helen. It's confidential at the moment, but Ned told me early this morning that he's proposed to Helen and she's accepted his proposal.'

'I beg pardon?' I think I said but Mr Waters didn't answer, just made his face smile and went back to whatever had been totally consuming his attention on his desk.

TWENTY-FIVE

Paris, 1997

ON THE WAY BACK TO THE CITY FROM THE AERODROME, Mark drove to the Pont de l'Alma tunnel on the right bank. The streets remained quiet. Only a few cars drove through, slowing at the site of the accident, whether out of respect or to see the damage, Victoria didn't know.

It was a part of Paris you wouldn't expect to find in Paris, all concrete and bitumen, softened only by the dozen or so bunches of flowers people had left on the roadway above. There were two lanes of traffic heading into the tunnel, with police at the entrance. Other than the flowers, there was nothing to communicate anything gentle or beautiful; nothing of Diana at any stage of her life here, except its ending. Nothing would warn you it was dangerous.

Mark drove through, pointing out the concrete pillar the car had hit, the site of impact hardly discernible. 'Over a hundred kilometres an hour, six feet of concrete. Not a chance,' he said. He turned around and drove back through the other way.

He parked in an alley and they walked back to the end of the tunnel.

Mark went to get some shots. Victoria walked down further and peered into the mouth of the tunnel. The walls were lined with once-white tiles, now greyed with exhaust fumes.

As she walked back out, she saw a copy of *The Sunday Journal* on the ground with the photo she'd seen weeks ago, a haunted Diana, those big kohl-rimmed eyes in that narrow face, looking as if she knew what was coming.

Victoria was standing on the bank outside the tunnel, watching the cars. She moved back further. It was a cool night, the earlier rain cleared. Looking up, she saw there, peeking up above the trees, the Eiffel Tower.

Had she looked up and seen it? Victoria wondered. After the crash, had she known she wouldn't live? Was she thinking of the two boys, longing for just one more moment with them? She was with strangers. She died with strangers, as alone, ultimately, as she'd ever been.

Victoria found tears in her eyes again. If she indulged them, she thought, they would never stop.

∽

When she checked in at the hotel, the receptionist gave her messages. Claire and Ewan had phoned.

From her room—hardly space for a bed and tiny shower, but redeemed altogether by what she knew would be a view over slate tile roofs to the Luxembourg Gardens in the morning—she called Ewan first. 'The vigil at the palace is getting bigger,' he said. 'There's been nothing from the family, though. Nothing at all after the first statement.' Ewan sounded a bit lost.

'Charles was here.'

'I know, but he hasn't said anything. And there's been nothing from the Queen. You know what they did?'

'No.'

'Sunday. Balmoral. They went to church.'

'Well, it's what they'd do.'

'The rector didn't mention Diana, Danny said. He got a couple of shots of the boys. You'd think nothing had happened.'

Victoria felt queasy suddenly. The boys. They were photographing them. '*The Guardian*'s blaming the tabloids.'

'Everyone's blaming the tabloids,' Ewan said. 'Even the tabloids. But Harry says there's no flag at half-mast at Buckingham Palace. Actually, there's no flag at Buckingham Palace at all, because the Queen's not there. But he's going to run a story as tomorrow's lead. I don't think it's a good time to do them over, but his instincts with them are better.'

'Yeah, I guess.'

'What do you think?'

'I just . . . I just think it's all a bit sick now.'

'It wasn't us, Victoria. No one could have predicted this.'

'I went with Mark. To the place.'

'What was it like?'

She looked out into the Paris night. 'It was like nothing, in a way. There are flowers. The thing is, I don't want to write any of it. I don't feel objective. I can't be objective,' she said.

'You're seeing everything. Just write that. Write what you're seeing. It will be enough.'

'Will it?'

'Yes,' he said.

Victoria wasn't so sure.

After she got off the phone and had a shower, it was nine pm. She sat down to write, hopeful as always that the words would come and form themselves together to mean something.

❧

When she looked up from her laptop screen, it was after midnight. She had written and edited, written and edited, and the time had flown. She didn't want to read it over again. Her writing was changing, she knew, and she didn't seem to be able to stop it happening. She had no idea if it was any good anymore.

She stood in the mirror sideways and looked at her belly. Other than the test results, you'd never know she was pregnant. She was queasy, it was true, and nervous, perhaps more emotional, and no period, but other than those things, which could all be placebo effect, she was exactly the same. Perhaps she wasn't pregnant, she thought then. She'd get another test when she returned to London.

Ben would still be on set in Bath. They were filming the night scenes there. He was staying overnight, he'd told her. If she was back tomorrow from Paris before he arrived home, he wouldn't even know she'd gone, except Ewan had told him. He hadn't called all day. Normally, he would have. He was angry, she assumed—angry that she'd gone at all, and now, as he'd see it, perfectly righteously angry because she hadn't told him.

She filed the story she'd written for *The Eye* with Ewan rather than the subs desk, hoping he was still awake to read it.

She called Ben's cell and left a message. 'I had to travel after the news today. Talk soon. Love you.'

He called back a minute later—between takes, he said. 'What did you want?' he said. His tone was curt. She was right. He was angry.

'I'm in Paris.' She was lying on the bed in a t-shirt and her underpants. She looked at her belly and felt like crying. She bit her lip.

'Princess Diana?' he said. He didn't mention the call with Ewan.

She felt her shoulders hunch around her ears. 'Yes,' she said. 'They want me to cover it.'

'Okay,' he said, although his tone suggested it was anything but.

'I am sorry, Ben. Last night, today, not calling. I don't know what's wrong with me.'

'Okay. I'm sorry too.' His tone softened. 'Marriage is a big change for anyone but this is even harder.'

'In what way?' In truth, she'd been wondering the same thing. She loved him, didn't she? He was everything she wasn't: brave, larger than life, funny. She loved him. Didn't she?

'Because of me and what I do. I'm used to it, but I forget that you're not. I'm going to do something about it.'

'What do you mean?'

'I'm meeting with Cal tomorrow.' Cal was his lawyer. He must be flying Cal over from New York.

What could a lawyer do? Even Ben had said the press were free to do what they liked.

'Okay,' she said, not wanting to argue again. 'I don't know when I'll be back, but I'll call in the morning. I should know more by then.'

'You don't need to do this, you know,' Ben said.

Back to not working again, she thought. 'Yes, I know,' she said, deciding to pretend he meant go to Paris rather than work as a journalist. 'But this came up.'

'Did they have to send you?'

'Yes,' she said. 'I'm the one they wanted to send.'

'Did you want to go?'

She hesitated. 'Yes, I did.'

He laughed, a small laugh. 'Well, at least you're honest. What can I say, Victoria? Come home soon as you can. We'll talk . . .' She heard a voice in the background, a woman. 'Gotta go.' The line went dead.

'If you beat me home, don't forget to feed Martha,' she said to the empty line.

He'd hung up on her. He was still angry for going away and not telling him, she thought.

She should have told him. He was right. She'd deceived him and it was wrong. She wasn't normal. He was.

Her phone rang then. 'I'm sorry,' she said.

'Why? What did you do?' It was Claire's voice.

'I thought you were Ben.'

'I figured. What did you do?'

'Nothing.'

'Well, I'm the one who's sorry. About this morning. Are you all right?'

'I'm in Paris.'

'How is it?'

'I just filed for tomorrow. Hardest job I've ever done.'

'I know. It's awful,' Claire said. 'She was just so alive, so real.' Claire was teary by the sound of her voice. 'It's a terrible shock.'

'I've been thinking of that story I wrote. Did it turn everyone against them?' Victoria said.

'No,' Claire said. 'Don't be daft. It was generous to both of them. You write about goodness.'

'Do I?'

'Well, yes, sort of. It's easy to make a living out of being mean. It's much harder to make a living out of being nice.'

'I don't want to be nice.'

'Well, what do you want?'

'I don't know. Truth?'

'So what are you going to write for the magazine?' Claire asked.

'I have no idea. There was a picture.'
'After?'
'Yes.'
'Jesus.'
'I know. No one's run it yet, but they will.'
'Harry would.'
'He doesn't know.'
'Thank God. Although, really, it hardly matters.'
'I had a fight with Ben just before you called.'
'I figured that too. Victoria, about today . . .'
'Please don't worry. I'm just all over the place,' Victoria said. She'd sat up and was looking at herself in the mirror again, her face now. She looked afraid, she realised. She looked terrified.

'I am a bit worried.'

'I saw her body,' Victoria said. 'The coffin, I mean.'

'About you. I'm worried about you. Are you all right?'

'I am. I really am, Claire. It's just nerves and all the changes and then Diana.'

'Why don't we have a coffee when you get back tomorrow?' Claire said.

'Of course. But I don't know when that will be.'

'Well, let me know, and we'll meet. I need to talk to you about something.'

'Are *you* okay?' Victoria had been so preoccupied by her own problems she hadn't even thought there might be something wrong with Claire.

'I'm fine, but I need to speak with you.'

~

Ewan phoned her at six am. She woke from a dream, afraid, saliva running out the side of her mouth onto the pillow, dry lips, sick in her stomach.

'Harry was right about the family,' Ewan said. 'The mood is definitely turning against them. There's a big to-do.'

'Who with?'

'Everyone really. The P.M.'s on it.'

'Daddy said yesterday Alastair had been sniffing for a phrase or something.'

'Well, he found it. She's the people's princess now. Blair made a statement late yesterday. Off the record, Alastair told me Tony's going to talk to the Queen, tell her to come home. *He's* going to tell *her* to come home,' Ewan said.

'It can't be easy on them. Did you get the piece I wrote?'

'Yes,' he said. 'It will run tomorrow.'

'Was it all right?'

'It was beautiful,' he said. Beautiful was not a Ewan word. 'Very moving. I wanted it for the leader, but Harry said it didn't catch the mood. People are really angry at the family.'

'I guess,' she said. 'I'm not though.'

'No. But Newswriting 101.'

'Find the conflict,' she recited, adding, 'Maybe conflict is overrated.'

'Maybe. Sells papers but.'

'I saw her coffin.'

'Mark got a shot.'

'That's not what I meant.'

'I know.'

'It felt like I was writing the truth, Ewan.'

'You are,' he said. 'But Harry isn't. And, increasingly, truth's not the job.'

TWENTY-SIX

Brisbane, 1981

I COULD HEAR DOGS BARKING AT ONE ANOTHER, AND IT put me on edge. I got out of bed and came out here and put the television on.

Diana Spencer has gone into hiding.

'Good girl,' I crowed when I heard that. 'Perhaps you're more wily than you look. Perhaps you'll hide for the rest of your life.'

It's possible she's come to Australia, they said; one of her sisters lives here. I hope she has. I hope she comes to visit me.

I heard the possums scurrying along the roof at great speed, and then a different sound, their little feet on the ceiling plaster. They're coming home.

I rang the hospital. No change, the nurse on the ward said. Is there someone who can come and sit with you, dear? she asked.

He's not my husband, I said.

No, she said. I know. But is there anyone?

I called Andrew Shaw then because I didn't know what else to do.

'Are you working today?' I asked.

'Who's this?' he said, more confused than annoyed.

'It's Maddie Bright.'

'Maddie?' he said, his voice still waking up. He sounded like a little boy right then.

'Are you coming over today?'

'Is something wrong?'

I might have sobbed. A noise came from me and I was not quite in control.

'I'm on the way,' he said. 'Can I bring Frank and Sally?'

'That would be lovely,' I said.

After I got off the telephone, I went out to put the kettle on. I could hear the kookaburras starting up. There's a group of them living in the gums at the top of the rise. They laugh at me every single day. I suppose they laugh at all of us. We are so terribly funny. Imagine their view of us from high in a tree, running around below them like giant ants. Perhaps they have sayings. They might call each other human-brain, and say, 'You're off with the humans today.'

Wouldn't that be a nice thing?

When Andrew arrived, I had already had a cup of tea, which brought what comfort it could. I poured him one, put his three sugars in.

'Ed,' he said, having settled the children in front of the television and some terrible cartoon whose central character appeared to be a bat.

'There's no change,' I said.

'No,' he said softly. 'No.' He drank his tea, looked as if he was about to say something, then didn't. He sat forward, looking at me.

'I lost everyone,' I said.

'I assumed,' he said.

'It's not that I haven't been happy. I have. But I lost everyone.'

He nodded.

'My father killed himself after the war. He couldn't find a way home.' I realised I was nodding. 'I wasn't there. I was . . . I wasn't there.'

Andrew Shaw put his hand over mine on the table. There were tears in his eyes and I appreciated the fact he would cry for me, or for my father, who had so much he never got to give. Writing, teaching. All lost with him.

Andrew Shaw told me then that he was very sorry, but he had some news he needed to tell me. He was so gentle I knew what he was about to say.

'It's Ed,' he said. 'Ed has cancer, Maddie. I think that doctor yesterday must have thought I was related to him. He took me outside to tell me. I think they thought you were too frail to hear it.'

'Ed didn't tell me.'

'It's possible he doesn't know.'

'Can we go and see him again today?'
'Of course. I'll take you up there and wait with the kids.'
'I knew,' I said. 'Everyone dies.'

※

We were leaving the house to go to the hospital. Frank and Sally were already in the car. I was dressed now and I took a cardigan so I could stay the day with Ed.

Frank and Sally were waving like maniacs at me from down in the car. I was so glad Andrew had brought them. Hope, that's what children are.

'Just . . .' I said, stopping before locking the door.

Andrew was beside me.

'I lost everyone.'

'I know,' he said, patting my hand which was still holding the key in the lock.

'My father,' I said.

He nodded, didn't say anything.

'The war. It was just too much.'

I saw the bird then, the baby crow who was fledging in my yard.

'Not Ed, though. Ed's been a constant.'

'He has,' Andrew Shaw said. 'He's been a good friend.'

'Did they say how long?'

'He's not coming home, Maddie. That's what they said.'

'I see. I lost everyone.'

'You did,' he said.

'We should tell his father.'

'Yes,' he said. 'Let me do that.'
'My father fought in the war.'
'Which war?'
'First.'
At the bottom of the stairs, I stopped again and sat down.
'There's more I have to tell you,' I said.
He sat down beside me.
'I don't think I can be forgiven.'

TWENTY-SEVEN

Perth, 1920

WE ARRIVED IN THE CITY OF PERTH EARLY IN THE morning after six days at sea. We'd taken a train from Albany where the ship had anchored the evening before. It was raining for our arrival in Albany and there had been showers on and off through the night during the journey north.

It was a relief to be on solid ground, although my legs still felt wobbly on and off that first day. The planned levée where the prince could meet people in Perth was moved into the station foyer due to the weather and, when I came onto the platform, I noticed the prince had been accosted by the governor and his wife, a portly, stern-looking woman who might have taken the prince to her bosom and embraced him given a chance. They had chased him down and caught him when he'd stopped to talk to a group of soldiers. As the prince shook their hands, he looked weary. There was none of the boy on the ship about him now. His face was glum. There had been no spider letters in the mail waiting for us in Albany. Mr Waters said it had left the prince very low.

I had spoken to Helen briefly before we left the ship while we were packing to leave.

'Mr Waters told me Ned has asked you to marry him and you've accepted him,' I said, incredulous.

'Yes,' she said. 'What of it?' She looked up at me and she was the hard-hearted Helen now.

'Why?'

She looked lost suddenly. She sighed. 'Maddie, I went to try to talk to Rupert like you suggested. If I were different, perhaps we'd have had a chance, or if he were less like himself, less loyal, less bloody convinced about David, perhaps we'd have overcome our circumstances. But that's all water under the bridge now.'

'But Colonel Grigg!' I said. 'You said yourself he doesn't believe in anything.'

'He's safe,' she said. 'I want to be safe.'

'And Mr Waters is not?'

'Maddie, you have to stop all this,' she said. 'I know you think it's simple. But you don't know anything.'

'I know two things,' I said. 'Colonel Grigg isn't Mr Waters and Mr Waters is who you love.'

What on earth was wrong with Helen? I thought. And how did Colonel Grigg in a million years conclude that she was interested in him? She just wasn't, and anyone could see it!

Except Colonel Grigg, who couldn't see beyond his own nose, and Mr Waters, who may as well have been wearing blinkers.

∽

There were no spider letters waiting in Perth and now it was clear that F.D.W. was going to stick to the plan to end her friendship with the prince. For his part the prince had written twenty-three letters on our six-day journey.

I was in the office set up at Government House with Mr Waters at lunchtime when the prince himself came in after the official reception in the town hall. Our office was much like the one in Sydney, although it was in a separate building from the main house, a cottage that was usually a guest cottage for the governor that had been converted into offices for the tour. We'd already set ourselves up and I was busy attending to letters for Mr Waters.

'That bastard Halsey has contacted the King about the India trip,' the prince said. 'He makes me sound weak. I'm in for it now, Waters. You know what my father will be like.'

'I don't think the admiral meant any harm, sir,' Mr Waters said. 'In fact, I'm sure of it. What he said to me was that no human being could endure what you'd endured and not feel it. I'm sure that's how he'll have put it to His Majesty too. It might be for the best.'

Whether or not the admiral had put the message to the King in the way Mr Waters suggested, the King blamed the prince. BE STRONG STOP YOU ARE POW STOP ENDS was the wire.

The prince had it in his hand. I already knew what it said as Mr Waters had told me when he first came in. He'd looked quite worried and had said we should focus on the job at hand today and try our best.

It was the governor himself who handed the telegram to the prince, the prince told Mr Waters now. 'How could my father do that, embarrass me in front of that buffoon? I have done so well. How could he, Rupert?'

Mr Waters had stood up and was leading him out of the office to go back to the main house. 'Let's go and talk to Godfrey,' he said. 'I'm sure His Majesty is trying to help. Godfrey will know what to do.'

The prince shook him off. 'Grigg tells me you wrote to your father, Waters. Did you?'

'I beg pardon, sir?'

'I said, did you write to your father?' He stressed each word.

'Well, yes, but not about the India tour.'

'You told him I'm struggling, didn't you?'

'I may have said the tour was asking too much. That's all.'

'Ned said Lloyd George told him that the King has it on very good authority from one of his men that I'm not stable. Was that your father?'

'No, sir. I don't believe he would—'

'Oh, forget it, Waters. I'm just sick of the whole fucking lot of you.'

He left.

༄

When Helen came over to the office, she wanted to know where Colonel Grigg was. 'I don't know,' Mr Waters said. 'Will you two be making an announcement soon?'

He said it coldly, as if he didn't care.

'I don't know,' she said, just as coldly. 'Ned wants to wait until we're back in Sydney so that Godfrey can tell the King. I said you could do that.'

It was as if they were daring one another not to care.

'Of course,' Mr Waters said. 'I'll send a wire today.'

'Let Ned decide,' Helen said. 'It's up to him really, not you.'

༄

Despite the frayed tempers and misunderstandings among the humans everywhere you looked, Western Australia was immensely beautiful. The Swan River had a sandy bank unlike the river in Brisbane with its mud, and so it was like being at the seaside. Although the rain had continued through our first day, it cleared briefly in the afternoon and I walked across to the riverbank and watched swans among rowing boats.

Here, I thought, here is beauty, and we humans do our very best to make it ugly.

༄

It was early evening when the prince came back across to the office. He had been to a second function in the afternoon, another levée where awardees were presented to him. Mr Waters was hurrying behind him. I heard their conversation. 'They are doing their best, David, and I know it wasn't what you'd hoped.'

The prince turned around, forcing Mr Waters to stop suddenly. 'They are not doing their best.' He said each word slowly, enunciating every syllable. 'We said *people*. We said I want to meet with *people*. Instead they gave me a blasted luncheon with that awful woman and then an endless droning list of idiots I did not wish to meet.'

I wasn't sure who the awful woman was.

Mr Waters glanced at me then said, 'Let's keep going and talk in your private office, sir.'

'What's tonight?' the prince asked, not moving.

'The ball, sir, here at the house.'

'Oh fuck, Rupert,' he said.

Mr Waters looked at me as if to apologise for the prince's language. With five brothers, I'd heard the word, and others besides, I didn't say.

The prince went on, still exercised. 'If it's a ball, the governor and his stupid wife are going to be there. She judges me. I swear she judges me. And they'll want me to dance with their daughter.'

'David,' Mr Waters said, 'it's not that hard to dance. We've done much harder things, sir.'

The prince laughed then. 'I'm not sure of that,' he said. 'I think this is worse than the war.'

He looked at me, cocked his head a little. 'You must come, of course,' he said.

I was so surprised I turned to look behind me to see who he might be addressing. Helen was there. Her eyes were not on the prince. They were on Mr Waters.

'Sir,' Mr Waters said then, 'poor Maddie has enough to do keeping up with the mail.'

I was nodding furiously, agreeing with Mr Waters, not daring to speak for fear I'd say something stupid.

Mr Waters continued: 'I'm sure—'

'I don't care,' the prince snapped at Mr Waters. 'I want her there. Will you? Would you like to come with us to the ball?' he said to me again.

'Well, sir, I do have a lot to do here.'

Mr Waters said, 'Yes, she does and, David, we'll never hear the end of it if we change the arrangements. Remember Sydney and Miss Little. They'll have tables organised—'

'Well, they can reorganise them. You don't have to work, Maddie. Surely you can have one night off for some dancing. Is Mr Waters such a bear?'

'I don't dance,' I said truthfully.

He laughed again. 'Well, that settles it. Dickie and I will teach you. Dickie, believe it or not, is an excellent teacher, although I am the better dancer.'

I saw Mr Waters look towards Helen, who was glaring at him. He looked away. 'Very well,' he said. 'I'll send word. But, sir, there are only so many times—'

'I know,' the prince said, his eyes hardening as he looked at Mr Waters. 'But this is one of them. Because, Rupert, I asked you to make sure I never had to put up with that woman again and she will be there tonight. Am I correct?'

'Well, she's the wife of the governor, sir, and it's his house.' Mr Waters looked around as if the governor might be listening right then. 'It's difficult to see how she can be kept away from the ball that's been organised to welcome you officially. We've cancelled the second dinner and arranged to hold one of the dances in Bunbury, where they won't accompany us.'

'And I asked you to fix India and instead you have my father dressing me down once again.'

'I am sorry,' Mr Waters said. His tone was curt. It was as close as I had heard him be short with the prince.

The prince didn't notice or didn't care. 'Helen, you'll have to lend Maddie something to wear. It will be a relief to have you two in my sights instead of those bloody women. Thank you,' he said to me, although in truth I didn't think I'd done anything but agree to come to a dance. And, really, I hadn't even done that.

To Mr Waters he said, 'Maddie can walk in with Dickie. Helen, can you come now and help me with my remarks?'

'Of course, sir,' she said. She shook her head at Mr Waters as she passed him, as if he'd done something wrong.

'I can't go to the ball,' I said to Mr Waters after they left.

'Leave it with me,' he said. 'This is more about his friend, Mrs Dudley Ward. She doesn't want . . . She's not writing to him and it's unsettled him.' He picked up the telegram the prince had left on his desk that morning and put it down again without looking at it. 'But you might have to go.'

'I don't have anything to wear.'

'We'll find something. Helen will have dresses.'

I laughed then. 'I've worn just about everything Helen owns, I believe.'

'Government House might have something then. Really, Maddie, it's the least of my worries right now.'

'Of course,' I said.

∽

Helen came to my room after dinner.

'I just can't believe it,' she said. 'Rupert should have done something about this, and he hasn't. Of course he hasn't. You'll have to come to the ball. But Maddie, darling, stay close to me. Do you understand? And if there's late night dancing, just say no, you're too tired.'

'All right,' I said absently. I wasn't really listening. I was too excited. The Prince of Wales had asked me, Maddie Bright, a nobody from nowhere, to a ball. He preferred my company to that of a governor and his wife. I couldn't believe it.

'Just make sure you keep your wits about you,' she said then. 'Tea. Think tea.'

I laughed. 'Helen, you're not really going to marry Ned, are you?'

'Why not?' she said. 'He loves me, and he says he does.'

'It's settling for less than you deserve.'

She smiled unkindly. 'As if you'd know.'

I felt the sting of it.

'Just stay with me tonight, all right?' she said.

'Yes, of course,' I said.

We went to Helen's room then to get dressed. She wore her cream silk dress and I wore a red one of hers and my own black slippers.

I told her how angry the prince had been, especially towards Mr Waters. 'Maybe it's the lack of letters,' I said.

'Rupert puts up with it,' Helen said.

'He doesn't have a choice.'

'We always have a choice,' Helen said. 'Always. His every waking moment is a choice.'

I stopped Helen at the top of the stairs. 'You can't have it both ways.'

'What do you mean?'

'You can't say I love Rupert but Rupert doesn't love me and then, when he asks for your hand, say no and then say yes to someone else.'

'Why can't I?'

'It doesn't make sense.'

'So? In my experience, most of life doesn't make sense.'

Downstairs the prince and Dickie were waiting in the lounge given over to our visit. When Mr Waters came in, he just stared at Helen. The look on his face! Helen was beautiful, and he loved her. Oh, I thought. He was so dear to me. I wished Helen had some jolly sense.

Colonel Grigg came in then and Mr Waters looked away from Helen. The colonel smiled over at Helen and while she returned his smile, I knew her well enough to know there was no love there. She loved Mr Waters. Oh, you fool! I wanted to say.

Dickie, in tails, said Helen and I were two-thirds of a Union Jack. 'Just a picture,' he said. He was smoking a cigarette. 'Aren't they, David? If only there was a blue one, we'd have all the colours covered.'

The prince laughed. 'Oh yes, Dickie, but Helen here is too old for you, and Maddie is beyond your brains, I think. You'll have to make do with the governor's daughter.'

'What about me?' Colonel Grigg said in a baby voice.

'You're the help,' the prince said. 'Like Rupert. You do what you're told.'

Colonel Grigg looked miffed. Mr Waters hardly registered. He'd been standing apart from the group, his hands in his pockets. He was so handsome in his tails. So handsome, and utterly undone, I knew.

'Well, at least tonight we'll have the ship's band and not the local fellows,' the prince said. 'Eh, Rupert?'

Mr Waters smiled. The prince seemed in better spirits and I was relieved.

The steward came in then and the prince went off to meet the officials, and so Helen and I were escorted into the ballroom by Dickie. The walls were papered in a soft green that set off the gleaming polished boards of dark timber. The tables, covered in ivory cloths, each had a centrepiece of native flowers, kangaroo paw and Geraldton wax. There were no streamers or flags, and no balloons. It was simple and elegant, just as the prince always preferred.

'Well, this is lovely,' I heard the prince tell the governor as I came in. He caught sight of me. 'And may I present Miss Madeleine Bright from my staff.'

'Charmed, I'm sure,' the governor said. But he hardly noticed me. I'm sure he knew that underneath my red silk there was nothing but a serving girl who couldn't serve him in any way, and so he ignored me.

Thinking of that night now, I might still recall the prince's beauty, his shining blond hair combed back, his eyes of that blue born only of blue-eyed parents, like a double dose, so light and piercing. And because I was in his orbit, I saw first-hand what it was like to have all the other planets spinning around you. It was exciting and exhilarating and a little bit dangerous.

I didn't know the tunes, and I certainly didn't know the dance steps, but Helen danced with the prince while I took lessons from Dickie, and then we swapped. I didn't know the prince was expected to dance with girls who'd come along expressly to dance with him. I hardly knew what to wear to a ball, let alone the protocol for an official ball such as this one.

I was dancing with the prince, and I'd managed the steps well. He turned me around at arm's length then pulled me close. I was sure I saw fondness in his eyes. He was fond of me. That's why he'd asked me to the dance, why he'd insisted, why he danced with me now.

And I was fond of him too.

'Let's get out of here,' he said in my ear, so close I could feel his breath and it gave me a thrill.

I looked around. Dickie had gone to get a drink. I couldn't see Helen or Mr Waters. 'Sir, I don't think you can. Everyone is watching you.'

'Hmm,' he said. 'We'll go out to the terrace. At least there I won't have to look at that awful woman.' He spoke loudly enough for those around us to hear, and I worried about what they'd think. I did as he asked.

He led me out to the terrace, which looked over the gardens, lamps illuminating flowers and trees. During the day, it had a lovely view over the river. I could still hear the band, louder each time the doors were opened. It was a fine, cold night. The perfume of flowers wafted up.

There were other people out on the terrace, but I noticed he didn't look towards them as we went over to the edge. He kept his eyes on the horizon, as if they wouldn't know who he was. Imagine that, I thought, not being able to go anywhere without people noticing you.

'Well, Maddie, a little escape,' he said, taking a cigarette from his case and offering me one. I shook my head.

'Do you know where Mr Waters is?' I said.

I felt nervous being out here alone with Prince Edward.

'I sent him upstairs to get my drumsticks,' he said. 'I'm going to play with the band tonight if it kills me. I'm not sure Newdigate squared will approve.' The governor's name was Newdigate Newdegate. Mr Waters had made a comment about it when we first arrived.

The prince sighed heavily. 'It's nearly over.'

'What is, sir?'

'For God's sake, call me David!' he said.

I must have looked frightened for he said more softly, 'We've been dancing with one another all night. I am not your sir.'

'All right,' I said. 'What's nearly over, David?'

'All of this.'

I could smell the tobacco smoke now and the rosemary down in the gardens.

He smiled ruefully. 'Oh, Maddie, I don't expect you have any idea what this is like.'

'No, I'm afraid I don't.'

He sighed. 'It's almost impossible to explain. I hate my life. I *hate* it.' He stopped abruptly and took a deep breath. 'Listen to me, telling you all this. I shouldn't, you know.'

'But why are you so angry with Mr Waters? He's so loyal and he works so hard for you.'

'Yes, well, Rupert is supposed to be my man. That's his job. But they are all such meddlers really. And we just want to have fun, don't we, Maddie?' He smiled then. 'Why am I going on and on about all this boring nonsense? You are a beautiful girl. A very beautiful girl.' And he leaned in and kissed me on the lips.

My heart was racing. The touch of his lips on mine had stirred something in me that I didn't fully understand. 'Sir . . .' I began. 'David . . .'

But I didn't finish the sentence because he leaned in and kissed me again, full on the mouth this time. He pulled back, slid his eyes left and right.

All at once I realised where we were, who he was. I looked around, worried about who might have seen us. What was I thinking, kissing the Prince of Wales in full view? The couples around us were not staring, thankfully. I don't know how they missed it. For me, it was as if an explosion had gone off right next to me.

Then I saw, on the other side of the terrace, Mr Murdoch from the newspapers—and he was looking straight at me.

'Oh, Maddie,' the prince said. 'My little Maddie. You must be the most beautiful woman I have ever seen.'

'Sir,' I said. 'I'm not sure . . .'

Just then I heard Helen's voice. 'Maddie!' she called as she came over. 'Here you are!' She hurried over to join us. 'David, what are you doing bringing the young staff out onto the terrace? They're all asking for you in there.'

'Where's Dickie?' he asked, smiling down at Helen.

She made a gesture to indicate drinking. 'They've taken him upstairs.'

'That was fast,' the prince said. 'He usually waits until I start playing with the band.'

'Not tonight. You are going to have to talk to him again, I suspect. Are you all right, Maddie?' She looked at me.

'Yes, just flushed from the dancing,' I said. 'It's lovely to be out here in the cool air.'

I looked over to where Mr Murdoch was standing, but he'd gone.

'Quite,' the prince said, looking at me slyly. 'So stuffy in there a body might suffocate without knowing.' He dropped his cigarette to the tiles and ground it into the grout with his shoe. 'Must I?'

'You must,' she said. 'Or I'll tell Rupert.'

'Please don't, Helen. He'll tick me off, and I've already been ticked off for dancing too much with you and Maddie. But really, what does he expect? That I'll dance with the daughter? No, thank you. Give me my people any day. Anyway, Maddie can actually move. Not like skinny boots.'

I laughed, for it was a funny description of the governor's daughter, who was very slim and wore a pair of red sparkly boots under her ball gown.

Helen looked at me and I stopped smiling. She started to say something, looked at the prince and back at me, then closed her mouth again.

TWENTY-EIGHT

London, 1997

VICTORIA CAUGHT A CAB STRAIGHT TO HER FATHER'S house in Twickenham from Heathrow. She had an odd feeling of unsafety, and she wanted to be near him. Not that she would tell him she was feeling that way, but she was unsettled still and couldn't understand why. She wanted to be with her father at home.

In the cab, she wondered if she might ask him about Ben, but she wasn't even sure what it was she needed to ask. She might have been able to ask her grandmother what to do, she thought, but not her father, not really.

Victoria had always felt she'd been a disappointment to her father. She'd left *The Guardian*, and now she wrote celebrity profiles. She was about to be married to a film star who made zombie movies. It probably wasn't what he'd hoped for. How could she tell him that, even in this, she was somehow losing her footing?

When the cab pulled up outside the house, Victoria felt sadness, deep in her chest. Diana. At first she thought of Diana. There were no tears, just this ache in her chest. The feeling became more intense.

Oh God, she wanted her mother back right then.

∾

Victoria had been eleven, nearly twelve, boarding at Marlborough, when her grandparents turned up one morning in the middle of term. They must have driven through the night to get there from Craster, although they didn't say that and Victoria wasn't old enough to think about things like distances.

She'd been called out of breakfast in the dining room. 'Take some toast,' her dormitory supervisor had said, although you weren't allowed to take food out of the dining room.

And then her grandfather was waiting for her in the headmaster's office, his face grave. 'Princess,' he said, smiling too brightly as soon as he saw her. 'We're off to London and you are coming with us.'

'Why?' she'd said, holding on to the toast.

'A whim,' he said, smiling still.

He held her hand too tightly on the way to the car where her grandmother was waiting.

They took her straight to the hospital, not to home.

Victoria still remembered her father in the waiting room. He was slouched in a chair staring out at the London morning. He stood when they entered the room, and she saw he was wearing his big old sweater, the one with a moth hole in the front, and his khaki work pants, not his suit.

'Mummy's gone,' he said, and his face crumpled, although there were no tears. He pulled her into a rare hug, wouldn't let go, even when she squirmed.

'Daddy, you're hurting me,' she'd said.

She couldn't make sense of what he was saying. She wasn't sure where her mother had gone. It was her father she was most worried about. He should be wearing his suit, his overcoat. Why was he wearing his work clothes?

'Daddy?' she said.

Her mother had told her about the knee surgery on the phone the weekend just gone. It was minor, and she would be home the same day, 'so don't worry, darling.' Victoria was eleven. Of course she didn't worry.

It was the anaesthetic, her father said. But it was weeks before Victoria understood. Her grandmother kept saying her mother was sleeping. And that's what she thought. At the funeral, the priest too had talked of sleep. Her mother was asleep, and she would wake up.

After the funeral, her father didn't speak of her mother. The next time he left the house he had his suit on again.

Over time, Victoria found herself unable to raise the subject of her mother's death. When she was young, she had thought him heartless, but as she grew older she saw the tenderness underneath, the tenderness he couldn't quite reach in himself. It didn't mean it wasn't there.

He was of his generation, she told herself in her teens, when she wanted to hear stories about her mother, in her early twenties when she wanted to know about men, in her thirties when she wondered if she'd have children. Her father wasn't able to talk about his feelings and, when he was deluged by grief, he cauterised his heart rather than try. He was affectionate, up to a point, and kind, but he wasn't really present. He was Joyce's Mr Duffy, living his life a short distance from himself.

Sometimes, she'd look up from reading and catch him looking at her, and she'd see the deep sadness on his face. She'd understand what he'd lost. She'd think, I look like my mother and it pains him. She wished she looked different. She cut her curls short, dyed her blonde hair chestnut, and took to wearing contact lenses instead of glasses.

It didn't make any difference. When she first took Claire to the house, Claire saw a picture of Victoria's mother and said, with Victoria's father there, 'Oh my God, is this you?'

As she went through the front gate, she had a stab of memory of her mother when Victoria was very small, nursery school-aged. There had been a dog that had got off its leash and had run at Victoria, right outside the gate. Her mother had pushed Victoria out of the way, putting herself between Victoria and the dog, and had been badly bitten on the hand. Victoria thought she'd be in trouble for somehow causing the dog to attack them. But her mother was laughing through her tears. It must have been the shock. 'Oh God, that was so wildly exciting,' her mother said, holding on to her injured hand.

When the dog owner caught up, Victoria's mother gave him a piece of her mind, but to Victoria she only said that she would always protect her like that. 'I'm so scared of dogs,' her mother said. 'Did you know that? Mummy is *so* scared of dogs. But not when they run at you, Victoria. Not at all. How's that for biology?'

She would know what to do now, Victoria was sure.

Victoria's parents' house had hardly changed since her mother died, the only addition the handrail they'd put in for the small flight of stone steps when her grandmother came to live with them after her grandfather died. The front door was still painted the same light blue her mother had chosen, faded now and grimy.

Victoria let herself in. 'Daddy?'

'In here, darling.'

He was in his study, as he always was, the only room that looked out across the front garden. Her mother had been the gardener and her father had left it untouched, save the gentle pruning done by Victoria after the neighbours complained. Victoria had also engaged a lawyer to tell the neighbours to leave him alone. It would have been easier to employ a gardener,

Claire had said, but Victoria didn't want to. The garden might be grown over now but it brought some comfort still, she thought. Her father would sit in his office and look out. If it made him feel even a little better, it was worth being a bad neighbour for. What did it matter to them anyway?

'What are you working on?' Victoria said when she saw her father. She threw her coat on the little chair that had been hers as a girl, parked her overnight bag next to it.

'Oh, this and that.' He smiled. 'A paper for the education wallahs.'

'I thought you were the education wallahs.'

He smiled genially. 'Used to be, but now they're in government, they're bringing in the young guns.' Victoria knew her father was less busy now because he called her more often. Not that he and Tony were no longer close. But everyone wanted to advise the new P.M., and her father had never been one to put himself forward. He'd wait until Tony called. Victoria suspected Tony was calling less and less.

'Will we have tea?' he said.

'Lovely.'

They went out to the kitchen. He didn't ask about Paris.

Victoria made tea and they carried their cups back to the study. Her father sat at his desk, turning the office chair to face her. Victoria sat in her old easy chair, too small for her now, so she was at a lower level.

She picked up the framed photograph of her mother from the table, the one Claire had assumed was Victoria herself.

Her father frowned.

'Daddy, do you miss Mummy?'

'Of course,' he said. He looked nervous, as if unsure what she was going to say next.

She put her cup and saucer down on the table beside the photograph. 'It's just . . .' She burst into tears.

'Victoria, are you all right?' His face softened. He pulled his chair towards her.

'Clearly not,' she said, composing herself as best she could. 'I don't know if I'm happy.'

Tears were still coming out of her eyes. She wiped them, took a breath in and held it until she stopped crying.

'At work?'

'I don't feel I can write anymore.' She tried her best to smile. 'I'm sorry. I didn't mean to arrive and fall apart. Probably not what you need at all.'

'Diana?' he said. 'It's upset you?'

She nodded.

'Well, you were always kind to animals.'

'I'm sorry?' she said, not understanding.

'You always wanted to take in stray animals. Remember the crow?'

When she looked up at him, it started her crying again.

'No,' she said, 'I don't.'

'It had fallen from the tree in the front, your mother's pear. Remember? The pear never produced any fruit. She was so much more hopeful than me.' He looked whimsical then;

sad, Victoria thought. She wished she hadn't come. She was only making things worse for him.

'Oh yes, I remember,' she said, smiling as brightly as she could. 'And I do know the tree. You can't see it anymore for the hedge.' She sniffed. 'We have a baby crow at home at the moment. I didn't remember that other one. I wonder why not.'

They sat quietly for a moment.

'I wasn't enough; I know I wasn't,' he said sadly.

'What made you think of the crow?' she asked.

'You're not tough, Victoria. Intellectually, you are, but there's something soft in you. Maybe you're in the wrong job.'

'I should become a vet?'

He laughed. 'No, but I know it hasn't been easy. I know I'm not easy.'

'No, you're not,' she said, smiling through her tears. 'But neither am I, and you were mother and father both. You did well, Daddy.'

He was shaking his head. 'I know that's not true, my dear, and I don't mind that it's not. I just wish . . .' He put his teacup down.

He extended his hand towards her but stopped mid-air.

'Nana and Poppy were there for the rest,' she said. 'I did fine.' She was smiling through the tears, which had started again.

'They were. Victoria . . .' He was frowning.

'Yes?' She looked up.

'Nothing. It's nothing.'

'Are you sure?'

He nodded. 'It's just this paper I'm working on. It can wait.'

'Okay, Daddy.'

The moment was gone.

She picked up her cup, sipped tea. 'You like Ben, don't you?'

He didn't answer straightaway. 'I don't know him very well,' he said eventually.

'But you like him so far?'

'I do,' he said. 'I do. Do you, Victoria?'

'Of course.' Why would he ask that?

He nodded. 'Good then.'

As she was leaving, he said, 'When your mother died, I couldn't write, not for months. The grief, I expect. The only other times I have trouble writing are when what I'm writing doesn't agree with who I am. I think that's what I was trying to say before.'

At first she thought he was criticising her, the kind of writing she did, but later she thought back to what he'd said. It was entirely true.

TWENTY-NINE

Brisbane, 1981

THE WESLEY HOSPITAL AT AUCHENFLOWER SITS HIGH above the Brisbane River. It's more like an airport than a hospital, with plush furniture, carpets and soft pinkly-papered walls. In the foyer there's a fancy cafeteria and a flower shop. I bought Ed a little bunch of daisies but gave them to a woman in the lift who was crying.

In the hospital, they didn't comb his hair right, parting it on the left when he always parted it on the right, and it made him look like a stranger. I didn't feel I knew him well enough to fix it myself, but I brought his comb and mirror and left them on the table with a picture of him.

He looked so small and slight there in the bed. 'I brought you a flask,' I said.

'You're the best, Maddie.'

They wouldn't give him alcohol because it was bad for his liver, but I couldn't imagine why they'd care. He was going to die. He wouldn't need his liver. I gave him the flask but he only took a tiny sip then put it away from himself.

The nurses kept thinking I was his wife, even though we had explained several times that we were neighbours. He blushed once when one of them said I could stay in the room overnight if I wanted.

༃

On the last day... Oh, I can't think of it without tears coming into my eyes. He was always thin but now it was like a different face, a different person who'd emerged from the Ed I knew.

His father had come to visit once and had sat there, stony-faced and likely drunk. I made Andrew Shaw go and tell him when Ed passed. There would be a funeral at the enormous church at Rosalie; Andrew and me, Ed's father, the Catholic priest and a nun from the convent. The children from the school formed a guard of honour for the coffin. I have no idea why. And he was gone.

༃

Ed was the only person I had told everything: partly because he was a drunk and unlikely to remember, and partly because there was something good in him that even drink couldn't destroy. I watched his eyes widen and narrow as I told the story from start to finish.

'That's the story you should write,' he said at the end, nodding slowly in the way of the drunk. 'It's a great story.'

I wondered then if he thought I'd made it up.

'It was me,' I said.

'It's a great story,' he said again, and I was left none the wiser as to what he meant.

The only thing I didn't get to tell him about was the letter and then it was too late. He'd probably have said it wasn't as good a story. People like stories about overcoming adversity, and they even like tragedies. I'm not sure what they think about trickery.

⁓

I didn't have the heart to keep going with the book after Ed died. My heart was somewhere else, I suppose; back with the dead. It's a place my heart knows well.

I stopped writing to Mr Inglis, too, as it seemed disrespectful to pretend to be Ed now that he'd passed, although you might wonder why I didn't think it was disrespectful to appropriate Ed's identity before he died. I stopped writing to Mr Inglis, put the book away and didn't reply to letters I received. I knew enough to know they'd give up eventually, as they'd done at the beginning.

I had written back to Helen. I thought of writing again, but I didn't know what to say.

I would let bygones be bygones, as I'd told her I would. I would make my forgiveness real. This is the choice we have in life. The Buddhists are entirely right, even as they are so damn superior about it. We can harden our hearts and miss the life that's ours, or we can soften and forgive and find something tender and real in the middle of ourselves.

◆

Lady Diana Spencer married Prince Charles in front of all the world but me, for I couldn't bear to watch. I took myself to bed and stayed there for a week before I picked myself up and told myself I must live the life I'd been given.

I didn't have Ed.

I didn't have my family.

I was afraid to take another step.

But Andrew Shaw and Sally and Frank needed me.

It was enough for a life. Surely it was.

THIRTY

London, 1997

VICTORIA HAD BEEN HOME FOR AN HOUR WHEN SHE heard the downstairs door, voices, Ben farewelling his driver. They hadn't spoken on the phone again since the night before in Paris. She heard his tread heavy on the steps. And then his key in the door. She looked up. There he was in the doorway.

She would never tire of that face, she thought, and it was followed so quickly by dread that it took her breath away. She couldn't at first speak to greet him.

'You're home,' he said, smiling.

He'd been drinking, she thought.

'I am,' she said, shaking off the fear.

He came in and leaned down and kissed her. 'Wanna eat out?'

'I have to work,' she said, waving her fingers over the keyboard of her computer.

He was fine, she thought, relieved.

Martha was winding herself around Victoria's legs, crying softly.

'Diana?'

She nodded.

'Okay, I'll go and get takeout.'

'Great,' she said. 'Are you all right to drive?'

'What's that supposed to mean?'

'Nothing,' she said, feeling fearful again. 'I thought you said you were having drinks tonight, and that's why you came home with the driver.'

'I always come home with the driver. Are *you* all right?'

'Fine,' she said. 'Trying to write this piece for the magazine.' Ewan had said he wanted an eyewitness account of Paris to lead with. 'It's harder than you'd think.'

'I bet,' he said. 'Come on, let's go out to dinner. We can go back to that place . . . what was it called? The high-end one?'

'Le Gavroche?'

'That's it.'

'You think they'll have us back?' She smiled.

He looked angry suddenly, inexplicably. 'What the fuck does that mean?'

Her smile died. 'Just that the maître d', that horrible fellow, didn't like us.' Her heart was racing now.

'You mean he didn't like me?'

He had raised his voice, and she realised she was afraid of what he might do.

She was afraid of Ben.

'That's what you mean, isn't it?' he said. 'They didn't like me. And you don't like me much either. You don't even tell me where you are anymore.'

Victoria chose her words carefully. 'Ben, that's not what I meant. They were the problem, not you.'

'Is that right?' he said.

She shook her head. It was as if a different person was in the room now. She did not know this person. It was not Ben.

But she did know this person.

She put her feet on the floor. She put her hands by her sides, made her shoulders relax. Somehow, she knew in her bones the one thing she mustn't show was her fear, a fear that raged under the surface of her skin and threatened to break out of her and fill the little kitchen.

Martha was crying in earnest now.

Victoria looked out the window. 'Ben,' she said, 'let's not do this. Not tonight. Let's have a night that's just you and me. Not our demons.'

He sat down heavily in the chair opposite her. Just as quickly as he'd entered the room, the monster had left. 'I'm sorry,' Ben said. 'I really am, honey. I don't mean to do this. I just . . . I love you so much, and I know the photographers are driving you nuts.'

'And I love you,' she said, looking him in the eye. 'We can weather the photographers. Can't we?'

She felt a flutter in her belly.

'We can,' he said. 'And Cal can help. I talked to him today. He's already written to *The Daily Mirror* about the last picture. And I called Brian Martin at the *Telegraph*.'

'What for?'

'To tell him we're engaged,' Ben said.

THIRTY-ONE

Perth, 1920

AFTER THE BALL, I WENT UPSTAIRS WITH HELEN TO GET changed. I was feeling embarrassed about what had happened with the prince, but also a little thrilled.

She sighed. 'Oh, Maddie, there's going to be trouble. How could you be so stupid? I told you.'

'What do you mean?'

'Don't pretend. For a start, the prince danced every dance with you and so now they want to know who you are and how he came to know you. I'll do my best,' she said, 'but you should have refused him.'

'But Helen, I—'

'Keith Murdoch told me he saw the prince kiss you. Kiss you! What were you thinking, Maddie? I'll do what I can but I have to warn you, it might get rough.'

'Rough?'

'There's the problem with your last job.'

'What do you mean?'

'You were fired. It won't take much digging to find that out. I imagine your cafe owner will be more than happy to talk to the newspapermen. I'll try with Keith. He's reasonable, but he saw it with his own eyes.' She sighed. 'David is not to be trusted, Maddie. Do you know what I mean? I've been trying to tell you that.'

'Do you mean he's a candidate for a pot of tea?'

'Exactly,' she said.

'But he danced with me because he likes me,' I protested. 'He likes both of us. We're on his team. He would never act improperly. Even Mr Waters says so. He's a prince, Helen, and he *is* fond of me. He and I talk.'

She laughed, not her lovely childlike laugh but a harsh laugh I didn't think I'd heard before. 'You need to wake up,' she said. 'There is no way on earth that's why he danced with you. He danced with you because he likes to dance with young women and that's not all he likes to do. Remember Ruby?'

I frowned. 'From Sydney?'

Helen nodded. 'Remember she left us after Canberra? Do you know why? Because of David and his stupid cousin. Do you understand what I'm saying?'

She had become so stern with me I felt like crying. 'Mr Waters doesn't agree with you,' I said. 'He also says you're wrong about the prince and F.DW., that she is his friend and he would never act improperly.'

'Mr Waters is a slave to the fucking prince,' she said angrily, 'and so he will tell you a whole pack of lies and sell you down the river. He'd sell his mother if it would make David happy.'

'Are you sure this isn't because the prince danced with me more than you?'

I simply didn't accept what Helen was saying, that the prince would be anything but noble. I had seen him with the soldiers and their families, his kindness and generosity. Helen was wrong, surely.

She laughed that hard laugh again and it frightened me. 'Oh, Maddie, I wish you hadn't said that. Our friendship matters to me.'

'It matters to me too,' I said. 'But why are you saying these things? You sound so angry with me.' I was feeling very upset.

Helen softened and I saw sadness in her eyes too. 'It's because I know the world. No, I am not jealous of you. David has picked you because you are young and inexperienced and he knows it. Freda's dumped him. You are sport to him. And if you think for one minute that it will be different with you or that I'm making this up, you are mistaken. You are not the first. You will certainly not be the last.'

She shook her head. 'I'll see what I can do with Mr Murdoch, but you need to stay away from David. Yes, he's a darling. Yes, we are terribly loyal to him. Yes, he endears himself to us. But, Maddie, do not think for one minute that you matter to him. You don't. None of us does. Not really. He will pursue you and then he will discard you. That is what these men do.'

I was crying now, thinking of how angry Helen had been with me, how disappointed. I wished I'd never gone to the ball.

'I'm sorry, Helen. He was so lovely to me, especially tonight. And I didn't think he was that sort of person. Is that what Mr Waters is like too then?' I said, through tears. It felt as if the world was not how I thought it was.

'No, of course not,' she said, more gently, looking upset herself suddenly.

'You know what I'm going to do?' I said then, wiping my eyes and recovering myself. 'I'm going to write your story.' I was smiling through my tears. I had suggested it in my letter to Daddy, more to cheer him up than anything, but now I knew what I could do for Helen and Mr Waters. 'I'm going to write the story of the brave ambulance driver who is my friend and her captain.' I could write their story, I decided, or what I knew of it, and they would read it and understand each other.

I leaned over and hugged her. 'Thank you for being my friend,' I said.

She held on. 'Oh Maddie, darling, you are so very young. It's sweet of you to try, but it wasn't simple.'

I withdrew from the hug. 'So? It's simple now, isn't it?'

'No, it's not.'

'He said he loves you. You said you love him, Helen.'

She softened again. 'I do, Maddie, and perhaps he does, but it's not enough. It will never be enough.'

THIRTY-TWO

London, 1997

BEN HAD LEFT EARLY AND VICTORIA WAS RELIEVED WHEN she woke and the flat was empty. She didn't want to talk to him. They'd shared the bed last night but it was as if she were sleeping with a stranger. She'd stayed awake half the night worrying. Martha spent the early-morning hours spooned around Victoria's head. It had felt protective. 'Good girl,' she said to the cat as she left for the office.

She saw Mac at the front desk on the way in.

'Miss Byrd,' he said, 'you were in Paris? You saw her?'

She nodded. For some reason, she thought she might cry.

'We went to St James's,' Mac said. 'We signed the book.'

'Of course you did,' she said, tears pricking her eyes. 'I'm glad you did. I'm glad there are people marking her passing.'

He walked her over to the lift. 'You take care now,' he said.

When she got up to the fifth floor, she went to see Ewan in his office.

'I haven't written anything more,' she said. 'I'm so sorry. You'll have to get someone else, Ewan. I can't do it.'

'You can't just not file, Victoria. Surely you know that.' He was sitting at his desk sorting through pictures. He hadn't looked up when she'd come in.

She didn't want to tell him about last night, about Ben.

'Well, I can't. I can't write about her anymore. I can't write about Diana.'

Now he did look up, seeming more curious than anything else. 'Is this because Harry didn't run the piece from Paris as the leader?'

'No—as if I care about that.'

'Then why not?'

'I've lost all my muscle. She's my age. She's . . . I saw everything in Paris and I wrote my heart out, but you're right. It's not what's wanted right now, and I'm finding I can't write to order anymore. Claire said yesterday she thinks it's us, our industry, that killed her.'

'That's like blaming a—'

'A cow for heart disease. I know. But maybe it's time we take responsibility. Even if people are demanding this stuff, it doesn't mean we have to supply it.'

Ewan sighed. 'Oh, Victoria, I can't have you go ethical on me. I'm up against a hell of a deadline. I need you.' He gestured to his desk. It looked as it always looked: like the desk of a teenager raging against the very notion of adulthood. 'I have to get the stories finalised and go to press within four hours of the funeral, so that we get the edition out before the others. We don't have a lot of flexibility here.'

'I know.' She forced herself to hold back her tears. She didn't want to cry in front of him and have him know how upset she was. 'I just can't do it, Ewan. I can't. It's something to do with Diana, and also me and those photographers. I can't. I'm so sorry.' She felt her voice falter. She still hadn't mentioned Ben.

He sat back and looked at her more carefully. 'No, I'm sorry,' he said, taking his glasses off. For a minute, she thought he was going to fire her, but he only said, 'Jeez, it's been a long couple of days.' He rubbed his eyes with one hand. 'Okay. Okay. You know you can only do this once, don't you?'

She nodded, not trusting her voice right then.

'I mean, I get it. This one has affected us all. So.' He sat there for a moment, thinking, put his glasses back on. 'How about I take you off Diana and we get you straight on M.A. Bright? I think we can run that as the November cover if Fin gets his contract in place. If that's not a story with your fucking name on it, Victoria, I don't know what is. It's you to a tee. You'll find your muscles again.' He made to flex his bicep, his arm skinny even in a long-sleeved shirt.

She smiled. The relief she felt was enormous. 'Have you heard from Finian again?'

The True Story of Maddie Bright

'Yes, as a matter of fact. He called me early yesterday. You'd think Diana didn't happen. He just went on and on about the new novel. Do you know what a lost baby is?'

'I think it's just that—a lost baby.'

'Okay. He sort of expected me to know.'

'Me too, but I think it's just a baby that's lost somehow. He said it's a trope.' On the flight back from Paris, Victoria had read the chapter Finian had given her. 'There's a baby left at a foundling wheel and it dies. It's very sad, maybe a bit overwrought. Not exactly uplifting as the start of a novel either.'

'Okay. Well, what I'm thinking is that you can go sooner rather than later. M.A. Bright will get out. It absolutely will get out and currently we're ahead of it. Frankly, I don't much care about the novel. From our point of view, it's an interview with M.A. Bright, and she's offering it to you. That's a story even if it's not really M.A. Bright. It's like that lord everyone tried to chase. What was his name?'

'Lucan?'

'That's it. Finding M.A. Bright is like finding Lord Lucan.'

He looked at her and smiled gently. 'It's going to be easier on you, I think,' he said.

'What will you do about Diana?'

'That's my problem. Maybe Harry will let us hold longer. I wouldn't mind that anyway. Maybe I'll write it.'

'Thank you,' Victoria said. She looked at him. 'Why are you doing this?'

He looked at her for a long moment. 'Why do you think?'

'Because I'm a good writer?'

He didn't answer straightaway but only looked at her again. 'Because you're my best writer,' he said. 'And . . .' He pushed his glasses up his nose and looked at her. 'Is everything okay, Victoria?'

'Yes,' she said, too quickly. 'I just . . . it was the . . . The photographers are at my place again today.'

'Who?'

'No one I know. Ben told them we're engaged.'

'I see,' Ewan said. 'You're engaged?'

'Yes,' she said. 'We were keeping it under wraps, but Ben thought it was a good idea to tell someone he knows at the *Tele*, so now they want pictures again because Diana will only be a story for so long. They'll need something else then. They'll run a story about the wedding, and I . . .'

'You?'

'I wanted to keep it private.'

'Yeah, well, it's a living.'

'I guess it is,' Victoria said. 'Anyway, thank you. I'll never forget you did this.'

'Do forget it,' he said, waving her off. 'I just want the old Victoria back.'

He looked upset then, and it scared Victoria for no reason she understood.

THIRTY-THREE

Perth, 1920

HELEN MANAGED TO CONVINCE MR MURDOCH THAT HE shouldn't mention me in his story about the ball. 'He said it wasn't your fault and he wouldn't put you through it,' Helen said.

She gave me a quick hug. 'We averted disaster, darling!'

When it came to the prince, though, Mr Murdoch was less disposed to be kind, Helen said. The piece he'd written after Sydney had now been published. In it he said the prince showed 'unnerving judgement in choosing pretty girls who were good dancers', but his mother might prefer he choose 'good girls who are pretty dancers'. Dickie thought it very funny but Colonel Grigg was hopping mad, apparently.

I hardly saw the prince the day after the ball. Early in the morning, he went with Mr Waters to inspect the train which would become our home for the first leg of the journey east across the continent. It was the train we'd travelled up from Albany on and not as comfortable or as elegant as the train from Sydney, as we'd learned the first night. The narrower gauge of the railway tracks meant the carriages were not quite as wide, and the train rocked more from side to side. They had built special carriages for the visit, Mr Waters had told me, making them as wide as they possibly could.

The prince's private chamber and dining room, which had been placed in the middle of the train to mitigate the rocking, were separated by curtains. Curtains also separated his office from ours. When Mr Waters returned to Government House, he said the prince wanted doors put in. Before long I heard him giving instructions to the carpenters.

At lunchtime, the prince took a boat trip along the Swan River to the town of Fremantle where there was another reception. Helen accompanied him, along with Colonel Grigg. I stayed at Government House drafting letters for Mr Waters, who was still trying to ensure the King changed his mind about the prince's trip to India.

I learned that the prince was to have barely three months at home before setting out again. Mr Waters said, in one of the letters I typed for Sir Godfrey's signature, that they feared the prince would not survive if put under this much pressure.

The mail was still being received in Sydney and we'd made arrangements for two bags to be sent by rail and car. Meantime, I was working my way through the letters we'd brought with us from Sydney and the few that had so far been gathered by the governor in Western Australia.

There were no letters with the spider seal.

Mr Waters wasn't short-tempered but I could tell he was feeling the strain. My loyalty for him was unwavering and had only increased over the time I worked with him.

Before he'd left for Fremantle, the prince had come into the office where Helen and I were working.

'No letters for me?' he said.

'No, sir,' I said.

'David, you might check with the steward,' Helen said. 'But we have work to do.' Her tone was curt.

'Oh, Helen,' he said, 'don't you want to have any fun?'

She looked at him and smiled. 'I don't think the tour is about my fun, sir.'

'No, quite right too,' he said.

After he left, Helen only said, 'I have told him he's to leave you alone, Maddie. I feel sure he will. He's a good sort, in his own way.'

I didn't say anything, but privately I had decided Helen didn't need to protect me. I had the skills a girl with five brothers would have—I knew how to defend myself with whatever was at hand; a pot of tea, for instance. I knew I'd been in danger at Christie's, even if I didn't actually know for certain in detail what the danger was (being without previous experience in that department!). But Helen was mistaken. The prince was fond of me, and I was fond of him. He liked talking to me.

He was a good man, just as Mr Waters said he was. Whatever had happened to Helen in love, it had coloured her thinking too negatively.

Helen and Colonel Grigg had made no announcement about their engagement. I'd heard Helen tell Mr Waters that Colonel Grigg wanted to wait until we returned to Sydney. Not that their engagement was a matter for royal protocol, but he didn't want the news to be out until those back in London knew.

I had thought more about my idea to write their story, Helen's and Mr Waters's. The title came to me late one night, *Autumn Leaves*, which I thought was so beautiful I immediately found Helen and shared it with her. She said it sounded like flannel nightdresses and hot chocolate, not romance. Also, she said, it was winter not fall. What was winter not fall? I said. Rupert and I, she said. Well, *Winter Leaves* is no kind of title at all, I said, and stomped off.

I had no idea then what she'd been through, what it had cost her. I would have been kinder had I known. I know I would have, even given my youth.

∽

The prince and his cousin returned by motor from Fremantle late in the afternoon, just as the rain set in. The prince had hardly any time between coming in from Fremantle and an evening event, I knew. I saw him rushing towards the house under an umbrella with Dickie. He looked exhausted. He didn't even come over to the offices to check for mail.

Helen had gone to the town hall to finalise details for a state banquet to be held the following day and she'd sent a message for Mr Waters to go and talk to the mayor about who would be sitting at the head table as there was some to-do about the plan.

I was in the staff lounge in the main house. I'd had a letter in the mail that day from Bert. It was full of news, but it was what he didn't say that worried me. He mentioned Mummy and the boys but not Daddy, who I knew had left Sydney early to return home. I hoped he was all right.

Just then, James came in and said the prince had asked for me.

I was making my way to the back door to grab a brolly and go over to the cottage when James said, 'No, miss, he's in his private chamber.'

I went up the stairs and to the end of the hall and knocked on the door.

'Come!' he called.

I opened the door and stepped inside. The room was lavishly furnished, with lounges and two chairs, a fireplace where a cheery little fire burned and large sash windows on two sides that faced out across the lawns. You would look straight to the river during the day, I thought.

'Sir, you wanted to see me?'

The prince was sitting in one of the easy chairs. By him on the table was the pile of draft replies I'd finished the day before. He got up and came over to the doorway where I stood.

'Maddie, darling, you have done a marvellous job on all these letters,' he said, closing the door behind me. 'Come in, you silly old thing. Sit, sit.' He gestured to one of the lounges and I took a seat.

'Was there something you needed, sir?' I asked. I had brought with me my pencil and notebook.

'David,' he said, gently admonishing. He came over to where I was but remained standing.

'David. Did you want anything, sir?'

'Talk. Can we talk?'

'Of course, sir.'

He gave me a mock-stern look.

'David,' I corrected myself. I put the notebook down on the table, the pencil on top of it.

I felt on edge, uncertain about him, or the room, which felt strangely sinister. I dismissed my fears, assumed it was the fire casting shadows.

'My father now wishes I were my brother Bertie,' he said. 'I'm telling you this because you are the only person on my staff right now whom I trust. Bertie has been such a good boy, and I have been a disappointment, he says. He's sending me to India.'

'I don't believe he dislikes you,' I said, relieved we were on familiar ground.

'You think fathers always like their sons?'

'I think any father would like a son like you.'

He laughed. 'Well, my father doesn't. He doesn't like me. He doesn't like my friends. He probably wouldn't like you!'

'Everyone likes you, sir.'

'Maddie, you really are the dearest dear.' He gave me a fond smile. 'The admiral is not my friend,' he said. 'None of them are. They're just sycophants. But you are my friend, aren't you?'

'Of course,' I said. I saw his dinner tray, the meal barely touched.

He sat down beside me now, taking one of my hands in both of his. His hands were warm and soft like a child's. I noticed the bruises on his right hand were less angry after the days at sea in which he didn't have to greet all those people.

I saw there were tears in his eyes. 'Are you all right, sir?' I asked.

'Oh, Maddie,' he sighed. 'Do you know what it is to love?'

'I think so, sir,' I said. 'I love my family.'

'But to love a man?' he said.

I shook my head. The prince was worrying me again now. He wasn't quite himself.

'I think, my darling girl, I might be falling in love with you.'

'Really, sir?' I said. I had an inkling he was going to kiss me again.

'David,' he said, and he leaned over and kissed me on the cheek. He sat back and grinned.

I felt an odd combination of nervousness and curiosity.

Helen's warning came back to me; he is not to be trusted.

Oh, what have I done? I thought then.

I stood, but the prince, who still had my hand, pulled me back down beside him on the couch.

'I must go, sir. I can't be here in your room with you.'

'Of course you can.'

'Sir, you have the races to attend tonight.'

'Ah, my little Maddie bossy boots, Rupert's little helper! That's where you're wrong. They've been cancelled because of this awful weather. So I am a free agent tonight.'

He swung around and kneeled in front of me, his hands on my knees. He looked at me, that smile. 'May I kiss you?' he asked.

I barely nodded. I was afraid, but I was still curious too.

He leaned forward and kissed me on the lips and then his tongue was in my mouth. I could taste tobacco and smell whisky.

I felt desire now, welling up from deep within my body. It was my body that began to respond.

'Oh, Maddie,' he said. He was still leaning over me, his hands moving up my thighs, outside my clothes.

He pulled at my blouse before apologising, smiling tightly, and moving to undo it. He lifted my skirt. He was breathing heavily, as if under considerable stress. He leaned back, rubbed his own thighs.

I watched his face. He wasn't looking at me.

He stood now, began to undo his belt, his trousers.

'I want you,' he said tightly. 'I've wanted you since the first moment we met. You're Emily's daughter. I want you.'

At the mention of my mother's name, my desire drained from me in a moment. It was fear that took over.

'Please,' I said. I could hear my voice as if from far away, high and reedy. 'We must stop this.'

I was having trouble getting breath into my lungs.

His body was over me now. 'We can't stop,' he said. 'Of course we can't.' His own voice was loud. He was tearing at my bloomers. And then he was hurting me.

∽

I stopped struggling. I became oddly calm, my body still as a mountain. He was nothing but this frenzied movement on top of me, and the pain was so great, I thought I might die under him.

Still, I did not move.

∽

After he had finished doing what he wanted to do, he moved off me and sat back on the couch, his pants around his ankles. I could feel the wetness between my legs. I didn't know what it was. I wondered if he'd urinated.

When I could move again, I sat up, tried to pull my skirt over myself to cover me. The firelight in the room, which had seemed dim when I came in, hurt my eyes now with brightness. The prince was puffing but his mood was calm, neither anxious nor upset. He said he was sorry. 'I didn't intend to . . .'

Perhaps he thought me willing. Perhaps he did. 'We love each other?' I said. I was trying it out, but the words were wrong as soon as I said them.

'We do,' he said.

'So it doesn't matter?' I said, trying again. 'I might have wanted it.'

'You did,' he said, looking at me oddly. 'I suppose you did. But you mustn't tell the others.'

'Why would I?' I said.

'Yes, good girl. It will be our secret. Helen said I mustn't . . . with you. I'd hate to disappoint her. But we couldn't stop ourselves, darling, could we? There's a good girl.' He grimaced. 'The fact is, I wouldn't have done that to you,' he said. 'I have had a very bad week. My father . . .'

'I know,' I said.

'Yes, of course you do. You're the only one who understands.'

'Mr Waters understands you, sir. He mentioned the letter that came from your brother. He was very upset for you.' I was trying to find the life I'd had before he did what he did, but it wasn't there anymore.

'Ah. Well, it seems I am yet again found wanting in comparison to Bertie,' the prince said. He was perfectly calm. For him, what had happened was entirely normal. 'The thing that rankles, of course, is that he is no better than me. He just knows how to play up to our father. Perhaps you are right. Perhaps Rupert understands me.'

I was shaking, I realised.

'He loves you, sir,' I said.

'And Helen?' he said. 'Helen loves her prince.'

'Yes, sir,' I said. We were both still only half dressed, I realised. 'She loves to write for you because you are such a marvellous speaker.'

I was worried suddenly that someone would come in and find us. I felt shame, shame at what I'd done. I felt terrible about Helen most of all. She had warned me. She had warned me and I had failed to heed her warning.

I was still shaking. I could not stop.

'But does she love me like you do?' he said. He seemed not to care if we were found.

'She loves Mr Waters.' I had started to fix my clothes. I noticed my notebook and pen there on the table but couldn't place them as mine.

'But you're cold, Maddie. Yes, let's get you dressed to warm you up.'

I wasn't cold. The fire was still burning in the grate.

'How do you know that?' he asked then.

'Know what?'

'That Helen loves Rupert. I thought she and Grigg . . .'

'In the war. You know the story.' I assumed he knew.

'What story?' he said, sitting up, looking interested.

'When Mr Waters was wounded. Helen was at the hospital. But he had to come back to you, sir.'

'That's nonsense,' he said. 'Rupert never loved anyone. He loves his prince!' He thought for a moment. 'What do you mean Helen was at the hospital? The first one? The French one? I went to get him and took him home. Helen was there?' He frowned. 'The rascal. That's why he didn't want to leave. It's why he made me appoint her to my staff. He told me she was excellent with the pressmen, but really he wanted her for himself. Why did he lie to me? I thought he was the only one who was loyal. But he's just like the rest of them, out for what he can get.'

There was a knock on the door then. Someone tried to open it as if to come in.

The prince made a face at me, a funny face. He was standing up now, buttoning his trousers and tucking in his shirt.

Whoever it was couldn't open the door, which was when I understood that the prince had locked the door behind me. He'd locked the door with me in his room.

I pulled up my bloomers and stockings and straightened my skirt as best I could. I wanted to be away from him.

'Who is it?' he said, trying not to laugh, looking at me. I was still shaking.

'Come on, David, open up—it's me.' It was Dickie's voice.

The prince went over and let his cousin in.

'Maddie?' Dickie said when he saw me.

'Oh, shut up, Dickie,' the prince said. 'You're a fine one to judge.'

'I wasn't,' his cousin said. 'Maddie, are you all right?' He didn't wait for an answer. 'David, they're looking for you.'

'Why?'

'You're supposed to be at the races.'

'I thought that was cancelled.'

'Apparently it wasn't. We've got to get you ready and get over there.'

'It's pouring rain.'

'Yes, but they can't run the Prince of Wales Cup without the Prince of Wales.'

'All right,' he said. 'Maddie, darling, thank you for looking after your little prince.' He lifted my hand and kissed it.

I left them then, Dickie calling for James to come to help the prince dress.

Soon I heard them leaving the house.

Dickie came to my room just before they left. 'Maddie, there's nothing you need to talk to Mr Waters about, is there?'

'Why would there be?' I said.

I had hoped to be able to come to my own room and get under the covers and feel safe. I had hoped to cry. But there were no tears. I had sat looking out at the rain without seeing anything.

Desire. That word desire that I see in books and magazines and on the television. Desire. That moment he had first leaned in and kissed me had awoken desire, hadn't it? Later, I would relive what happened, over and over, moment by moment, in every cell of my body, but I would never feel desire again.

'Good girl,' Dickie said. 'Mum's the word when it comes to these sorts of things.'

'Of course,' I said, as if I understood everything about the ways of love.

He'd locked the door. That's what I was thinking. He'd locked the door. Why would a person do that?

THIRTY-FOUR

London, 1997

'I'M GOING TO COME RIGHT OUT WITH IT,' CLAIRE SAID. 'Ewan called me yesterday after you left.'

They were meeting at Torino's in the banking district, as Claire had lunch with a client. She was dressed in a black suit with a bright pink blouse. Today, she looked the picture of a modern businesswoman, Victoria thought, nothing like the day before other than the pink of the blouse echoing the fuchsia of the t-shirt.

'Some days a milk-vending machine, today an idea-vending machine,' Claire had said when Victoria commented.

'The bastard,' Victoria said about Ewan. 'I mean, I know I'm having trouble, but what did he call you for?'

'Trouble with what?'

'And, yes, I had to go in this morning and beg off the Diana story. I've never done that before. I've always filed to deadline. But Diana. I couldn't do it. Why call *you* about it? The bastard.'

Claire laughed. 'Why the fuck would Ewan call me about *your* writing?'

'Oh,' Victoria said. 'Then what did he call about?'

'He's pretty worried about you, as it happens.'

'Why?'

Claire just looked at her.

'Ben?' Victoria said.

'Look,' Claire said, 'I know Ewan hates anyone who's successful as a matter of course, and Ben's successful, and I've always thought Ewan had a little crush on you himself. But something's wrong. I know it is.'

'I see,' Victoria said. 'Well, you and Ewan have put two and two together and got five. I know Ben isn't the sort of fellow I've been with before—let's face it, they've all been more like Ewan really. Maybe it's like me and Tony. Ben will get used to you like Tony got used to me and then we'll be back to normal.'

'Did I push you away when I first knew Tony?' Claire said.

'I don't know.'

'Believe me, I didn't,' Claire said. 'I know Tony has his problems, but he's not like Ben. Ben's got all the signs.'

'Signs of what?' Victoria found herself getting angry at her friend.

'He was lovely to start, wasn't he?'

'Yes.'

'Swept you off your feet.'

'So?' Victoria wasn't sure where this was going. 'We fell in love,' she said.

'You did,' Claire said. 'I know you did. Except . . .'

'Go on,' Victoria said, her mouth set tight.

She gave a little sigh. 'He is different from the other guys you've dated, but that's not it. What did you first like about Ben?'

'He couldn't care less what anyone thought.' And she *had* liked that about him, she thought.

She recalled their third date. It was what they'd nearly fought about last night. He'd wanted to take her somewhere special, he said, so he booked Le Gavroche.

'But sir must wear a jacket,' the maître d' had said to Ben at the front desk.

'Why?' Ben had said, tilting his head, smiling slightly. 'It's not cold out.'

The waiter had looked flummoxed. Clearly he was accustomed to being obeyed. 'Never mind, sir. We can lend you one.'

'No thanks,' Ben said, exaggerating his American accent, Victoria thought.

'But it's a requirement,' the maître d' said firmly, placing himself between them and the dining room.

Ben reached into his jeans pocket, took out a bill. 'You sure about that, bud?'

Victoria, who'd been standing behind Ben, grabbed his hand. 'We'll eat somewhere else. Come on.'

He looked at her. 'No,' he said. 'We're eating here.' It wasn't said angrily. It was just a statement of fact, the way he put it.

It should have been a warning. He lacked . . . was it respect for old things? Was it affection for tradition? Whatever it was, he lacked it, and when faced with whatever it was, he was not embarrassed, as Victoria might have been, but belligerent.

They'd dined at the restaurant, Ben the only one without a jacket. For Victoria, it was excruciating.

What might have saved him was his final gesture. He left an enormous tip and, on the way out, he said to the maître d', 'Thanks again, bud. Good food, by the way.'

Victoria told Claire about that night now. She left out what had happened later, after they got home, when Victoria had asked him why he'd insisted on dining there.

'Don't you fucking tell me what to do.' He'd shouted that, hadn't he? He'd shouted at her. That was the truth.

Victoria had told herself that she was the one with the problem, that he didn't let all the trappings of stupid English propriety get in the way, that she, Victoria, had let him down not the other way around.

She looked at her friend. 'He's just not bothered by all the nonsense. It's refreshing.' But even as she told the story, she saw the seeds of what she'd seen last night, self-belief and confidence turned to rage.

'What's wrong?' Claire said.

'Nothing,' Victoria said. 'Nothing. Go on.'

'Okay,' Claire said. 'I am in your corner.' She held her hands up. 'If he's the one, I'll be clapping you into the bridal waltz. But I want to say this, even though you might hate me for saying it. You have no promise to keep to him, Victoria, and no promise to anyone else. Your dad won't care if you don't marry him. I won't care. The world won't care. You have to be sure.'

'Were you sure with Tony?'

'I was.'

'Totally?'

'Okay, not totally. But I knew I was safe. I don't think you know that.' She smiled across at her friend, tears in her eyes. 'I never try to change people. First, you're a grown-up. Second, you've never listened to me anyway, and, third, why should you? You're perfectly happy, by your own account.'

She nearly told Claire then. I'm pregnant. I'm terrified. But something stopped her. Once she said it aloud, it would become real. It would become the truth.

'Yes, I am,' Victoria said. 'And this is all just pre-wedding nerves. Ben and I wondered if you would be matron of honour.'

'Of course,' Claire said. 'Anything.'

'Well, that's great—and now, I must away.'

'Just know this, Victoria,' Claire grabbed her friend's arm as Victoria stood. 'I'm here when you need me. I am totally here when you need me, and Tony has your back. Ewan too, okay? We're all on your team.'

Victoria looked over and saw that the tears had filled Claire's eyes now and were running down her cheeks.

THIRTY-FIVE

Perth, 1920

IT WAS SUNDAY NOW AND THE PRINCE WAS TO REST UNTIL the afternoon, when we would depart Perth for the south again. I hadn't seen him since the night he'd called me to his room, and sometimes in my own mind, I had trouble believing anything at all had happened.

After breakfast in the main house on my own, I thought I would go into the office and do as much as I could to get the letters typed for Mr Waters. I thought if I had something to concentrate on I would feel better, more anchored. Helen came in as I was finishing breakfast and sat opposite me as she usually would. 'Are you all right, Maddie?' she said when I stood to leave.

'Of course,' I said. 'Why do you ask?'

'You seem to have lost your spirit a bit. Last night was so deadly dull. I wished I'd been able to stay back here. We could have had more fun playing skittles.'

They had gone off to a state dinner the night before, Helen and Dickie and the prince and Colonel Grigg. I had wondered if I would be invited too, but I wasn't. Mr Waters didn't go either. He and Sir Godfrey had gone back to Albany by train to pick up mail and to meet with the admiral about the tour of India before the ship left. They had only returned late the night before, and I hadn't seen them.

I had wanted to tell Helen about what had happened with the prince but I found I could not. I was sure I had done something to make the prince do what he did. Of course I had. I shouldn't have gone to his room. I shouldn't have kissed him. And underneath my shame was fear. I would have moments of panic—I was having one now, with Helen—and I would have to stop whatever I was doing until I could get breath into my lungs again.

The moment passed. 'I'm really fine,' I said when Helen stood and made to catch me if I fainted. 'Just tired.'

Dickie came in to the dining room then to say that he and H.R.H. were playing tennis and did Helen and I want to join them?

'Oh God, Maddie, let's,' Helen said. 'I'll start seeing double if I have to read another newspaper story about the flowers on the table at the banquet last night.'

'Why?' Dickie said. 'What was wrong with them?'

'They were flowers native to Western Australia and apparently that's important.'

'I don't remember them,' Dickie said.

'No, but that doesn't stop the newspapermen noting them.'

Like Helen, Dickie didn't remark on my absence the night before. Perhaps, I decided, my attendance the first night had been the aberration and they didn't expect me to have been invited. I wondered if the prince had told them what had happened. Perhaps they all knew, I thought.

When we went outside, the prince was already on the court serving balls to no one. He was dressed in his usual sports attire and he smiled and said good morning. It was the first time I'd seen him since that night in his room, and it was as if nothing was different between us. And, yet, everything was different.

My thoughts remained all jumbled. I told myself I loved him and he loved me and it was our love that had led to what had happened. But the moments of fear I felt had no home in love, and love surely was not full of shame. The way he had been, animal and frightening. That wasn't love.

We played a set. I don't know how I managed. I kept looking at the prince. He had once been so kind. I kept searching for a sign, some acknowledgement of what had passed between us, but he gave none. There was nothing of the boy about him now to my eyes.

The prince partnered with his cousin. Helen and I were no match for them. Dickie suggested we split the teams. 'I'll take Helen. You can have Maddie.'

'No,' the prince said. 'I'll have Helen.'

Dickie looked at him and then came to my side of the court. I didn't understand how the prince could do this.

Dickie was terribly kind to me, I noticed, although I wanted the prince to be kind, not his cousin. And then the prince caught my eye once and he smiled sheepishly and gave me a little wave, and I thought perhaps we'd be all right.

Still, I was terribly confused.

Mr Waters came by on his way from the garages to the office. He was dressed in his suit pants, shirt and vest, his tie around his neck not tied.

'Welcome back, stranger,' the prince said. His voice was very loud.

Mr Waters looked over at him.

'Your turn for tennis, Rupert,' the prince shouted. 'You can play with Maddie and I'll play with Helen. Dickie needs a break.'

'No, I don't,' Dickie said. 'We're fine, aren't we, Maddie?'

'Actually, sir, I have things to do,' Mr Waters called and kept walking.

'Oh, come on, man, are you scared of losing?'

'No,' Mr Waters said. 'I just need to see the admiral about something.'

'Is this about the King?'

Mr Waters turned around. 'Yes, sir, I'm afraid it is. There's been a further cable about India. Please don't concern yourself. We're still hopeful.'

The prince laughed, more a sneer. 'Come on, Ruples. Play tennis instead. My father's not going anywhere.' He was drunk, it occurred to me then. Something was not right about him.

Mr Waters had stopped. 'I'd love to, David. Just not now.' And he resumed walking towards the main house.

The prince had walked over to the gate out to the grounds. I watched as he took a ball from his pocket, tossed it high in the air, then slammed it towards Mr Waters. It hit him in the back with considerable force.

Mr Waters hardly flinched. But he turned and said, 'You have to learn to control yourself.'

He kept walking towards the house.

Helen didn't go after Mr Waters. None of us did. We all just stood there.

'It was a joke,' the prince said finally.

No one spoke for a few moments and then Dickie said, 'David, you have to say sorry to him.'

'Why?'

'You hit him with the ball on purpose. Why would you do that?'

'He lied to me. He wrote to his father about me. And he's a liar.' The prince was looking at Helen and then at me.

'He's your most loyal man and you know it,' Dickie said. 'Now, go and say sorry.'

'Loyal?' And he looked from me to Helen again. 'Hah! Let's play,' the prince said.

'Not me,' Dickie said. 'Not until you've made up for that. That was beyond the pale.'

'He didn't care.'

'If you think he didn't care, you're blind, old chap. Of course he cares. He's your man, David.'

∽

We left Perth that afternoon to travel overnight to Pemberton. I was feeling even more wretched as what I'd done settled in my consciousness. I was sure that my telling the prince about Helen and Mr Waters had angered the prince and increased his rage towards poor Mr Waters.

I spent the afternoon in the office with Mr Waters, pretending to be drafting letters, but my mind wouldn't focus.

Mr Waters looked over his spectacles at me. He was very tired, I thought.

'It seems I need to speak with you, Maddie,' he said.

The winter sun was slanting through the window, illuminating in deep red the leather armchair and dust motes above it before heading out the other window to soften the view of the trees.

I felt guilty, as if I had let Mr Waters down, as if he knew what I'd done.

I felt afraid, too, for I knew what had happened to Ruby Rivers. 'Mr Waters, I'm very sorry. It wasn't—'

'What?' he said. He was looking at me. 'What on earth have you done, Maddie?' He was smiling. 'I only wanted to tell you that H.R.H. is busy working on his remarks for Tuesday, so he's asked me to go over the letters with you on this trip.'

'Oh,' I said. 'I'm sorry. I was thinking of something else.' During the sea journey, the prince had taken to talking directly to me if there were changes to the letters I'd drafted. I had only involved Mr Waters if I had concerns. The prince was using Mr Waters to avoid me after what had happened.

'Mr Waters, can I ask you a question?' I said then, desperate to understand what I'd done, fuelled by my shame and worried now that I had hurt poor Mr Waters.

He put his pen down, nodded. 'Yes?'

'Do you know why the prince hit you with the ball this morning?'

My voice was unsteady. Mr Waters regarded me carefully.

'Maddie, you are a certainly one to ask difficult questions, and that is no exception.' He sighed. 'The prince is under enormous strain. And we have all this.' He gestured towards the papers on his desk.

Mr Waters frowned. He wasn't one to take drink, but he'd taken drink this afternoon, I noticed. The whisky decanter was out on the table and there was a glass on his desk.

He looked sad then, staring out the window as the trees rushed by.

'When we were boys, my grandfather—my mother's father, that is—made me a rocking horse,' he said finally. 'He carved it himself from a single piece of wood. It was for my birthday.

He painted it black and white, after the racehorse that had won for the King at Ascot.'

He smiled. 'I've never sculpted myself, but ever since, whenever I see a tree stump or a big log, I think back to how he created a horse from that lump of wood. He carved its legs and body and head. He made a horsehair tail and mane and real leather reins. He mounted it on rockers.

'On the day of my birthday he couldn't be there. He was a doctor and he had surgery. He left it for me and I thought I had never seen a thing so beautiful. I think I didn't get off for the whole day.

'The next day, David and Bertie came for my birthday party. They gave me a picture atlas, I think. David got on the horse. He could see how much it meant to me, how proud I was.

'"I want it," he said. He was five or six at the time, and I suppose a five-year-old might say that, mightn't they? But after he left, my father said it would be a lovely gesture to give David the horse. Even his nanny had said, "David, you can't have his horse," but my father served the King. He knew what our responsibilities are.

'So I gave it to him. I did what Father said. My grandfather was honoured, he said, that the prince would have the horse. My parents said I'd been such a good friend.

'Do you know, I don't think I ever saw David play on the horse? It sat in the nursery and then went up to the attic.'

He smiled sadly.

'Once, when we were boys, he told me my father was the most stupid person he'd ever met. And you're just like him, he said. He didn't mean it. He said it to wound me, for I was older, and he didn't like that I could do so much more because of age.

'This may seem strange but I have always thought he would trade places with me if he could. It's not something I would say about the King, and perhaps as H.R.H. grows into himself, it will be less the case. There is a steeliness in his father I haven't yet seen in the son. I was frightened of the King as a boy, and I was never on the receiving end of his temper. I used to imagine growing up with that. I often thought perhaps that's why David . . . Oh, I don't know.

'His life, Maddie.' He had put his pen down now and he was looking across at me. 'We were in France together. I never saw him shirk a difficult task. He needs me. You know?'

He looked crestfallen. I didn't dare say anything.

'Helen doesn't understand that this is what I have to do,' he said. 'Ned's a different kind of man. But I was born to this. Helen doesn't see value in that, not in any way. If only she did . . .'

I had all but forgotten the story I'd planned to write, my stupid, childish *Autumn Leaves*, but I looked at Mr Waters now and I understood what had happened to tear them apart. It was this, his sense of duty, his most endearing quality that was also a terrible weakness. It meant he was unable to act when Prince Edward lashed out that morning. And he was also unable to act to show Helen she mattered to him more than the prince. And perhaps she was right; perhaps she didn't.

I also knew now that there would be no way Mr Waters would take my part if the prince decided against me. I was all alone with what had happened. That was the truth.

'I think H.R.H. will bring change,' Mr Waters was saying. 'I think he will change the way we see the monarchy. But that's not the question you asked. The answer is, I don't know. Every now and then, he just gets angry with me. I do my best to ignore it.'

'He's a cad,' I said, my voice angry, not at what the prince had done to me but at the way he treated poor Mr Waters.

'He's the Prince of Wales,' Mr Waters said, collecting himself. 'We'll speak of him with some respect.'

All lives are conscripted. If there *is* divinity, if those Jehovah's Witnesses and Latter-Day Saints and Pentecostals are on to something, then God either has a nasty sense of humour or a penchant for cruelty.

THIRTY-SIX

London, 1997

IT WAS THE FOLLOWING SATURDAY NOW, THE DAY OF Diana's funeral. Victoria arrived home after lunch. She used to love this walk from the station up to the flat in the afternoon, the smells of cooking coming down from the houses, making her wish for the warmth she imagined lay within them. It was what she once thought marriage might be, one of them cooking dinner for the other, sitting in the kitchen sipping red wine, laughing at a toddler.

When Victoria tried to imagine that scene now, she felt despair. She knew that she needed to act. She just didn't know what action to take.

She'd planned to watch the funeral on the television at the Ainsleigh Arms with colleagues, but instead she'd walked to Hyde Park alone and, from there, she'd wandered the parks until she found a spot. She was on her own as part of an enormous crowd. It was strangely soothing.

She could have been writing the story, she thought. She could have been covering this, the biggest news of her life, probably. At first, she felt the pull of it, that need to bear witness, to describe to others what she saw, stretching always towards the truth of a thing. She thought of phrases and words for what was around her, but she soon let them go and gave in to the experience. It was a relief.

She was not in the front of the crowd but she could see enough as the coffin passed on its way to Westminster Abbey. She'd have been in the media scrum if she were still on the story. She wondered if that's where Ewan was. He'd taken over from her and hadn't once been resentful about it. He'd made a joke about putting Des on the story, but she knew he wouldn't do that.

The silence was eerie, all those people together in a public place without speaking. People had been angry at Diana's death and Harry Knight had given them someone to be angry at. They were angry at the Queen, Prince Charles, the family. Public anger, stoked by the tabloids, had forced the family to come down from Balmoral finally to grieve publicly. They'd brought the boys out of the palace to see the flowers left at the gates and the folk waiting there. They were criticised for hiding the boys and then they'd put them on show and were criticised for that. But now their anger had given way to silent mourning, to reverence.

Victoria caught sight of the carriage long before it passed, flowers piled on top, joining up with flowers thrown before it by members of the crowd. Behind the carriage, she saw Prince Philip and Prince Charles, Diana's tall brother Charles Spencer in the middle of them, the two boys, Diana's sons William and Harry, on either side of him. Victoria watched as the boys marched slowly past, flanked by grown men.

She didn't stay for the service, which was shown on enormous screens in all the parks, but on her way down the mall to the station she heard what at first she thought was thunder but soon clarified as the sound of applause.

She caught an almost empty train home. Everyone else was still at the funeral.

∞

When she opened the front door, she thought she was alone, and in truth she was relieved more than anything. She hadn't seen much of Ben in the days that had passed since they'd fought again, and she had no idea what she would do now. The baby. That's what kept coming into her head. They were having a baby. She'd made herself not think about it. She hung up her coat and slipped off her shoes and walked up the stairs to the kitchen.

'The prodigal returns.' Ben was sitting in the kitchen.
She jumped.
'God, you startled me,' she said. 'I didn't know you were home.'
He didn't get up, didn't turn his head to acknowledge her.
'Ben?'

'Yeah,' he said, still not looking at her.

'I didn't know you'd be home.'

'Where have you been?' he demanded. He turned to her now, a grimace on his face.

'Work,' she said. 'Ewan wanted me to edit a piece for the magazine.' She'd had to cut down the Kate Winslet interview because it would no longer run as the cover story. 'I went in early and stopped on the way home to watch the procession.'

'Did you?'

'Yes,' she said, feeling guilty now, as if she had done something wrong. She wasn't lying, but she felt as if she was. 'The funeral ... Diana.'

He made a noise, almost a grunt. 'I spoke to Daniella today. Turns out you're going to Australia next weekend, which came as news to me. It made me look like an idiot, Victoria. I'm here because of you. You think I want to be in that stupid movie?'

She didn't respond. She was about to say, I haven't had a chance to tell you, but she didn't.

'I talked to Cal again today,' he said.

'About?' she said, not sure where this was going.

'About us. He said I'm letting you get out of hand.' The way he said it. The words themselves. Did his lawyer actually say that? Victoria had never met Ben's lawyer, but she couldn't believe anyone would say this.

'Ben?' She sat down opposite him and tried to make eye contact. She was finding herself afraid again. Without thinking her hands went to her belly.

He noticed that but didn't remark on it.

'We're moving, Victoria,' he said. 'We have to.' He looked a little more like himself now, around the eyes at least. 'I can't protect you here. I thought if I told them we were getting married, they'd show you some respect . . .'

'I wish you hadn't told them,' she said, before realising that would only make him more angry.

He looked at her as if she didn't understand the most simple thing. 'I told them because Cal thought it would help. But it seems you've become interesting in and of yourself, Tori.' He handed her a copy of *The Daily Mirror*. 'Page three. You're the page-three girl.'

She opened the paper and saw the picture. It wasn't her face. It was her backside. They'd taken a picture; it must have been in the park at the top of the street. She'd been running and she was bending over in a stretch and her running shorts had pulled down enough to see her underpants. HOT VICTORIA was the headline. *Does boyfriend Ben know she trots it out at the park?* the caption read.

Victoria just stared at the picture. She couldn't speak.

'I told you to let me handle this. But you knew better. You wouldn't move. You wouldn't have security. Did you want this?'

Victoria looked at the picture again. They'd used a telephoto lens. The photographer could have been a mile away. No amount of security would change that. This had nothing to do with being rich enough to lock yourself away. She was about to tell him as much but something made her hold her tongue.

She took a breath in. She thought she might be sick. It passed.

'So now I'm in charge,' he said. 'Enough fucking equality.' He was not himself. Or perhaps he was himself and the other Ben was the act.

She didn't know anymore.

She only knew that now she was in danger.

Her baby was in danger.

'My bodyguards will take you to work tomorrow,' he said matter-of-factly. 'You drive from now on, no public transport. I've asked Cal to buy the place I looked at while you were in Paris. We'll move as soon as we can. You'll just have to cancel Australia.'

'Hang on,' Victoria said. 'I don't like this, Ben.' She gestured to the picture. 'It's me they've photographed here, not you. I don't like it, but I'm not going to fix it by hiding.'

'Fuck, Tori!' He stood then and took a step towards her and she thought she might faint. She saw his hand go up to strike her before the blow and she knew, suddenly.

She knew him.

Oh God, she knew him.

The blow—openhanded, she would write if it were a fight or a court case she was reporting on, but it wasn't, it was her life—the blow landed on the side of her head. She could feel her ear ringing, wondered was there blood. Her brain rattled in her skull a little before she could think straight. She licked the side of her mouth.

It was not a warning. It was a smack across the side of the head, designed to hurt. And it wasn't the first time. The night before Diana died, and another night, a month ago.

She knew him.

Later she would tell herself it was the child within her, the developing foetus who had a better instinct for survival right then than Victoria herself. Later she would marvel at those few women who can see what's coming and get out. Later she would understand courage in a way she'd never understood it before.

But for now she was going to rely on a child who was yet to form tiny hands in order to get out of the way of the monster in front of her whose hands were forming into fists as her brain calculated too slowly what she should do.

She would not cry, she decided, because whatever else he was, this monster wouldn't like to see weakness.

She looked up at him and forced herself to smile. 'Ben, I'm so sorry. You were right. I really messed this up.' She made eye contact with him, his hand still raised for another blow, this one on the other side. She had to act quickly. 'Ring Cal now. Tell him to come over and we'll sign the contract together.'

This was new. He was momentarily discombobulated. She had taken away his reason for anger. Would it work? She had no fucking idea. What would a three-month-old foetus know?

He stood there, menacing.

He stood there, ready to hit her.

He stood there, revising himself in space.

He didn't strike her again.

He sat back down. 'All right,' he said. 'I just love you, Tori. I couldn't stand to see you hurt.'

'I know,' she said. 'I really do.' She had a feeling in her stomach then, the fear she would not indulge, combined with something else she couldn't name. She squashed both down, felt the nausea that followed fear. 'So call Cal and we can see him tonight.'

He nodded, breathed in and out. Then he stood up and walked past her to the bedroom. The bulk of him as he passed made Victoria queasy again.

Anger. The other feeling she would not indulge was anger.

She had less than a minute.

She grabbed her purse, ran down to the door, grabbed his keys, her own, deadlocked the door and ran down the three flights of stairs to the street. She had no shoes on.

She looked back up to the kitchen window of the flat. It was a mistake. There was Ben, his head and half his body out the window looking at her, not yelling, just watching her, his face. The look on his face. He'd been tricked, he knew.

It terrified her. She thought he might jump out the window after her.

She ran down to Brockley Road and hailed a taxi.

The driver started singing, 'Put your shoes on, Lucy . . .'

'Huh?'

'You okay?' the driver said.

'Fine,' she said.
'So where are we going?' he said.
Where was she going?
She gave him Claire's address.

THIRTY-SEVEN

Western Australia, 1920

WE HAD LEFT PEMBERTON THAT MORNING TO HEAD BACK to Perth on the train. The day before, the prince had toured a sawmill and logging camp with his cousin and Colonel Grigg. Showers had blown in through the day. I'd remained on the train. I didn't even offer to accompany them.

I hadn't seen the prince on his own at all since that night in his room. It was as if everyone else was as they had always been, and I had changed fundamentally. I could never go back. I knew that much.

By mid-afternoon, we'd reached the town of Manjimup, where the train slowed to a crawl so that people could wave to the prince. But he didn't come out of his car as he normally would to the observation platform at the back of the carriage and James signalled for the train to speed up and we went on.

Mr Waters and I were sitting at a table in the office going through the day's letters together. He'd told me that morning that his pen, on the barrel of which was engraved *Dear Rupert* in the same lettering as the brand of the pen, Waterman, had been given to him by the prince when they'd returned from France. It made it look as if his name was Rupert Waterman. 'He's always been very generous with gifts,' Mr Waters said, looking at the pen fondly.

Mr Waters had not mentioned Helen again, or Colonel Grigg, but I knew underneath his heart was broken. Everything was wrong. It was all so terribly wrong.

It was like a spell, the way the prince affected us all. He took your wooden horse, I wanted to yell at Mr Waters.

The train had slowed down at several points, crawling along the tracks. It slowed again now, and then came to a complete halt. It was always unnerving, the noise of the train on the tracks suddenly quieted. I looked out the window but could see no town or settlement, just the giant trees we'd come through the day before.

'Where's H.R.H.?' Mr Waters asked James, who was standing at the sideboard with his polishing cloth.

'Resting,' James said.

'Well, let's hope the stop doesn't disturb him,' Mr Waters said.

The prince hadn't asked for me, hadn't spoken to me, and I was sure he would tell Mr Waters and I would soon be dismissed, like Ruby Rivers. We were birds of a feather, Ruby and I. While I had silently judged her from the very first, we were not so different. We were curious. She was more curious. That was all.

Earlier that morning, Dickie had come and taken the draft letters for signature to the prince. Dickie was his usual jolly self, although there was something new in his smile when he left me, a smugness I didn't like. Perhaps I'd imagined it but I was sure he and the prince had talked about me.

The night before, Helen had asked me again was I all right. I'd told her I was fine. But my mind could not form a coherent picture. He was a prince and yet he was no different from other men, from the fellow at Christie's. Then I told myself it didn't matter because it had been what I'd wanted. But that wasn't right. I hadn't wanted what had happened. I hadn't wanted it at all.

Mr Waters turned to look at the door at the end of the office, panelled in oak, which led to the prince's private study and chamber. We were still stationary.

'I wonder what it is this time,' Mr Waters said, just as a guard came into the carriage.

'There's a cow on the track, sir,' the guard said. 'The engineer is shooing her off and we'll be away soon.'

Just then, the train started up again.

'There it is,' the guard said, steadying himself as the train lurched forward. He left.

The door leading to the study remained closed.

'Thank goodness,' Mr Waters said to me. 'We have to be back in Perth for the reception at five. We'll telegraph if there are further delays.' He looked at his pocket-watch again, closed it and put it in his fob pocket. 'Now, as I was saying . . .' He smiled, picked up his pen again and began reading. We were gaining speed. I could see the plume of steam sailing past in a cloud that appeared solid. It reminded me of the poem that sounds like a train, 'Death and His Brother Sleep'.

Mr Waters was still smiling when we heard an awful noise—as if someone had screamed, I thought, or a wild animal was in pain. I felt a bump. I thought we'd hit the cow. Then a long sad wail and the train began to slow again.

Then I was falling.

I grabbed an ashtray, a heavy glass thing, from the table as it began to slide to the right. It was seconds but it felt much longer. Then the shattering of crystal, warmer than glass, the chairs tipping onto two legs, the light of the sun flashing suddenly in through the window, the smell of something—oil, grease, alcohol; a decanter for claret tipping its contents onto the carpet—and Mr Waters, looking at the door leading to the prince's quarters.

And all of a sudden, as if the world had righted itself, we were back to where we were, eerily still, just the creak of metal settling into place.

Except that we were not where we were. We were on the windows. When I looked up to the ceiling, there were the windows on the other side, and above them the sky, those enormous trees now leaning in menacingly.

I knew immediately we had derailed. The carriage had gone over and with it the desks and tables and chairs. The office was a shambles.

'David,' Mr Waters said, getting up, finding his balance only slowly and heading for the back of the car, clambering over fallen furniture.

I followed. 'Are you all right?' I asked.

'Yes,' Mr Waters said. 'Are you?'

I noticed as he turned to look at me that his hair had fallen onto his face. He was breathing fast. 'I'd better . . .' He pointed towards the end of the carriage. He opened the door without knocking, calling, 'Sir, are you all right? Sir?'

There was a whisper of something within, a person moving about.

Mr Waters half crawled through the prince's dining room and study, everything upturned, the smell of whisky strong, the metal smell of the wheels grinding on the tracks. Hadn't someone said something about this, the narrower gauge unable to take wide carriages? We were on one side, lurching, the slow groan of metal suggesting this carriage hadn't quite come to rest. I could smell deep rich earth. Water was coming from somewhere and dripping on our heads.

Mr Waters called the prince's name but there was no answer.

Oh God, I thought, where are the guards? The police?

Mr Waters turned to me. 'James has the key,' he said. 'Go and find him.' But then he moved back and kicked the door, the door he'd had the carpenters install. It held fast on the first kick but gave way on the second, flipping open. We climbed through to the prince's private chamber.

The prince was standing up, although he was dishevelled, as if he'd fallen. He was wearing a silk dressing-gown tied tightly around his slim waist, no trousers. I can still remember the sight of his skinny calves. In one hand he held a decanter of what was surely whisky and in the other a glass. 'I managed to save what matters,' he said, smiling. The chamber around him was a mess, his bed overturned, books fallen from the little table, his writing desk on its end.

He looked at me and then his eyes left me. I followed his gaze. There to our right was Helen, crouching in the far corner looking disoriented, her clothes askew, no shoes on her feet.

'Do something will you, Waters?' the prince said. 'It doesn't look good.'

Mr Waters's hand came back and found mine. I held it and tried with all my might to put kindness into that grip. I looked at him a moment and I'm sure he saw what was in my eyes for I thought he might collapse.

He turned back to his prince before he spoke. 'Maddie, you must go for help,' he said. His voice was a whisper. 'I will stay here.'

Already there were voices outside the carriage. *Are you all right, sir? Your Royal Highness?*

'Tell them he's getting dressed,' Mr Waters said to me quietly.

Helen was looking at him, wide-eyed with fear.

'Tell James to keep them out of here,' Mr Waters said, his voice breaking.

THIRTY-EIGHT

London, 1997

IT WAS COMFORTING TO SIT ON THE FLOOR WITH JORDAN and Tony playing Lego, to do this simple thing, to watch Claire's gentle useless husband loving his son. It soothed Victoria. She felt safe, she realised. She felt safe for the first time in months.

When Claire had answered the door, Victoria only said she and Ben had fought and she'd stormed out.

Claire had looked at her bare feet and then at her face. 'He hit you,' Claire said softly, as if she were trying to calm an upset child or a frightened animal.

Victoria nodded weakly, let Claire pull her into an embrace, sobbed.

'He does love me, Claire,' she'd said when she regained her composure.

Claire looked her in the eye. 'Victoria, you didn't storm out,' she said, still quietly. 'You ran from danger, honey. We're not going to talk tonight.' She smiled and her smile was full of love. 'I'm going to call Ewan and he and I will sort out what to do. But tonight we're just going to get you feeling safe. I want to call your daddy as well.'

Victoria shook her head. 'No,' she said. 'Please.'

She watched Tony and Jordan now. This was what you'd hope for, she thought, a hapless useless husband full of love.

Claire tucked her into bed in the room with the baby Max. She woke a few times during the night when Max did, Tony or Claire coming in to soothe him. She heard Tony singing a lullaby in the other room at some stage, and then she slept.

༄

It was the next morning now, and Ewan had turned up at Claire's with Mac, the security guard from Knight News. Claire had telephoned Ewan after she put Victoria to bed and they'd come up with a plan.

The four of them were sitting in Claire's loungeroom, toys strewn over the floor. Tony had taken the boys for a walk to the park on Claire's instruction.

Victoria didn't want to tell Ewan anything, so she just said she and Ben had argued. Already she had begun to compose herself, to explain away what had happened.

'I'm sorry, Miss Byrd,' Mac said, 'but you can't go back there.'

'Of course she won't,' Ewan said. 'She's not stupid.'

Victoria shook her head. 'Please don't worry. I'll be fine. It's the stress. He can't stand what the photographers are doing to me.'

It was Claire who spoke. 'Victoria, you can't keep giving him excuses.'

She realised they all knew. Claire had told them. Ben had hit her. His anger wasn't just bad temperedness, as Victoria had told herself. Claire was right. Something was terribly, terribly wrong.

But Victoria hadn't told any of them about the baby. Last night, the baby might have given Victoria the energy to run, but today it was the baby that made her know that no matter what, she was now tied to Ben. One way or another. There was no escaping that fact. She was carrying his child.

Claire told Victoria she couldn't return to her flat until Ben was gone.

'Ewan and Mac will go over tonight to tell him to leave,' Claire said. 'Then we'll organise for a locksmith to change the locks.

Victoria listened without speaking as Claire and Ewan outlined the plans they'd made. When they finished, she said, 'I'll have to go with Ewan and Mac. He has to hear it from me or he won't believe it. I know he won't.'

Her friends were right. She couldn't stay with Ben the way he was. But she wasn't sure she could leave either.

THIRTY-NINE

Western Australia, 1920

WE ALL STOOD THERE FOR A MOMENT IN THE WRECKAGE. And then I heard the voices of the guards who would soon find their way through the windows above us or through the door we'd broken.

I knew the first thing we had to do was get Helen out of the prince's bedchamber. I also knew Mr Waters was in no state to protect anyone from anything.

If we went out through the same door we'd come in, we couldn't be sure there weren't press men or government men.

'Mr Waters,' I said, 'I'll help Helen. You need to go outside, sir, with the prince. It's the prince they're coming for. Mr Waters?'

I looked at the prince then. His expression was hard to read, as if the enormity of what he'd done was still forming in his features.

Mr Waters was standing next to Helen. Oh, the look on his poor face. I couldn't long watch him. Helen was the love of his life, and she had been with his prince.

I looked over to the prince again. 'Please, sir,' I implored him.

'Rupert, dear chap,' the prince said quietly, not meeting anyone's eye, 'let's you and I form a decoy. We'll go up to meet them and give Maddie a chance to clean up. Maddie, darling, you're a dear to lend assistance.'

He'd managed to don his pants and shrugged out of the robe so that he was more or less dressed.

He looked about him, grabbed the decanter of whisky he'd been holding when we walked in and his cap. He put the cap on his head and picked up some papers from the floor near the desk, then called to the guards, whose shouts from somewhere above us on the bank were quite frantic now. Soon they would be upon us.

'We're here!' he called out, waving the papers through the window above our heads.

Mr Waters did his best to secure the door leading to the back of the carriage, pushing a chest of drawers against it and nodding to me.

With that the prince stood on the upturned sofa and put his head out the window that was now the roof of the carriage. He placed the decanter and his papers on the glass and used his arms to heave himself out of the carriage. 'Here!' he called. 'I've managed to rescue what's important, at least.' I heard the clink of the glass decanter and relieved laughter from the men.

'And, finally, we've managed to do something that wasn't on the bloody schedule!' More laughter.

'Quickly,' I said to Helen, who was still crouched in the corner. 'Into the bathroom. We won't have long.'

She still didn't move so I put my arms under hers and began to lift her.

She let out a sob. 'Oh God, what have I done?' she said.

'Helen,' I said gently. I could smell whisky on her breath and the prince's cologne, which made me queasy. 'You'll have to stand for me.' This she did, still sobbing. We made our way to the bathroom. We were slow, as I had to steer her clear of any broken glass because she was not wearing shoes.

Like the rest of the carriage, the bathroom was on its side. It was lined in white marble, and what was once a wall was now the floor. I took a monogrammed towel, which was still hanging from the rack that was now on the ceiling. I turned on the faucet—the water ran straight onto the floor, not into the sink—and soaked a corner of the towel in cold water. 'Here,' I said. 'You wipe your face and I'll find your shoes.'

'Maddie,' she said in a broken voice.

'Yes?'

'Do you hate me?'

'I could never hate you, Helen,' I said, and I meant it. I hugged her then as tight as I could. I felt so much. 'You're the best friend I've ever had. Ever,' I repeated and did my very best to smile.

I went back out to the prince's bedroom and managed to find Helen's shoes, a toe sticking out from the upturned bed. I knew

I had to get her shoes on her and get her out of the chamber and back into our office.

I could still hear voices above us.

The prince: 'I can't let anyone in there until Rupert has cleared the sensitive papers. But we're all fine. What about the carriage aft? Have we counted the government men?'

This would buy us a few minutes at most. I went into the bathroom and said, as gently as I could, 'They'll be here soon. We need to get to the other side of the door.'

Helen nodded meekly, let out a tight sob, closed her eyes and began to pull a shoe onto her foot.

FORTY

London, 1997

WHEN VICTORIA ARRIVED AT THE FLAT, SHE DIDN'T FEEL nervous. Ben would have calmed down, she was sure, although thoughts of his face at the window as she'd run, the focused determination in his features, could still make her heart race.

She was glad Claire had insisted Ewan and Mac come with her now.

'Harry says we're going to cover you at home for a couple of weeks,' Ewan said.

'What do you mean?'

'I think we're going to give you a bodyguard,' Ewan said. 'Can you sing like Whitney?' He started on the long wail of the chorus from the movie *The Bodyguard*.

Victoria smiled. 'That's ridiculous, Ewan. I won't need that.'

'Ben has power, Victoria, and money. Guys like that . . . We're going to get you through this,' he said. 'We're all going to get you through this.'

It was this kind of talk from Ewan, from Claire, that unsettled her most. It was as if they knew something she didn't.

Victoria told Ewan and Mac to wait outside the door to the flat, which she'd leave ajar. 'If you come in, it will just make it worse,' she said. She realised she was speaking quietly so that Ben wouldn't hear.

Ewan started to object but Mac put his hand on Ewan's arm and said, 'I'm right here, Miss Byrd, you understand?'

She nodded.

'Let her do it her way, Ewan,' Mac said. He was the perfect person to have here, she realised.

But Ben was contrite, gentle, sorry for what he'd done. There would be no violence from him, Victoria was sure. It was hard to believe there ever had been any. Perhaps she'd imagined it, she thought, or perhaps she really was so stubborn she would drive anyone to fury.

At any rate, she hardly needed Mac and Ewan. He didn't know they'd accompanied her. She wished now they hadn't. She could do this on her own, she thought. If only everyone would leave them alone, perhaps they'd be all right. It was the photographers that had made this so difficult.

'I'm about ninety per cent what she gave me,' he was saying, talking about his mother. 'But there's the other ten per cent.' He sat down, drank from his water glass.

She watched his Adam's apple rise up and down with swallowing.

'And it's the ten per cent we gotta be scared of.' He was opening and closing his left hand in a loose fist on the table. She noticed that and felt a moment of fear; it passed. He wasn't that other Ben anymore.

'I haven't been back on set,' he said. 'I've just been here thinking about what I did. I'm so sorry.' Tears ran down his cheeks as he spoke.

Victoria thought she understood now what it felt like to know a person and not know them at all. He was Ben, the boyish film actor she'd fallen for. And he was someone who hit women. If she tried to concentrate, to keep those two thoughts in her mind at once, she couldn't. His smell. His smell was a smell she loved. It confused her now.

There was only a moment when she saw that other Ben. 'Were you at Claire's?' he said coldly.

She didn't answer.

Victoria probably wasn't the first woman he'd hit, she thought now, and she wouldn't be the last. It had taken a while for her to believe that. This was the insidiousness at the core of violence, she'd read in a story Claire had dug up for her. It was about funding schemes for domestic violence, and Claire had written it when she was with *The Eye*. You start to second guess yourself, one woman said. You think it must be you. And when they look at you with those eyes you fell in love with, you believe them. And your own confidence is so smashed by the blows that you just believe them, whatever they say. Claire said it explained everything.

It didn't.

'I know all that,' Victoria said now. 'But you have to leave, Ben. I'll make you leave if I have to.'

She was trying to be kind.

'You and whose army?' he said then—not angrily, just trying for his old humour, she thought. His eyes were pleading, if anything. Please don't do this, they were saying. I love you.

'My army.' Mac was standing in the doorway to the kitchen. He and Ewan must have been worried by what Ben said. Strangely, it hadn't worried Victoria. Was she blind to what he could be like? she wondered. Again she wondered were they all seeing something she couldn't?

Mac moved closer. Ben stood and Victoria could see what would happen next.

'Don't!' she said.

Mac stopped where he was. She looked at Ewan, who'd come in behind Mac. 'This is not what I wanted,' she said. 'This is not fair. He . . .' She was crying, she realised. 'Ewan, I want you to wait for me downstairs.'

'I won't,' he said fiercely. 'You can't think I will.'

'Please,' Victoria said. 'Mac, you go with Ewan. I'll be down directly.'

'Victoria . . .'

'Please,' she repeated.

Before he left, Ewan turned to Ben. 'One hair on her head and I'll kill you myself, slowly, and using every bit of power I have as an editor. I know you understand me. I know you understand that, you cunt.'

'Fuck off,' Ben said. But he was calm, Victoria knew. The fact she'd asked Ewan and Mac to leave meant he wouldn't hurt her, not now, not again. He wouldn't. She was sure he wouldn't.

Was that what it took, bringing Mac along, a physically stronger presence? Was this all violence was, a show of strength? Surely not, Victoria thought. Surely we've evolved further than that.

After Mac and Ewan went outside, Victoria went and sat at the table opposite Ben. He refused to meet her gaze. His eyes were full of tears.

'So,' she said. 'This really is the end of our road.'

'Were you scared of me? Is that why you brought those guys?'

He looked up and she saw what she'd loved in him at the beginning, that softness.

She still felt the pull. 'I brought them because I did. You have to get help, Ben.'

'Of course I will. If only—'

'No,' she said, tears running down her face. 'You have to get some help.'

'Please, Victoria. I'm going to change. I promise. Please give me a chance. Just one chance. I love you so much. I will be better. I promise I will be better. It was my dad. It was how he solved his problems. It's not me. I can change.'

Later, when she thought back, she wished that she hated him. It would have been so much easier. But she didn't hate him. She even loved him still that night. She loved him still and couldn't bring herself to stop loving him, not now.

'All right,' she said. 'All right.'

FORTY-ONE

Perth, 1920

'I'M SORRY I LET YOU DOWN,' I SAID. 'I WISH I'D SLAPPED him.'

Helen laughed. 'Is that all you did?' she said. 'Failed to slap the heir to the throne? It's hardly a crime, Maddie. I did ask you, when we first met, not to turn out a Fenian.'

'I wish I'd stood up for you,' I said. 'I should have.'

We were back at Government House. We'd left the train and had come back by motor. The overturned carriages would be unhooked, their contents packed into the remaining upright carriages, and the train would come back to Perth once the track was repaired. The track had subsided in the rain, someone told us, the carriages too wide and heavy for the bend.

We were sitting on the bed together in Helen's room. I hadn't left her side. She was remarkably composed. I don't know if

I wanted to comfort her or I wanted comfort from her. I couldn't put it all together, but I was sure it was my fault, all that had happened. Telling the prince about Helen and Mr Waters, going to his room instead of refusing. I blamed myself, for all of it.

And now Helen had been with the prince.

On the way up the stairs with Helen, who was still shaking at that stage, I had heard Colonel Grigg on the telephone, saying all was well and we were lucky that the train had been travelling slowly. 'We went down an embankment where the ground was soft. Not a hundred yards further along, there was a steep cliff. We'd have lost him if it had happened there.' I didn't know who he was talking to. Seeing the colonel there reminded me that Helen and he were engaged, that she didn't love him. And poor Mr Waters, who loved her truly, who she loved truly, had now seen her with his prince.

Life was altogether too cruel, I thought.

The doctor had seen to Helen's forehead. She had a cut, but it didn't need stitching, the doctor said. Other casualties included the guard who'd come to explain the delay—he had been between carriages when we went over—and a government minister who'd been locked in the toilet when the train went over and whose ego was very bruised.

James had been knocked unconscious in the office. Helen and I had found him and helped him out of the carriage.

In truth, we were all still shaken up. By the time we came out of the train, the prince had already been escorted off to a waiting car. We hadn't seen him since the crash. I heard one of the stewards tell the housekeeper that we would be delayed an extra day in Perth at least. The prince's schedule for the next day had been cancelled. The admiral had ordered a medical examination for him. I heard Dickie telling Colonel Grigg that the prince was furious at being made to submit to an exam when there was nothing wrong.

'Helen, I wish . . .' I sobbed then, for I was thinking about myself, what had happened to me. I still hadn't told Helen.

'Are you all right, Maddie?'

I nodded. 'Are you?'

'Of course,' she said. 'What a nuisance this all is.'

I didn't understand. 'So you are in love with the prince?' I said.

'David? Don't be daft.'

'I saw.'

'You saw what?'

'In his carriage.'

'You saw what?'

'You were there.'

'Yes.'

'You and the prince.'

'No,' she said emphatically. 'David is a poor boy with no idea of what being a grown-up person is.'

'So what were you doing? Pouring tea?'

She laughed. 'I don't know if I needed to pour tea. He's not like that with me. He was talking, but . . . he . . .

'Hmm,' she said then. 'How do I put this? David is a very odd person. You probably know a little of that. I still wouldn't say I understand him. He's not like that fellow in your cafe, but he's nothing like Rupert. Nothing like Rupert. Rupert is so very . . . decent.'

She smiled weakly. 'What should I tell you?' She looked hard at me. 'I should tell you the truth.' She lit up a cigarette, dragged an ashtray across the table, threw the match in, took a long draw and breathed it out.

'On the ship on the way to Australia, David had a breakdown. It's all hush-hush and you mustn't tell anyone because the Prince of Wales can't possibly break down; of course he can't. Rupert and the admiral very nearly turned around and went back to England because when I say he had a breakdown, I mean he entirely dropped his bundle. And he's the Prince of Wales. You couldn't have had him do any formal functions the way he was. He went to bed and would not come out of his state room. It went on for a week. He didn't eat. I'm fairly confident he hardly slept. He looked like a ghost by the end of it, like the shell of a person.

'It was Ned who refused to let them go home. He contacted the P.M., who spoke to the King, and the King commanded the admiral to continue with the tour.

'The prince was largely unaware of all this. But that's why Rupert and the admiral are so careful with him. It's very hard to understand if you haven't seen him when he's not well.

'When he recovered, Rupert and the admiral settled down but Ned told me I was to keep a careful eye on the prince and report any signs of weakness. I had got to know David better anyway, just as you have. I saw him do some enormously wonderful things, showing this great generosity of spirit he has. We lost a sailor near Barbados. He came on deck as soon as the alarm sounded. He joined the search and, when it was in vain, he demanded the entire ship attend the funeral. He wired the sailor's family. He will visit them when he returns to England, and see they are cared for. He will do things like that in a minute. There is this spirit in him that is childish in a way but still generous.'

She took a draw on her cigarette, held in the smoke, breathed out. 'He and I were working on a speech, probably Barbados actually, and he started to cry. I mean, really cry. He was sobbing like a child. It had something to do with his family. I don't remember what exactly. But he looked at me and he talked in a very little voice and asked would I please give him a little cuddle. Actually, he said "widdle cuddle" in a baby voice. It sounds odd to say it aloud to you, but it didn't seem odd there with him, if you know what I mean.

'Honestly, there was nothing except affection in it. It was like he needed a mother, like any child who's feeling a bit lost. I gave him a cuddle, just as I might a child. And so, from time to time, when he felt the need, I would visit his chamber and he would just lie in my arms on the bed and cry his heart out. Half an hour of that and he would be fine. I didn't mind. Afterwards, he was always calmer, better able to manage the tour. Sometimes I'd even sing a lullaby, just as a mother might. It was really very sweet. I never said a word to Ned. I've never told anyone until now, not even Rupert.

'Anyway, as you know, he was devastated when Freda wrote and broke it off. That's why I was worried about you. I thought he might transfer his feelings for Freda to you. You even look a little like Freda, tiny with those curls. She's smart too, and young. You have such a future ahead of you, Maddie, and I thought . . .'

She looked entirely undone. I didn't know why. But I felt a stab, wanted to tell her the truth. 'Helen?'

'Yes?'

I hesitated, then said, 'Nothing.' I just could not make the words come out of me. 'So that's what you were doing in his room today?'

'That's right. Except . . .' She paused.

'Except?'

She grimaced. 'Today, he tried to kiss me—a proper kiss; a man's kiss, not a child's. Perhaps he was just lonely. Perhaps he was just seeing if he could. But I said we must stop. The look on his face, Maddie. Such pain. I was afraid then, afraid of what I'd be asked to do, because I knew I didn't want to do it.

'Luckily for me, the train derailed. I didn't have a teapot handy, as it happens, but I was saved by the narrow gauge.' She smiled bitterly.

'So Mr Waters is mistaken,' I said slowly.

'Yes, he is.'

'Well, tell him then.'

'No.'

'Why not?'

'For one, he won't believe me.'

'Of course he will,' I said.

I knew I wouldn't tell Helen what had happened to me now. What happened to me hadn't happened to her. She'd been alone with the prince many times and it hadn't happened to her. She'd managed to make sure it didn't.

Helen was crying, I saw, her breath catching. 'He... I shouldn't have let him kiss me.'

She paused then, her hand over her mouth, before composing herself once more. 'I don't think I can stay now, Maddie. I don't think I can work with him anymore. And more than that, I have been here these three months, and the truth is that Rupert and I will never be able to resolve our past. His loyalty will always be elsewhere. If I didn't know it before, I surely know it now. I had hoped so much that his goodness would be enough, but it won't. And if I don't leave, Ned will fire me.'

'He doesn't have to know about you and the prince. Also, you're engaged to him. He can't fire you.'

She just looked at me. 'Of course he'll know. I'm sure Rupert will tell him. And we're not engaged. I told him no.'

'But he told Mr Waters...'

'I know. I did say yes to him. Stupid! It was after that night on the ship when Rupert was angry with me, and Ned came to offer comfort. He apologised for the way Rupert spoke. He was so very gentle with me and I thought, yes, I could do this, I could marry you. But even before you spoke to me, I knew it was a mistake. I have told Ned no. Several days ago. He's angry with me. He will love this as an excuse to fire me.'

'Mr Waters won't tell him. He wouldn't, Helen. He's a different kind of fish.' Then I said, 'Did the prince ... with Ruby?'

'I expect he did,' Helen said. 'I'm sorry if I've been cross with you. I really didn't want it to be you. I love you, Maddie. You're a darling dear, and an exceptional young woman. Surely we can save one. That's what I thought. Surely we can save this bright little one. It's what's sustained me through all this.'

I didn't say what I wanted to say: it's already too late.

'I never dreamed it would be me!' she said. 'I'm too old for a start. And he thinks of me as his mummy, not his lover.

'But Rupert,' she said, and she let out another little sob on his name. 'Of course he won't believe me.'

'Mr Waters doesn't know that Prince Edward is like this.'

She smiled weakly. 'No,' she said sadly. 'Poor Rupert has no idea.'

She'd had a dream the night before she said, of a child, a little girl with curly blonde hair like hers. The child couldn't speak, just looked at her as she called to it. It was easy in the way of dreams, but she woke up with tears on her cheeks.

'What happened in France?' I said.

'All right, I'll tell you,' Helen said. 'I'll tell you the whole story. But you won't want to write it anymore, that's for sure.'

'Why not?' I said.

'Because it's sad,' she said. 'Too sad for any soul to bear.'

From *Autumn Leaves* by M.A. Bright:

France, 1918

He had not returned.

It was three months and he had not returned. There had been no word from him, not a letter, not a telegram. Nothing.

It shouldn't matter, but it did. It shouldn't matter because it was what she expected, but it did because it was him. It did because now it was about more than the two of them.

She was with child, three months gone, the doctor in Soissons had told her.

Is everything all right? the doctor had asked.

Yes, she'd replied confidently, wearing a ring enough like a wedding band.

Now she'd been to see Madame Fox in the village. She told Madame Fox she had a friend who had a problem; did Madame know someone who could help?

The True Story of Maddie Bright

There is a woman, Madame Fox said.

She went to the woman without thinking because thinking was impossible.

Still no word.

The woman had a clean apartment, a room where she did her women's work and, mercifully, ether.

That night in her own bed in her quarters she felt the dull ache in her loins, as if within her was the pulse of the world.

The next morning she took off the bed covers and went to stand. She collapsed just as she saw the bright red on the sheets, dripping now onto the stone tiles.

༄

It was Miss Ivens sitting by the bed. She didn't know how much time had passed. It wasn't her own bed. It was a bed in the hospital.

'You're awake,' Miss Ivens said gently.

'What happened?' she asked. It was hard to make her eyes focus.

'A haemorrhage,' Miss Ivens said. 'We operated. You'll be all right now.'

Did Miss Ivens know? she wondered.

'I'm sorry,' she said.

Miss Ivens took her hand. 'I wish you'd known you could have come to me.'

Tears pricked her eyes then.

'You're a good girl. Rest now.'

Miss Ivens kept hold of her hand until she drifted off.

When she woke she felt stronger. Miss Ivens was by her side again, or perhaps she'd been there the whole time.

'I want to go back to work.'

'No,' Miss Ivens said. 'You've lost a lot of blood. I need you to rest, let the nurses care for you and then, when you're strong enough, don't fear; I will order you back to work quick smart.'

'What about the school?'

'Iris is filling in and says she looks forward to your coming back. She thinks you are a marvel with children. She said you must get well soon as she is not a marvel with the children.' Miss Ivens gave her an impish grin.

She smiled back and then remembered. Children. A child. Don't think.

∽

Miss Ivens was there again. 'I have to tell you something now,' she said gently, 'as your doctor, I mean, and then we don't have to talk about this again. All right?'

She nodded.

'The person who did this to you, who started the bleeding . . . I need to find them and give them some training. You were lucky there is no infection, but your bleeding was very serious.'

She looked at Miss Ivens. 'Of course,' she said.

'Thank you. And there is one other thing I need to talk to you about when you feel ready,' Miss Ivens said. 'As a doctor.'

'I'm ready now,' she said.

Miss Ivens nodded, looked towards the window out to the sunny cloister where the patients gathered in the mornings. 'As you know, we had to stop the bleeding,' Miss Ivens said.

'Yes?' she said.

Miss Ivens held up her hand. 'Please. You see, the only way to do that was to remove the womb.'

Miss Ivens regarded her carefully.

'I see,' she said.

'All right, then,' Miss Ivens said, businesslike and brisk again. 'You're a good girl. We'll have you back on form in no time, my dear, and I can say that, from my point of view, you will be most welcome and much valued. From all points of view, actually.'

She could feel the tears welling in her eyes, the constriction in her throat. They'd taken her womb to stop the bleeding, Miss Ivens had said. She knew enough to know what that meant. It meant she would never now have children.

∞

It was a month later. He was standing at the door to the garages.

She'd been about to go out. There had been heavy guns the night before to the north. They would need more cars at Criel this morning.

She'd kept herself busy. She'd told Miss Ivens she couldn't run the school anymore, if that was all right. She didn't feel well enough.

She didn't feel worthy. That was the truth.

Miss Ivens had said she could have an extra week, that Iris would cover but then she would need to go back to the school. 'The children miss you,' Miss Ivens said. 'And we can't have that.'

It had been Miss Ivens who had walked over to the stables to tell her he was here. 'The British officer with the arm,' Miss Ivens said. 'He's here to see you.'

She panicked for a moment. 'You didn't tell him . . .'

Miss Ivens was shaking her head. 'Of course not.'

☙

'I didn't see you when we left,' he said lightly, as if it didn't matter.

'Oh well,' she said.

'H.R.H. is a hard taskmaster.'

'I imagine.'

'The war will end,' he said. 'I wanted to come and see you, to ask . . . I meant what I said that night, the night of the pantomime. I want to marry you.'

She looked at him. 'My hand is taken,' she said.

'I don't understand.'

'I can't marry you,' she said. 'I don't love you.'

'But you said—'

'I didn't. I don't. That was just talk.'

All she had to do was to walk across that floor. Ten feet. Walk across that floor to him.

She couldn't.

The True Story of Maddie Bright

His eyes the colour of truth, his blond hair flopping over his forehead, his slight frame. She felt such a world of emotion.

'Is there someone else?' he asked.

'Yes,' she replied. 'And I want you to leave.'

'I don't believe you,' he said. 'After what we shared. How can you be so heartless?'

'I said you would be sorry. And so now you are.' She smiled tightly.

She stood then and made her feet walk her body out of the room and away from him.

FORTY-TWO

Brisbane, 1997

VICTORIA FLEW FIRST TO HONG KONG, DESCENDING OVER rooftops at dawn. The landing was bumpy and made her wish she hadn't come at all. She spent nearly three hours in transit at Hong Kong airport, watching the buses and planes never quite collide on the tarmac. It was like a Chinese restaurant, she thought: utterly chaotic from the outside but very well organised in its own way.

Ben had said of course she could go to Australia. He had been wrong, he'd said, to be angry about that. And of course she'd be upset by the photographs, especially that most recent one, which crossed a line. He had been possessed of a madness, he said. He'd been blaming himself and then blaming her. He needed help, he agreed. He'd taken the first step, made an appointment to see a psychologist in Los Angeles while she was away. He'd

The True Story of Maddie Bright

already spoken on the phone to the psychologist and it had been reassuring. The psychologist had dealt with people like Ben before, she assured him. Telling the truth was the first important step. It would make all the difference, Ben told Victoria.

It gave her hope.

They would do their best to stop the photographs, Ben said. But of course she could stay in her flat. He hadn't realised how important it was to her. Simple. He would buy the block of flats she lived in and, as soon as the tenancies expired, they'd convert it back into the house it had been. She could do whatever she wanted.

It was such a grand gesture, Victoria thought. He would change. He *had* changed. He hadn't been angry again since they talked. He'd been so loving. He was going to see this psychologist, he said. He was going to be better.

∽

Claire had called more than once. Victoria hadn't returned the calls.

Ewan hadn't said anything, but she knew he'd spoken to Claire.

Mac was the only one who spoke to Victoria about it. She'd come in to work on the Wednesday and he'd said, 'Miss Byrd, nice to see you back.' He'd looked around. 'This is my number,' he said, handing her a card with two telephone numbers. 'Home and pager. You call me any time, day or night. Do you understand?'

She nodded.

'Any time,' he said, 'and I'll find you.'

What was she supposed to do? she wanted to say to him, to Ewan, to Claire. There was a baby now, Ben's baby, and she had to make the relationship work. Of course she did.

Still, she didn't tell Ben she was pregnant, not even as he took her in his arms and kissed her to say goodbye at Heathrow.

She would use the break in Australia to come to her own decision about the pregnancy. There was still time.

She called her father before she left, told him she was off to Australia to do an interview.

'I won't make Sunday this week,' she told him.

'That's all right,' he said, adding, 'I love you.'

It was odd. He wasn't usually given to expressions of emotion.

'I'll see you next Sunday?' he asked. He sounded old.

'Yes, Daddy,' she said.

'Victoria?'

'Yes?'

His voice was strained. 'No matter what, we'll be all right.'

After she hung up the phone, she realised Ewan must have called her father and told him. Or Claire. One of them had.

Oh well, she'd deal with it when she returned, she decided. She'd deal with all of them when she returned.

∾

Ewan had written the cover story for *Vicious* about Diana's death. Victoria had read it over for him before she'd left London. He'd used some of her own story from Paris and given her a by-line with his, which was generous, for it was his writing that saved the story from becoming either retribution or schmaltz which Ewan would never indulge.

He showed her the spread. There were shots of the two boys in their grief, the envelope on top of the flowers on her coffin with the word *Mummy* written on it—someone among the funeral organisers thinking to turn it face up so the photographers could get the shot—the immense crowd outside the cathedral and in the park and across the bridge and throughout the city. Only two thousand attended the actual service but two and a half billion watched on television.

'Don't use the shot of the boys,' she'd said.

'Why not?'

'Everyone else has. Your story's too good for it.'

'Okay,' he said. 'Are you sure?'

'Never more,' she said.

Ewan's story made Victoria so proud she worked with him. He was an extraordinary writer. She'd forgotten that about him. She gave him the copy back. 'I wouldn't change a word,' she said. 'It's the best thing you've ever written.'

'Really?' he said, genuinely surprised.

'You've done exactly what journalism is supposed to do. You've kept yourself just out of the frame, but remained involved enough so that we feel what we feel because of you. You've borne witness. It's beautiful, Ewan. I couldn't have done that, even on my best day.'

She flew the shorter leg with the Australian carrier Qantas. The attendants were so friendly, the opposite of the British Airways flight she'd started on. 'Can I get you a drink?' they asked repeatedly. What was worse, many passengers did drink, even though they must know they were arriving in Sydney early in the morning local time. Most of them were Australians coming home. They were loud.

Victoria tried, unsuccessfully, to sleep and instead watched the movie. It was Ben's first zombie movie, the film that made him famous.

Victoria hadn't watched it before. It was silly. You could tell what was going to happen, and it didn't really require very much acting, just a lot of running and looking grave.

'I love him,' one of the flight attendants was saying to the other when they came with breakfast, pointing to the screen.

'He flies New York–London all the time,' the other said. 'Up the front, of course. Marjorie got to serve him.'

'I'd like to serve him,' the first one said more quietly.

'Is he English or American?'

'American, but I think he's dating an English girl.'

'Lucky English girl.'

Lucky English girl. That wasn't right, was it? It's what everyone thought, even Claire at the start. Not Ewan, maybe not Victoria's father, but everyone else. You lucky thing.

His anger, his temper, wasn't his fault. He'd said it was his father. Victoria knew from stories she'd written that men who hit women always had an excuse, but Ben had said he'd get help. That's what would make a difference, Victoria believed. She was willing to trust him.

But she hadn't told him about the baby . . .

∾

They landed at dawn in Sydney, where Victoria spent several hours waiting for a domestic connection to Brisbane. The light was wrong, sinister in some way she didn't quite understand. She felt frightened again. She shouldn't be frightened, she told herself. It would be all right. There were no photographers here. No one would hurt her.

Andrew Shaw was waiting at the gate in Brisbane. They'd agreed he'd be carrying a copy of *Autumn Leaves*, but it wasn't the edition Victoria was familiar with. She'd picked him anyway: tall, muscled, early forties, faded jeans and a polo shirt tucked into them, carrying a novel.

He had blond hair and very blue eyes, Victoria noticed. When he smiled, as he did now, you wanted to smile back.

'I was trying to pick which one was you coming off the plane,' he said, taking her wheeled bag, leaving her with just her satchel over her shoulder.

'Did you have any near misses?'

'Not really,' he said then. 'You're very pale for Brisbane. But you still don't look like I thought. I'm glad you recognised me.'

'What did you think?'

'Harder,' he said, 'tougher. You're a journalist.'

'Are journalists hard and tough?' she said.

'Yes,' he said. 'Aren't they?'

He took her down to baggage collection before she realised. 'I don't have any other bags.'

'You travel light,' he said.

'Yes,' she said.

She wasn't sure she liked him. He had a knowing nature. Was that what Ben had been like at the start? She couldn't really remember.

They walked out of the terminal into a bright warm day. Victoria took off her jacket and carried it over her arm. She thought she might be sick. Tired, she was so tired. It was only eleven am and yet it felt as if the sun had been up forever. 'Isn't it your winter?'

'We're having an early spring,' he said.

She stopped walking then. They were on a path to the car, under a tin roof, which was marginally cooler than in the sun. The warmth might be lovely if she weren't so tired. 'I need a minute,' she said.

'Jet lag,' he said. 'Gets you at the start.' He took her satchel and jacket, put his arm under hers to support her. 'There's a seat just inside where it's sure to be cooler. Reckon you can make it?'

She nodded.

He almost lifted her with his left hand, pulling her bag and carrying her other bag and jacket with his right.

He sat her down and said he'd be back. He took her bags with him. Good God, she thought. He might just run off with them.

Soon a silver pickup truck pulled over near where she was. He jumped out, holding a paper cup and water. 'It's just from the water fountain by the elevator, so not very cold, but it will help,' he said.

She took a small sip. 'Thank you,' she said. 'I think you're right. It's a long way.'

'Morning sickness?' he said.

'I beg pardon?'

'Oh, I'm sorry. I assumed. I'm so sorry. Forget I said anything. I'm just a bit nervous about all this.'

She just smiled weakly. How had he known?

He opened her door for her and helped her into the truck and then put her bags into the back. They were soon on their way.

They drove along the riverside. The river was wide, like parts of the Thames, and brown.

'How long have you known Madeleine?' she asked.

'Maddie. We call her Maddie. Ah, gee, at least a decade. More. Frank was four when she took us in and he's nineteen now. Decade and a half then. That went fast!'

'How did you meet?' Victoria wasn't exactly suspicious of Andrew Shaw, but she was cautious. The stories of people exploiting old folk were well known. Finian Inglis had said he wasn't sure what Shaw's interest was.

'I'm a builder. I did work for her. Well, actually, I did work for her neighbours first.' He sighed heavily. 'They were horrible people in the end. He was a lawyer, told me this story about

Maddie wandering around her backyard half naked. I knew it was complete nonsense. She'd never have done that. She's a very private person.

'They put me on to do some renovations and then they got it into their heads I should check out her house. It was pretty rundown, and they worried it was going to fall over onto their house. I came to really like Maddie, and she didn't like the neighbours much. But I thought they might be right about one thing, that her house might actually fall down around her, or burn down with the ancient wiring. So I offered to help, and after a bit, she accepted.

'She's not the most trusting person in the world, and nor am I, so we were a good cautious pair. After Ed passed away, Maddie looked after the kids for me while I worked on her house, and then she continued to look after them when they started school. They're good kids and they know what she's done for them. She's been their mum, no doubt about it.'

'Ed—is that Ed McIntrick?'

'Yes.'

'Her agent?'

Andrew Shaw looked at her. 'Hmm,' he said. 'Anyway, she liked the kids more than me, I'd have to say.'

He smiled, a likeable smile. She thought of Ben then, who also had a likeable smile. You never had any idea who people were.

'Where are the kids now?' she said.

'Frank's at the university doing architecture, and Sally's in year twelve. She's going to do journalism. Maddie's influence.'

'You must be very proud,' Victoria said.

'I am,' he said, looking over at her suddenly. 'And very grateful to Maddie. She's been there pretty well their whole lives. I'd do anything for her.'

'Of course,' Victoria said.

'What I mean is, me and my kids, we'd never let anyone hurt Maddie.' He took his eyes off the road again, long enough to make eye contact with Victoria.

She nodded. She got the message.

'So their mum's not around?' she said. Was she interested? She couldn't be interested.

'Divorced,' he said. 'And then she died.' The way he said it didn't invite discussion.

'I'm sorry,' Victoria said.

He nodded.

He was very good-looking, and he had these hands. She imagined he'd built houses with them, but they were really beautiful in and of themselves. He used them to gesture, touched his face, pushed his hair back.

'Do you play an instrument?' she asked.

She was definitely interested.

'Drums,' he said.

'I nearly said drums.'

She was jet-lagged, tired, pregnant to another man, the man she was engaged to, and she was interested.

'How on earth did you know that?' he said.

Was he interested?

'You have hands.'

He looked at her and burst out laughing, and it was even better than his smile, one of those infectious laughs that makes you want to join in. 'Doesn't everyone?' he said.

'Fine,' she said. 'Yours are just . . . intriguing.'

'Well, I've never had anyone tell me that.'

'Are we off to see Madeleine—Maddie—now?'

'No, I'm taking you to your hotel so you can rest for today.'

'I'm not tired.' She wondered why he wouldn't take her straight to Madeleine Bright. She wished she'd had a chance to speak with Finian Inglis before she left. 'We can go today. I'm only here a week.'

'You are,' he said, pulling into the driveway of the Heritage Hotel.

∽

She had a room looking over the river. The light was still all wrong, she thought. It was far too much day. She closed the heavy drapes. She turned on the air conditioning and got in the shower, which was more like a waterfall, as if there was so much water in the world you didn't need to care. It was heaven.

Dressed in the hotel robe, she lay on the bed and called Barlow Inglis, caught Finian just as he was leaving.

'Did you tell me Andrew Shaw worried you?' she asked.

'Well, it's just that Madeleine Bright is so old. It's possible he's found a manuscript and he's somehow trying to make money out of it.'

'He wouldn't take me to see her today, although I asked. So I'm a bit stuck and I'm only here a week.'

'Oh, that's not good,' Finian said. 'On the other hand, if he was doing something untoward, he wouldn't want a journalist involved. For now, just take him at face value. You might be more tired than you think.'

She decided to lie down for five minutes.

When she woke and looked outside, it was dark, which was all wrong in the opposite way to earlier. She went back to sleep, and when she woke again she could see the beginnings of dawn making the cliffs across the river turn gold.

She had been tired, she realised. It wasn't just the jet lag. She'd been exhausted by everything that had happened. Having slept, she could see more clearly. The world was less sinister now.

She took a walk through a university campus and then into the city, where she found a coffee shop. She had breakfast with tea; she couldn't stomach coffee. The tea was appalling. Weak, lukewarm, with milk that tasted like cream.

As she walked back to the hotel, she realised there were no photographers here to worry about. They wouldn't know her in Australia and the English photographers wouldn't come this far to get a picture. She was known in London, because of Ben, and maybe Los Angeles, because of Ben, but not in Australia. It was such a relief. It made her think again that being with Ben, even if he got help as he'd promised, would mean a life of watching everything she did in case someone was taking a picture. Never bending down to stretch after a run, or wearing shorts, or coming out of her flat without being ready for them. Was that the life she wanted? Would they stop eventually, as Ben suggested? Or would it just get worse and worse?

When she checked for messages back at the hotel, Andrew Shaw had called to say he'd collect her at ten to take her to Bright.

She could hear a voice in the background, female, as he spoke on the message machine. She didn't know if it was his daughter, a girlfriend or the television.

The fact that she wanted to know should worry her, she thought. The fact it didn't worry her should worry her too.

He had guessed she was pregnant. She didn't look pregnant yet, and he hardly knew her, but he'd guessed. He'd known her as she was.

Ben hadn't. Ben hadn't known at all.

FORTY-THREE

Perth, 1920

THE NEXT MORNING, MR WATERS CAME TO SEE ME AT THE office in Government House. 'I can't thank you enough, Maddie.'

'Oh no,' I said, 'I didn't do anything. And Helen—I don't think she meant to . . . I think you misunderstood what we saw, sir.'

He held his hand up to stop me speaking. 'Helen is leaving us, Maddie. She's going back to Melbourne today.' He looked as if it took considerable effort to keep his voice even.

'Did Colonel Grigg dismiss her?' I couldn't believe Mr Waters would let the colonel do this. I couldn't believe the colonel would do it. Mr Waters loved her! Colonel Grigg had proposed to her! How could they just abandon her?

'Helen decided to leave, Ned told me. And he's broken off their engagement too, he said, in light of recent events.' Mr Waters almost smiled when he said the second bit!

'No, Mr Waters, she broke it off with him. She doesn't want to marry him. She never did. She loves you. Mr Waters, I don't think . . .'

'You don't think what?' he said sharply.

'I don't think it's what you think, sir. I don't think she and the prince . . .'

He just looked at me.

'I don't think she did what . . . The prince, he . . .'

He was glaring at me now. 'Maddie, I don't want to hear any more about this. I think we know where Helen's heart is, and where it isn't. It's my own fault for pursuing her. I will not be so unwise again.'

'But you love her.'

'Stop!' he said. He gathered his composure. 'The reason I told you what's happened is that Colonel Grigg wants you to take over from Helen. He wants you to staff Prince Edward, help with his remarks. There's Bunbury tomorrow and a couple of train stops en route to Adelaide. That should get us back to the ship.'

For the first time, Mr Waters looked as if he couldn't care less about staffing Prince Edward or the trip or any of the things he was responsible for.

'What about the letters?' I said. I didn't want to have anything more to do with the prince.

'We'll just have to manage. I'm sure we can. We can leave the letters until we're back aboard ship and go through them then. We'll do our best.' He smiled weakly. 'Maddie.'

'Yes, sir.'

The True Story of Maddie Bright

'I did try to get her to stay. I can't believe he . . .' He didn't finish the sentence.

~

I found Helen at the front gate, waiting for her taxicab.

'How will you get home?' I asked. I felt awful for her. She looked so small in her overcoat, her valise to one side. She had told me the story the night before, what had happened to her and Mr Waters. My heart was breaking for her.

'I've booked a train to Adelaide tonight and then on to Melbourne tomorrow,' she said. 'And then, home.'

'London?'

'Temporarily.'

'What will you do? Can you go back to *Vanity Fair*?'

She nodded. 'I'm sure they'll take me back. I'm actually a very good editor.'

'Did Colonel Grigg fire you?'

'No. I quit before he had to.'

'How can he possibly be angry with you? What a hypocrite. I don't think Mr Waters told him.'

'Well, bully for Rupert. But someone did. James, Dickie. One of them did. And Ned was just itching to get his revenge. Anyway, I can't stay. It's all over.' There were tears in her eyes. 'I tried to explain to Rupert, Maddie, but it was no use. He doesn't love me, he said.'

'He's just angry because of what he saw, Helen. He'll be all right. If he knew the truth, I know he wouldn't give the prince another thought. He would be by your side. Can I tell him? Can I give him *Autumn Leaves* if I get it written?'

Helen just smiled. 'Of course you can,' she said.

∽

Back in the office, there was a spider letter. I didn't know the content of the letter but the prince's happy mood after it was delivered told me his mistress had changed her mind. I didn't speak to him myself, but I heard him making jokes with Dickie. Mr Waters was still reserved with the prince, and the prince didn't come near us. I wrote remarks and asked Colonel Grigg to talk them through with the prince. He was only too happy to take over, found me easier to manage than Helen.

It was three days later, on the train east, that the prince asked if I could come to see him about the day's letters for signature.

I went to his study but he wasn't there. I called out, 'Sir?' and heard him call back from his private quarters.

I went towards the door, and I felt afraid. I knew I had to go in, but I didn't want to.

I decided if anything happened, I would kick him as hard as I could and run back out.

I went in.

It was dim in the prince's private study, despite the brightness of the day outside. The shades were drawn and the prince was sitting in an easy chair, pen in hand. He was sipping from a glass.

'Sir?' I repeated.

'Maddie,' he said, looking up and smiling. 'Maddie, dearest, these letters today are the best of the best. And Ned tells me you wrote my remarks for this morning. Marvellous work, my dear.'

'Thank you, sir.'

He stood then and put down the letter in his hand, the glass. 'Drink?' he offered.

'No, thank you,' I said.

'Rupert seems unhappy with me,' he said, smiling.

'I don't know, sir,' I said. 'Perhaps he is.'

'He'll come round, I should think. Always does.'

I didn't respond.

He stumbled a little on his way to the decanter on the side table, poured himself a drink, took ice with tongs and dropped it into the glass. 'Hear that?' he said. 'I love that sound.'

I did not speak, only looked at him. He disgusted me.

I don't know if I had somehow communicated my feelings, but it was the last time he asked for me personally.

FORTY-FOUR

Brisbane, 1997

M.A. BRIGHT LIVED IN PADDINGTON, WHICH WAS NOTHING like its London namesake. It was hilly and darkly green, more jungle than suburb, pocked with little wooden houses on legs, mostly painted in a uniform cream with dark green and dark red trim.

Stumps, Andrew Shaw had said in the truck on the way. The legs of the houses were actually called stumps, not legs. The houses were up on the legs—stumps—because of floods, he explained. 'Brisbane's a river city.'

M.A. Bright's house was built high on a block that rose steeply at the front. It commanded a view over the neighbourhood. If it flooded, Victoria said, the entire city would be under. There was a rock wall and stairs leading up. In another climate, colder, mistier, it would be haunted.

'Maybe it started as a way to mitigate flood and it became the Queensland vernacular,' Andy said. Victoria liked that he used that word, vernacular.

They went in—Andrew Shaw had a key, Victoria noted—and found the writer just inside the door, sitting in a big comfortable chair on the enclosed front veranda, a crocheted blanket over her knees.

She was like an aged writer in a novel, Victoria thought, the kind the word *wizened* was invented for. Victoria had known Bright was in her nineties, yet had expected someone larger, more imposing. M.A. Bright was tiny in the big chair, her face wrinkled so much there were more wrinkles than face. White hair fell in wisps about her skull.

Inside, her cottage was well maintained and neat, a rug on the floor. It looked as if someone was caring for the place. On the table next to her was a signed picture of Diana, Princess of Wales, and another picture, a young woman Victoria didn't recognise, Bright herself, Victoria assumed.

She remained seated in the chair but smiled up at Victoria warmly, extending her hand, which Victoria took.

'Miss Bright, it's an honour,' Victoria said.

'You're the writer,' M.A. Bright said. Her voice was certain, and she gave the appearance of spryness, but the thing that would stay with Victoria was her eyes. They were a blue-green or hazel, and they looked directly at a person, directly at life, Victoria thought.

'No, you're the writer—I'm the hack,' Victoria said, laughing.

The old woman was staring up at her intently. 'I had a friend who said that once,' she said. 'She said I was a writer and she was a hack.'

'Well, in this case, there's no false modesty. *Autumn Leaves*, which I've reread on the flight over, is so very beautiful.'

'It has a happy ending.'

'It does?' Victoria said.

Victoria had wept when she read the last pages of *Autumn Leaves*. It was awful for the young ambulance driver, awful for her captain. They had been at cross purposes and had lost one another.

'It was a story handed to me,' the writer said. She laughed then and said, 'Literally!'

'Wow! You would only get one story like that in a lifetime. Shall I sit?' Victoria wanted to get her tape recorder out so as not to miss anything.

'Oh, please do,' Miss Bright said. 'Where are my manners?'

Andrew Shaw, who'd gone further inside the house, came out then with a teapot.

'I made tea, Maddie,' he said.

'Oh dear,' she said. 'At least there's Sally's banana cake. You may have to ignore the tea itself, Victoria.' She laughed and then said, 'Actually, we can't have that, Andrew, can we? We can't drink tea that tastes like an old boot. Victoria's from London!'

The old woman stood up—she *was* spry—and led them through the house. The interior was painted white, with

The True Story of Maddie Bright

gleaming honey-wood floors and high ceilings of pressed metal. It was really rather charming, Victoria thought.

M.A. Bright moved slowly but efficiently, tipped out the tea Andrew Shaw had made, washed the pot, put more tea in, boiled the water, took down cups.

Andrew took a tray from a cupboard. It was obvious he knew his way around the kitchen and was accustomed to Maddie being in charge.

Maddie looked at Andrew at one stage and Victoria thought she saw fear. 'I don't know if I can,' she said, perhaps thinking Victoria couldn't hear.

'Course you can, Maddie. It's just information, remember?' He looked across at Victoria then and smiled. Victoria wondered again if the old woman might have been coerced into the interview, into publishing the book, and Victoria didn't want any part of that. She wished Andrew Shaw would leave so she could talk to M.A. Bright alone. He'd said he would but now he was hanging around.

Andrew carried the tray back out to the veranda. Maddie followed, Victoria behind.

Victoria noticed on the way out from the kitchen a little desk with an old typewriter just inside the door to the enclosed veranda, pencils in a mug and a sheaf of papers, probably the manuscript for the new novel. The writer's desk. She'd get them to photograph that for the story, she thought, and the backyard off the kitchen where she'd noticed chickens, a vegetable patch.

Andrew Shaw set the tray down on the little table between the two chairs out on the veranda. 'Maddie, I'll leave you to it.'

'You won't stay?' Maddie asked, her eyes wide.

'Nope.' He bent down and took her in his arms for a long moment, might have whispered something. Victoria worried again the poor old woman was being coerced, although the fact that he was leaving made it less likely. And the writer did not look easy to coerce.

∾

'I like sitting out here and watching the street,' Maddie said after Andrew had left. There were louvre windows all along the front wall of the veranda. They were open to the street now.

'Yes, it's lovely,' Victoria said. It was a perfect blue day and the air was crisp. Maddie was wearing a cardigan and long woollen slacks with little red boots. Victoria had missed them before because of the blanket. 'I like those boots,' she said now.

'Oh, that's Sally. She keeps me up with the trends.'

'Miss Bright . . . May I call you Madeleine?'

'Maddie.'

'I'm Victoria.' She thought of Tori.

'Yes, I know.'

'Will we stay out here for the interview?' Victoria looked around. The street was quiet, although crows were cawing every now and then. She had taken out her little cassette recorder to tape the interview.

'Yes, I think so,' the old woman said. 'And then our thoughts can scatter to the air and not worry us.' She made little dances in the air with her fingers.

Maddie had brought out a thin manila folder, Victoria saw now, which she set on the table between them. Victoria sat opposite her, angling her chair to face Maddie. Maddie continued to face the front windows.

'All right.' She pressed play and record, and surreptitiously put the recorder on the table nearer Maddie than herself.

'I never met Mr Inglis,' Maddie said, seeming not to worry about the tape recorder. Often people became momentarily shy when it went on. 'It was Mr Barlow who looked after me. Did you say you are from a magazine?'

'Yes, I work for Knight News, for a monthly magazine in the UK called *Vicious*.'

The old woman laughed at that. 'I'm not sure I'm ready to be in a magazine called *Vicious*.'

'Oh, we just pipped *Vanity Fair* in sales.'

'*Vanity Fair*,' she said. 'I knew someone who worked for *Vanity Fair*. My father . . .' She smiled. 'It doesn't matter now.'

'Of course it matters,' Victoria said. 'Do go on.'

'My father was a poet.'

'Ah,' Victoria said. 'So writing is in the blood?'

'You might say,' Maddie said, smiling. 'What do you write?'

'Me?' Victoria said. 'Actually, mostly I write profiles on people who've achieved something and, sometimes, people who haven't achieved something.' She smiled. 'But in your case, we're speaking of an enormous achievement. *Autumn Leaves* is a wonderful story, and I understand from Finian Inglis that—'

'It's a sad story,' Maddie said.

Hadn't she said it had a happy ending just before? 'Yes,' Victoria said. 'Tragic.'

'Just like Diana.'

'Yes. So, as I was saying, I reread *Autumn Leaves* on the plane. Shall we talk about that first?' Victoria knew writers were often difficult to draw out on new work, and she also wanted to get to know Maddie before she broached the new novel and Andrew Shaw's role.

'*Autumn Leaves*,' she said. 'Wasn't I lucky to find Mr Barlow? That was Mr Waters. He did that.'

'Mr Barlow from Barlow Inglis?'

The old woman nodded.

'And Mr Waters?'

'Mr Waters was still the prince's man then.'

'Ah, yes, so there has always been speculation about *Autumn Leaves* being autobiographical.' She thought she'd chance the difficult question.

'Well, of course it was,' Maddie said. 'Not autobiographical, but based on two real people. Everything's autobiographical when you're a writer, isn't it? But really, it went from them to me to you, and nothing can survive that sort of journey unmolested, so it hardly matters, does it?

'I read your story on Diana and Charles,' Maddie went on, changing the subject without missing a beat, 'and I liked that you gave her power no one else was giving her. You rewrote her story for her and I think it would have made a difference to her. I hadn't thought of her that way before, and it brought me comfort that she could have power over her own destiny even after everything that happened. I hope you were right. I hope she had found her power.'

'Yes,' Victoria said. 'Thank you. And so, getting back to the two characters in *Autumn Leaves*?'

The old woman looked at her, smiled and shrugged. 'What I did with *Autumn Leaves* was to show them their story.'

'And so who were they?'

'Mr Waters and Helen,' she said, as if Victoria should already know this.

Was M.A. Bright addled? Victoria thought then.

'And now we come to the exploiting part,' Maddie said, smiling across at Victoria. Her gaze became intense. 'You have the loveliest cheekbones.'

'Thank you,' Victoria said, unsure where this was going. 'My mother's. But no one's ever said that. Getting back to *Autumn Leaves*, it was published in 1922, is that right? And you wrote it after the war?'

She nodded. 'Now, of course, I'd change the ending. I'd give it a happy ending.'

Okay, back to the happy ending. 'But it's poignancy lies in the tragedy for the two protagonists.'

'Yes, and the war had plenty of tragedy. My father for one. My brothers. I lost everyone.'

'And it was hard to write after that?' The interview was getting away from Victoria, she thought.

'Who cares about writing?' she said. 'I mean, really.' Maddie Bright stared hard at her. 'Who cares?'

Victoria smiled. 'I think I know what you mean. So *Autumn Leaves* wasn't based on your life at all?'

The old woman just smiled.

'*Winter Skies*?'

'Yes,' she said. '*Winter Skies* would be my story.'

'It's a true story?'

'As true as any,' Maddie said.

'Barlow Inglis are very excited about the lost baby.'

'Yes,' Maddie said, becoming serious suddenly.

'That first chapter is heartbreaking.'

'Yes,' Maddie said. 'It was. I'm not doing very well, am I?' She took a sip of her tea, offered the plate of cake. Victoria took a piece, put it on her saucer. She didn't feel like eating.

'I think you're doing splendidly,' Victoria said. 'I have to tell you that I was a little intimidated. I don't think I've ever interviewed someone like you before; someone who's never been a public presence and yet has changed so many lives.'

Victoria noticed the picture of Diana on the table again, and next to it the picture of a pretty young woman in a woollen suit, blonde curly hair. 'Is that Princess Grace?' she asked.

'No,' Maddie said. Then, 'Will you write something more about Diana?' She glanced at the picture herself.

'I don't think so.'

'Did you watch the funeral?'

'I did, from the street. I watched the coffin pass. It was . . . It was hard to fathom.'

'I couldn't bring myself to watch on the television,' Maddie said. 'I sat in my own backyard and looked at stars. When I found the Southern Cross, I latched on.'

She sighed. 'Well, here goes,' she said then.

She sat up straight, crossed her hands in her lap. 'I need you to turn that tape off now. I do have some news, but it's only for you.'

Victoria picked up the little recorder, pressed pause.

M.A. Bright leaned over then and reached for the folder, took out a single piece of paper and handed it to Victoria.

FORTY-FIVE

1920

WE TOOK THE TRAIN TO ADELAIDE WHERE WE JOINED the *Renown* for the journey to Tasmania. There were mercifully few speeches and the prince seemed to have lost interest in doing them anyway. I would write the text and Colonel Grigg would go through it with the prince. Mr Waters never commented on the fact that I would not go through the remarks with the prince myself. He never once suggested we do it differently. He and I continued to work together closely.

Mr Waters never mentioned Helen either. You would not even have known of his feelings unless you had started writing a story about them. Once Helen left the tour, I started the story that became *Autumn Leaves* in earnest. I made a study of Mr Waters, his most endearing mannerisms, the way he looked up from his work sometimes, so hopefully, the way he paused with his pen mid-air when considering the exact right word. I wrote Helen from my fond memory of her. I did my best to find the best truth of them.

From Tasmania, we sailed back to Sydney. The prince's moods continued to fluctuate as they'd always done, up and down, up and down, with the flow of letters from Mrs Dudley Ward. He left me alone.

Mr Murdoch came to see me before he left. He was going back to England but only temporarily, he said. 'I can't tell anyone yet, but I've been offered the editorship of the Melbourne *Herald*. I'll be looking for writers. I'd be happy to have you join us.'

'Why?' I said.

'Because you write well,' he said, as if it were obvious. 'You think I didn't listen to the speeches or read the statements? I know you wrote them. Ned Grigg isn't at that level. And I want women on my staff for the paper,' he said. 'I'd have asked Helen too if she'd been here.'

I looked at him.

'It's nothing like that,' he said. 'Women are the majority of my readers. I want women writing. You can start as a cadet.'

I couldn't answer him straightaway, couldn't trust my voice. 'All right,' I said finally. 'Yes.'

'I'll start in January,' he said. 'I'll be in touch.'

It was the day I was leaving his service that Mr Waters told me that bad people and good people look the same, that you couldn't tell them apart, that people he expected to be good had turned out to be bad. I don't know if he was talking about Helen or the prince, or even me. I didn't ask him.

But Mr Waters was right about that. Bad people and good people look exactly the same.

We docked in Sydney and took a train to Brisbane, stopping en route so that people in dozens of towns could come to see the prince. I went home as soon as we arrived and when Mummy asked me, I told her lies about the tour, the prince, everything. Grand was the word I used repeatedly. Everything was grand. Mummy asked me what I had thought of Prince Edward. Your overall impression, she said eagerly.

There was hope in her features, I could see, almost a desperation. The world she'd grown up in, the world she'd had to flee; surely, it remained on the side of goodness, she seemed to be saying. She'd lost her son, her husband for that world. It couldn't have been for nothing.

So when she asked me my overall impression of the prince, I swallowed hard. I swallowed down the very last vestige of the child I had been, my mother's child, and told her, 'Mummy, he was the most beautiful creature I have ever seen.' This was not a lie. Much was said later about the prince, and much of it was true. And, after his death, the biographers raked over the cold coals of his life, trying to make a flame, of love or hate or pity—how he would have hated that last. They pitied him, a fool for love of a woman not worth loving. That's what was said.

I often thought later of my mother. She had no rudder to guide her but her own upbringing, which was so steeped in loyalty to the Crown, fealty to the monarch, that she couldn't change direction. She could no more have imagined the Prince of Wales as he came to be than I could. Her own young life was so prescribed she had no need of the tools most young women have need of. She had no idea what the world was really like. The only man she'd ever known was Daddy, and he was a good man.

But my mother asking. My mother! 'Beautiful,' I said again. 'Like a creature of the deep we can imagine the beauty of but never know.'

Daddy was quiet, and at first I thought he was angry that I'd gone on the tour, but the truth was that by then he had too many demons of his own to care. He wasn't getting better, as Mr Waters had said he would. He was getting worse.

On my own, I cried and cried. I was glad to be back with my family, back with the little boys, but I felt so different from the Maddie who'd left them that I wasn't sure I was home at all. It was as if I had changed but they had too. The earth under my feet had changed. Nothing would ever be the same, although I didn't know that at the time.

I went to see Mr Waters at Government House in Brisbane when they came back from a trip to the west of Queensland. The prince was in bad shape, Mr Waters told me, and they were taking him out to a farm for a few days before they sailed for home. It was as if the whole incident with Helen had never happened. They were back to normal, managing their prince for the good of the empire. There were three daughters at the farm, I read in the paper.

I remember thinking that for Mr Waters, this was life. Perhaps he even knew what the prince had done, if not to me, then to Ruby Rivers. He knew what had happened to Helen. He knew what his master was capable of. Helen was right. It almost made him worse.

I gave him the story that became *Autumn Leaves*. 'You need to read this,' I said. 'It's written about you. It's the truth.'

He looked alarmed.

'It's all right. I'll keep your secrets. But read it, Mr Waters. It's your story.'

'Maddie, he does his best.'

'I'm sure he does,' I said. 'Thank you, Mr Waters. I've learned so much.'

∾

It was a month after they'd left that I realised I was with child. I knew from Mummy's pregnancies the symptoms and I figured out that what he'd done was how you made children. He had made a child in me. I knew I couldn't tell my mother. I certainly couldn't tell my father.

I hadn't told them about Mr Murdoch's offer and I was glad I hadn't now because I knew that I would not be taking it up. Mr Murdoch had written before he'd left to go back to London. In my reply I thanked him but was sorry to inform him that I would be taking up another position.

I told Mummy I wanted to go and visit Bea. I'd made enough money from the tour to get us through to the end of the year, and so they were happy to pay the train fare. I took what extra I could without telling them. It wasn't much.

Saying goodbye was awful. They thought I was going off to Sydney for a week, but I thought I would probably never return home again.

I told Bea a lie too, that I'd been offered a position with the prince's staff and I didn't want to tell Daddy about it because he'd say no—not because it wasn't a good opportunity, but because he had a set against the royal family. I told Bea I could study at the university in London. She was more than happy to buy me a berth on a ship and to explain to Mummy and Daddy why she'd done it. 'Are you sure you're all right?' she did say on the night before I left.

I felt certain that if I told the prince of my condition, he would help. The baby was his, and he would help me. That's what I believed. He may have been weak, but he would take responsibility for his own child. Surely he would. He was a prince.

I arrived in London after six weeks at sea. I don't think I've ever missed my family quite as much as I did in those weeks, the little boys especially. I wanted them when they were smaller, one on each knee telling me stories. I wanted to read my father's rat essays and call him gently back to us.

By the time I disembarked, the pregnancy was beginning to be obvious. I knew I wouldn't get work in my state and I had little money with me. I found a hostel near Buckingham house and set out the next day to go and see the prince.

I had thought it would be easy. He'd always been so available to his staff on the tour, I assumed seeing him would be the easy part. I went to the gates and found a guardhouse to one side on the left where there was an army captain. He came out of his booth and looked at me. He noted my mid-section. I asked for Mr Waters.

He told me to wait.

A man I didn't know came out after about twenty minutes. 'I believe you're looking for Mr Waters?' he said.

'Yes.'

'You can talk to me.' He didn't give me his name.

'I can't,' I said. 'I must speak with Mr Waters. I must see Prince Edward.'

He smiled. He was a short man with a face like a rabbit, beige hair and large ears. 'His Royal Highness the Prince Edward is not here,' he said. 'And nor is Mr Waters. But at any rate . . .' He looked at my belly. 'At any rate, they wouldn't be able to see you.'

I went back three or four times to no avail. Eventually, the guards got to know me and stopped sending anyone down from the house. It dawned on me that they wouldn't help me.

Mr Waters wouldn't help me.

The prince wouldn't help me.

I was all alone, pregnant and in a strange place with no money.

The True Story of Maddie Bright

I thought of contacting Helen but I had no idea where she was. I went to the office of *Vanity Fair* but they said she hadn't worked there since 1919.

On my fourth visit to Buckingham house, I saw Sir Godfrey Thomas coming out and called to him. He saw me and looked as if he might recognise me, but once he saw my belly turned stony-faced and went back inside.

The next day, there was a guard I hadn't yet met and I asked to see Sir Godfrey Thomas. He told me to wait and the same man who I'd seen on the first day, the rabbit man, came out and told me Sir Godfrey wasn't there. I told him to check again as I'd seen Sir Godfrey myself the day before. He started to rabbit away, so I said I would wait for as long as it took. I spread my two palms over my belly. I was afraid. I was desperate.

The man went away and then, after what seemed an age, the guards glancing slyly my way whenever they could, he came back and led me not into the palace grounds but across the road to St James's Park.

There was Sir Godfrey seated on a bench in the park. At least he had the decency to look pained.

I told him the child was the prince's. He looked around us and then told me I couldn't say things like that. It wasn't possible, he said.

Even aid was beyond them, I realised, even aid to those they'd harmed, to the prince's own child. There was no goodness in any one of them.

'Maddie, can you not see that if we give you money, it's as if we agree to your preposterous story.'

'My story is not preposterous,' I said. 'Where is Mr Waters?'

'Rupert is no longer serving H.R.H.,' he said.

I went back after the child was born, and Sir Godfrey met me in the park again. It was he who first told me about the foundling wheel at St John of God Church, the one the nurse at the Sally Ann gave me directions for.

'I'd like to help,' he said, 'but you know that if I help you, it looks as if this is something to do with H.R.H.'

If you are ever in trouble, Maddie, you come to me, the prince said to me once, when I first knew him and he was upset about what my father had suffered.

He meant a different kind of trouble, I suppose; the kind he did not cause.

∽

Mr Barlow was the first person I told the story to. He came to the Sally Ann two weeks after I'd read in the paper that my baby had died. I was in a terrible state. I had entirely given up on life. Mr Waters had given Mr Barlow my manuscript of *Autumn Leaves* and had told him where to find me. I couldn't believe Mr Waters would do this. It meant he knew where I was after all.

I remember noting this at the time. The good people and bad people look exactly the same as one another, Mr Waters, and you looked like a good person. But you were not. Not in any way. You must have known I had come to Buckingham house, and you did not help me. Perhaps you thought getting my story published would help me but, even so, that wasn't the help I needed.

The only thing that had stopped me from ending my life before then was my little brothers at home and the cord that tied me to them, to my earthly form. Those strings of attachment that tethered me to this world and that those Buddhists would have me eschew. I thought of the twins and wept and wept. But I had no means of getting back to them and no wherewithal to find work.

I may have said this to Mr Barlow, whom I had never met before. I am a woman who killed her baby. I have nothing to lose.

Mr Barlow only looked at me sadly, as if he understood the weight of my situation and would do anything to make it not so.

The second time he visited, he brought his sister, who got me out of bed and washed and dressed me. They took me to a hotel to stay until I was strong enough to travel home.

Mr Barlow told me he would publish *Autumn Leaves*. He would be so proud, he said. We would together remove the names of the characters—I'd hardly used them anyway—but he must publish, he said, to show the truth. 'It's going to cause something of a ruckus with the royal family,' he said. 'But I don't care.'

I must write that other story too, he said. It must be shared. He didn't care what anyone thought, even Mr Waters.

Not because it's a true story, he said, but because it tells the truth.

∽

After I arrived home in Brisbane, my berth paid for by dear Mr Barlow, I saw my father's condition had deteriorated. Instead of getting well, he was more disturbed. In his study, he talked to people who weren't there, lined the walls with his rat drawings. Mummy was afraid. The boys were the selves they'd changed into to accommodate him, doing their best.

Within a year, Daddy was gone physically as well as mentally. He took his own life, hanged himself under the house, right about under where I sit to write. A mercy, really, for our father was long gone by then. I missed him so much and for years, even the person he was after the war, who would sometimes show glimmers of his old self, who might have grown happy even if he remained afraid of life. I kept seeing signs he was getting better after I arrived home, but it was just my wishing it were so.

We never as a family recovered, and I was in no state to help. Daddy was so much the centre of our happiness. We were like a centrifuge then, spinning, but its only effect was to separate us into our component parts. Mummy died, a cancer that started in her left breast. I cared for her through her last days. She knew, I think. She knew I'd had a child. I don't know how. We never spoke of it, but I felt in her eyes there was a knowing. I'm sorry, she said on her second-last day. I'm sorry I didn't protect you.

I did my best to raise the twins, but really I only raised them so that the empire could take them too. And then Bert died in

1949, a heart attack from an inherited condition none of the other boys had lived long enough to discover, and John just two years later in a house fire.

And so I was alone. There was never enough money to live on from the royalties the book earned, of course—it was even banned for a time, Mr Barlow wrote me—and so I trained as a teacher down at Ithaca, and thank goodness I did.

In my first month home from London, I used to visit the orphans' home in Petrie Terrace. I would go to the nursery. You could just wander in and sit down. There was a cut-out in the wall and you could sit on a bench and watch the babies sleeping.

I imagined taking one of those babies home with me. Not having the baby—I didn't think about that—just getting up and walking into the nursery and picking a baby up and walking out.

But I knew they'd come and find me. They'd know what I'd done to my own child, and that would be that. I'd go to prison. Here were all these babies with no home to go to, but no one would give them a home with me.

I think of their journey, those babies. I think of where they've come from and are going. Not one of them asked to be born into a world where they would have no roots other than those they put down themselves, where they might pass through life so quickly. This was not a choice any of them made, not my baby, not my brothers, not any of us really. That's what religion should help you ponder, but it doesn't.

You learn to accommodate the past, I suppose, or perhaps the present accommodates you. I must have decided—I mean,

I don't remember deciding, but I must have decided to stop thinking about what had happened, to block it out altogether. Perhaps that's not quite what I did. But something like that.

Teaching helped, the children; not because it was a child I lost but because children are hope personified. I didn't want to write, to find the demons there, but teaching was perfect. There was a time when *Autumn Leaves* started to earn money and my accountant told me I could leave work now and live off my earnings. I just nodded and smiled. Teaching saved me. I was not about to give it up. I instructed the accountant to separate me from the book's earnings and completed my will. When I died, the money earned by *Autumn Leaves* would go to children separated from their parents by death. To orphans. My money would go to orphans. I hope it makes them rich.

∽

Any teacher with a brain will be able to tell you, within broad parameters, where the children in the class are heading in life: this one to medicine, this one to marriage and children, to alcoholism, despair, to law or bricklaying or murder. It's not that I believe in destiny exactly. But we become a close enough approximation of the person we are on the road to becoming from an early age, and destiny exists to the extent that there must be a great ledger somewhere with it all written down long before any of it happens.

The prince's future was more set down than most. You might forgive him a great deal if you understood the weight he carried from the time he was a small child. A destiny was written for him, a destiny he ultimately sidestepped but never truly escaped.

When he grew old, to me Edward, then Duke of Windsor, most resembled his father, King George V, more than any of the other boys in the family. He had abdicated and so it was a difficult comparison. His father had spent his adult life as the monarch, duty his principal driver, whereas Edward had done so for less than a year before he'd abdicated and married the divorcee Wallis Simpson, driven by some other feeling than duty.

When I knew him, he saw himself as a different man from his father, a modern man. I think we all saw him that way. But he looked like his father in the interview I watched and he expressed a deep concern for making sure things were done properly, the thing he had despised most about his father. He talked a lot about the 'Establishment' as if, in 1970, he'd just discovered it existed. I wondered then at his stupidity, for I had never thought him stupid when I knew him.

I don't believe Edward VIII abdicated for love. Perhaps he wasn't someone who could love, I think now, for love requires of us that we see another person and I'm not sure he could. Perhaps the prince was missing some part of his humanity that must form when we are very young, the capacity to take love in that allows us to give it back.

If Edward's destiny was largely written for him ahead of time, when I first met him, my future was only lightly written, hardly marking the page at all, a journey with many potential roads. I began with such opportunity, in Australia, where we were more free to do as we pleased than in England, where I might have been born to nobility. I began life amid enormous optimism, as big as the sky over Australia, with a good and decent father who would do anything to feed that optimism in his children. I might have studied history and worked for the library as Bea planned for me. I might have been a writer, which was what Daddy wanted me to do.

But then Daddy went to war, and when he came home there was no chance of education, and Edward was gone from us. And then I went with the prince and Mr Waters and learned the true nature of men.

It comes down to choices we make, I suppose, within the constraints of the hand we're dealt. I'm a terrible bridge player. I never managed the strategy. I think the prince might have been a terrible bridge player too, if it came to it.

The prince's men though—Sir Godfrey Thomas, Colonel Grigg, even Admiral Halsey, Mr Waters—understood how a hand of bridge might be won or lost. They made sure it was the former when it came to their prince. When I knew him, the prince was twenty-six years old and full of what I mistook for idealism. But now, looking back, I can see he was nothing but a soul in search of a conscience. That soul was run entirely by men who understood how to get what they wanted from the world and did so.

What I have done is skirted the life I might have lived, or perhaps I have lived within it, some small version of it so that the me I would have been surrounds me. I can see her there sometimes as I'm falling asleep. She has such courage. She is pouring tea on them again and again whenever they dare bother her. She is strong, invincible. They cannot harm her.

FORTY-SIX

Brisbane, 1997

SHE RANG CLAIRE. SHE DIDN'T KNOW WHAT ELSE TO DO.

'Maddie Bright is my grandmother.'

'What?'

'M.A. Bright, the writer, is my grandmother.'

'Victoria, slow down. It's three in the morning. Where are you?'

'Australia. I'm sorry. I just . . . I have to call Daddy, and I don't know what to say. And Ben.' She sobbed. 'Oh God, it's like a bolt out of the blue, Claire. You were right. I'm sorry I couldn't see it before. I've met this fellow.' She was crying now. 'I don't even like him much, but in two days, he's shown me what's wrong, why I have to end it with Ben. The baby, we'll just have to work it out, but I can't go back to him.'

'Well, that's good. Hats off to whoever he is.' Claire was

bleary. Victoria could hear Tony in the background. 'It's Victoria,' Claire said. 'Go back to sleep.'

'Andrew,' Victoria said. 'Andrew Shaw.'

'Who?'

'That's who's made me see,' Victoria said.

'What baby?' Claire said then.

'He's just a normal fellow. We flirted. It wasn't like Ben. It wasn't anything like Ben.' She knew she'd woken Claire up. She knew she wasn't making sense. But she didn't seem to be able to do anything about it. She'd spent time after her meeting with Maddie Bright wandering through the Botanic Gardens. She'd left without waiting for Andrew Shaw and walked until she found a taxi.

There was a tree, an African tulip, she was told by a gardener, and she stared at the purple flowers for a long time. It was like being drugged.

'I'm pregnant, Claire,' she said to her friend now.

'Oh, God!' Claire shrieked. 'No, nothing, Tony,' she said. 'Go back to sleep.' Then she said, more quietly, breathlessly, 'Of course. Of course you are. No wonder this has been . . . Oh, Victoria, I should have noticed. How stupid. I wish I could give you a big hug. I'm so sorry.'

'No, don't be,' Victoria said. 'It's all become clear now. Yes, it's been a big upheaval. But you were right, Claire. It's not going to work. It's . . . He can't come back from what he did, even if he gets better. What was I thinking?'

'That's right, and we can work this out. I'll help. We'll help.'

'I don't want an abortion.'

'That's fine. Of course. Have the baby. Whatever. You can join my bad mothering club, membership of one so far, and be unhappy about everything you do, really. Tony can look after it. Well, to the extent he looks after his own kids. Seriously, we'll make it work, Victoria. Whatever you want, we'll make it work. Where did you say you were?'

'I'm in Australia. I'm sorry I woke you. I just had to talk.'

'No, that's fine, I'm up now,' Claire said. 'I'm going to make coffee. So if Max needs breastfeeding, too bad. But can we back up? Did you say at the start of this phone call when I was still asleep that M.A. Bright is your grandmother?'

'Yes.'

'Okay, that's what I thought you said. You mean M.A. Bright the novelist from the twenties, don't you?'

'Yes!'

'You have to explain that one. I'm glad I asked, actually. If I'd got off the phone without asking I'd have figured I dreamed this, because M.A. Bright is a man.'

'Well, she's never been a man, but now she's also my grandmother.' *Grandmother.* The word had kept repeating in Victoria's head.

'Claire, you couldn't put it in a novel,' Victoria said, 'because no one would believe it. M.A. Bright wrote *Autumn Leaves*.'

'I knew that much,' Claire said.

'Autumn Leaves is about the army officer and ambulance driver who fall in love during the great war. It's based on a true

story. M.A. Bright, Maddie, actually met the real people the characters of *Autumn Leaves* are based on during a royal tour of Australia in 1920. I don't know how much of the book is real, but Maddie worked for Prince Edward—he's the blond one who later abdicated—as some sort of secretary, and so did they, the couple, except they weren't a couple then. *Autumn Leaves* is their story, Rupert Waters and Helen Burns, or it would be their story if it were true. Am I making sense?'

'Not really. So you're related to them, or to her?'

'Her. Both. They raised Daddy and pretended to be his parents and my grandparents, but they weren't.'

'The Byrds?'

'Yes. They changed their name to Byrd after the explorer. Poppy was a history nut.'

'Hang on. So the Byrds—your nana and pop—were the Waterses? Your nana? I loved your nana, the American. She was funny.'

'Yes. My grandparents were Rupert and Helen. Maddie said those names today, when she was talking about *Autumn Leaves*, and I swear, Claire, I could almost feel it coming towards me. The truth. It's woken me up.'

After the gardens, she had sat on a bridge on the river. Someone stopped, wondering if she was contemplating suicide, she realised only later. I'm fine, she told them. I know the truth.

And the truth was what had become clear.

'I didn't know their first names,' Claire said. 'Are they named in *Autumn Leaves*?'

'No, they're not. Remember, the nameless hero and heroine? Jack did a thesis on them.'

'Jack?'

'Boyfriend. Cambridge.'

'Oh yes, scruffy. So the Byrds are the Waterses. And how does M.A. Bright come into it?'

'She had sex with Edward.'

'Who's Edward?'

'The prince. Edward, the one who didn't want to be king. Mrs Simpson, but years before.'

There was a long pause on the other end of the phone.

'Are you still there?' Victoria said.

'So, fuck, Victoria, you're a princess.'

Victoria laughed aloud. 'Yes!' she said. 'I suppose I am.'

'But how did the Waterses, the Byrds, end up with the prince's baby?'

'That's the bit that's a cracker story,' Victoria said.

'Yes, because none of it's a cracker story so far.'

'I suppose so, but it gets better. It turns out you were right. They are the mafia.'

'Huh?'

'The royal fucking family. Maddie was pregnant to the prince, and she followed him to London. When she got there, no money, no anything, he refused to help her. He wouldn't even see her. She was pregnant and, Claire, they planned to kill the baby.'

'Hang on. Who planned to kill the baby?'

'The Queen's men.'

'The Queen wasn't born.'

'Not this queen, Mary, the one married to George V.'

'Of course.'

'I'm serious!'

'Okay,' Claire said, 'so then she had the baby and they planned to kill it, and your grandparents intervened to save the child and ran off with it. How could they do that?' Claire sounded incredulous.

'Rupert Waters found out from the prince's private secretary that there was a child and the Queen's men were watching Maddie. He, Rupert that is, was furious at the prince. Are you with me so far?'

'Sort of,' Claire said.

'Okay. He was going to leave the prince anyway after he read the draft of *Autumn Leaves*, but then he found out about Maddie. So he had her watched too, separately from the Queen's men. It was Rupert who went to the church where Maddie was going to leave the baby and he told the rector he was acting at the prince's behest. He arranged for them to report it as a death. They even buried a sack of potatoes in a pauper's grave and told police they'd buried the child.'

'How do you know all this?'

'Maddie told me today.'

'And she reckons the baby is Michael Byrd, Tony Blair's adviser and a dyed-in-the-fucking-wool republican?' Claire said.

'Yes,' Victoria replied.

'And *Autumn Leaves* is the story of your grandparents who aren't really your grandparents. Meanwhile M.A. Bright thinks she *is* your grandmother?'

'Exactly.'

'Hang on. Why are you even there? In Australia, I mean?'

'Ewan had a call from the publisher, M.A. Bright's publisher at Barlow Inglis. There's supposed to be another book, a sequel that tells this story, called *Winter Skies*. Awful titles aren't they? They asked for me by name.

'I came here thinking I was doing an interview with the writer. Turns out there is no *Winter Skies*, just a chapter she wrote over and over again when she believed the baby had died.'

'And you believe all this?'

'No, I know it. I'm sure.'

'How?'

'I have the letter. It's Nana's writing. It explains everything.'

'Wow! I mean, wow! So when did she write that?'

'After Poppy died, 1981. M.A. Bright got me over here to interview her for a new book but really it was to tell me the truth.'

'Okay, but if your nana wrote in 1981, why wait until now to contact you?'

'I think she wants to meet Daddy. I think she knows her time is coming and she wants to meet her son.'

'Good luck with that.' Claire knew Michael. She'd interviewed him for *The Eye* when Labour released its science and education policy.

'I think he will. He might be reserved but he's terribly kind. And she's ninety-five, Claire. Her whole family died. I mean, it changes everything for me and for him. I've lived a lie. That's the fucking truth.'

'It is, Victoria. It is.'

FORTY-SEVEN

IT WAS THE NEXT DAY NOW. VICTORIA HAD HARDLY SLEPT after she'd hung up from Claire. She'd been to talk to Maddie again early in the morning. They sat where they'd sat the day before, in the chairs out on the front veranda.

'I'm in trouble,' Victoria had said.

Maddie looked at her. 'What sort of trouble?'

'I'm engaged, and he . . . he isn't right.' She let out a sharp sob, held her breath to stop from crying. 'He hit me,' she whispered.

'Oh, my dear girl,' Maddie said, taking her hand. Maddie's was cold. Victoria grabbed it with her other hand and held on.

'Oh,' Maddie said again with such love.

Victoria started crying in earnest now. Maddie pulled her into an embrace and said, 'There, there.'

Victoria sat down on the floor at her grandmother's feet and cried then as she hadn't when she was a little girl, when her mother was gone. She cried and it felt like she would never stop. She said this, her nose and eyes running, the tissue Maddie handed her of no use to stem the tide.

'Well, that's possible but unlikely,' Maddie said. 'In my experience, we cry for as long as we need to, and not a moment longer.' She kept her hand on Victoria's back.

Maddie didn't ask questions and that was a relief. When Victoria had cried herself out, finally, she blew her nose on Maddie's handkerchief and wiped her eyes.

'Better?' Maddie said.

Victoria nodded.

'You'll be leaving him,' Maddie said, as a statement not a question.

'I know. There's a baby.'

'I see,' she said. 'How lovely.'

∾

It was later that same day and Andrew Shaw had collected her from Maddie's and taken her out to a wildlife park. She'd said she'd like to see a platypus, but now she had a koala in her arms. It really was dear, with a sweet stupid face and chubby little legs, the softest fur, although it smelled musty, like moss after rain. It didn't look at her. It stared front and centre, like a teddy bear preparing for a photo shoot.

As they were taking the photograph, it pooped in her hand. She didn't know what to do.

'Oh dear,' Andy said afterwards, brushing the poop to the ground. 'That's not very respectful of an international visitor.'

Earlier they'd seen the platypus in a tank. It was much smaller than she thought it would be.

'If you were here another week, I'd drive you up to O'Reilly's,' Andy said. 'There's a creek on the way where you usually see them.'

'They're the strangest animals,' she said.

'The platypus?'

'All of them.'

'That's why I like Lone Pine,' he said. 'They're making the animals available for people to see.'

'Maddie told me they gave the prince animals on his tour,' she said. 'A kangaroo they took on the ship with them and a koala, but it belonged to a little girl who was devastated to lose it so he gave it back. A lizard. They returned them all before they went home to England. Probably a good thing.'

'I came here with Maddie a lot when the kids were small,' he said. 'She never told me that.'

They sat on the riverbank and ate the picnic he'd brought: egg sandwiches and tea in a flask.

'Maddie's better,' he said. 'What I mean is, she's more settled than she was.' There were tears in his eyes. 'She might not live much longer but she'll know she has nothing to be forgiven for.' He wiped his eyes on his sleeve. 'She's very religious. I think she thought she might be going to hell. You were kind about all this.'

'Kind?' Victoria said. 'It wasn't her fault.'

'No, but she thought it was.'

The True Story of Maddie Bright

'I don't know if my father will come and see her.'

'I don't think it matters. You did.' He looked at her. 'Is it hard, knowing? Would you rather not know?'

'Do you care?'

'I do,' he said. 'I thought about it before we did this. I wondered, would I want to know? I decided I would.'

It had been Andy's idea to contact Victoria and not Michael. It was easier to ask for a journalist and he figured Victoria, being one generation removed, might find it easier. Poor Finian Inglis would be disappointed there wasn't another book, Victoria had thought, although she wasn't entirely sure there wasn't a book. There was a manuscript on Maddie's desk and Victoria wondered if it told the story after all. She had been itching to have a closer look.

'It's the deception that most rankles,' Victoria said. 'I was close to my grandmother growing up, and yet she never told me.'

'I guess once she'd told Maddie, she felt she'd done what she should. And they were different times. They were scared of the royal family.'

'Yes.'

'Not now though. They'd never do that now.'

She looked at him. 'No, although you never know. I have a friend who thinks they're worse than the mafia.'

He laughed. 'Is that your fiancé?'

'No,' she said.

'I notice you're not wearing a ring,' he said.

She hadn't worn her engagement ring since arriving.

She looked at her hand. 'I'm working it out,' she said finally.

He nodded. 'Let me know when you have.'

'Why?'

'I might want to know.'

She laughed. 'You never remarried?'

'No,' he said. 'I tried a couple of dates when the kids were a bit older, but none of them . . . Women don't generally want two kids from the get-go.'

'Some might,' Victoria said.

'Well, it's not *The Brady Bunch* out there.'

∾

'My father might not want to meet you,' Victoria had said to Maddie that morning.

'I know.'

'Will that be all right?'

'It will have to be.'

'How do you stay happy, given everything that happened?'

'Ah, well, I don't know much about happiness. The children saved me, first the children I taught at Ithaca and then Frank and Sally. It's impossible to be anything but in the moment when you have forty youngsters to contend with.

'What I know is I have these gifts. First, Ed, then Andy and Frank and Sally, and now you. You've arrived and now I know I can meet my maker and I won't have to account for killing a child. You're a beautiful girl and Diana is at peace. And there's a baby!'

From *Autumn Leaves* by M.A. Bright:

Addendum

London, 1921

The knock was so soft on the front door she might have missed it. But then the wailing started up and she didn't miss that.

She went along the narrow hallway past the study, opened the door.

It was him.

In his arms, he carried a child. The child was the one wailing.

'Where have you been?' she said, taking the child from him without thinking.

'Not with you,' he said. 'I'm so sorry. I've left David's service for good.'

'No, I mean, where did you get a baby?' She lifted the child onto her shoulder and began to rub its back. Wind? Did it have wind? It settled there at any rate.

She remembered the women of Asnières, their soldier husbands gone back to war, leaving them with children. She'd done what she could to help, carrying babies around the little schoolroom while she taught to give the mothers a break, her own heart on her sleeve.

'How did you find me?' she said now.

'I'm the government.' But he was smiling as he said it.

Something had changed in him, she thought, and then no, she decided. Nothing would change in him. Her heart hardened momentarily. But then he took his hat off, his hair falling straight into his eyes. She felt a sudden pull of tenderness.

'Whose baby is it?'

'Ours,' he said, pushing his hair back.

'Ours?'

'We can't ever say anything different.'

'What do you mean?'

'Will you marry me?'

'I don't understand.'

'I don't have a ring yet.'

'I still don't understand.'

'I love you. I've resigned.'

'What about India?'

'Some other fool will go to India.'

'Won't David need you?'

'No.'

'You've resigned?'

He took from his coat pocket a piece of paper. He unfolded it, a page from *The Times*. He pointed to a story. 'This.'

She took it in her right hand, leaned back so that the baby didn't fall forward. She read. 'A baby died?'

He shook his head, gestured to the child. His eyes were filling with tears.

'This is the baby? But why?'

He put his finger over his lips. 'We can never tell.'

'All right,' she said.

'Maddie,' he said. His voice choked as he said it.

'And David?'

He nodded tightly. 'Godfrey knew.'

'I'll kill David. How could he?'

He shook his head. 'No,' he said. 'We'll do what we can do. Maddie's all right. She's on her way home. I've seen she's looked after.'

'Does David know?'

'About the child?' He nodded.

'What were they going to do?'

'What do you think?'

The baby, who had fallen into a deep sleep on her shoulder, stirred now. 'They wouldn't.'

He nodded, almost imperceptibly. 'They think they did.' He gestured towards the newspaper.

'Godfrey?'

'No, the Queen's men.'

'Oh,' she said. 'All right,' she said.

'All right, we won't tell, or all right, you'll marry me?'

'Both?'

He grinned. 'I'm about the happiest man on earth.'

She smiled. 'Our child?'

He nodded.

'All right.'

From *Winter Skies*:

Epilogue

Brisbane, 1997

She saw him like new as he walked up the air bridge to where people waited for loved ones. He looked lost, reminding her of that other morning, when her mother was gone, and for a moment it felt as if her mother had died all over again that very day and he was returned to that place of grief.

He came slowly, thoughtfully. He was wearing his travel clothes: neat dark grey slacks, white shirt, navy coat. His curly hair, gone grey, was clipped short and he wore his reading glasses.

He carried a copy of *Autumn Leaves*.

He looked like his mother, Victoria thought, like Maddie. The spitting image of her in the face.

'Daddy,' she said. 'I'm so glad you've come.'

Andy had waited at the house with Maddie. She was nervous, she said. It will be fine, Victoria had told her. I know it will be.

But Victoria didn't know. She knew how difficult her father could be, how much this mattered.

※

Maddie stood. He was in the doorway, a foot taller than his mother.

Neither spoke.

They moved towards one another.

On Writing

H.R.H. Edward Prince of Wales visited Australia in 1920 and had a train crash. While I researched what has been written about Edward, all the characters in *The True Story of Maddie Bright* are fictional. Fidelity to history is not the job of the novelist. We tell plausible whoppers, as Margaret Atwood has said, and that's what I have done. True story!

This is my sixth plausible whopper and seventh book with Allen & Unwin and if it were my last, I would mark the moment. Before I was a novelist and after I was (briefly) a cadet journalist, I worked for mathematician Dennis Gibson who was a university vice-chancellor. My job was to write his correspondence and speeches. I learned to be the voice of someone else, and we both loved books. Before I worked for Dennis, I worked for Brian Waters who was the registrar at the university, and I learned about duty and possibly semicolons.

My agent Fiona Inglis took me on nearly ten years ago after she read the original manuscript for my book *For a Girl*, published in 2017, which tells a true story from my young life. It takes a certain kind of heart to do what Fiona did. Some people who have read no other books of mine but *For a Girl*, or who listened to the ABC *Conversations* interview about the book, wrote to me and trusted me with their own stories. I am proud to count myself among you.

I don't think I knew how to write a novel until about the fourth one, but my publisher at Allen & Unwin is Annette Barlow, and she and her team have maintained the same dedication and care to make my plausible whoppers more plausible for twenty years now, which would be a feat in any circumstance but is mighty given the disrupted state of their industry in these first decades of the twenty-first century.

Like universities, you will find extraordinary people in publishing if you stop and regard them: editor Ali Lavau, who keeps a writer from her most wrongheaded impulses, earlier Catherine Milne, a notable editor now a publisher, and long ago, Sophie Cunningham, a publisher now a writer. Nada Backovic designed beautiful covers for my earlier books, and her work is honoured here by Lisa White. Aziza Kuypers, a final reader of the manuscript of this novel, managed to avert an implausible whopper almost at the finish line. And senior editor, dear Christa Munns, has made sure we all do what we're supposed to do while wrangling 115,000 words and nearly as many changes penned across them, twice. Annette Barlow herself is gentle and generous in her spirit. She was the first reader and editor of *The True Story of Maddie Bright*, and I'm so grateful she is the one.

Readers. Colleagues Belinda Ogden, Jo Fleming and Sasha Marin read the early novels in draft and Kris Olsson was a reading friend for a long time. My uncle Tony Lynch and aunt Jill Lynch have come to every one of my book launches. Wendy Brealey has read every one of my books. Sharon Cameron and her bookclub gave *The True Story of Maddie Bright* shape and she and Cass George are the kind of bookclub folk you wish ran the world. Some readers send me kind emails.

It takes a village and when you are a writer they should all be certified psychotherapists. Louise Ryan and Gerard Ryan and Lib Fletcher have been there for most of my life; Suzi Jefferies, Theanne Walters and Lenore Cooper too now. Rebecca Lamoin has been an unexpected gift to my creative soul, and Andrea Fox makes me think differently. Kim Wilkins has supported many writers including me and is my sister on the road.

The Banff Centre and Wild Flour Bakery Cafe were a mother's arms when I needed them. Stace Callaghan is the invincible summer in the quote. Shar Edmunds has restored my faith in a good world which I find I do not want to live without. Cathy Sinclair walks up a mountain with me and doesn't give advice, sometimes not even if I ask for it. Merlo Paddington, you know what you do.

David Mayocchi has walked a long road beside me and it has cost him, and all the good men in my novels rely on him for lessons about how to be a person.

As readers of *For a Girl* will know, I have two children, one named Otis and one I named Ruth who has another name now. I love them both and that is the antidote to despair.

Mary-Rose MacColl
December 2018